BoogaMedia Publishing

First published in 2023

ISBN: 978-06488160-8-9

An imprint of BoogaMedia

To everyone that help me take control of my story and passion, this book is for you.

Go out, live, and write your own story.

Lightning Jump
Collision of Worlds

By Ben Fjord

Chapter One

The rain hits the window like a thousand tiny pellets, creating a rhythm. Rayleigh finds herself lying in bed, pulling the blanket up, and sinking further into the mattress. Listening to the rain soothes her thoughts.

Trying to will her body into action – *You got this* – she slips out of bed, trying not to make it rock.

Her stomach turns at a small movement next to her. Tom stirs, but he quickly settles and the feeling in her stomach subsides.

As the grogginess fades, she scans the room looking for her running gear. With an uneasy sway, she pushes herself up, quietly tiptoes around the room and collects her running gear. She pulls her clothes on as she heads towards the door.

The lock clicks as she turns it. Once the door cracks open, the cooler air of the hallway comes into the apartment.

"Crap." She pauses, realising her phone is by the bed.

Turning away from the door, Rayleigh begins to sneak back through the apartment, moving like a ninja to grab her phone from the bedside table. She sneaks a look at Tom, who is still sleeping soundly.

What a goof. He'd sleep through anything. Looking at him, she is reminded of the safety and security their relationship brings, realising how lucky she is as the warm feeling swells in her chest.

She leans over and kisses him on the cheek, whispering her love. Tom murmurs but doesn't wake. Rayleigh makes her way to the door, pausing briefly to look back at Tom before heading out.

When she reaches the front door of the building, the weather greet her with a slap to the face. She shivers, trying to shake off the cold as it bites into her. As she stares into the downpour, her body fights her, not wanting to take that first step out into the rain. *Surely lying in bed cuddling would be much better?*

Her body adjusts to the cold and she kicks herself into gear.

Go for five minutes. If you don't like it, go back and cuddle.

The water seeps into her clothing within the first few steps, but she pushes deeper into the rain. Her clothes cling to her more with each step. The harshness of the pavement pushes back against her feet as they hit the ground. With each impact, her body loosens up.

Rounding the first corner, she settles into a steady pace and her breathing becomes stable. Her feet thud as they bounce through puddles. Running is the thing she does for herself to prepare for the day and the world she must face. No matter what happens, it's her morning run that helps get her through. It keeps her sane in a chaotic life.

She approaches the park, where she can see others braving the weather, out for their morning exercise. She finds comfort in seeing that it isn't only her out braving the weather. She gives a smile and a nod as she passes another runner and heads into the park.

The latch of the metal gate clanks as it closes behind her. There's loose gravel underfoot as she moves from the footpath to the park grounds. The unevenness of the park ground is gentler beneath her feet compared to the harshness of the concrete path.

Moving through the park, she sees a couple of familiar faces, but she pushes on, slipping into a meditative state, focusing on her breathing and body.

The ducks are playing in the pond, unaware and uncaring of the downpour. They don't even acknowledge her presence as she continues around the pond.

She follows the path to the exit. Upon leaving the park, the firmness of the ground changes as she returns to the hard footpath.

Gentle, Rayleigh tells herself as her knees protest.

She starts to hear the crashing of waves, as she closes in on the beach. The weather has stirred up the swell, bringing in monster waves. The thunder and ocean try to outdo each other, each attempting to show their dominance. Rayleigh stops running at a sudden crack of thunder close by.

Rayleigh eyes the lightning with rising alarm. *Maybe it's time to head back.*

Not feeling ready, she pushes the thought aside, continuing to run along the footpath running parallel to the beach. The waves crash and thunder continue to echo each other. At the end of the street, she turns away from the beach and begins the journey inland, back to the apartment.

She slows to a walk as she reaches her street. Her muscles ache.

She checks her phone, then smiles to herself as she pushes through the front door. She's taken ten seconds off her time.

Nothing has moved or changed in the apartment since she left. Through the open door to their room she sees Tom still in bed, looking blissfully happy.

She strips off her wet clothes in the doorway to make sure she doesn't drip water throughout the apartment. She drops them into a tub at the front door, then slips into the bathroom, closing the door behind her.

The heated floor beneath her feet feels amazing. She takes a moment to bask in it, and the heat from the lamp above her. The shower hums when she turns on the water. She tests the temperature before jumping under the stream. The heat of the shower washes away the bitter chill from outside, thawing her out. She lets her thoughts slip away, enjoying and appreciating the heat. She begins to hum to herself.

Going through her morning routine, she takes the towel from the rack, relishing its softness as she wraps it around her.

It's the simple pleasures.

She sees a coffee on the basin as she steps out of the shower, and smiles.

He is good to me. Realising Tom must have had slipped it into the bathroom, not wanting to disturb her routine.

She smells the aroma of the coffee as she cups it in both hands, instantly reassured that the day has begun and that she's lucky. Hearing the sounds of activity coming from the kitchen.

She smells the food before she sees it. *Mmm... eggs and pancakes.* Skulking around the corner, she creeps up on Tom in the kitchen, trying to pounce on him like a tiger.

"Morning, hun," Tom says over his shoulder, before she can jump him.

"Ah man, how did you know?"

"Honey, you couldn't creep up on anyone." He throws an arm around her and kisses her on the forehead.

They hold each other tightly, taking in each other's presence, only to be distracted by the food sizzling away on the stove.

"Quick, go get dressed so we can have breakfast," Tom says as he turns back to the food which is on the cusp of burning.

"Clothes? Well, that's no fun." She drops the towel and stares at Tom.

"Oh, you're evil. Don't you have a big day? I'd hate to make you late." Tom picks her up and squeezes her tight, smothering her in kisses. She cries out in delight.

In fits of laughter, she scurries to the bedroom to get dressed. As she bounces through the room she relaxes as she begins to think of her day.

She flicks through the contents of her wardrobe, eventually settling on something to wear. Slipping on her favourite pencil skirt and a blue business shirt, she heads back out to the dining table for breakfast.

Tom has laid out an amazing array, including pancakes and fruit – everything her heart might desire. She sits at the table, surveying the spread. She's overwhelmed with happiness and satisfaction. What a life she has.

They begin to talk about their day as they tuck into the food.

Tom looks up at the clock, then breaks through the breakfast chatter. "We should probably get going."

"Oh crap," Rayleigh responds as she sees the time.

They both spring to action, tidying the table.

"You go finish getting ready," Tom says.

"Thank you." Rayleigh gives Tom a quick kiss on the cheek before heading to the bathroom.

When she emerges from the bathroom, the table has been cleared and the kitchen looks perfect once again. Tom walks out of the bedroom, dressed for work. He takes his bag from the chair and meets Rayleigh at the front door. They continue talking as they head out together, taking the lift down to the street they head outside into the street. With a gentle kiss, they wish each other a good day and go their separate ways.

***

Rayleigh finds herself in the kitchen at work, thinking about her current project while the coffee machine brews her drink.

The client is looking for more of a rustic feeling... so I guess maybe the high chair would be better... and I should go for more wood and subtle colours.

"Well, you look deep in thought," Rayleigh's colleague chimes in, grabbing her attention.

"Huh? Oh, yes. Sorry about that." Rayleigh quickly collects her coffee and moves aside. "I was thinking about this current project, and what furniture I should go with."

"I'm a little jealous you got that one. I would have loved to work on it," the colleague responds, taking their coffee from the machine.

"It is a great project. I feel lucky to have the opportunity," Rayleigh responds before taking a sip of her coffee. "How's your project going?"

"It's going well. A couple more weeks and it should be finished."

"That's awesome. Maybe we should speak with Margret to see if you can work with me when you're done?"

"If you could, that'd be amazing."

They both pause, sipping their drinks.

"I guess I should get back to work. I need to take off early today," Rayleigh says, nodding to her colleague before turning to leave. Rayleigh nods greetings to two other colleagues as she heads back to her desk.

As she moves through the office in a daze, Rayleigh continues to think about her project. She realises she left her phone in the kitchen, and heads back to collect it. She slows as she nears its doorway, as she can hear her colleagues talking.

"Everything seems to always work out for her. It's like she gets everything she wants. It doesn't seem fair."

"She does have a perfect life."

They stop talking moments before Rayleigh walks into the kitchen.

"Hey. Have you seen my phone?" she asks, trying not to let on that she heard them.

The three of them look around quickly, before one of them sees a phone on the counter.

"This one?" they ask, holding it up.

"Yep. That's it – thank you."

Rayleigh takes it and heads out of the kitchen again. As she walks away, the colleagues start talking again. "Do you think she heard us?"

As she walks back to her desk, the words ring in Rayleigh's head.

What's wrong with a perfect life?

A knot grows in her stomach at the thought. She dives back into her work to push the thought aside.

Chapter Two

Waking with a start, Rayleigh sits bolt upright in bed. Rolling thunder moves into the distance. Collapsing back onto the bed, she rolls over to look at Tom. Her heart is racing, and her body is hot and flushed. As she breathes, the tightness in her chest subsides, and she begins to calm down.

She glances at her clock to see she's beaten her alarm by a couple of minutes. She reaches over to switch it off so it doesn't wake Tom. He looks so peaceful.

She lies in bed a little longer. *Come on, Rayleigh – you've got this*, she recites to herself, then pulls herself out of bed.

She recoils at the coldness of the floor against her feet, before letting them touch it again. With each breath, the world around her comes into existence. Her body responds to the sound of the rain beating down outside, trying to drag her back into bed. She takes a couple more deep breaths to break the chains of slumber and move into the world.

She looks through the window at the bleak weather: rain, lightning and thunder continuing their war from the previous day. She slips into her running gear, putting on an extra layer to stay warm and, hopefully, a little drier.

At the entrance to the building she experiences a sense of déjà vu as she looks out into the world. Pulling her jacket a little tighter, she steps out into the rain. After a couple of steps, she builds to a jog, then picks up her pace, pushing herself. She longs for summer, when the mornings are warmer and the rain less frequent. But this isn't the time for such thoughts, so she pushes them from her mind, and sets herself to the task at hand. Putting one step in front of the other, inhaling and exhaling. The rhythm of her footsteps soon calms her nerves and she gets into sync with her run.

As she makes her way through the park, she jumps as a large bolt of lightning strikes nearby. Looking around to see if she can see what it struck.

"That was close."

Rayleigh pushes on. At the end of her run, there's still uneasiness in her stomach. Restlessness bites at her, as an energy swirls in her body, so she decides to keep going. She turns right, heading away from the park and down towards the beach.

The waves are lashing the sand, the giant swell continuing to be built up by the storm. Standing on the edge of the sand, she takes in the power of the waves and the ocean. She's unable to tell the difference between the sound of the waves and the thunder. With a small part of her wanting to hide away, at the sight of the raw power they display.

Rayleigh's brain chimes in, spurring her to keep moving. She swings around making her way down to the sand, and starts running along the beach.

Her body begins to call out for a shower as it reaches its limits, and the cold burrows into her. She slows, preparing to turn back towards the apartment.

The sky lights up, as lightning cracks close by.

Blinding Rayleigh with a wall of white, her stomach swirls and she fights the urge to throw up. Her skin tingles.

She stops to gather herself.

"Hold on. Who are you?" says a soft voice from behind Rayleigh, catching her off guard.

She jumps slightly. "Sorry, who's there?"

Rayleigh rubs her eyes. Steadying herself and with the sickness in her stomach subsiding, the world swims back into view.

As her vision returns, confusion begins to sink in.

Where's the beach? The waves are no longer crashing in the background. The sick feeling in her stomach returns along with her confusion.

The rain has stopped. She's hit by a strange smell in the air, almost metallic. Rayleigh's body continues to tingle. Fighting panic, she notices tall buildings all around her.

"Where am I?" Rayleigh whispers under her breath.

She takes in the black ominous skyscrapers, seeing the glass stretch in to the heavens. Lifting her hands, Rayleigh can see black soot on them, looking around the ground and buildings appear to be covered in a thin layer. Giving an industrial layer to the buildings, with an underground feeling to the place. She has a feeling she's being watched. But can't make sense of where she is. Her stomach is still turning over.

"Is this your first jump?"

Rayleigh turns in the direction of the voice. "Jump? Hang on, who are you?"

Looking at the woman standing before her, she is busy with a device in her hand. Wearing a large coat that covers her almost head to toe. The stranger pays Rayleigh no attention, but pauses every now and then to look around, as though searching for something.

"Okay. We don't have time for this. We need to go." Rayleigh can hear the urgency in her voice. "That way." She looks off down the side street. "Come on," she says with a little more urgency. "We need to go."

"Sorry – I don't know you," Rayleigh replies, looking at her blankly, shifting her weight, while wondering where to go and what to do.

"It's up to you, but I'm leaving.," the stranger says. She turns to head in the direction she had indicated.

"Stop!" a voice booms from behind them.

Both Rayleigh and the stranger turn. With figures in uniform streaming onto the street in front of them, their guns trained on them.

Without hesitation or waiting for a response, the officers open fire.

Rayleigh's body shuts down, fear taking over with the bullets screaming towards her.

Before she has a chance to do anything, Rayleigh is pulled into an alleyway.

"We can't stay here," the stranger yells at her, pulling a weapon from under her coat, she begins to return fire. "Cover your eyes and ears," she calls out.

The stranger pulls something from under her coat and hurls it at the officers. There's a loud crack, and the world lights up. Rayleigh's ears ring, and once again her vision goes white.

Rayleigh can feel herself moving, but she can't see. She tries to fight back and break free. With each step, her vision returns a little more. Seeing her new companion in front of her, pulling her down the street.

"You can stay and die, or come with me," she says, looking back at Rayleigh. "I'll explain later."

Rayleigh's stomach does another somersault, at the thought of dying. She gives in, letting herself be pulled along. Rayleigh begins to run alongside the stranger, which allows them to pick up their pace. As they reach the end of the street, they turn, picking up speed again and putting distance between them and the officers. Ducking and weaving over fences, through alley ways and diralect buildings.

As they move through the streets, the world seems foreign to Rayleigh, yet somehow familiar. In her confusion, she's unable to put a finger on what is happening.

She's quick, Rayleigh realises as she struggles to keep up. The stranger doesn't hesitate at all, turning and darting quickly around corners, each turn action made with confidence. Rayleigh's muscles protest at the effort required to keep up.

She has lost track of where they are, feeling as though they are running around in circles. After several kilometres, the stranger pulls up at a street corner. Rayleigh's body takes the opportunity to collapse to the ground.

How can she be doing this so effortlessly?

"How are you holding up?" the stranger asks.

"I'll manage," Rayleigh replies, trying to put on a brave face.

"Okay, we should be fine if we can make it to the forest." She turns her attention to the device in her hands.

Rayleigh sits, taking in her new companion. She appears to be of similar build to Rayleigh, but with the coat it is hard to tell. There is an air of confidence about her, that Rayleigh wishes she can have. With a gentle face, Rayleigh finds herself believing that she is safe in her presence, which surprises her. Rayleigh is caught off guard when the she looks down at her.

"Let's go," she says, reaching down to offer her hand.

Rayleigh stares up at her, then takes the hand, pulling herself up. They're off again before she has the chance to think, darting around the corner and over an open field.

When Rayleigh sees a fence, she hesitates, wondering how they will get over it. It towers over them both.

Her companion doesn't even slow down; several steps from the fence, she launches herself up on top of it. From this perch, she turns back to Rayleigh, who is now nearing the fence, and she lowers her hand, gesturing for Rayleigh to take it.

Rayleigh is baffled by what she has just seen. The woman is now sitting like a bird on its roost, as though this was her natural habitat.

Rayleigh finds herself reaching up without thought, and before she has a chance to work out how to get over the fence, she's hurtling through the air. Baffled by the stranger's strength, and the ease with which she's lifted her. In the blink of an eye, they are on the other side of the fence and catching Rayleigh as she falls.

A hot flush comes over Rayleigh as she finds herself in the stranger's arms, looking up at her face.

"My apologies," the woman says as she places her down gently.

Stunned, Rayleigh stands looking between the fence and her, trying to work out what just happened.

"Come on, we need to go."

"Hold on. You need to explain what's happening first."

"I will explain more once we are safe."

They hold Rayleigh's gaze for a moment, during which time a sense of peace comes over Rayleigh. There is something about this woman that puts her at ease.

Rayleigh watches as the woman turns and ducks into the forest. Without thinking, Rayleigh follows her. As they make their way through the forest, Rayleigh does her best to keep up.

Exhaustion soon kicks in, muscles starting to cramp up. Her companion continues moving ahead, casually jumping trees and ducking under branches. Rayleigh is struggling, falling behind, frequently hit in the face by branches. She pushes herself harder to keep up.

Abruptly, Rayleigh comes rushing out of the bush, bumping into them, having stopped in the middle of a small clearing.

"This will do," she says, looking around.

She pushes her hand into her pocket, and pulls out a small item throwing it onto the ground. With a click and a whirr, the device begins to grow.

Rayleigh takes a step back, afraid. *What is this?*

To her surprise, after a few moments, Rayleigh sees a small door half the height of her is in front of them. Before Rayleigh can ask what is happening, the stranger disappears through it.

Rayleigh looks around at the forest. She feels silly, standing there alone. Taking a deep breath, she crouches to step through the doorway. When she rises, she is in a small single room with no windows. Turning back, to look outside, she can see the stark contrast of the forest outside through the open door.

A fire in the centre casts gentle light over the room, which is small. There are cushions all over the floor, giving it an almost tribal feeling. There is a small table between the cushions to one side of the fire. The lick of the flames gives Rayleigh a sense of safety, triggering a memory of trips Rayleigh had taken with Tom to their cabin in the woods. There is a small cabinet in the back, that Rayleigh assumes is there for storage.

The stranger gestures to Rayleigh to move further into the room. Then she closes the door behind her.

An uneasiness comes over Rayleigh's body as she realises that she is standing alone in a room with a stranger. *What am I doing?*

The stranger jostles her slightly, trying to pass her to reach the other side of the room. She begins to remove her heavy outer coat and a small jacket underneath.

Rayleigh studies her new companion. *Wow, she is stunning,* she thinks, before she can catch it. Feeling herself blush, she turns away, trying to hide it.

"Here are some dry clothes," the stranger says.

Rayleigh turns to see her holding out some clothing. She realises she's still wearing the wet clothes from her morning run. She takes the offered clothes, then looks around for a place to change, but the door outside is all that Rayleigh can see. In confusion, she turns back to the stranger to ask where she can change.

But she has already turned her back, trying to give Rayleigh some privacy. Not wanting to delay, Rayleigh quickly changes out of her wet clothes and into the warm dry ones. Pulling on what appears to be some sort of work trousers, based on the thick fabric. Followed by an undershirt and a button shirt of the same material.

Rayleigh flops onto the cushions, surprised at how soft the clothes are despite the thickness of the fabric. *What is this made of?* She runs her fingers over the cloth, trying to determine the fabric. Warming up now that she's in dry clothing, she begins to relax.

"Are you feeling better?" the woman asks.

"Yes, much better, thank you."

"That's good. My name is Tailia, by the way."

"I'm Rayleigh." She feels like she's back in school, meeting someone for the first time. She hesitates, unsure where to start. Questions swirl in her mind. "What is going on here? Where am I?"

"The room is made of nanites, which can build any design programmed into them," Tailia explains, excitement creeping into her voice.

Rayleigh looks over at the door. "Won't a door in a forest be weird, if someone walks by outside?"

"It will disguise itself to fit with the surroundings. I'll also be monitoring the forest, just to be safe." Tailia holds up a small tablet looking device for Rayleigh to see.

Rayleigh senses that her next question is most likely a dumb one. Finally, she asks, "Where am I?"

"I'm going to assume dimensional jumping is not something that exists where you are from."

"Wait, what?" A world of new questions appear in Rayleigh's mind, at hearing 'dimensional jumping'.

Tailia lets out a small sigh. "Let's start at the top. There are countless dimensions, each with different planets, systems, races and species. You have jumped from your dimension into this one, through a hole, a portal. It happens naturally between dimensions, but it's also possible to create a hole artificially using a jump device." She points to the device strapped on to her arm. Rayleigh looks over the device quickly, seeing a big screen in the middle that looks like a large phone, with some small dials and buttons next to it.

Rayleigh's head is swimming with all this information. "Hang on... wait – what?"

Tailia chuckles, then relaxes into her spot next to the fire, and begins to explain. "Imagine a sphere, like a planet, that is a dimension. Then within each dimension, there are universes, systems and planets. Just like there are different sized planets, there are different sized dimensions. Some will contain a handful of planets, others have hundreds or thousands of planets. These dimensions sit next to each other, and when they touch, they create a portal from one dimension to another. This is a naturally occurring jump point. Some dimensions will always be in contact with the ones next to them, creating permanent jump points. Others will float around and create temporary jump points when they touch. Finally, if dimensions are close enough, with the right technology and enough power it's possible to create an artificial jump point." She pauses, waiting to see if Rayleigh is following along.

14

Rayleigh nods half-heartedly.

"When we met, I was running from I.D.T." Tailia pauses again. "The Institute for Dimensional Travel. Its officers police dimensional travel, more or less. They've been hunting me down for a while because they believe travel between dimensions should be outlawed, which makes me a criminal, in their minds. When you arrived, I was getting ready to jump in an effort to escape."

Rayleigh tries to take this all in. "So I've jumped from my dimension to this one?"

Tailia nods.

"Which means that if I want to get home, I need to go back and jump back through that portal?" Rayleigh says, trying to walk herself through the thought.

"Well..." Tailia stops looking down at the device on her arm, pushing several buttons. "Sort of. Unfortunately, when using naturally occurring portals, it's not possible to know where you'll end up. It's sometimes more an educated guess than a science. Also, this is an unmapped sector."

"Unmapped?"

"When a sector is mapped, it's possible to a certain degree to know where you're jumping to, based on the dimensions that are nearby. Unfortunately, my device doesn't have a map of this sector. So I have no idea where I was going to jump to, or how to find the portal again."

Rayleigh's heart sinks, and she's overwhelmed by all this talk of jumping, dimensions and mapping.

When she looks up, Tailia has pulled out what appears to be some snacks from her backpack, and offers them to her. Raleigh raises a hand to turn them down. Given the sick feeling in her stomach and her swirling head, eating is the last thing she wants to do.

"Let's just say I believe you," she says. "If that is the case, how do I get back to my sector?"

"That requires us to find out your sector and a map, so we can work out how to get there. I feel it's safe to assume you don't have that information?"

"Nope," Rayleigh responds, feeling utterly lost.

"That's okay. I know some people that might be able to help."

"Right." Excitedly, Rayleigh stands up. "When do we leave?"

"We need to head to Sector 14, and the next jump point is in a few days," Tailia says, looking down tablet device for their surroundings. "Don't worry. We're safe here, and we have enough food and supplies to wait."

Rayleigh's disappointment bites into her. Exhausted from the emotional rollercoaster, she sits back down on the pillows again.

How can this be possible? she thinks. *Who is this woman?*

Despite the absurdity of everything that's happened, Rayleigh fights against the drowsiness and shock of the situation. She decides she should probably eat something, so she takes some of the food that Tailia has placed on the small table in front of them. One item appears to be a kind of dried fruit that looks a bit like an apple with the shape and colour. She takes a bite, enjoying its sweetness, noticing that it tastes more like a berry.

She breathes deeply, trying to calm herself. With each breath, she settles more, beginning to take in the room around her and replaying the events of the day.

Rayleigh studies Tailia properly for the first time. She's slim, with a slight tinge of purple to her skin. She moves smoothly, with no sudden movements, giving her a gentle presence. Rayleigh remembers how she moved earlier when they were running, and is amazed at her strength, despite them being similar in size and build. Her long hair is pulled to one side over her shoulder to drape down her front. Rayleigh finds herself captivated by her, having to catch herself, to make sure she isn't staring. Tailia is laying down, casually throwing food into her mouth, looking over at Rayleigh from time to time. This gives Rayleigh the impression that she would have the same calm demeanour in any situation.

As she reaches for another piece of fruit, Rayleigh finds herself thinking of Tom. *How is he? What is he going to think, when she doesn't come back?*

As these thoughts skim through her mind, she settles in for a wait and shifts the conversation to other things in an attempt to try and take her mind off everything.

Chapter Three

"Come on Rayleigh, it's time to get up." Tailia's voice reaches into Rayleigh's sleep, and she feels herself being gently rocked awake. She stirs and opens her eyes to see Tailia staring down at her.

"We need to go if we're going to make the jump," Tailia says, before turning away to continue packing her satchel.

"What time is it?" Rayleigh asks. She rolls over and starts looking for her clothes.

"We are one-fifteenth into the day," Tailia answers without turning.

"One-fifteenth... I'm just going to take that as early," Rayleigh says to herself, just above a whisper.

As she puts on her clothes, Tailia finishes up with her satchel and throws it over her shoulder and prepares to leave.

While they've been living in the small room, there hasn't been a lot of space to escape from each other, so over the last few days they've had to find ways to move around while not stepping on each other the confined space. Nodding to each other, they head for the door to outside.

When she steps through it, Rayleigh finds herself in the middle of a dense jungle. It's a stark reminder that she is in another dimension. A weight coming over her, as she remembers her old life, and Tom. She's a little confused. *Why haven't I thought of Tom?* Reflecting the previous days in the small room with Tailia, she's uncomfortable at the thought.

Tailia bumps into Rayleigh as she tries to exit the room. "Sorry about that," she says as she steps past.

"That's okay," Rayleigh replies, moving out of her way.

The sounds of the forest filter in as they take in their surroundings. Tailia turns back to the door and presses a button on the side. Rayleigh looks on in amazement as the small door begins to fold in on itself, crumbling in front of her eyes. Tailia collects the device from the ground once it's finished packing down. She slips it into her jacket, then looks at the jump device on her arm, to work out which direction they need to head.

"This way," she says, and starts walking off into the jungle.

Collecting herself, Rayleigh trundles after her.

They are no longer in a hurry, so Tailia moves at a pace that Rayleigh can keep up with, which gives Rayleigh the chance to explore the sights and sounds of the forest.

The trees stretch up into the sky, swaying softly. Rayleigh hears their clicks and cracks as they dance with each other. The calls in the distance make her wonder what sort of strange animals might be making the sound, and whether they might be dangerous. She picks up her pace slightly, wanting to stay within safe distance of Tailia.

As time passes, they settle into a rhythm as they move through the forest, bending under branches and stepping over fallen trees. They don't talk much, as Tailia is focused on the jump device and Rayleigh looks around, noticing that the forest appears to be thinning out.

When they reach the edge of the forest, a field is visible beyond it. Rayleigh hesitates not sure if stepping out of the cover is safe, coming to enjoy the forests cover. She can see animals grazing in the field, resembling deer, however with their antlers growing downwards over their face and creating something that looks like a beard below their heads. As she steps into the field, she can hear the animals in front of them grunting and playing with each other, bunting their antlers against each other which creates a cracking sound. It almost sounds as though they are communicating and joking around with each other. As Rayleigh and Tailia walk forwards, a silence comes over the animals, as they stop to take in the two strangers that have walked into their herd.

What kind of animals are these? Rayleigh wonders to herself, pausing in confusion at what she is seeing. Up close she can now see, that the animals have 'antlers' covering their bodies, almost like a cage around it. *I wonder if that is for protection.* The thought crosses her mind.

Tailia is too busy looking at the device in her hand to even acknowledge the existence of the animals. Rayleigh realises she is being separated from Tailia, and she steps forward cautiously, feeling like she has just walked into a stranger's living room as an uninvited guest.

The herd of 40 animals separates slightly to let them through. Rayleigh returns the look. *They must be four or five metres tall.* She weighs up their height now that she is up close.

She feels no malicious or ill intent from them, as they casually go about their business. The sounds of their breathing become calming with each step she takes.

Looking at them, Rayleigh feels like she should be scared or at least disconcerted by their appearance. However, the big eyes looking back at her, while they continue to chew, make them adorable. If it were not for their size, she would almost want one as a pet.

Tailia stops suddenly. "This is it!" she says, and puts the device away. She looks up, taking in her onlookers for the first time. She raises an eyebrow, as though she's caught someone staring at her.

Suddenly, one of the animals lets out a loud cry, and then they all run off in every direction, heading for the tree line as quickly as they can.

Rayleigh's body tightens jumping into fight or flight mode. *What spooked them?*

"This may tickle a little bit," Tailia says as she turns to Rayleigh and takes her hand. Rayleigh feels the hairs all over her body stand on end, and a queasy sensation in her stomach.

With a thud and a crack, everything turns white.

***

Coming to, Rayleigh registers a soft surface beneath her body. She pushes herself on to all fours to get out of the sand, stifling the urge to throw up.

She can no longer see the lush grass or jungle in the distance. It's hot, the sun beating down on her. Its bright light forces her to squint.

Tailia stands tall next to her, once again looking at the device in her hand.

"How are you feeling?" she asks.

"A… lit… tle… sick…" throwing up what little she had in her stomach, before taking a few deep breaths, "but more importantly, what happened to the jungle?" Rayleigh pulls herself up off the ground, grabbing Tailia for stability.

"We've jumped to the next place," Tailia replies, pulling a tablet device out of her bag. Rayleigh can see her looking over what appears to be a map.

"Where is that?" Rayleigh asks, looking around.

"We've jumped to the next sector, Sector 14. This is Planet 39 within this sector. We need to be careful here. This is not a normal planet, and you shouldn't trust what you see."

Rayleigh stares at Tailia blankly.

"We're here to get information on the Hu Thus, hopefully," Tailia says. She walks away, still looking at her device.

Rayleigh trots along after her, not wanting to fall behind. "Who are the Hu Thus?" she asks when she catches up.

"An ancient race with extensive knowledge of jumping between dimensions."

As they walk, Rayleigh looks around the barren environment. The plant life is sparse and there isn't a lot of vegetation. The few plants are small and harsh, without many leaves and with a hard outer shell.

As they walk, the scenery changes from a desert landscape to a rocky valley and cliffs. Stepping over rocks and sliding around boulders, as they try to make their way through the cracks in the terrain. They come to a cliff face, by now, Rayleigh is several metres behind Tailia, keeping pace while trying to process everything on this new planet.

Rayleigh watches as Tailia walks head first into the cliff face without hesitation, simply disappearing from view. Rayleigh stops walking, unsure what she has just seen. She approaches the cliff face and puts her hand against the surface. It's solid.

She begins to wonder if she imagined Tailia vanishing into the cliff. Turning around, she looks back in the direction they had come from. *Did I lose her somewhere?*

Not quite sure what to think, and with the uneasiness of being alone working its way into her body, Rayleigh pushes the cliff face again, but it is still solid.

She looks around, hoping to see Tailia hiding somewhere. With no idea what to do next, Rayleigh looks back at the wall.

Tailia's head pops out of the cliff face. "I'll be back in a moment," she says casually, before vanishing back into the cliff.

Rayleigh rubs her eyes. *Did I imagine that?* She reaches out her hand again, this time putting more weight behind her push. Still nothing changes.

"Tailia! Tailia!" she calls out, looking around. Walking down the cliff face, to see if there is a cave that might explain it.

Questioning her own sanity at this point, she turns and begins to walk in the opposite direction, supposing she must have missed something. When she reaches the crack they came through, she turns to see Tailia reappear.

"Where are you going?" Tailia asks, a confused look on her face.

"I... um... was..." Rayleigh finds herself lost again before noticing the man standing next to Tailia. He is neatly dressed in what appears to be a uniform. It looks like something out of one of the old western movies Tom watches. The gentleman approaches Rayleigh, then raises both his arms in front of his face, as if he is about to play a kid's game of peekaboo.

"We r lc le om el e av tr," he says, with a slight bow before lowering his hands again.

Rayleigh stares at him in disbelief.

"He's welcoming you," Tailia says from behind him. "He 's about to check if you are allowed access. You're safe and have nothing to worry about."

Sure enough, the man pulls from his pocket a gadget that looks like a monocle, and hands it to Rayleigh. After she takes it, he makes a circle with his finger and places it over his eye, indicating that she should put it on.

Rayleigh places the glass over her eye and looks at him through the glass, feeling a little silly. She had expected something to happen, but she sees nothing but him staring back at her. She starts to ask if something should be happening, but stops when the man extends out his hand, gesturing that he would like the device back again. Rayleigh, completely confused, hands the monocle back. The man takes it, pulls out a long rod from his pocket, then places the monocle on the end of the rod. As he turns it over in his hands, a holographic screen flicks into view and Rayleigh sees images flashing up on it.

They are pictures of Tom and Rayleigh's life, back home. Questions flood her mind, but before she can speak, the man shuts down the device and turns back to Tailia and says, "Le ee ve nc on ra lea cl."

Tailia nods.

He turns back to Rayleigh. Then, without warning, he sticks something into her neck. Rayleigh feels the pinch of the needle, then pain runs down her spine.

"Hey," is all she can get out before her head starts to spin and she begins to feel faint. She reaches out, grabbing the man's forearm to try and stabilise herself.

When the feeling subsides, Rayleigh realises she is still holding the man's arm. He is giving her a surprised and uncomfortable look. Quickly, she pulls her hand away.

"Sorry about that," she says.

"That is okay. Please follow me." He turns to walk back towards the cliff face.

"Hang on… what was that?" Rayleigh blurts out.

"The shot I gave you contains small robots that translate our outsider or first level language for you."

Small robots... does he mean nanites?

Before Rayleigh can ask any more questions, both the man and Tailia disappear into the cliff face. Rayleigh stands alone, stunned.

"Are you coming?" Tailia calls out, poking her head out of the cliff.

"But I..." Rayleigh begins, but Tailia vanishes before she can finish.

Rayleigh approaches the wall and places her hand on the cliff face. *This is silly,* she thinks.

Her hand disappears into the cliff. She withdraws her hand quickly and almost hits herself in the face. Gently, she reaches out again, and her hand disappears into the cliff.

She turns her hand around. There is no resistance, no sensation against her hand. Her arm and the cliff have become one.

Something grabs Rayleigh's hand, and she is pulled forward. Before she has time to react, she dives into the cliff face. The muscles in her body tighten, and she half expects the cliff to smack her in the face.

However, she continues through the wall, following the rest of her arm. When she regains her footing, she finds Tailia holding her hand.

"The entrance isn't a toy," Tailia says with a smile.

Rayleigh looks up, and goes to speak but notice the city living behind Tailia. Looking in awe at it all, she can see technology that appears to be light years ahead of what she had expected. There tall buildings stretching deep into the mountain, with trains, and small vehicles moving about. People go about their business, with a bustle of a metropolitan city. The stark contrast between the desert outside and the interior of the mountain is like night and day. There are hums and clicks of sliding doors opening and closing around her, as people come and go out the buildings around her.

Inhabitants gather around her. She begins to feel uncomfortable at all the eyes looking at them, as if judging them both.

Tailia's voice interrupts her thoughts. "Welcome to Annie Ingles."

The monocle man gestures for Rayleigh and Tailia to follow him. As he walks off, Tailia falls in behind him. With her head on a swivel, she tries to take in all the sights, fighting back the uneasiness of being in such a place. Rayleigh doesn't want to be left behind, so takes off behind them.

As they walk through the structure, Rayleigh is amazed at its size. It looks as though the city takes up the entire mountain. *Was the mountain here first?* Rayleigh wonders. *Or the city?*

Rayleigh tries to count the windows, to see how tall the buildings are. Built losses track as she tries to count and walk, settling that there would be fifteen to twenty levels on the tallest buildings. The ceiling to the city is hundreds of metres above the buildings.

The locals stop what they are doing and turn to face them as they pass, raising their hands over their faces like the man did earlier. Like a wave in the ocean, the hands drop as they pass. Rayleigh hears them mutter in the same jumbled language.

That must be their local language? What did he call it, outsider or first level. Rayleigh remunerates, trying to remember what he had said.

What is this world?

Moving through the streets, Rayleigh quickly loses her bearings. She scans the city and the people around her. Tailia is calm and casual, taking everything in stride, with the confidence that Rayleigh has come to expect from her companion.

Rayleigh sees and hears children running and playing in the background. They skip and dart at the corner of her eye. They play with the mischievousness of all children, trying desperately to see these new people within their community.

She finds the children's energy and the familiarity of their play comforting. Caught up in her own thoughts, Rayleigh walks into Tailia, and catches hold of her briefly to stabilise herself. Tailia places her hand on Rayleigh's gently.

"How are you doing? Are you okay?" Tailia whispers, holding Rayleigh's gaze.

"Oh, yes. Sorry, I wasn't paying attention."

"That's okay. We're here."

Tailia lets Rayleigh's hand drop as she turns to head through a doorway. Rayleigh follows her into a small bar where a handful of people are sitting around, drinking and conversing. Nobody acknowledges their entrance. The bar is small, cosy and intimate. Rayleigh notices some of the people are smoking from unusual pipes with purple smoke coming out.

Tailia doesn't pause, heading straight towards a group at the far side of the bar. As they approach, Rayleigh takes them in, hesitant due to their appearance. They are all human except for one of them, who has reptilian features and is small with grey skin, sucking on a pipe and exhaling purple smoke from their mouth and nose.

There appear to be small diamonds on their face. *How did they get there?* Rayleigh wonders. A large scar runs down the left side of their face, giving them a dark, sinister appearance. Rayleigh slows and moves behind Tailia.

The creature flashes their teeth in a snarl, allowing the smoke to creep slowly out of their mouth and nose.

"You couldn't scare a bee off a flower, Rutherian," Tailia quips, like a parent to a child who is misbehaving.

The creature slithers under the table out of sight, then pops up on the same side as Tailia and Rayleigh. Rayleigh realises that they must be only a few feet tall, though with a solid build.

"Tailia. Welcome, welcome. What brings you down into the slums?" Rutherian says, giving Tailia a hug around the waist. Rayleigh senses a shift in Rutherian's attitude, shifting from snarling and fierce, to a gentle embrace between friends.

Tailia reaches down to pat the creature on the head, as if greeting a child.

"Be nice to her, Rutherian," Tailia says. She crouches down next to them, looking in Rayleigh's direction. To Rayleigh, she says, "Don't let Rutherian give you crap. They're a big sweetie with a heart of gold."

"A heart of gold and blood of diamonds." Rutherian chuckles, then looks around at the bar. "But hey, don't say it too loud. It's a pleasure to meet you. If you are with Tailia, then you have my life." Rutherian reaches out a hand, its back towards Rayleigh.

Unsure what is happening, Rayleigh copies the action and touches the back of her palm against Rutherian's.

"How can I help, Tailia?" Rutherian asks, darting back under the table and slithering back to where they had been sitting. Gently placing the pipe back in their mouth, the purple smoke begins to flow again between mouth and nose.

"We would like some information," Tailia begins. "Rayleigh has jumped, and we need to work out where she's from."

"Interesting," Rutherian muses. They lean forward, looking Rayleigh up and down. After a moment, they settle back into their seat. "Guess you want to speak with Groggy." After a pause, they continue, "Are you sure that's wise??? But hey, I trust you know what you're doing." Rutherian takes another puff of smoke before pulling out a small knife. They push it under one of the diamonds on their face, slicing it off.

Shocked, Rayleigh looks between Tailia and Rutherian, wondering if this behaviour is normal. As she watches, the mark on Rutherian's face begins to bleed but stops quickly, closing over again with another diamond.

"Here, you'll be needing this," Rutherian says, throwing the diamond to Tailia.

"Thank you, Rutherian." Tailia swipes the diamond mid-air.

"Do you need anything else?" Rutherian slips the knife back under the table from where it came.

"How is the family?" Tailia asks as she tucks the diamond into her pocket.

27

"The fighting continues, and we have lost too many already," Rutherian replies in a sombre tone. Everyone at the table and in the rest of bar seem to pause in response. "But we live on," Rutherian adds, then throws back the last of their drink.

"My thoughts are with you. Please let me know if you need me," Tailia replies in a hushed tone.

Rayleigh shifts her wait, unsure where to look, as the two of them appear to share a moment.

"The Queen of Rain offering her services..." Rutherian chuckles. "Be careful. I might take you up on that."

Tailia turns to face Rayleigh. "We should get moving."

Why does Rutherian call her the Queen of Rain? Rayleigh ponders, looking up to catch Tailia looking at her, so she nods, unsure what she missed. She notices Tailia turning back to Rutherian, placing her left hand over her eye and the other on top of her head.

"Until we meet again, good friend," she says to Rutherian. "May your cup be full."

"And the same to you," Rutherian replies, mirroring the gesture.

With that, Tailia turns and starts for the door. Rayleigh wonders whether she needs to perform the same action, but pushes the thought aside and follows Tailia into the bustling street.

After the quietness of the bar, the street seems alive with people, even though there are only a dozen or so people, with some standing by the doorway have a smoke.

"What now?" Rayleigh asks Tailia.

"Not here," she replies under her breath. She makes for the front gate.

As they move through the crowd, the pair do not exchange any words. Rayleigh senses Tailia's urgency. She walks with purpose and ease, weaving in and out of the crowd, not touching a soul.

Rayleigh, on the other hand, seems to be bumping into everyone, as if she is barging through the crowd like a bull as she tries to keep up. When Tailia's hand slips into her own she's startled, and unsure what to make of the gesture.

28

Without warning, Rayleigh finds herself in an alleyway, pushed up against Tailia.

Hang on. What just happened? She can't understand how they went from the street to the alleyway in the blink of an eye.

"We're being followed," Tailia says in a hushed voice, before Rayleigh can speak.

"How did..." Rayleigh begins, but Tailia cuts her off by placing a hand gently over her mouth.

Then Tailia is moving down the alley, dragging Rayleigh along, still holding her hand. When they reach the end of the alley, they dart across to the other side of the street. Again, Tailia moves expertly through the mass of people.

"There's a secret exit up ahead. We'll take that," Tailia whispers over her shoulder as they enter another alley. Rayleigh nods in agreement. They stop briefly two or three intersections so that Tailia can scan down the streets. Rayleigh has been watching as the roof, slowly makes its way down to their leve, as they come closer to the edge of the city. When they reach the wall of the city, they stop next to it. Standing before it, it looks like a normal cave wall, *how does she know this is the place,* she pounders trying to find any sign or detail that might distinguish that this is the place.

"Do you trust me?" Tailia asks as she switches between looking at Rayleigh and down the length of the wall, as if searching.

"Ah, yes," Rayleigh replies after a slight hesitation.

"Okay. This is going to be uncomfortable. To get through the wall, we need to be close to each other, very close. We'll be trying to confuse the wall, so we need to be close enough so it can't distinguish between us. This should hopefully allow us to pass through. Also, I'm sorry. The nanites need your body make-up to allow you to pass through the wall. Unfortunately, I don't have a chip for you, so we'll need to use mine," Tailia continues, all the while looking around.

"Oh, like at the entrance," Rayleigh says.

"Yes. But this isn't authorised, so only smugglers and runners will have access," Tailia whispers, as though she's trying to avoid publicising what they are about to do.

"Okay, do what you need to do," Rayleigh says, relaxing into it, trusting in Tailia.

Talia takes Rayleigh's arm and raises it to place a small pen like device onto it. There is a small click and a pinch as something bites into her. Pulling her arm away, Rayleigh sees a small amount of blood swelling. Tailia takes the device and sticks it to her own arm, flinching slightly as the device pinches her in turn.

"We need to give it a second." She places the device back into her bag. "For this to work, you'll need to be closer then that," Tailia says. She holds out her hand.

Rayleigh pauses, having a flash back to her first date with Tom, before they kissed. The thought makes her tense up, scared of what is about to happen next. Tailia slowly creeps in closer, and Rayleigh's heart skips a beat. Taking Tailia's hand, she steps forward into Tailia's personal space. Tailia slides her arm around the back of Rayleigh, pulling her closer, feeling the contact between them, Rayleigh's heart races. She feels Tailia's breath against the side of her neck as Tailia slides her head across her shoulder, Rayleigh returns Tailia's tight hug.

"Are you ready?" Tailia whispers into her ear.

Rayleigh's response gets stuck in her though, as she tries to respond. Giving up she nods subtly. With that, she finds herself falling towards the wall.

Unlike the wall at they used to enter, Rayleigh can feel the wall as it touches her arm. Like touching Jelly, there is some resistance and then gives way to them, allowing them to pass through. As they move through the wall, Rayleigh feels a slight pull all over her body as the wall pushes back. It is one of the strangest things Rayleigh has ever experienced, and the sensations over her skin and body are entirely new to her.

Before she knows it, they are through the wall and standing outside again. Tailia is still embracing Rayleigh.

"Are you okay?" she asks.

"Yep, I think so," Rayleigh says, checking over her limbs. "That was weird."

"Sorry if I invaded your personal space."

"Oh no. Not that. It felt like the wall was pushing against me."

Tailia turns away slightly, and Rayleigh gets the impression she is trying to hide the fact that she's blushing. "Ah, yes. I have been told that can be a strange sensation." She pulls the jump device out of her pocket and looks at it. "Okay, we need to go this way," she says finally, before putting it away.

The two of them begin their journey into the valley, moving through the desert once again.

After a while, Rayleigh notices that they haven't spoken since they left, which is strange, because since they met there hasn't really been any silence. The two of them have chatted back and forth easily. Rayleigh notices tension in her own body. *Why am I frustrated?*

Thoughts begin to pile up in her head, and she loses track of the world around her. With a thump, Rayleigh walks into Tailia's back as she stops to look at the jump device.

"Oh, sorry about that," Rayleigh says, stepping back.

"That's okay. Please be careful. We need to be mindful of the people following us," Tailia says, gazing between the device and the landscape.

Why is she being so distant? Rayleigh wonders.

"Are we lost?" she asks. Then she catches on to what Tailia said. "Hang on... people following us? Who is following us?"

"The I.D.T. have officers stationed in different dimensions, planets and cities. I noticed some officers as we moved through the city. I've been tracking their movements to see if they noticed us." Tailia puts the device away. "I think we've lost them now. Sorry I've been so distracted. I wanted to make sure we were safe before we jumped to the next location."

So that's why she was quiet, Rayleigh thinks.

"Are you ready to jump?" Tailia asks, placing a hand on Rayleigh's arm.

Silently, Rayleigh nods.

Tailia turns and takes Rayleigh by the hand, then walks forward. Rayleigh feels her hairs stand on end, and her stomach turns. With a flash, they vanish to their next location.

Chapter Four

When her vision returns, Rayleigh looks over the field around her. At first glance, it appears to be a corn field, with long rows of crop stretching far into the distance. But rather then ears of corn, the crop has a fruit that looks like a raspberry the size of a basketball, hanging off the side of it. Poking one of them, it pops, before settling back again. Rayleigh can see the outline of skyscrapers towards one side of the field, with mountains reaching up beside it. The city looks like it has small flies buzzing around it. *They must be some sort of transportation.* Rayleigh thinks, trying to rationalise what she is seeing.

"Okay. We should be safe for now," Tailia says.

Rayleigh nods before returning to looking at her surroundings.

If it wasn't for the city and the 'flies', this could almost have been her home dimension. The fields stretches into the distance. Rayleigh catches sight of something hovering over the field, appearing to be harvesting the crop. *Is that one of those flying things?* Rayleigh wonders to herself, trying to get a closer look. It turns in their direction, heading towards them, she can see that it has five robotic arms hanging below it. It appears to be picking up speed, making Rayleigh step back. Trying to put Tailia between herself and this 'robot'. It has a giant ball like head/body, with several red glass orbs around the sides. *They must be it's 'eyes'.* Rayleigh studies the device as it slows up in front of them.

"Please vacate this property. This is private property," an automated voice calls from above.

six metres in diameter, its size is threatening, and Rayleigh begins to wonder what it will do with them.

"Stand down. I'm authorised to be here. Agent Rita Ronald," Tailia responds. She pulls out what looks like a badge from her jacket and holds it up to the robot.

The robot pauses, as if weighing its options. Suddenly, it drops down to be level with them.

"My apology, agent," it says. "How can we be of assistance?"

At this height, Rayleigh can finally see the robot clearly. It isn't as threatening when it's level with them.

"We need transport to the city," Tailia says curtly, with an air of authority in her voice.

"Transport has been arranged. It will arrive 800 metres northeast of this location. How can we be of assistance?"

"That is all," Tailia says, waving her hand to signal to the robot that it can leave.

With that, the robot raises into the sky again and disappears into the field, returning to its work of tending to the field.

"Come. Our transport will be here soon," Tailia says, turning.

As they walk through the field, Rayleigh sees more robots flying overhead. They appear to no longer be paying them any attention. However, Rayleigh still can't shake the feeling that they are being watched. The robots appear to keep the vicinity around the two of them, by flying around or moving away when they approach.

The plants tower above them, making it hard to see more than a few metres ahead. However, as always, Tailia walks with purpose, as if this was completely normal. Before long they exit the field to enter a small clearing. There are several flashing lights around its edge, giving the impression that it's some kind of landing pad.

Before Rayleigh has the chance to speak, a beep sounds from above them. Looking up, Rayleigh sees a craft coming in. Tailia puts an arm across Rayleigh's front protectively, in an effort to keep her out of the path of the incoming craft.

The craft slowly touches down. With a gentle hiss, the door opens up wards like a wing, revealing a comfortable-looking interior with couches and a small table.

Without saying a word, Tailia climbs into the craft. Not wanting to fall behind, Rayleigh follows her inside, taking the seat opposite Tailia. As they settle into their seats, the doors hiss closed. There is a small click, and Rayleigh can see them starting to rise into the sky.

"Destination?" asks an automated voice.

"Leonard Loren Lockle of the Lockle Emporium," Tailia responds curtly. "Please activate codes 56, 42 and 36. This is agent Rita Ronald, badge 920517. Please confirm."

"Confirm. Codes 56, 42, and 36 activated."

Rayleigh looks at Tailia in confusion, questions running through her mind. *Where are we? What are all these codes? And who is Rita Ronald?*

"We can speak freely now," Tailia says. She drops her authoritative posture and relaxes. "Sorry about back on Annie Ingles. Annie is surrounded by nanites. That's how they've protected themselves from outsiders. They will only allow you through the wall if the nanites have your genetic code." She takes a small flask out of her bag.

"That explains the injection," Rayleigh replies.

"When your genetic code mixes with mine, it gives us a small window where the nanites are confused because they can't tell which is my genetic code and which is yours. During that period, both genetic codes are accepted by the wall. Unfortunately, it doesn't take long for them to work out that the new genetic code is foreign, and then denies access." Tailia offers the flask to Rayleigh, who refuses.

"So what are we doing here?" she asks, looking out the window, at the world passing them by as they zip over it. "And who is Rita?" she adds.

Tailia chuckles to herself. "Rita is one of my aliases. And we're here to see if we can find information on the Hu Thu." She places the flask back into her bag. "If anyone will to know about your sector, it's the Hu Thu."

The craft touches down. The door opens with a click.

"Thank you for travelling with us," says the automated voice over the speaker.

"Who are..." Rayleigh begins, but Tailia cuts her off with a raised finger and a slight shake of her head. Rayleigh sees Tailia has straightened up again, taking on her more authoritative posture. Rayleigh pushes her questions aside.

Following Tailia outside, Rayleigh finds herself standing in the city she had seen earlier. The buildings still tower over their heads, even though the landing pad is hundreds of metres above the ground. Rayleigh gawks at the size and scale of the buildings, which stretch far into the heavens.

There must be hundreds of storeys in this building, Rayleigh thinks. *Who made these buildings?*

Noticing that Tailia has already begun walking across the platform, Rayleigh decides she had better follow or risk falling behind. As she takes off after Tailia she hears the beep and click of the craft behind her as it locks before taking off.

The doors to the building slide open as they approach. Inside is what appears to be a small holding cell. Without pausing, Tailia steps into the room, so Rayleigh follows. The doors close behind them.

A sound from the wall behind them attracts Rayleigh's attention. Turning, she sees two robes slide down, popping out of the whole that is opened in the wall. The robe in front of Rayleigh is green and Tailia's is purple.

What is this? Rayleigh wonders.

"Throw it over your clothes. We don't have long," Tailia says, pulling her robe over her head. It covers her from head to toe and drags slightly onto the ground. There is also a small head scarf, which she pulls around her head and over her face.

Rayleigh follows Tailia's lead. As she finishes up, there is a click and the wall on the far side of the cell opens.

Rayleigh could never have imagined the interior. It's like the inside of a beehive and a forest all at once, and Rayleigh struggles to grasps its structure and the freeness of movement within it. People in robes are moving everywhere, going about their business, forming a sea of different colours. Rayleigh can even see robed figures flying up the open middle of the space, travelling between levels and different areas of the building. Some stop to take in the forest stretching up the middle of the building, while others move quickly as though they are running late for a meeting.

Rayleigh is fascinated. Not knowing where to look, she steps forward onto a platform, walking towards the rail in the centre of the large space.

"Hey, watch where you're going," says a voice. A robed figure almost runs into Rayleigh, stopping only at the last moment, then pivots around her before moving forwards again.

"Stay close," Tailia says as she begins moving along the platform.

Rayleigh finds herself in a trance, looking around at the wonders. The massive inside garden stretches as far up into the building as she can see. Figures move around on each level, and flying between the levels. Turning, she sees a purple robe moving away from her, and panic sets in. *Is that Tailia? Or someone else?* Time seems to stand still. After a further quick scan of the area, Rayleigh determines there are no other purple robes. *I guess it's her,* she reassures herself before taking off after the purple robe.

When she joins the figure in the purple robe, a familiar voice says, "I thought I'd lost you there."

As they move along the walkway, Rayleigh wonders how the robed figures are flying, why they are all wearing robes, and what everyone is hiding underneath.

Tailia catches her off guard as she stops in front of a solid smooth wall, then stares at it as if waiting for something. After a moment, an outline appears in the wall, a small opening appears, and Tailia places the diamond that Rutherian gave her into the opening. It closes again, and when nothing happens Rayleigh wonders if everything has gone as planned. As if hearing her thoughts, a new outline appears the size of a door, the wall clicks and slides open. Tailia barely lets it finish opening before walking through. Rayleigh jumps, not wanting to be caught outside before the door closes again.

The room seems to be some kind of store, with items on shelves and laid out all over the room. It is a little sparse. *Maybe it is some sort of antique store.*

There are small plants around the room, and an item that Rayleigh has never seen before. Curious, she moves around the room, while Tailia moves directly to its far side.

"How can I be of assistance to the agency?" says a raspy, slightly metallic voice from behind Rayleigh.

Turning around, she sees a yellow robe behind her. Its wearer almost appears to be bowing, but Rayleigh can't tell for certain because of the robe.

Startled, she simply points a finger at Tailia. The figure in the yellow robe turns to follow the direction of her finger, before turning back to her again.

"Confirmed. Good day to you," the voice says, then the figure begins to back away.

Rayleigh sees Tailia turn to face in her direction, which she takes as a sign to head over to her. Scanning the room out of curiosity, wanting to see all the different items, she wonders what her friends and family would think about all this.

Approaching Tailia's robe, another door opens in the wall nearby, and several robes exit. Making their way for the main entrance, where it closes behind them. The new room looks smaller than the one they are in, and Rayleigh can see another robed figure inside moving around. The figure finishes putting away some paper, before heading in their direction.

"Goddammit. What are you doing here?" The figure removes their robe, seeming flustered. "You shouldn't be here."

Now Rayleigh can see the wearer of the robe for the first time. It has an almost ape-like appearance, with longer arms. It hovers on a metal round disc, that is roughly 30 centimetres thick. They rub their temples as they float towards Tailia.

Rayleigh notices the figure in the yellow robe she had been speaking with earlier is now behind her, holding what she can only guess is some kind of weapon, which is pointing at her. She squeals and raises her hands, feeling like a criminal.

"Come on, Groggy," Tailia says, pulling off her face scarf. She raises her hands too. "Is that any way to treat a friend?"

"Friends! You took my wings! And you want to be called a friend?" Groggy responds. Rayleigh's gaze shifts to his back, where she can see two stubs on the right side, and two scared wings on the left. The stubs are moving slightly, in unison with the remaining wings. Rayleigh has to look away, before she is sick; with her heart tugging at her in sympathy.

"Because of you, I will never fly again," he continues huffily.

Tailia gestures. "Come on. You're flying now, aren't you?"

"Seriously? Gah. I don't even," Groggy continues in distress.

"I'm sorry, Groggy—" Tailia begins.

"You're sorry? Pft." Groggy veers from frustration to sadness. Rayleigh feels the tension in the air and debates internally whether there is anything that she can do – but she doesn't dare to move because of the strange-looking weapon.

"Come on, Groggy," Tailia continues, trying to win them over. "I know a dimension that is making advances in genetic growth. I might be able to help."

"You know I don't like that name," he responds finally, though seeming to be calming down.

"Come on, Leonard. I can help, if you let me," Tailia says.

The tension in the room shifts again.

"What do you need?" Leonard responds after a moment, the last of the anger dissipating from their voice.

Tailia stands upright, more confident now. "We're looking for the Hu Thu."

Leonard looks Tailia up and down, then at Rayleigh. "Who's the newbie?" he asks, sizing her up.

"I picked her up on the way. We're trying to get her home."

"You always were a softy," Leonard says. "Come on." waving them through, indicating for the yellow robed figure to release Rayleigh, who darts over to Tailia as Leonard begins moving to the back of the main room, reaching out to place his hand on the back wall.

Once again, there is the familiar hiss of the door opening, and when it finishes they move through the new doorway into a smaller room, letting the door close behind them.

There are papers and drawings all over the walls; it looks like the inside of someone's mind. Rayleigh can hear the Tailia and Leonard talking, but can't quite make out what they are saying.

Pausing in front of the back wall, Leonard looks over at Rayleigh and Tailia, then at the yellow robe.

"You didn't get this from me," Leonard says finally, pressing his hand against the wall. It dips inwards and then pops outwards. Rayleigh is surprised to see Leonard pull a section out like a drawer, placing it on a desk.

Rayleigh is fascinated to see that in the drawer is some jewellery. It's gorgeous, sparkling in the light. No one else is looking at it. Leonard is reaching into the hole where the drawer had come from. After a moment, he pulls out a small twig with what appears to be a glowing orb attached to it. Gently, Leonard places the twig down on a nearby desk next to the draw.

Rayleigh is captivated by the twig. She can't work out how it can still be alive if it has been inside a wall, but it glows with life.

Leonard begins playing around with the orb, and after a few moments a list of coordinates and figures pops up on the desk next to the orb. Rayleigh realises the orb is casting the information onto the desk.

"These are the ones I know of," Leonard says. "But I don't know if they are still there." They look up at Tailia.

Tailia looks at the list. "These three don't exist any more," she says, gesturing, "but I've not heard of this one. So maybe it's still good." She takes note of the coordinates. "Thank you, Leonard. I owe you one."

"Owe me one. I think that list is quite long, and growing every day. I'm looking forward to the day I get to cash in all these favours," Leonard says with a smile. Before returning the twig to its place in the wall. Leonard picks up their robe again and throws it over themself. "Was there anything else I can help you with?"

"That is all. Thank you," Tailia says, pulling her scarf back over her head. She adds gently, "Be careful. The I.D.T. are on our path." Rayleigh can hear the worry in her voice.

"When are they not?" Leonard replies with a smirk.

With that, they rises back to their original height, higher than everyone else.

Tailia turns to Rayleigh. "Come on. Let's go," she says, making her way to the door.

When the door opens they are again presented with a sea of robes rushing past. Rayleigh realises now just how peaceful the store was, compared to the outside. There are several robes standing at the entrance, apparently waiting to get in. With the door having opened, they push past to take the opportunity to rush into the room.

The yellow robe and Leonard begin engaging with the new people, trying to help them and show them the different items in the room. Rayleigh and Tailia exit, working their way back to the flight deck, Rayleigh allowing Tailia to clear a path through the crowd but staying closely in step with her. As they approach the wall of the flight deck, the door opens.

After they enter the room, they remove their robes. Tailia places hers in an opening in the wall, and Rayleigh follows suit, watching as the robe disappears into the darkness. Rayleigh can see Tailia speaking with the wall on the far side. *What is she doing?*

She's about to ask what is happening, but she's cut off by the wall opening next to her. Through the opening she can see a craft landing on the pad outside. This vehicle is slightly larger than the last one, but otherwise similar. When Tailia walks out onto the deck, Rayleigh follows her.

They climb into the craft and take their seats for the journey. Rayleigh's stomach turns slightly as the craft begins to climb into the sky, and she finds herself wondering what dimension they will be visiting next.

Chapter Five

Rayleigh stumbles as she steps through the jump hole, her foot caught on a tree branch. Her stomach is still doing somersaults and her skin tingles all over. Fighting the urge to throw up, Rayleigh tries to walk it off, looking at the dense rainforest.

There are strange birds and animals calling from their hiding places. Something moves in the trees, but Rayleigh isn't able to see. There are loud crashes and cries as animals go about their lives. This sense of the life of the rainforest makes her feel at home, triggering memories of hikes with Tom. The sounds of the animals, are nothing like she has heard before, the plants are tall, towering above them with their orange and red leaves, there is unusual sweet odour which reminds her that this is not her home. This is indeed an alien planet.

"Are you okay?" Tailia asks, not looking up from the jump device in her hands.

"Yep. That one was easier," Rayleigh replies.

"That's good. I just wanted to quickly mention: you're safe. You don't need to be afraid of them." She places the device back into her inside jacket pocket and looks at Rayleigh.

Rayleigh is about to ask what Tailia is talking about... but then she sees a tall figure standing behind Tailia. They are easily 10 feet tall, with grey skin all over. Despite there size, they are slender, with arms and legs to do not look they should support their size. Rayleigh notices the staff in their hand, which between the tribal robes and mud over their clothing and body. Rayleigh is structure by the primitive tribe though, which grips her, like being stuck in concrete, Rayleigh fights against her a fight or flight impulse, trying to not to be overwhelmed. *Are these Hu Thu's?* she wonders, looking around at them as they emerge from the forest into the clearing they are in.

Tailia turns to greet the figure, and begins talking with them in a series of clicking and knocking sounds. *That must be their native language.* Rayleigh is amazed at what Tailia is able to do. Remembering what Tailia said, and seeing how casually she's interacting with this stranger, Rayleigh feels the tension leaving her body.

The tall Hu Thu has slender arms and legs. They move with fluid movements, like water. Moving their hands and gesturing to Tailia as the two of them talk. Tailia and the creature finish talking, with both of them looking in the same direction as the Hu Thu points into the distance. There is a smaller group nearby, holding spears, bows and arrows.

Though their tunic appears old and almost falling apart, with all the dirt and mud, it is holding together. Small circles and lines cover not only the clothing but also the Hu Thu's skin.

Suddenly, Rayleigh realises she has been staring, missing the whole conversation between Tailia and the Hu Thu, and that they are now looking at her wordlessly, as if questioning whether she is ready to move.

Collecting her thoughts, Rayleigh looks at Tailia, nodding in an attempt to give Tailia confidence that she is focused and ready to go. But no one moves, creating doubt in Rayleigh about what to do next, responding, "Ready when you are."

Tailia and the Hu Thu look at each other, before turning and beginning to walk towards the edge of the clearing, stepping into the jungle.

Making their way as a group through the forest, Rayleigh notices mounds and walls hidden in the forest. The trees and vegetation have claimed the remains of old buildings, covering them with moss, trees and vines to a point where the buildings are almost unrecognisable.

Rayleigh finds herself jumping and looking in the direction of every sound, unsure what is lurking in the undergrowth. Tailia and the Hu Thu continue their conversation as they walk. At times the Hu Thu appears to be laughing, which sounds like a series of faint clicks in quick succession.

Rayleigh notices that the other Hu Thu's that were visible in the clearing, have vanished. *When did they leave?*

Despite the Hu Thu's size, they move through vegetation with ease, stepping easily over logs and trees, trickling through the forest like water making its way through a rocky crevasse, shifting and moulding to the surroundings. Rayleigh and Tailia have to push through the foliage to keep up with their guide.

After pushing through a bush, Rayleigh is surprised to find herself standing on the edge of a clearing, looking out over what appears to be a village amongst the ruins of a city. The tall skyscrapers and buildings appear to be hundreds of years old, held up by trees and vines that wrap around them entirely. Rayleigh can see that the trees have now become places for people to live. Seeing the trees forming into soft outlines of houses and apartments, with people coming and going.

The village existing in the rumble of the ancient skyscrapers and buildings, with life returning through the trees and the Hu Thu's in a small section of the city where nature and civilisation have combined to create a home.

She's becoming lost in her thoughts once again. Tailia and the Hu Thu have already begun to walk down the road to the village. Rayleigh hurries after them.

Coming to a cliff face, vines and trees have grown down the side, creating a path several metres wide down the side of the cliff. Rayleigh notices the locals moving freely on the path, giving them a wide berth as they pass.

The structure of the path suggests that it is by design, but Rayleigh fights to understand how that would even be possible. Wondering whether whole village and path is by design or if it is naturally occurring, she studies the village, the vines and the trees.

The guide stops in front of a hole in the wall, then raises an arm to gesture for Rayleigh and Tailia to head inside.

Pulling back the veil of vines at the entrance, Rayleigh follows Tailia into a room that is cosy and warm. A small fire licks away in the centre, and Rayleigh is surprised to see that while the furniture is made of trees and vines, all the normal items one would expect to see in an apartment are present.

Not wanting to block the doorway, she moves further into the room, amazed that all the items appear to be made or grown in place.

Tailia takes a seat at table in the room, while the Hu Thu that led them there remains standing in the doorway. With a small bow, they turn and exit, leaving Tailia and Rayleigh alone.

Rayleigh takes a seat next to Tailia, with aches and pains all over her body, she flops into the seat next to Tailia.

"What makes you think they'll be able to help?" Rayleigh asks.

"The Hu Thus were once a mighty race. Before the Arrilian War, they moved freely across dimensions, mapping and exploring wherever they could. When the I.D.T. overthrew them, the Hu Thu were forced to dispose of all their technology for their safety, and they went into hiding. I'm hoping they've been to, or have mapped, your home dimension."

Rayleigh hears some clicks coming from behind her. She turns to see the Hu Thu from earlier standing in the doorway.

"They are ready to see us," Tailia says to Rayleigh, collecting her jacket from the seat and heading for the door.

Quickly, Rayleigh gets up and follows her. After exiting the room they turn left and continue their descent down the cliff further into the village.

Chapter Six

They come to a stop before a large tree. Rayleigh cranes her neck to look up, uncertain if there's even a top to it, as the tree disappears into the canopy of the forest. There is a large hole in its side, which the Hu Thu and Tailia disappear into. Rayleigh follows.

Upon entering the tree, Rayleigh sees several Hu Thus sitting around a large pool in the centre of the space. They appear to be meditating, producing faint clicks and hums. They do not react as Rayleigh and Tailia enter, and Rayleigh wonders if their presence has even been noticed.

They move towards the pools, stopping short of the group. Rayleigh studies the inside of the tree, watching as the hollowed out tree disappears overhead. The vines run up the inside of the tree, disappearing hundreds of metres above them.

She notices a chair behind her, which appears to have grown up from the ground. *When did that happen?* Rayleigh thinks. The others have taken seats, so she follows suit.

One of the Hu Thus from the group around the pool stands and walks towards them. Rayleigh shifts in her seat, sensing a strong aura from the Hu Thu, as if they have all the knowledge in the universe. It makes her want to hide away, while at the same time feeling like being wrapped up in a blanket and hugged. Rayleigh has never felt this before.

The Hu Thu joins Rayleigh, Tailia and their guide, taking a seat on a chair that grows from the ground. As Rayleigh watches, a table grows before them. Some members of the group put their hands on it. *This is incredible,* Rayleigh thinks.

Tailia begins talking to the group in the Hu Thus' native language. She hands the Hu Thu the monocle given to her by Annie Ingles. Rayleigh catches Tailia looking over at her, and she blushes as she realises Tailia has been talking about her.

Now everyone is looking at her, and Rayleigh starts to feel like a lab rat. After a few moments, they resume their conversation. The Hu Thu turns the monocle in their hands as if studying it.

When they place the monocle on the table, with vines coming out of the table, to swallow the monocle, Rayleigh watches in astonishment as it vanishes into the table.

The Hu Thu adopts a relaxed posture, closing their eyes. Rayleigh looks around the group uncertainly. After a moment, the Hu Thu opens their eyes and looks at Rayleigh.

"Hello and welcome to Hu Thu," they say. "My name is—" They quickly change to their native language. "—but you can call me Dit3. I hear that you are looking to return to your dimension?"

"Yes, if that is possible."

"Yes. I believe it is," Dit3 says. "Looking at the information that Tailia has provided, we believe that we can assist you. Unfortunately, the 'knowledge well' that contains the information relating to this specific dimension does not reside here."

"Where is it?" Tailia asks.

"It is on 5-438-A-2. Which I believe is familiar to you."

"Seriously?" Tailia asks.

"Yes, it is."

Tailia chuckles. "Sorry, that was directed more towards myself than you," Tailia responds, using Dit3 native name. "I trust in the 'knowledge well.' It is just not somewhere I really wanted to go back to." She pauses, as if turning the information over in her mind. "How do we access the data when we get there?"

Dit3 seems puzzled by the question. They look back and forth between Tailia and Rayleigh, before finally turning to an aide standing nearby and speaking in their native language.

"We will assign a 'knowledge well'..." Dit3 trails off, then switches to their native language to talk quickly with Tailia.

"Monk is probably the closest translation we can come up with," Tailia responds.

"Hmm... Monk will do, I guess. We will assign a 'knowledge well monk' to help with the data extraction," Dit3 concludes.

"Thank you for your assistance. It is greatly appreciated. Please note, we will need to visit another dimension before we can go to 5-438-A-2. Is that okay with your 'monk', and with you?" Tailia asks. Rayleigh hears some hesitation in her voice.

"We would prefer not to interfere with other dimensions, but as a member of our **family**, we trust in your **foresight** and **processing**. So if you decide this is necessary, we will approve it."

Rayleigh is surprised to hear the word 'family' mentioned, and isn't quite sure why they emphasised the words foresight and processing. She finds herself wondering what relationship or shared experiences Tailia has with these Hu Thus.

"The—" Dit3 pauses. "—**council** looks forward to having this convergence of knowledge returned."

"Thank you for your trust," Tailia says, standing from her chair and bowing slightly to Dit3.

Rayleigh watches the monocle resurface from the table, as the vines pull away. Tailia picks it up and places it back inside her jacket, and the table recoils back into the ground.

"If you head back to the room, we will have the monk join you there."

"We should go," Tailia says to Rayleigh. She says a few words in Hu Thu and they bow to each other.

With that, Tailia and Rayleigh are left with their guide, who gestures towards the opening in the tree. As they move towards the entrance, Tailia strikes up a conversation with the guide in Hu Thu. Feeling excluded, Rayleigh lets her gaze wonder, noticing the glowing orbs stretching high into the top of the tree. Watching them, they appear to flicker, creating a ripple affect as the light wavers.

Moving with the group through the village, Rayleigh notices some children playing nearby. While they are the same height as her, they are playing a game with sticks and a ball, that reminds her of children playing in the street outside her place. *What game is that?* she wonders.

Hearing the locals go about their daily conversations, Rayleigh still feels like everyone is aware of their presence, the conversations slowing or going quieter as they approach. The kids are the only ones that appear to not care, as they run in and out of the grown-ups.

Rayleigh realises that she has slowed down slightly, and the others are starting to get away from her. She jogs after them. Catching up with them at the bottom of the pathway leading up the side of the cliff, she pauses for a moment. Looking around at the houses, people, and life that is happening around her, a heaviness comes over her as thoughts of home float across her mind. She never imagined she would see such things.

Looking for jump portals, other dimensions and different races. Am I dreaming? How is Tom doing? What must he be thinking? Rayleigh finds herself wrestling with the thoughts that stir within her. A desire coming over her, to be back on the couch with Tom, cuddled up and watching a show together. With the loss and loneliness getting stuck in her chest, she looks out over the courtyard of the village. *Do they feel this way as well?* She ponders, before turning to take off after the others.

"Sorry I fell behind, I got caught up looking at everything," she says quickly, catching up with the others. Slowly down, she finds herself suddenly flying forward, as her foot catches on the vine. Reaching out she grabs onto the guide to stable herself.

The Hu Thu stops, looking down at Rayleigh and then at her hand on them. Rayleigh senses the Hu Thu tighten up, startled by the sudden interaction.

Tailia breaks the awkward silence. "All good. This the room we will be staying in." She raises her hand to gesture through a door to a place overhanging the village and courtyard below.

Rayleigh heads into the room, wanting to move on from the awkwardness. The apartment is the same one they stopped in earlier.

Tailia speaks a few final words to their guide, who bows and heads back down the road. Tailia joins Rayleigh in the apartment.

"It sounds like we might be here for the night. We should settle in," Tailia says, throwing her jacket over the table, and taking a seat next to Rayleigh. "Is everything okay? You seem distracted."

"Oh, it's nothing." Rayleigh looks up to see that Tailia is still looking at her. "I'm thinking about my old life. Wondering whether people are missing me, or what they think has happened."

"I'm sure they are missing you and will be excited to have you back." Tailia places a hand on her shoulder. "Maybe you should get some sleep. It's been a long few days." She gestures to an internal doorway.

"Maybe you're right." Rayleigh places her hand on Tailia's. "Thank you for everything."

"No problem. Go, rest. I have some things to do, so I will join you later."

"Sure thing."

A wave of exhaustion hits Rayleigh as she pulls back vines to reveal a bed. Like the rest of the apartment, it is made from plants. *This will be interesting,* Rayleigh thinks, and wonders how comfortable a bed of plants can be.

She's surprised as she flops down onto it and finds it warm and gentle. It grows up around her, creating an even more comforting experience. Exhaling deeply, she drifts off to sleep.

Chapter Seven

Rayleigh stirs from her nap, responding to the sounds of voices nearby. In a daze, she looks for the alarm clock. She fumbles around the bedside table but can't seem to locate it. She rubs her eyes, and the world swims into view. *How long have I napped?*

The room filled with vines and plants remind her that this is not her apartment.

Low voices are coming from the next room. It was the Hu Thu's language that she had heard. Not the alarm clock. Rayleigh experiences a flash of embarrassment, and she is happy that no one is around to notice.

Pushing away her embarrassment, she climbs out of bed and places her feet on the floor. She waits for her legs to wake up, giving them a jostle of encouragement, feeling the life return. She pushes herself out of bed, quietly wiping away a little bit of drool from the corner of her mouth.

The sun is hanging low in the sky, making her realise she'd napped for an hour or so. But the rest has given her more energy, bring her back to herself. She stumbles a little as she makes her way over to join Tailia and their new guest at the table.

"Hello, my name is…" the Hu Thu pauses, cocking their head slightly, looking as though they are in thought. "You can call me DitDit42." They stand to bow to Rayleigh as she takes a seat at the table.

Tailia slides what appears to be a hot drink over to her. Rayleigh takes it, then looks over at their guest, responding with a polite bow before taking a sip of the drink.

As the warm liquid sinks into her body, Rayleigh recalls the coffee Tom would make her each day. Pulling the cup closer to her at the thought, she takes another sip, breathing in its smell with hints of caramel and coffee.

"I would have liked to avoid this, but we will need to go to 4-921-C-35, otherwise known as Tarillia. There are some people there that we will need to ask for help. Hopefully, they're still there." Tailia pauses, looking up at the ceiling, before continuing. "Wahita or 5-438-A-2, isn't the most welcoming place, so we need assistance."

"Okay," DitDit42 says with a nod, taking an orb from their robes and turning it over in their hands, as if it's a Rubik's cube they're trying to solve.

"Who are we meeting there?" Rayleigh asks Tailia.

"Trouble and mischief," Tailia replies with a chuckle and a smirk. "Get some rest. We will leave in the morning. DitDit42, make sure you have everything you need. We might not be back for a while."

"How are you able to speak our language?" Rayleigh asks DitDit42.

"The knowledge well imparted this language to me earlier this day," DitDit42 replies.

"But you speak so well. That makes no sense."

"The knowledge well has an infinite source of knowledge. I was of the impression you were not able to speak Hu Thu, so surmised that I should learn your language. Was this not correct?"

"No, that is correct," Rayleigh says as she stands from the table. "I don't speak Hu Thu. I'm just surprised you can learn a language so quickly."

"The Hu Thu can retrieve information from the wells as they require," Tailia says, taking a sip of her drink. "But there will be time for this later, as we travel. DitDit42, can you begin your preparations?"

DitDit42 responds with a polite bow. "Of course. I will complete level 4 preparations."

"Maybe level 6 is best, for both Tarillia (4-921-C-35) and Wahita (5-438-A-2)," Tailia adds.

DitDit42 pauses as if in thought. Finally, it says, "I will consult with the council on this matter." It bows again and turns to the door.

"Thank you for your knowledge," Tailia replies, bowing in turn.

Tailia and Rayleigh watch DitDit42 leave before beginning their own preparations.

***

The sound of the rain overwhelms everything else, and stirs Rayleigh from her sleep. She lies with her eyes closed, listening. The rain is almost hypnotic and gives her a sense of warmth and security.

She slides her hand across the bed, searching for Tom's hand. She finds it and pulls, sliding under the arm as she rolls over. She presses herself backwards, nuzzling against the warm body behind her. She can feel the warmth of the body, as their skin touches, being held gives her a sense of peace and safety.

She slips back into sleep.

***

The rain continues outside as Rayleigh wakes from her sleep. She is alone in bed now, and she pulls the blanket tighter around herself, trying to keep warm, taking in the beautiful sound of the rain, like a thousand tiny symbols all playing softly at once.

As she regains consciousness, she hears clicking in the background. Did she leave the clock in the bedroom again? Sitting up in bed, Rayleigh rubs her eyes. The room comes into view.

She sees DitDit42 and Tailia, through the partially open doorway, at the table, talking.

Feeling exposed, she pulls the blanket tighter, trying to cover herself.

Tailia notices the movement and looks over at Rayleigh. Her smile puts Rayleigh at ease. She allows the blanket to loosen around her again.

She slides her feet over the side of the bed to touch the soft, lush undergrowth, which makes Tailia's and DitDit42's conversation fade from her awareness.

You've got this, she tells herself as she pushes herself out of bed.

The blanket slips away, releasing her from its embrace.

54

Her clothing has been neatly folded in the corner. She doesn't remember putting it there. The realisation that she isn't wearing much spurs her into action. She begins dressing so that she can join the others at the table.

As she pulls on her shirt, she freezes. *Wait – was last night a dream, or…* Her breath quickens and shortens, and she blushes as the memory comes back into her mind. The comforting embrace wasn't a dream, and neither was it Tom. Calming herself, she remembers how nice it felt and how safe she had been. Memories of Tailia and her, flood into her mind of the laughing and joking the night before. They had shared some local fermented concoctions while eating the local food. It had been the first time in a long while that she had allowed herself to relax; she had forgotten all about the dimensions and the fact that she was not at home.

Once again, she had felt safe and happy.

Embarrassment swells within her as she pulls on the last few items of clothing. Wanting to push the feelings aside, she walks into the other room to join the others. As she approaches, DitDit42 switches from Hu Thu so that Rayleigh can join the conversation.

"Morning," Tailia says. Rayleigh tries to avoid eye contact, still embarrassed about what happened during the night. Tailia continues, "There's food in the kitchen, along with a local hot beverage which should help fight the effects of Fu Fa from last night."

"Thank you," Rayleigh says, still avoiding eye contact with both of them.

Tailia comes closer and whispers, "Is everything okay?"

"What happened last night?" Rayleigh asks sheepishly.

"I think we might have had a little too much Fu Fa," Tailia replies quietly. "Sorry – I hope I've not upset you."

"Not at all. It's just that I felt safe for the first time in a while… but I don't really know you."

"You mentioned that last night as well… It was nice to hear about Tom. It sounds like you love him very much." Tailia places a hand on her elbow. "I was surprised how affectionate you became after a few drinks. It was as if a weight had been lifted; it was a side of you I hadn't seen. But there's nothing you should feel bad about. It was nice to see you happy and laughing. As for the cuddling, in my culture that is completely normal. I'm humbled that you felt safe enough to allow me in. So there's nothing to be embarrassed about," she concludes.

Listening to Tailia talk, Rayleigh has relaxed.

"Come," Tailia says. "DitDit42 has everything we need now, so we can leave when we're ready." She turns to head back to the table, where DitDit42 has been sitting patiently.

"Thank you," Rayleigh replies. "I'll grab some food and join you."

Tailia continues talking with DitDit42, leaving Rayleigh to head to the kitchen to get some food. As she joins them at the table, she looks down at the food. *What is this? Is it scrambled eggs? It doesn't smell like eggs.* She searches for courage and, finding it, takes a first mouthful.

DitDit42 and Tailia's conversation distracts her from the food as she chews. It doesn't taste like it looks, but while the taste is unfamiliar she finds herself enjoying it. She hurries to take a second mouthful, realising how hungry she is.

"We have been permitted to use level 6, so I have been provided with the appropriate knowledge for this mission," DitDit42 says.

"That's great to hear, and it will be a big help," Tailia says. "So, the plan is to head first to Tarillia (4-921-C-35) to get some assistance for the journey to Wahita (5-438-A-2). The last I heard, they were drowning their sorrows in a bar there."

"Who are these companions?" DitDit42 asks.

Tailia chuckles. "Trouble and mischief. We met during one of the wars." She takes a bite of her food. "They now run the lanes, working for different—" She stops to cough. "People trying to make ends meet. If anyone can get us into Wahita (5-438-A-2), it's them."

Rayleigh finishes her food before speaking. "Are you sure we need them?"

"Our chances will be better if they're there. I'd definitely recommend it."

"Sounds like we should take the time to go get them," DitDit42 adds.

They each look around the table, nodding to one another. At a sound from the door, they all turn in unison.

"I've come to wish you well, and for the knowledge to be bestowed upon you," Dit3 calls out from the doorway.

"Fantastic. Thank you for everything," Tailia says, approaching them. She stops short, bows and clasps her hands together in prayer.

Dit3 returns the gesture, before straightening and walking through the door, flanked by two other Hu Thus. Their heads are covered, and they make no sounds or gestures to the group.

When Tailia looks back at her, Rayleigh decides it must be time for action. Pushing herself up from the table seems to stir DitDit42, who follows suit. Rayleigh collects the small bag Tailia had given her, for her belongings, from the bedroom before joining them at the front entrance. Tailia pulls back the vines to reveal the outside world, then allows Rayleigh to step onto the road outside, the others following.

The sight of towering trees, and the flow of water from the rain earlier, takes Rayleigh's breath away. She still can't believe the world she is now living in. The rain has created waterfalls within the village. The newly created waterfalls, sound as though the village is clapping to say goodbye to the three of them.

They each bow to Dit3 as they pass and begin their climb to the top of the village.

Chapter Eight

The waterfalls fade as the forest embraces them, bringing with it new sounds. The three of them move through the forest without a word. Rayleigh notices that DitDit42 is smaller than their first guide, appearing to struggle more moving over trees and navigating the forest. DitDit42 is still moving more ease then Tailia and Rayleigh, gliding through the forest, as the forest appears to be working to allow DitDit42 through. Tailia and Rayleigh continue to push their way through the forest, branches whacking into them frequently.

Memories of walks with Tom pass through Rayleigh's mind. They took countless hiking adventures, seeing hundreds of waterfalls. It was one of their favourite things to do together.

Birds fly overhead and Rayleigh can hear the calls of animals around her, adding to the familiar sense of being in the wild.

They pass through a small group of trees to find themselves at the edge of a clearing.

"This is it," DitDit42 says.

Rayleigh can hear Tailia breathing heavily, and there is sweat on her brow. *So I'm not the only one.* Rayleigh pauses, trying to catch her breath and looking up at their guide. DitDit42 reaches out an arm, holding their staff horizontally. Tailia and Rayleigh each take hold of the staff.

There is a flash of light and a crack of thunder. Rayleigh's body jumps, and she feels sick as a tingle runs across her skin. She is becoming used to the sensation of a jump.

As the sensation subside, Rayleigh notices asphalt underfoot. There is a faint burning smell in the air, and she hears the clanking of metal in the distance.

"You're getting better at that," Tailia says, pulling out her jump device from her clothing. Satisfied with its reading, she puts it away again and says to Rayleigh, "It might be best if you don't talk to anyone. DitDit42, it might be best if you conceal yourself. I'm not sure this place will be friendly to Hu Thus."

"As you wish." DitDit42 bows, then turns.

"I'll be in contact when we have what we need," Tailia calls out as DitDit42 walks away.

Then she turns to Rayleigh. "Let's go."

Rayleigh nods. She turns to say goodbye to DitDit42, but to her surprise they are no longer there. Confused, she turns back to find that Tailia has also started moving, and she hurries to join her.

As they walk, Tailia hands a trench coat to Rayleigh. *Where did this come from?* Rayleigh wonders as she pulls on the coat. She's even more surprised to see another coat, which Tailia puts on herself.

They walk into a busy street, pushing through people mindlessly going about their lives.

As they walk, Rayleigh looks at the people, who appear to be lifeless, almost zombie-like drones. They all wear the same drab clothing, and none of them talk or interact with anyone. They purchase food from the vendors of small stalls without a word.

Buildings tower above them, dwarfing them, almost stripping Rayleigh and Tailia of their identity. Within the landscape they are ants, moving along with all the other insects.

The buildings appear old, old enough that they ought to be demolished. Yet Rayleigh can see hot metal being poured inside some buildings, only to then be hit by massive metal hammers. The air is cold, but the rain is warm to the touch. Rayleigh isn't sure if she would describe the day as hot or cold.

Tailia moves with confidence as usual, making Rayleigh wonder how she knows such a place, only to push the thought aside. Being confident is likely Tailia's default state. Rayleigh moves through the sea of people, keeping an eye on Tailia, trying to make sure she doesn't loose her. When she bumps into the occasional person, she goes to apologises, only to see a lifeless face staring back, scaring the life out of her. She stops the apologetic words from forming in her mouth, and moves on without speaking.

After turning into a dark alleyway Tailia appears to hesitate, scanning the street they've just walked down before moving on.

"We aren't being followed. So we should be okay," Tailia says quickly.

Rayleigh turns to scan the street, mimicking Tailia, looking at the tops of the building and the people and lanes around them. Satisfied, she turns and hurries to catch up with Tailia, who has started down the alleyway. Tailia looks up and down the walls as they walk, as if checking for something. She stops before a wall, tracing the line of bricks. After a moment, she swivels her hand and pushes on one particular brick. Rayleigh watches in surprise as the brick disappears. With a click, the bricks begin folding in on themselves, starting at the one that was pushed.

Tailia scans the alleyway once again, as does Rayleigh.

Rayleigh is fascinated to see the wall vanishing, to be replaced by a doorway. A metal latch slides open and a set of eyes appear in the opening, scanning them both, and then Rayleigh hears a grumble from behind the door. With the sound of a metal latch being lifted, the door opens.

Tailia takes a final look into the alleyway, and steps through, followed by Rayleigh. A hooded figure is operating the door. They have a huge frame and move slowly as they work to close the door again. Rayleigh hears a rumble, and wonders if it is made by the bricks closing up again.

They are in a speakeasy, where a bustle of bodies go about their business, murmuring to one another. Tailia is already making her way to the bar, taking off her jacket as she walks. She gestures to the waiter and takes a seat at the bar. Rayleigh follows her, not wanting to fall behind. She tries to guess the backstories of the people present.

She pulls off her jacket as she takes a seat next to Tailia. The waiter places a drink in front of Rayleigh before she can speak.

"I think you'll like this," Tailia says with a faint smile.

Rayleigh lifts the mug, which is warm. As she raises it to her mouth she detects the smell of vanilla. The muscles in her body relax in response to the familiar smell.

"That's a great decision," says a voice next to her.

A man is standing next to Rayleigh, smiling and gesturing at the drink in her hands. Smiling back, Rayleigh takes a sip. Warmth courses through her body.

"What's the smell you got?" the stranger asks.

Rayleigh looks at him in confusion even as the drink takes effect, relaxing her body even more.

"Vanilla," she replies.

"Oh. Not sure I know that one."

"Would you like to try it?" Rayleigh asks.

"No, that's okay. The drink has a psychedelic in it, which triggers your tastes. It means everyone gets something different with that drink. So I'd taste something else," he says with a wink. "Hi. My name is Allgery," he says politely, raising his hand to take Rayleigh's.

"Ha. Don't believe those lies," Tailia scoffs from behind Rayleigh. "That, Rayleigh, is 'trouble'… and the gentlemen in the corner, well… that's 'mischief'," Tailia says, gesturing to both Allgery and another man in the corner.

"Come now, Tailia… I'm not 'trouble'."

"Seriously."

"What about Tatterian? Or Bauther?" Tailia says, walking behind Rayleigh to stand in front of him. Rayleigh isn't sure if they are going to fight or hug.

"Well, okay, you have me…"

"And Yaather?"

"Hey. That one wasn't me," Allgery replies. He looks up to the ceiling as if in thought. "It is good to see you, Tailia."

"You too, Allgery."

They embrace, holding one another for longer than seems normal, each clasping and patting the other's back. Allgery has to bend over slightly to account for Tailia's size. Rayleigh concludes there is a strong connection between them.

"Good to see you two are still travelling together," Tailia says, looking over at Allgery's companion sitting in the corner.

"I keep saying he doesn't need to follow me, but he keeps insisting," Allgery replies.

They move towards the back of the room. Rayleigh collects her jacket and follows. When they reach the table where Allgery's companion is sitting, his attention is taken away from the conversation with the others around the table and drink, and he looks up. Noticing Tailia, he smiles, jumping up from his seat and almost knocking over the table. When he sees Rayleigh he stops, which makes her uncomfortable. *Is he going to hug me?*

"Hello, I'm Bellery."

He begins to extend his hand but then withdraws it, before extending it again. Confused, Rayleigh puts out her hand to greet him. "Hello, my name is Rayleigh."

Bellery takes her hand and gives it a good shake. It's strong enough to make Rayleigh wonder if she might lose her arm.

"Pleasure to meet you. Any friend of Allgery's is a friend of mine."

He releases her hand, then Rayleigh watches as he turns and performs the same steps with Tailia. Finally, he takes a seat at the table next to Allgery, who whispers into Bellery's ear, "You've met Tailia before," which turns Bellery's face red with embarrassment.

"It's okay, Bellery," Tailia says.

"So, what trouble have you brought me now, Tailia?" Allgery asks.

"We need to go to Wahita (5-438-A-2)."

This makes Allgery break into laughter, making Rayleigh feel even more uncomfortable about the situation, and even more out of the loop.

"Why would you want to go back to that hellhole?" Allgery asks.

"We're looking for information to get Rayleigh home."

This turns Allgery's attention in Rayleigh's direction, though it also calms his laughter.

"You do love a lost cause," he says. "Things have been a little boring… Why not?" He downs the last of his drink, and looks to Bellery, who quickly finishes the last of his. "I guess we—"

There is a loud crack, and the room erupts and the air is sucked out. The explosion rips through the front door, throwing people into the air. Allgery and Tailia turn in unison as the speakeasy erupts into chaos, everyone climbing and scrambling over each other, trying to get away from the door.

I.D.T. officers storm into the room as the vacuum of the explosion dissipates.

"You are under arrest!" an officer yells across the room.

Then the officer's head explodes. Rayleigh retches. She isn't sure who fired the shot, but everyone in the bar has pulled out weapons and are now firing in the direction of the hole in the wall, where the door use to be.

"Let me guess – they're with you," Allgery says to Tailia. He overturns the table over and pulls a gun from his jacket, firing in the direction of the entrance like everyone else.

"Can't say I know them," Tailia replies.

Rayleigh is terrified, and can't understand why they're speaking so casually. Tailia, too, has pulled two hand guns from underneath her coat.

"And you say I'm trouble," Allgery yells at Tailia over the noise, even as he takes out two officers coming through the front door.

"Guess sooner is better than later. Bellery, we need out." Allgery calls out.

"Yes sir," Bellery replies. He pulls open a compartment in the seat armrest. His hand move over the controls in the armrest, and to Rayleigh's surprise, the chair vanishes into the floor, leaving behind an opening and a stairway down.

"Come on, this way," Bellery calls to Rayleigh, who is crouching on the floor behind Tailia and Allgery.

Panic surges through Rayleigh's body.

"Hey, it's okay," Bellery says. "I've got you." He walks amongst the hail of bullets to crouch next to Rayleigh, and she takes his hand.

"Where did you find her?" Allgery yells to Tailia as he ducks behind cover.

"She found me," Tailia responds, then she stands to continue shooting at the officers storming into the bar.

"Please, by all means, your majesty," Allgery calls, gesturing towards the stairway with a curt bow.

"Ha. You're such a doofus," Tailia says, before dashing through the opening, followed by Bellery and Rayleigh.

With a smile and a few last shots at the officers at the entrance, Allgery ducks into the opening behind everyone.

Bellery, Tailia and Rayleigh stand in the underground passage, waiting for Allgery. When he comes down through the doorway, Bellery nods to him and closes the door.

"Come on. This way," Bellery calls out. He turns from the door controls and runs along the hallway.

Looking at each other, Allgery, Tailia and Rayleigh take off after him.

***

Rayleigh find herself once again amongst the lifeless people on the street. With their hoods pulled up, the group begin moving through the crowd of people.

Rayleigh pauses as she sees Tailia staring into the sky. Rayleigh notices the streetlights flashing, bumping into someone she turns towards them.

"I'm sorry," Rayleigh says to the lady.

They scurry away with fear in her eyes. Her mouth open, but not a single sound leaves it.

"Come – we need to go," Tailia says, appearing at Rayleigh's side and taking her by the arm.

"Where are we headed?" Tailia asks Allgery as they move along the street, people parting in front of them.

"Hangar 38." Allgery continues scanning the street for officers.

Tailia pauses and looks up at the sky again. "DitDit42, can you make it there?" she asks, as if speaking to herself.

The group stops, all looking up at the sky too. The streetlights flicker.

"What about DitDit42?" Rayleigh asks Tailia.

"All good. DitDit42 will meet us at the hangar," Tailia replies.

She pulls Rayleigh to the side of the road, joining Bellery and Allgery at the edge of the street. They all head down an alleyway, away from the crowd of people.

"The person I bumped into… why did they look so scared?" Rayleigh asks Tailia.

"Let's talk when we get on the ship," Tailia replies, smiling at Rayleigh before turning back to give a signal to Allgery.

***

Tailia stops to scan the streets and buildings, signalling to Bellery and Allgery to continue to the a wall on the opposite side of the street. Rayleigh tries to copy her movements, looking for any sign that someone might be following them, as they cross the street to join them.

"This is it," Bellery says under his breath, pointing at the door that they need to enter.

"Okay. Rayleigh, you're with me," Tailia says, crouching down next to the others.

"We'll head around the back," Allgery says, nodding to each of them in turn.

Tailia and Rayleigh creep forward, scanning for any sign of life. When she reaches the door, Tailia pulls an item from her clothing, placing it on top of keypad next to the door. After a few moments fiddling with the door, there is a small pop and click and the door swings open. Tailia ducks inside, and Rayleigh follows suit.

There are three ships in a row on the far side of the massive warehouse. There is also some odd-looking robotic machinery, looking strangely humanoid with two big arms and some legs, Rayleigh finds herself wondering about its use. The silence is eerie, and Rayleigh can feel her heart beating in her chest as excitement races within her. She looks at Tailia, waiting for her signal.

Rayleigh catches sight of a figure falling from the ceiling nearby, and they both jump. Before Rayleigh can react, Tailia is sprinting in the direction of where the figure would have landed. Rayleigh takes off after her, catching up as she rounds a collection of crates .

"Woah, woah, easy." Allgery says, as he and Bellery come out with hands raised.

Rayleigh and Tailia relax at the sight of them, before they collectively look over at the ship.

"Did I hear you say DitDit42 earlier?" Allgery asks Tailia.

"Yep. We have a Hu Thu travelling with us," Tailia replies, holstering her weapons and turning towards the ship.

"You're full of surprises," Allgery says with a sigh as he and Bellery follow her.

The spaceship appears old, but having never seen a spaceship before, Rayleigh isn't sure. She can see dents in the metal and a patchwork of different colours.

"How many people can it hold?" Rayleigh asks Bellery.

"It has beds for twenty, but we'll be the only passengers for this trip" he replies, looking up at the ship.

The metal ramp touches down onto the concrete warehouse floor with a crisp click, followed by the clacking of Bellery's and Allgery's feet as they walk up the ramp. Once inside, they stow their weapons and wait for Tailia and Rayleigh. Tailia stows her bag and weapons without asking permission. *Has she been here before?* Rayleigh wonders.

The ship's engines begin to power up. Bellery straightens up quickly and looks at Allgery with a confused expression on his face.

"Who's touching my ship?" he demands.

"Let me guess. Your friend?" Allgery says to Tailia,

Tailia smiles and winks at Allgery as she places her jacket in the bay.

"Bellery, it's okay," Allgery says as Bellery tries to move past Allgery and towards the doorway. "It's a knowledge monk. Who knows, maybe they've made improvements." He places a hand on Bellery's shoulder, but Bellery looks even more scared. He breaks free and takes off through the doorway.

"We should probably go after him," Allgery says.

Rayleigh and Tailia follow him to the command deck, where the door swings open to reveal Bellery hovering around DitDit42, trying to look over their shoulder to see what they are doing.

DitDit42's eyes are closed, and they don't appear to have noticed Bellery looking over their shoulder. They appear to be praying, their hands held over the top of the controls. They are muttering to themselves, and Rayleigh can see the controls moving as if responding to DitDit42's voice.

"A thousand pardons. We have company, so I believed it best to start the ignition sequence," DitDit42 says in response to the unasked question, bowing their head as Bellery and Allgery walk past.

"Company?" Allgery responds.

"Yes. In one minute and 30 seconds... 29... 28..." DitDit42 continues to count down in a calm repetitive voice.

"Well, then... I guess that's our cue," Allgery says. "Bellery, if you could be so kind?"

"Yes sir," Bellery responds, strapping himself into the chair next to DitDit42.

"Buckle up everyone," Allgery commands as he takes his seat at the desk.

Tailia directs Rayleigh to the seat next to her and shows her how to strap herself in. Rayleigh looks in response to a rumble, and through the front viewscreen she sees a fireball erupting on the far side of the warehouse. *Crap, what now?*

"Bellery," Allgery calls out as figures stream into the warehouse. As they get closer to the ship, it becomes possible to identify them as the I.D.T. officers. They flow into the warehouse like ants over prey, spreading out through the warehouse to close in on the ship.

"Yes sir," Bellery responds. His hands move over the desk with purpose and familiarity.

The whole ship shakes as the engines take on the weight of the ship, lifting it off the ground. It climbs slowly, turning towards the large door at the far end of the hangar. They watch as the doors finish opening, clicking into position as the ship moves towards them.

With a roar, the engines hurl the ship into the air and through the giant doors, out into the gloom of the day. Rain beats down on the screen at the front of the command deck as the ship roars through the clouds, breaching them to reach clear blue skies above.

The spaceship makes a small twist, as they head for the darkness of space. Rayleigh takes deep breaths to calm herself, her heart racing due to excitement. When she looks out into the darkness of space, realisation sets in. *This is space.* Her heart stops. *How did I get here?*

"So what's the plan?" Allgery words break through Rayleigh's thoughts, returning her to the group.

"I've just sent you some coordinates," Tailia responds as she taps away on the commands control panels in front of her. "This is where we can jump from."

"That's several weeks away," Allgery responds, looking at the coordinates Tailia sent through.

"It will give us time to prepare." Tailia looks at Rayleigh.

"Hang on. Why will it take so long?" Rayleigh asks, confused.

"This is a big dimension, and the place we need to jump to is on the other side. It will take some time to cross this dimension," Tailia replies. She turns back to the group. "We should teach Rayleigh how to protect herself. We'll need all the hands we can get."

"Sure thing," Allgery says. "Bellery and I can run her through firearms."

"I'll be happy to help ease her mind," DitDit42 chimes in.

Tailia nods in agreement. "Come on, Rayleigh. I'll get you set up." She passes Rayleigh's chair, heading for the doorway of the command deck.

Unbuckling her belt, Rayleigh slips off her chair and heads out.

***

"I've made some adjustments to your ship's software, which should allow it to run more efficiently," DitDit42 says to Allgery as he approaches.

"See, Bellery, the monk has helped improve the ship already," Allgery calls out to Bellery, who is staring intently at the controls.

DitDit42 gestures to the ship. "With your permission, I would like to make some further improvements over the coming weeks."

"Have at it," Allgery replies. He turns to the desk behind him. "It might be wise to keep Bellery updated. I'm sure he will be fascinated to see what you do, as well."

"As you wish," DitDit42 responds with a polite bow and clasped hands. They head for the door, leaving Bellery and Allgery alone on the command deck.

"Are you sure you want to do this?" Bellery asks now that they are alone.

"Something feels off. My gut is saying this won't end well," Allgery begins, then pauses. He gets up from his seat and walks over to stand by Bellery. "But after everything she's done… I would go through hell for Tailia. So I'm all in," Allgery pats Bellery's shoulder, looking out into space. He reaches into his pocket to pull out his watch. He turns it over in his hand, before slipping it back. "I owe her as much," he mumbles to himself. "She knows pain that we will never understand. If I can help, or ease the burden she carries, I'll do what I can."

Bellery is silent for a moment, then says, "I will do all I can to help."

"Thank you, Bellery. Come now, we have planning and preparation to do," Allgery says with gusto, turning to leave the command deck. "I'm hungry as hell… it's time to cook up a feast."

"Sir, I've told you. I don't think hell gets hungry… It's a place."

Allgery chuckles. "Oh Bellery, you beautiful soul. Come on."

The two of them laugh as they make their way to the kitchen, talking of old adventures and everything to come.

***

Rayleigh and Tailia are sitting at the table in the kitchen as Allgery and Bellery enter. Allgery and Bellery nod to them as they walk past, but continue to the cooking area.

"Looks like we're in for a treat," Tailia says. "The boys are going to cook for us."

"That sounds nice," Rayleigh says.

"Bellery and Allgery are great chefs. We're in safe hands."

"Earlier today, the lady in the square freaked out when I spoke to her. What happened?" Rayleigh asks, picking at the snacks on the table as she speaks.

Tailia sips her drink. "Communication is outlawed on Tarillia (4-921-C-35)."

"That's ridiculous. How can communication be outlawed?"

"Centuries ago, speaking without permission or authority was outlawed to prevent civil unrest. Punishable by life in prison, or even death. Only those with permission or who are in a position that gives them authority to speak, will speak. That woman thought you were trying to trick her into speaking, which would have been a death penalty, which is why she was terrified of you."

"But we were talking in the bar," Rayleigh says.

"The bar was full of 'jumpers', smugglers and outlaws... They don't exactly care about what is allowed," Tailia says, twirling her drink in her hand.

"But I'm not an outlaw."

Tailia laughs. "It's all a matter of perspective. You're a jumper and you spoke, which are both crimes, so to others…" She raises an eyebrow and takes a swig of her drink. "You're an outlaw."

Rayleigh sits back, taking in what Tailia said. She has spent her life trying to do what's right, and has never broken the law. Now she finds herself on the run, a criminal and an outlaw.

"But come now," Tailia says. "That's a problem for another day. Now we need to give you some training so that you can be ready for what's to come. I'll teach you hand to hand combat and Allgery will teach weaponry. As for the monk, they will need some time with you. Not sure how to explain it, but DitDit42 will help you with decision and flow."

Rayleigh feels exhausted just hearing what they will be doing over the coming weeks, but also a little excited about the new challenges that she will face.

Sounds begin to filter from the kitchen, pots and pans banging away, making Rayleigh wonder what Allgery and Bellery might be doing.

"I'm excited to see what he makes this time," Tailia says.

"Do they need help?"

"Those two? They don't like others in the kitchen when they're cooking. It might be best to stay out. After dinner we will get an early night, so you can get some rest."

Rayleigh nods. They both get up from the table and head back to their quarters. Rayleigh thinks about what she has in store for her over the coming weeks, learning about combat and defence. Uneasiness rises within her at the thought of combat. *Will I be ready? What have I got myself into?*

Entering her quarters, she closes the door behind her and crashes onto the bed, looking up at the ceiling trying to work out what is ahead of her.

***

"Morning," Tailia says, stretching out on the mat.

Rayleigh walks into the room, which appears to be a small gym. DitDit42 is sitting cross-legged at one side of the room with their eyes closed. They appear to be in deep meditation, their hands in front of their chest, moving slowly through different hand gestures. They are humming hypnotically and clicking to themself. Rayleigh is captivated.

"Ship to Rayleigh," Tailia says, breaking Rayleigh's focus.

"Morning," Rayleigh replies.

Tailia looks at DitDit42 in the corner, before turning back to Rayleigh.

"Come on, let's begin," she says, moving into the centre of the mat. "This might hurt, as we will need to build repetition and memory in your body. We'll be pushing your body in ways it has probably never been pushed before."

"I've done some self-defence classes." Rayleigh chimes in, pushing back at the idea that she doesn't know anything.

Tailia raises an eyebrow. "Let's just start from the beginning. This is a technique that I learned from… This is something I learned that should be useful," Tailia says. Moving Rayleigh's body, so there is a slight bend in her knees and her hands raised in front of her, at stomach level. "We will create a base and build upon it from there. We'll begin with some simple moves, and then you will practice, going through the movements over and over until they come without thought."

Tailia begins to show her the first few movements. Rayleigh follows along, trying to mirror her motions. She struggles to keep up with some movements and stumbles over others. They continue through the five different movements. As they go, Rayleigh notices Tailia's fluidity and elegance. After a few repetitions, Tailia steps aside and begins to direct Rayleigh, helping her when she forgets a movement, or when she does one wrong. As time passes, Rayleigh begins to settle into the movements, becoming more comfortable with each one. She still feels rough, and she doesn't have the same flow as Tailia.

Movement one. Movement two. Movement three. Movement four. Movement five. Rayleigh talks herself through the different steps.

Though she's unsure how long she's been going, she notice her muscles beginning to shake. She's sweating and her body aches. Finally, she collapses to the mat.

Lying on the floor, Rayleigh stares up at the piping and metal of the ceiling. The humming and clicking of DitDit42's meditation interrupt her thoughts. DitDit42 pops into view, looking down at her.

"I guess it is me now?" DitDit42 says to Tailia.

"She's all yours," Tailia replies, picking up her gear and heading out of the gym.

"I'm not sure I can do anything," Rayleigh says to DitDit42. She's still lying on the mat, struggling to move a muscle.

"That is okay. We can work from where you are." DitDit42 lies on the mat next to Rayleigh. "We are here to work on your mind… What do you see?"

"The ceiling."

"What do you feel?"

"Tired," Rayleigh says.

She expects another question, but for some time there is only silence.

"Your mind is a wealth of information. We choose what information is taken in and processed, and what information is removed. You say that you see the ceiling and you feel tired – because this is all your brain wants or is able to process. You need to dive deeper and take in more information. More data. Take in *more* of the ceiling, take in *more* of feeling tired. See the details, the lines, the pieces, the details of the ceiling. It moves, it breathes, it speaks to you." DitDit42 is speaking slowly in a hypnotic voice.

"But it's a ceiling. It doesn't move, breathe or speak," Rayleigh says, turning her head to look at DitDit42.

"It is speaking, if you are willing to listen to it. Open your mind. You need to allow the information to come in. If you do not listen, you will not hear. If you do not feel, you cannot understand. We make decisions based on the information we have available. If you do not have all the information, you will make poor choices. What do you see?" DitDit42 asks again.

Rayleigh is silent for a while, trying to understand what DitDit42 is saying.

"I see… I see…" She trails off, feeling silly about looking up at the ceiling and trying to feel something. *What is DitDit42 on about?* "I see, pipes, wires, lights… I see where one wall meets the next."

"Good."

"But I don't feel anything."

"Meaning and understanding will come. For now, absorb the information. Take it all in. What do you feel?"

"I feel… I feel the mat. I feel the pain in my muscles, the sweat running down my brow. I feel the twitch in my leg muscle, gravity pulling me to the mat, air passing over me…" Again, she trails off.

As she lies there, her mind reaches for all feelings and sensations present within her body. The tightness of her clothing, the pain, the exhaustion. She even questions if she feels DitDit42 beside her. She loses track of time as she dives into herself, trying to notice all the different feelings.

"That is probably enough for today. I want you to be conscious of taking in the world around you. As you go about your training, be aware of the information you are ignoring, and the information you are taking in. Open your mind to take in all the information, so that you can make the best decision," DitDit42 says.

Rayleigh opens her eyes, only now aware that she had closed them.

"But we only just started!"

DitDit42 turns to Rayleigh, smiling. "Actually, it has been several hours. I believe you may have napped."

"Oh, I'm sorry," Rayleigh says, embarrassed.

"Not to worry. Listen to your body – it knows what you need. If it tells you to nap, then nap. I believe Allgery and Bellery are in the armoury, waiting for you."

DitDit42 closes their eyes and begins a meditative chant.

"Thank you," Rayleigh says, pulling herself up from the mat.

As she takes her first few steps she feels a little giddy, and reaches out to the wall to stabilise herself. Her muscles protest at being asked to move again. Beside the door, Rayleigh drinks water from a tap, enjoying its coldness.

Open my mind, Rayleigh repeats to herself, trying to remember DitDit42's words.

As she steps through the doorway of the armoury, Rayleigh sees Allgery and Bellery standing in the shooting range. They fire down the range with casual ease, making it look like second nature. Unsure if they have noticed her, she continues to walk towards them.

"Hey, glad you could join us," Allgery calls out without looking around, catching Rayleigh a little off guard.

"Hey. I'm ready to learn," she says. "But I'm not sure I have the strength for firing a weapon." She demonstrates lifting her arms.

"Good. That's the best time to train." Allgery puts his gun down to greet her. "When we are tired, that's when we get sloppy. So being able to hit a target when you're tired is important to staying alive." He takes a gun from the rack. "We will be focusing on accuracy. We'll start small and build up from there."

Bellery laughs. "Accuracy! You couldn't hit the broadside of a barn."

"Don't listen to him," Allgery says.

"Don't worry. I won't disturb you," Bellery says, walking past them to place his guns back on the rack. Waving goodbye, he exits through the armoury door.

"You'll be fine," Allgery reassures Rayleigh as he guides her to the firing range. "Now, I'm sure Tailia has said the same thing: this is going to take repetition and practice. Once you've spent time with the monk, you should come here and practice. It's important that you are able to hit the targets you are trying to hit. We don't need any stray bullets in our backs." Allgery points down the range, then steps behind Rayleigh. "Let's see what you can do."

Rayleigh fires off a few shots, then she and Allgery look down the range to see what she hit – but she missed target, hitting the back wall.

"No stress," Allgery reassures Rayleigh. "It's all about your breathing. Try to keep breathing calmly, and ease into it. You look like you're scared of the gun at the moment. We need to work towards making you comfortable with holding it and shooting it. That will take practice and time." As he talks, Allgery makes small adjustments to try and tidy up Rayleigh's shooting stance.

"Try again," he says, moving behind her again.

Rayleigh misses everything again.

"Again," Allgery says.

"I'm not sure I have the strength," Rayleigh says.

"If we're in a fight, not having the strength will get you killed." Allgery looks at her blankly. "Again."

Rayleigh returns to firing her weapon. Over and over again, she continues to try and hit the target. As the afternoon passes, she does improve slowly. She fights her increasing exhaustion. She fights to keep her body functioning.

"That's probably enough for today," Allgery says, looking at his watch. "We should rest and eat. I'm sure you will sleep well tonight, and you'll need it, because we'll do it all again tomorrow." He takes the gun from Rayleigh and places it back in the rack.

Rayleigh looks down the range, disappointed with herself that she wasn't able to do it. Throughout her life things have come easily to her, so the thought of not being able to do something stirs annoyance within her.

Pushing the feeling aside, she joins Allgery at the doorway to the armoury and they head towards the kitchen, making idle conversation. Rayleigh isn't really paying attention; she's thinking back over the events of the day, trying to remember everything that the others have been trying to teach her.

Her stomach growls, bringing her back to the present. She notices the smell coming from the kitchen. *Is that beef stew?* Memories of home come flooding into her mind. As she enters the kitchen she sees that everyone else is already there, waiting for them to arrive.

Allgery and Rayleigh find their seats at the table. Rayleigh looks over the food that has been prepared, trying to make sense of what she is seeing. *Is that a roast, and vegetables?* The food is strangely coloured, but her stomach takes over and she stops caring. She begins to fill her plate, her hunger rising and the desire to eat building within her.

As they eat, stories of war, love and loss are passed around the table. Rayleigh listens, appreciating the connections and bonds that they have formed. She sips on her drink and relaxes.

DitDit42 moves through the group, collecting items from the table and cleaning up as they go, taking care of them all and ensuring everyone has what they need.

***

"She's asleep," Bellery says, looking over at Rayleigh, who has hunched over in the chair.

"Did we push her too hard?" Tailia asks, taking a sip of her drink.

"It's her best chance of survival," Allgery says. "So what's the plan?"

Tailia looks around at them all. "I'm concerned. From what DitDit42 has told me, the knowledge well is in an underground cave. In theory, it should be closed off from outsiders, so it should be safe."

"Only those with correct access rituals will be allowed to enter," DitDit42 says, entering the room from the kitchen and joining them at the table.

"That means we will need to work our way through the ruins of the capital to this location," Tailia says, pulling up a map of the city on a holographic display hovering over the centre of the table, flickering and giving off a faint hum as it displays the planet. She points to three routes in turn. "We can approach from one of these three locations. The last information I have received is that the planet is run by three gangs."

"Three gangs control the whole planet?" Bellery asks.

"There were hundreds, but over the last thousand years, three have risen to the top. Each specialises in a different type of warfare. They've reached a stalemate that has lasted for one hundred years, none of them able to overthrow the other. There is also a significant I.D.T. outpost. The I.D.T. have classified two of the gangs as 'Repudium' or void, because they have brought technology from other dimensions to use in this war."

"Sounds like a party," Allgery quips, smirking.

"I thought parties were supposed to be full of friends having fun? So is this really a party?" Bellery says to Allgery.

The group all look at Bellery, unsure about his statement.

Allgery chuckles. "Oh, Bellery," he says, patting him on the back.

"I believe we should land here, and come in through this route," Tailia says, pointing. "We should have minimal resistance if we go this way,"

"As we get closer, I will be able to get more information," DitDit42 chimes in.

"Sounds good," Allgery says.

"Until then, we try to help Rayleigh as much as we can. We will be throwing her in the deep end," Tailia says, looking at Rayleigh, who is still asleep with her head resting on the table.

"Sure thing, your highness. Should I carry the princess to her room?" Allgery stands up, pointing at Rayleigh.

"No. I have it," Tailia replies.

"Okay. See you in the morning," Allgery says. He nods to Bellery and the pair leave the dining area together, heading towards their respective rooms.

DitDit42 and Tailia sit for a moment, sipping their drinks. Tailia glances at the sleeping Rayleigh.

"Thank you for dinner," she says.

"It was my pleasure."

Rayleigh shifts slightly before settling again.

"I've not cooked before," DitDit42 says. "It was nice to use the knowledge from the well to prepare something. Food is fascinating."

"It still amazes me that the knowledge well can imprint directly into your brain. The food was amazing. It was as if you've been cooking all your life." Tailia takes another sip of her drink. "Am I making the right decision?"

"All we can do is try. You have made decisions based on the information available. Nothing more can be asked of you," DitDit42 replies, reaching across the table to place a hand on Tailia's.

"It's strange – you remind me a lot of Dit3. It feels as though I'm speaking with him now."

"The information I collected for this mission includes Dit3's experiences with you, as part of the level 6 information request. In essence, there *is* a part of Dit3 with us." DitDit42 looks up at the ceiling. "Your adventures, and your connection with each other, is special."

"What will you be teaching Rayleigh?"

"She will go through the same training that Dit3 completed with you."

"Good. She'll need that, in the times to come."

"You should also remember what Dit3 taught you. Open your mind and listen to your instincts."

"Thank you. My body tells me I need sleep." Tailia chuckles and places a hand on top of DitDit42's. They both sit for a moment before standing and letting their hands drop. They give each other a hug and DitDit42 exits.

"Rayleigh," Tailia says, rocking Rayleigh gently, trying to wake her. "Rayleigh, you should sleep in your room."

Rayleigh stirs slightly.

"You're exhausted," Tailia whispers. *She looks so happy.*

"Rayleigh. You need to rest." Tailia tries again to stir Rayleigh from her sleep. "Don't make me carry you."

She gives Rayleigh a small push. Rayleigh grumbles slightly and lifts her arm gently.

"Alright." Tailia chuckles, reaching down to scoop Rayleigh from the chair. She swings her up with ease and moves towards Rayleigh's room.

She moves carefully through the ship to ensure that Rayleigh doesn't bump her head or that her sleep is disturbed.

Reaching Rayleigh's room, the door slides open and Tailia turns sideways to move through the door. Gently, she places Rayleigh on the bed on the far side. She pulls the blanket over her and moves the hair back from her face.

"Good night. You did well," Tailia says.

She heads for the door, then pauses in the entrance. She smiles and ducks outside, allowing the door to slide closed behind her.

With the day done and everyone asleep, Tailia moves through the ship to her own room.

Crashing into bed, Tailia welcomes the rest that is to come. She thinks over the last few weeks, on the run from the IDT, to bumping into Rayleigh, and ponders on the possible futures for the weeks to come.

"You've got this," Tailia says to herself with a smile, then closes her eyes to get some rest.

Chapter Nine

Over the next few weeks, Rayleigh's practice with the crew continues. Each day, she practices over and over, trying to master the skills the team teaches her. Each evening, she falls asleep before everyone else, tired and sore.

Rayleigh and Tailia begin to practice hand to hand combat, helping Rayleigh understand what it is like fighting against another person. They move through the movements, from one through twenty. Practice and repetition.

Every time, Tailia is able to beat Rayleigh, throwing her to the floor. Rayleigh becomes increasingly frustrated and annoyed with herself.

Once again, Rayleigh finds herself lying on the mat, looking up at the ceiling, yet again having been defeated by Tailia. DitDit42 appears next to her, having stopped their meditation in the corner of the room.

"What are you doing down there?" DitDit42 asks.

"Looking at the ceiling." Rayleigh lets out a sigh. "She's too good."

"She has more information than you do." DitDit42 looks over at Tailia, who is standing beside of the mat, watching Rayleigh. "She has information from years of training and fights, and from the weeks of training with you," DitDit42 adds, offering a hand to her.

"How can I compete with that?"

"You can't. So stop trying to. Work with the information that you have. Make a decision based on what you know, rather than trying to predict what you don't know. You are not able to access the information Tailia has. You need to stop trying to access her knowledge and focus on your own." DitDit42 hands Rayleigh some water.

Rayleigh tries to take in what DitDit42 is saying, but isn't sure she understands.

"It isn't about winning. It is about surviving. With each moment you learn more and collect more information. This allows you to make better decisions, as new information becomes available. You have more information today than you did a week ago, so use it."

What is all this nonsense? Rayleigh thinks. She looks over at Tailia, then back at DitDit42. She walks out onto the mat, facing Tailia for the next round.

A strike, a swing, a duck. It goes on and on. DitDit42 watches on from the sidelines as blows are exchanged. Pain ripples through Rayleigh's body. The ache from the strike, the pain and exhaustion from the training. Her arms are weak, her muscles scream, but she pushes on.

A left hook connects with Rayleigh's face, dropping her to the mat.

"Breathe," DitDit42 calls out. "Open yourself to the years of information that Tailia is giving you. Embrace it, take it in. What do you see and what do you feel? Collect it."

Rayleigh stands and turns back to Tailia. The two of them go back and forth, over and over. With each blow and each swing, Rayleigh tries to open herself up. She tries to notice the ways Tailia moves, and the attacks she makes, all of which come from decades of combat experience.

Rayleigh reminds herself that this is only practice. In the field, it will be different. The sore muscles and the blows to the body… these things will heal. Now she needs to learn, to grow. With each round, she *is* growing, she *is* improving. With each day that passes, the rounds get longer and longer. Tailia may still be able to beat her, but Rayleigh is getting better.

After her session with Tailia ends, Rayleigh collapses on a chair next to the mat. She looks at DitDit42, who is in deep meditation. Rayleigh notes the aches within her body, then tries to observe the movements and life that the room is offering. There is movement from Tailia and DitDit42, the gym equipment and noises from the room and ship.

Rayleigh can feel the blood running down her fingers as it drips to the floor. The sweat flowing down her face and back. The protest of her legs when she thinks of standing. The cool chill of the water container in her hands. The bruises on her body where Tailia has hit her.

DitDit42 stirs from their meditation and beginning to move. Rayleigh feels movement next to her, and raises her hand to catch the towel that has been thrown at her. Turning, she sees Tailia smiling at her, raising her water container in a 'cheers' salute. Tailia exits the gym, leaving Rayleigh to sit on the chair, holding the towel.

What is this feeling? Rayleigh ponders. She can sense that DitDit42 has begun moving in her direction without looking. Turning, she sees DitDit42 is only a few steps away.

Smiling, DitDit42 sits next to Rayleigh, looking a little out of place on the small chair, given their long body, like an adult sitting in a child's chair.

"You caught it," DitDit42 says, looking down at the towel in Rayleigh's hands. "You can feel it, can't you?"

"I feel I'm being assaulted with information from everywhere." Rayleigh exhales, looking down at the towel.

"Now we focus on moving from reactions to decisions on instinct." DitDit42 stands and moves onto the mat. "Now that your brain is collecting all the information from the world around it, we need to train it to process and make decisions. At the moment, you react based on unprocessed information. We need to process the information so that your decisions are intelligent." DitDit42 adopts a meditative crossed legged pose on the floor.

Rayleigh pulls herself off the chair and takes her place next to DitDit42. Closing her eyes and placing her hands in front of her chest, she opens her mind to the world around her.

"Start categorising the information you are receiving. What is it? What can be done with it? Is it safe, or dangerous? The better we understand the information, the better our decisions. The pain in your muscles... acknowledge it, feel it, categorise it, decide. What does it mean when Tailia throws a punch at you? Acknowledge it, feel it, categorise it, decide." DitDit42 continues to break down the items in the room, the feelings and sensations after the fight with Tailia.

"But there's too much information... How do I process it all?"

"With practice, we improve. If you place your hand in the fire, you will pull it away instantly," DitDit42 says calmly, opening one eye.

"But that's instinct. I don't think about it."

"At some point in your life, you acknowledged fire, you determined it was hot, categorised it and decided what it could be used for and what response it needs. Just because you do not think of it now doesn't mean you didn't think of it previously. Now we want to expand this to the entire world. With time, you will respond to everything in your environment with the same speed and certainty as when you place your hand in a fire."

Closing her eyes, Rayleigh begins to categorise the things around her. She assesses and decides on the feelings and experiences that are coming to her, moving through them one by one.

She senses movement nearby, and opens her eyes to see Allgery enter the room.

"Are you coming to practice?" he asks her.

Rayleigh looks at her watch. She has been on the mat for hours, having lost track of time.

"Thank you, DitDit42. Please excuse me," she says quietly with a bow to the monk.

DitDit42 returns the gesture and returns to their meditation.

As she stands, a sense of peace comes over her Rayleigh. She looks around the room. Something has shifted, but she isn't quite sure what it is. Brushing the thought aside, she heads to the door to join Allgery, who has already begun walking to the armoury.

Rayleigh jogs to catch up with him, and they walk in step, talking.

Bellery is already in the armoury waiting for them.

"We will do the same combat drills," Allgery says. "You will move the drill, and hit only the targets that have weapons. Remember, not the 'innocent' targets." He provides this explanation even though it is not Rayleigh's first time through the course. He chuckles and gives her a pat on the shoulder at the mention of 'innocents,' to nudge her along.

"Okay, okay. I got it," Rayleigh says, collecting two pistols from the rack, which have become her favourites, and moves into the combat field.

"Three… two… one…" Bellery counts down. "Go."

Rayleigh begins walking through the combat course. While the layout changes with each drill, she has become familiar with the situation. She moves calmly and silently through the field, looking for targets that she can hit.

With a crack, the first target drops. A clean hit.

Creeping forward, she searches for the next target. *Crack*, second target.

The shot was a little wide. "Come on, Rayleigh. Focus," she mumbles under her breath.

Crack. Another target. An 'innocent'.

"Bugger," Rayleigh says to herself in annoyance. But she pushes on, moving through the field, trying to find the remaining targets, taking down the targets as they pop up, then moving on to the next target.

"Okay, that's all of them," Bellery calls out over the microphone once Rayleigh has moved through the entire field. As she enters the drill command station above the course, Rayleigh notices DitDit42 standing at the back of the room, watching.

Rayleigh holsters her weapon and heads to the stairs that lead to the viewing stations from which Allgery and Bellery have been watching her.

"Nice work," Bellery says, consulting the report on the screen in front of him. "You were able to shoot all the targets, although some of them weren't kill shots. You're getting better each time. Unfortunately, you still did get some of the 'innocent' targets."

Allgery jumps in. "You've come a long way. Don't forget that."

"My apologies," DitDit42 says, stepping forward. "Is it possible for the targets to fire back at Rayleigh?"

"Yes, we can configure that option, but that's more advanced," Bellery replies before Allgery can respond.

"Could we enable that, please?" DitDit42 asks politely, clasping their hands and bowing slightly.

"I guess so," Allgery says doubtfully, looking at Bellery.

"Thank you," DitDit42 says, then turns to Rayleigh. "Rayleigh as we discussed, open your mind, collect the information, process and decide. In combat, you are looking for items that are categorised as death or danger. These are the targets you must shoot."

"Ah… right?" Allgery says, confused about what DitDit42 is on about.

"Death and danger," Rayleigh says, bowing slightly to DitDit42 before moving her way back to the course entrance. As she walks down the steps, she reflects on what she has been learning. She exhales as she walks onto the field, trying to absorb all the information that she can see and feel, preparing herself for the drill.

Bellery counts down. "Three… two… one… go."

The drill begins. Rayleigh draws her weapon and begins moving in to the course, searching for the targets. The layout of the course has changed yet again, so she pauses, trying to take in the new surroundings. She becomes aware of her breathing; it is short and sharp.

"Breathe. You've got this," she says to calm herself. She pauses to focus her mind.

"Collect," she whispers as she exhales.

She can feel her surroundings, and she is beginning to 'sense' the layout, even though she has never seen it.

"Breathe," Rayleigh says again, edging forward as Allgery has instructed. She's covering her points and making sure that she can't be crept up on.

Crack.

Rayleigh cries out as pain shoots through her body. Electricity courses through her. As she collapses to the ground, she reaches for her injured shoulder.

"Breathe, Rayleigh. Breathe," DitDit42 says over the comms in her head. "You're fine. Collect. Process. Decide."

She tries to slow her breathing, moving through the different phases that DitDit42 has shown her.

"Pain is information. Embrace it," she says to herself through gritted teeth. "Breathe."

She gets onto all fours and continues to take deep breaths to stabilise her breathing. Pain continues to course through her body, spreading from her shoulder.

"Process," Rayleigh says, moving to the next step of DitDit42's teachings. She runs through the mantras and phases, helping her take in information and process it.

With each breath, the world swims back into view. Rayleigh resumes capturing and feeling her surroundings, taking in the layout. The movement of the spaceship, the sweat on her brow, the pain in her shoulder.

She rises from all fours to a crouching position, trying to take in more information about the world around her. She is back in the drill and taking in everything that she can. She steps forward, trying to get back in the flow of the drill.

Her shoulder screams in pain, but she knows now is not the time. She has to focus on the task at hand.

Danger! The thought jumps into her mind. A crack rings out as the bullet leaves her gun. Rayleigh hesitates before looking, worried that she might have shot an 'innocent' yet again.

The shot was clean, and it was indeed a target that should be shot. Rayleigh lets out a sigh of relief and begins to creep forward again. Slipping back into her meditative place, taking in the world around her, she moves through the drill.

There! her senses shout. Rayleigh registers movement, but she hesitates.

Danger! her senses scream a moment later. The danger is in another direction. Rayleigh points her gun towards it – too slow. Pain courses through her body yet again, but she gets off a shot, hitting the target.

Bending over in pain, Rayleigh catches herself before she falls on all fours again. She braces herself with her free hand on her knee.

"Well done," DitDit42 says over the comms.

"Let's call it there," Allgery says.

Collecting her thoughts, Rayleigh pushes herself up and begins moving towards the stairs. Climbing up the stairs, her body aches; the training and exercise has pushed her to the limit. She hands the gun to Bellery before she drops it on the floor.

"You've done well," DitDit42 says, crouching next to her. "You hit the first one, realised the second wasn't a danger and, even after being hit, you were able to take out the third. That is an incredible effort." DitDit42 hands Rayleigh a container of water.

"Those shots don't tickle, either," Allgery comments, walking over to stand behind DitDit42. "Few people can withstand two in a single session."

DitDit42 places a hand on Rayleigh's shoulder to comfort her. "You have it in you. Now it just requires practice."

"Thank you," Rayleigh says with a smile, placing her hand on DitDit42's arm. "I think I understand what you've been trying to teach me. I need to be open to the world and to trust myself."

The two of them sit in this position for a moment. Then DitDit42 bows their head to Rayleigh and stands, breaking their connection. They head for the door, leaving Rayleigh, Allgery and Bellery in the armoury.

***

Rayleigh continues her training with Tailia, Allgery and DitDit42, each of them taking their turn to improve Rayleigh's skills so that she will be ready for the fight that is coming. Rayleigh continues to improve, getting better at both hand to hand combat and weapons training. She takes in and begins to understand what DitDit42 is trying to impart to her.

As the ship approaches Wahita, DitDit42 begins to scan for communications and transmissions from the planet, gathering any information about the planet might help with the mission.

"DitDit42 has been able to get more information about the planet," Tailia says to the group sitting at the table in the dining area, pulling up the map of the planet. She looks around at them all to make sure they are paying attention. "It looks like one of the factions has been wiped out, and their territory has been taken over. That should mean we have one less player on the field. However, the I.D.T. have increased their presence and are now at war with the main faction. It turns out, the main faction imports highly advanced technology from another dimension which has allowed them to decimate the competition. The I.D.T. have responded in full force. There has been heavy bombing around the building above the entrance the knowledge well, and it looks like the route we wanted to use isn't feasible. So we'll be going in this way." She points at a point on the map.

The group tries to take in what she is saying. Bellery is following along eagerly, taking note of key pieces of information. Allgery sips from his cup and throws food into his mouth, acting as though this was a casual game of cat and mouse for children. DitDit42 nods their head, confirming that the information Tailia has provided is accurate.

Tailia looks at Rayleigh to ensure she has been following along. Rayleigh has been nodding and asking questions. Tailia can sense nervousness within the group, despite them trying to hide it. Her training with Dit3 allows her to sense the subtle changes of energy within the group.

After she has concluded her briefing, the group disperses to perform their own activities, and Tailia approaches Rayleigh to check on her.

"How are you holding up?" she asks, sitting down next to her.

"Ah. We're invading a planet with rival factions and a warring I.D.T., looking for some well that has information so I can get home," Rayleigh says, looking down at the table and playing with the cup in front of her. "To think that, several months ago, the biggest problem I had was whether I should do an extra yoga class each week."

"It's been a strange time. But hey, you've taken it all in stride. You've become more confident and you seem at peace, despite everything that's happened."

Tailia remembers her nerves before her own first battle. She felt like a wreck before hand, and she'd had years of training before that point. Rayleigh has only had a couple of weeks.

"I'm glad we met, and I will do what I can to keep you safe," Tailia says, breaking the silence.

"I'm glad we met as well. I don't know how I'll go back to normal life after this."

Tailia laughs. "What's *normal*?" she jokes.

They both start laughing. The sound brings Allgery back into the room.

"What's so funny?" he asks, sitting at the table with them.

"Just life," Tailia replies. She stands and takes cups and drinks out of the cupboard.

Rayleigh perks up when she sees the bottle in Tailia's hand. "Oh. You have more Fa Fu."

Tailia pours each of them a drink, and they each take a cup.

"Life," they all say in unison, raising their cups and banging them together.

"Hey. Where's mine?" a voice cries out from the door. Bellery is standing in the doorway, looking sad that he has been left out.

"Come on, Bellery," Rayleigh calls.

Tailia takes another cup from the cupboard for Bellery.

"Excuse me. Is that Fa Fu?" It's DitDit42's voice, from the hallway.

"Yep." Tailia chuckles and grabs another cup for DitDit42.

They all find space at the table, and Tailia pours drinks for Bellery and DitDit42.

"To life," Rayleigh calls, raising her cup.

"To the adventure," Allgery says, raising his cup to meet Rayleigh's.

"To the people," comes DitDit42, bringing their cup to the others.

"To chance," Bellery finishes off, bringing his cup up.

With that, they all say "Cheers", then drink. The mood has shifted now that they have let their guard down. They begin talking amongst themselves, laughing and joking, enjoying the time they have together before they make planetfall.

***

"Does anyone have any final questions?" Tailia asks, looking around the group.

Each of them glances to their left and right to see if there are any questions, but they all remain silent.

"Let's get ready." Tailia begins giving directions. "Bellery, can you take us in, please? DitDit42, can you assist? Allgery, can you help Rayleigh get kitted up and ready to move out?"

They all nod as she points to them in turn, then they stand and run off to accomplish their assignment.

"Rayleigh," Tailia calls out, jogging over to her. "Stay close when we're down there. I'll look after you."

"Thank you."

Rayleigh notices her heart pounding in her chest, with her hands getting sweaty at the thought of what is to come. Her breathing shortens and she can feel nervousness climbing up inside of her. Her body begins to tingle. She tries to calm herself down by taking deep breaths and moving through her mantras.

This is what the last few weeks have been for.

Having settled the unease in her stomach, she heads to the armoury to meet up with Allgery. As she walks along the hallway, she reflects on her life with Tom. The trips to cafes, movies and holidays all flash back into her mind.

"Breathe," Rayleigh says to herself.

"Focus." DitDit42 pops their head out of the doorway of the command deck as Rayleigh approaches. "You've done all you can. Open your mind, and you will be fine. We will do what we can to look after you." Placing a hand on Rayleigh's shoulder, which helps remove some of the doubt from herself.

Rayleigh responds with a half-smile, unsure if she believes them. "Thank you."

As quickly as DitDit42 appeared, they disappear back into the command deck. Rayleigh can see Bellery fretting over the controls as he prepares the ship for entry into planetary orbit.

Rayleigh continues towards the armoury, focusing on her deep breathing. She has a sense of déjà vu, remembering the breathing techniques she learned in yoga class. The memory brings a smile to her face.

The flickering of the ship's lights snaps her attention back to the present. Looking up, she sees that the warning lights have been turned on.

"We must be coming into range," Rayleigh says to herself. She jogs towards the armoury, wanting to make sure she is able to do her part.

As she reaches the armoury door, Bellery's voice comes over the ship comms. "They know we're here, and have begun firing." His tone is as casual as Rayleigh has come to expect from him.

Allgery looks at Rayleigh standing in the doorway. "Don't worry," he says. "At this range, they can't get through the ship's shields – but it's about to get bumpy." He starts putting on his combat gear, then calls Raleigh over. "Come on. Let's get you ready. We've decided to give you pistols, which are close to the training weapons you've been using. They should also allow you to fight using DitDit42's techniques. For hand to hand, there's the stick here, which will extend to full length, and a combat knife." Allgery points to each item one by one. "I believe Tailia has been training you with these items?"

"That's correct."

"Your armour will protect you from small-calibre weapons, and some blades. It should also reduce impacts. It's good practice, however, to try to avoid being hit. It can only take so much."

Rayleigh watches as he attaches the last of the equipment. A thrill builds up within her. Tailia enters the armoury, and Rayleigh watches as she straps on her armour with confidence and familiarity. She has the same armour as Rayleigh, which reminds Rayleigh of the padding that footballers use to protect themselves: armour over the chest and shoulders, but the arms left open so that they can move freely. There are several pieces of armour on each leg, which double as holsters for her weapons.

Rayleigh notices that Tailia has two swords strapped to her back, and she finds herself a little scared at the idea of them being used. As she watches Tailia finish up, she finds the contrast from elegance to combat-ready hard to comprehend, even though she has seen Tailia in both modes.

"We must be getting close," Allgery calls out as the ship begins to buck and weave. Small clicks come from the metal above their heads.

"We're close enough for particles to get through the shield," Tailia says.

They all pause, looking up at the ceiling.

"One minute," says DitDit42 over the comms, before their voice vanishes again. Rayleigh, Tailia and Allgery all look at one another, then return to their work.

By the time she has finished putting on her armour, Rayleigh is struggling to stand upright. Allgery and Tailia are swaying with the ship's bucking motion with ease, like trained sailors. A violent shift throws Rayleigh off balance, and Allgery's arm shoots out to stop her from falling. Embarrassed, Rayleigh reaches out to the nearby locker to pull herself back up, using a support rail to hold herself steady.

There is a sharp upward change as the ship engines roar slowly their decent suddenly, almost throwing Rayleigh off balance again. The ship whines in response to the hard landing.

"Thanks for the heads up," Allgery calls out to the ceiling, addressing Bellery and DitDit42 in the command deck.

"Our apologies, sir," Bellery says, running into the armoury with DitDit42 behind him.

"The ship's defences have been activated, and set to the armour codes you are wearing," DitDit42 states.

"Thank you," Tailia responds.

Rayleigh hears gunfire from outside the ship. She wonders if it's the ship defences or someone trying to get in.

"Let's move," Allgery calls out. Bellery collects his weapons from the rack and joins them as they begin filing out of the armoury.

Allgery turns and heads for the cargo bay and the exit, moving through the ship with purpose. Allgery has taken the lead, with Tailia following. Wanting to stay close to Tailia, Rayleigh has fallen in behind her, with DitDit42 behind her and Bellery following up the rear.

The ship's defences fall quiet, which they take as the sign to move out. Rayleigh's heart jumps as she steps onto the ramp, following the others. At the bottom of the ramp, she doesn't even stop to look, but follows Tailia to their position as practiced. Reaching it, Rayleigh looks up to scan her surroundings, trying to search for any movement.

The smell of gunshots and explosives are the first things she registers. A dozen or so bodies lie around the ship. Her stomach turns at the sight of blood. She pushes her nausea down; she doesn't want to let the team down.

In contrast to the smells that are assaulting her senses, the planet doesn't look particularly strange. It's a warzone, but the remains of the buildings could be from any skyscrapers or city buildings back home. Most have been destroyed, but every other one still remains. It's not what she predicted, having expected something more alien.

"That way," Tailia says, pointing to the far side of the landing area.

Without a word, Allgery begins moving, and the team spreads out behind him.

Rayleigh turns to see DitDit42 behind her, but Bellery has disappeared.

"Bellery?" Rayleigh whispers, scanning the area.

"Don't worry – he can look after himself," Allgery says over Rayleigh's comms. "Don't fall behind."

The rest of the group has already moved forward, so Rayleigh quickly jogs after them.

Allgery and Tailia crouch behind the wall of the closest building that's still standing.

Rayleigh catches up and crouches down next to Tailia. DitDit42 is standing on the other side of the street as if casually waiting for something. They are looking down at an orb in their hands, which has a faint green glow. Rayleigh notices that DitDit42 has no weapons or armour. They are still clad in their traditional tribal tunic and holds a staff that Rayleigh hadn't seen since they first met.

Allgery begins moving, breaking Rayleigh's focus. She turns to follow Tailia, keeping several steps behind.

"Focus," Rayleigh says to herself. "Keep your mind open. What do you see? What do you feel?"

"We should keep speaking to a minimum," Tailia says over the comms, and Rayleigh realises they have all been able to hear her muttering to herself. Embarrassment rises up, but she tries to push the thoughts out, to stay focused on the task at hand.

As she moves through the building, Rayleigh uses the techniques taught to her by DitDit42 to take in her surroundings just as she had been able to know the layout in training, she begins to sense the space around her.

The buildings are in ruins, looking as though the city had been bombed back into the stone age. There is very little movement or signs of life as they move through the streets, heading for the cave that Tailia and DitDit42 had indicated during the briefing. They duck in and out of streets, demolished buildings and laneways, moving quickly and quietly.

What is this feeling? Rayleigh thinks as she tracks Tailia.

As she steps into the street behind Tailia, something drops next to her. Spinning around, she sees a body similar to the ones she had seen earlier lying on the ground.

Rayleigh panics. *Wait... where did that come from?*

"Are you alright?" Bellery says over the comms.

"What?" Rayleigh responds, stunned, still looking at the body.

Tailia places a hand on Rayleigh's shoulder, snapping her out of her trance. Gently, she guides her to the wall of a nearby building.

"Are you okay?" she whispers.

"Yes, I... err..." she looks around, as if searching, before settling on the body again. "but it wasn't there when I looked the first time," Rayleigh stammers.

"Bellery saw them approaching and took them out," Tailia whispers. She takes Rayleigh's hands in hers. "Deep breaths."

Rayleigh reminds herself of what she has been learning with DitDit42, but her brain wants to shut down at the thought of her near miss.

"Breathe," Rayleigh repeats. She and Tailia hold each other's gaze.

"Trust yourself," Tailia says, before turning and giving a nod to the others, to prepare them to move again.

Rayleigh takes a moment to continue her steady breathing before beginning to move on. She draws her weapons. "I've got this," she says to herself as she falls in behind Tailia.

The group continues moving towards their destination, scurrying their way through the ruins. They approach the building that they are looking for, pausing on one side to make sure everything is safe before they cross the street.

"Looks clear," Allgery whispers as the others huddle around him. Bellery is still nowhere to be seen.

"Let's move in," Tailia says.

Allgery nods and begins moving toward the building.

Rayleigh strafes towards the right, following Tailia's direction for them to span out as they approach the building. Crouching, Rayleigh edges forward, hugging the wall of what appears to be some sort of café, with some overturned tables out front that look like they haven't been used in decades.

When she steps out from behind the wall, Rayleigh's whole body tightens.

There! her body cries, and she throws her arm out, gun drawn.

She pauses. Turning her head, she can see a child hiding behind a table that has been pushed over. Rayleigh sighs with relief at the fact that she has been able to stop herself.

The child huddles behind the table fearfully, tears streaming down their face and holding a teddy bear that has seen better days. Rayleigh's chest grows heavy at the sight of seeing a child in such a place.

"You poor thing," she whispers to herself.

Danger! her body screams. Without hesitation, Rayleigh throws her arm in the other direction, towards the building they are approaching, and fires. After a crack and a thud, something cries out and falls ahead of them.

Rayleigh looks at the child again. They have crouched down even further, terrified at the sound of Rayleigh's gun.

"What was that?" Allgery says over the comms.

"Danger!" DitDit42 responds as they rush out into the middle of the street without hesitation, slamming their staff into the ground with a giant swinging arc. As the staff hits the ground, Trees and plants explode outwards from the staff, shooting out from the location of impact.

Trees and plants stretch out growing from the centre of the junction, into the courtyard and the surrounding buildings, growing up into the sky and creating small defensive walls.

Bullets and laser rounds fill the air.

Rayleigh turns back to the child, but they have disappeared. She hesitates. *Should I go find them?* But several rounds whizz over her head, bringing her attention back to the fight. She turns back to the task at hand and moves to the closest wall, created by DitDit42's trees.

Rayleigh recalls her training, scouting for targets and firing as they present themselves. She creeps forward, poking in and out of the shelter and protection that DitDit42's staff has created for them. She sees Tailia and Allgery returning fire in the direction of the building.

Rayleigh fires as she makes her way towards Tailia. Reaching her, she crouches down beside her. Tailia appears focused but relaxed, firing and responding without hesitation.

Turning, Rayleigh sees that Allgery has opened with his large calibre weapon; it is tearing chunks out of the building, removing places where the enemy might hide. He moves without thought for himself, standing out in the open, not caring to hide from the volley of bullets.

As quickly as it started, everything falls silent. Allgery stops firing. Tailia stays behind cover. DitDit42 still stands in the street, holding the staff that has brought life to this lifeless place.

Rayleigh glimpses movement within the building. She raises her gun, but Tailia stops her, pulling it down.

"Clear," Bellery says over the comms. He pops out from a window at the top of the building. He must have crept into the building behind them, and he was responsible for the movement Rayleigh had seen. She realises there is still more to learn. The all move forward as a group again, returning to moving as one, with each knowing their roles.

They move from cover. Rayleigh looks back at the café. *Is the child okay?* she wonders.

They reach the front of the building. Parts of the walls continue to crumble and fall after Allgery's assault on the building.

"How are we looking?" Tailia asks as Bellery joins them, a large gun slung over his back. He holds a large combat blade in one hand and a pistol in the other. Rayleigh's vision struggle to settle on him, and she's hardly able acknowledge his presence.

"His cloak will stop your eyes from wanting to settle on him. It's best not to force it," Tailia explains looking at Rayleigh.

"We're good," Bellery says. He points. "There's a doorway down to the lower levels, this way."

"Let's move. Someone will have heard the firefight," Tailia responds, directing the group to move towards the door.

They move back into their positions to creep into the building.

Allgery has switched to a smaller rifle as he takes point and moves in the direction Bellery indicated. As they move, the members of the group scout out every angle, doorway and access point.

The building creaks and moans after the fight. Some walls crumble and collapse, no longer able to support themselves.

Rounding a corner, Allgery and Bellery fan out into the room in front of them, allowing Tailia and DitDit42 to move forward. Pushing the door open, Tailia and DitDit42 disappear.

"Clear," Tailia comes in over the comms.

Allgery nods to Rayleigh. She creeps into the darkness of the doorway, followed closely by Bellery and then Allgery.

The room is dark and damp, as if it had not seen the light of day in decades. Desks and papers are strewn over the floor. Rayleigh's nose twitches at a faint musky odour.

Without a word, the group moves towards a doorway on the far side of the room. DitDit42's staff begins to glow faintly. bBreaking a branch from it, to handDitDit42 hands it to Rayleigh. Taking it, she uses it to light her way.

Deeper and deeper they go. Allgery and Bellery take point, scanning rooms as they pass ensuring they are clear, knocking down doors as they go.

Allgery and Bellery pause in front of a doorway, scouting down the hallway, keeping a vigilant eye on each of the possible entry points. Rayleigh and Tailia press themselves against the wall outside the room, watching as DitDti42 passes them to enter it.

Rayleigh hears a deep rumble like thunder during a storm and a crushing sound from within the room. Rayleigh feels a sensation like a small earthquake, the walls rumbling.

"Clear," DitDit42 whispers over the comms.

Tailia indicates for Rayleigh to follow her. She nods to Allgery and Bellery before turning into the room.

As they enter, Rayleigh can see that there is a hole in the wall on the right. Arround the outside of the hole, there are vines and roots, appearing as though the hole has been riped open by them. Rayleigh is reminded of the plant explosion that came out of DitDit42's staff in the street. She realises that DitDit42 has been able to create a passage with the roots and plants from their staff.

Without hesitation, Tailia heads into the hole in the wall, nodding and placing a hand on DitDit42's arm as she passes. DitDit42 bows politely, then turns to face Rayleigh, gesturing for her to follow. Rayleigh steps forward and into the hole behind Tailia.

As she moves through metres of earth and rock, Rayleigh examines the intricate detail of the weaving roots that have made the tunnel. She is amazed at how beautiful the pathway is, and reaches out to touch the small orbs hanging down, like fruit hanging from a tree, they glow providing light for the tunnel.

Coming out the other side of the tunnel, she finds Tailia looking at the ruins of an underground village within the cave. Rayleigh is humbled by the size of the cave, seeing it stretch far into the distance, she wonders how something so big could go undiscovered. The small, dim orbs are throughout the village, lending an eerie green tinge to the ruins. Rayleigh finds herself wondering how they can still give off light, and what might be powering them.

Noticing that Tailia has holstered her weapons, Rayleigh follows suit. Turning, she sees the others emerging from the tunnel to join them at the opening to the cave at the tunnel exit.

"If you would be so kind, please follow me," DitDit42 whispers, walking past the group and heading into the village comfortably and with purpose. The group follow them.

It's clear the village hasn't been disturbed in centuries. There are trees throughout the village, giving a sense of life in the village, and she wonders how this is possible underground. The trees and plants are still flourishing within the village, and have overrun most of the village.

The group moves in quiet reverence, not wanting to disturb the peace within the deserted village. In the centre of the village stands a massive fountain with water flowing within it. Rayleigh, Tailia, Allgery and Bellery stop, allowing DitDit42 to move on alone.

DitDit42 halts before the fountain and begins to speak in the familiar clicks and hums of their native language. They begin to move through the hand gestures that Rayleigh has seen during their meditation, before bowing to the fountain.

Tailia, Allgery and Bellery are still scanning their surroundings for movement or possible threats. Looking back at DitDit42, Rayleigh sees they have placed the staff into the fountain and it is glowing, casting light over the entire village.

DitDit42 continues their hand gestures and appears to be speaking to the staff.

Rayleigh notices that the plants and trees around the edges of the village are beginning to wither. As DitDit42 continues, more and more of the trees and plants wither and die. Slowly recoiling to the fountain at the centre of the village, the trees and life of the village dying off.

Rayleigh looks to Tailia uncertainly.

"Hu Thus store information within the plants and trees," Tailia explains in a whisper. "As the information is taken into the staff, the plants are no longer be able to live."

Rayleigh realises that was where the plants from the street had come from: the information within the staff.

"So why not leave it?" she asks, sad to see the life being stripped from the village.

"The Hu Thu have not lived in this village for centuries, and they can't allow this information to fall into anyone's hands," Tailia says in a hushed voice, gesturing that they should be quiet.

The plants continue to wither and die. A small part of Rayleigh is sad to see the life leaving the village, as there was something beautiful and peaceful about the village.

As the last few trees and plants recoil, the fountain stops flowing. DitDit42 continues their gestures and words for a while longer, before stopping and standing, bowing to the fountain before retrieving the staff. Its glowing subsides and the staff returns to its normal state.

DitDit42 turns and bows to the group with clasped hands, and each member of the group returns the gesture, Rayleigh a beat behind the rest.

"We should go," Tailia says.

With nods of agreement, they turn and begin their journey to the tunnel. Rayleigh takes stock of the withered life within the village, shedding a tear for the life that was stripped from the village.

"Do not be sad; the life is not lost," DitDit42 whispers from beside Rayleigh. "When I return the information from here to our village, the life and memories from this village will live again."

Taking stock of DitDit42's statement, a peace comes over Rayleigh.

At the entrance of the tunnel the group looks back at the village before stepping into the tunnel. Ralyeigh stops at the tunnerl, looking back to see DitDit42 looking back at the village. Bowing to the village once more, they touch their staff to the ground. After a momnet the ground begins to shake, and the cave begins to rumble. DitDit42 stands and watches as the cave begins to collapse, engulfing the village, removing all trace of the Hu Thu's existence.

"Come on, we should leave." DitDit42 says to Rayleigh as they approach her.

Stepping into the tunnel, DitDit42 touches the plants holding it open and begins to walk after the others. DitDit42 and Rayleigh move through the tunnel, as it closes behind them, sealing off any access to the remains of the village. As they exit the tunnel, the roots retract completely and the dirt caves in, closing the tunnel.

The group leaves the way they came, heading for the ship, which they hope is still there.

They pass the café where the remains of their battle still linger, they work their way back through the streets, encountering small groups of resistance as they go. Moving on quickly after dispatching the groups, trying not to get tied down. Making it back to the ship faster then expected, they reach the safety of their ship, and feels like she can sense the relief of the group asa they begin to put away their equipment and weapons.

"Can you get us out of here?" Tailia asks Bellery as she takes off her armour.

"On it," Bellery responds curtly before turning and heading to the command deck.

Without needing to be asked, DitDit42 follows him.

"You did well," Allgery says to Rayleigh as she stows her items.

He is probably just saying that. Rayleigh thinks to herself, upon hearing his comment.

Rayleigh looks up to see Tailia nodding in agreement. Rayleigh tries to find the words to respond, but Allgery turns and leaves before she can get anything out, leaving Tailia and Rayleigh alone.

"No need to be hard on yourself. You've done well," Tailia says, placing a hand on Rayleigh's shoulder. Rayleigh sees a small smile on her face, with a relaxed look, bringing comfort and gentleness to Tailia's eyes.

"You've done well," Tailia repeats, before turning and heading out the door, leaving Rayleigh to finishing stowing her items.

Chapter Ten

"So… good news or bad news?" DitDit42 begins as the group settles down at the table in the dining area.

"Good news?" Tailia says hesitantly.

"We have information on Rayleigh's dimension," DitDit42 responds cheerfully.

"And bad news?" Allgery chimes in.

"It appears the dimension operates on a different pattern than most. It hasn't been seen for a while and doesn't play by the same rules as other dimensions," DitDit42 explains, pulling up the dimensional display map. They point to their location. "This is our current dimension. From what I can see, Rayleigh's dimension is here somewhere." They zoom out to show a section of the map.

"What do you mean, somewhere?" Rayleigh asks, confused still by the whole concept of dimensions.

"The Hu Thu's from the village we came from were aware of your dimension. However, because their dimension and your dimension do not cross paths, they were unable to map and find jump points," DitDit42 explains, looking at Rayleigh. "This means we need to jump to this dimension here to get information on jump points," they add, zooming in to highlight the new dimension.

The group fall silent, absorbing this information.

"Is that Dimension 8?" Tailia asks, peering at the map.

DitDit42 zooms in further. "It is."

"Great. I have someone that might be able to help us," Tailia states. "Bellery, can you take us to 8–21–D–35 (Yultina)?"

"Sure. We should be able to get there in a few days – if we can get the right jumps," Bellery replies, studying the map.

"Great. Let's do that," Tailia says. She turns to the group as a whole. "Any questions?"

They all look around at each other, as if waiting for someone to speak.

With nothing further to be discussed, they each break from the table, to head off to begin their tasks. The Bellery and DitDit42 heading for the command deck, and Allgery towards the armoury.

"How does DitDit42 know so much about dimensions?" Rayleigh asks Tailia as she makes to leave the room.

"Join me," Tailia says.

Rayleigh nods and heads out with Tailia.

"I don't have the full story," Tailia says, "but from what I've heard, millennia ago the Hu Thus moved freely between dimensions using advanced technology, and they enjoyed prosperity few species have known. Unfortunately, in their journey to explore the dimensions they came across another species that had also mastered dimensional travel. Let's just say they had a difference of opinion about dimensional travel. The resulting war crossed dimensions, decimating everything it touched. In the end, the Hu Thus went to ground in order to survive. The knowledge wells retain all the information they collected during their previous life."

"So why do they live like nomads?" Rayleigh asks, confused why a technologically advanced race would have little to no technology.

"Their technology can be traced, so they avoid all technology for their own protection. There are rumours that some Hu Thus have been able to seal off a number of dimensions for themselves, which is where they live. The Hu Thus outside these protected dimensions have been tasked with protecting any information that might lead to the discovery of these locations, which is why DitDit42 destroyed the village."

As they reach Rayleigh's room, Tailia concludes, "They're a secretive group, so it might be best to not ask too much about it."

Rayleigh nods in agreement. Tailia begins to walk away.

"Wait," Rayleigh calls out.

Tailia turns in her doorway.

"Who did they meet?" Rayleigh asks, suddenly afraid of who might have pushed such a race into isolation.

"The I.D.T."

Rayleigh processes this information. Before she can ask any further questions, Tailia has turned and continued along the hallway, leaving Rayleigh alone with her thoughts. Her heart aches as she thinks about what the Hu Thus have been through, pushed from their homes and into exile, living in hiding on the run.

***

Tailia joins Allgery and Bellery on the command deck, as they come into view of Yultina (8–21-D-35). Having been able to find jump holes in space, they were able to make good time and have reached the planet within a few days.

"We're being hailed," Bellery states.

"Let me speak with them," Tailia replies.

A voice comes over the comms. "This is the Royal Palace of Queen Yutintie. Please identify yourself and state your purpose."

"This is Princess Tailgarian Butar of Dimension 3," Tailia responds in a commanding voice. "I am here to speak with her royal highness."

"Is saying we are from another dimension a good idea?" Allgery asks, when the comms drop off.

Tailia looks sideways at him with a raised eyebrow, making him think better of saying anything more.

"Please proceed," comes the voice over the comms. "The Queen looks forward to speaking with you."

"Ye of little faith, Allgery," Tailia says. As she leaves the command deck she hears Bellery receiving instructions over the comms about entry and where to land.

Turning towards her room, she sees Rayleigh in the hallway, walking with DitDit42.

"Do you have any plans?" Tailia asks Rayleigh.

"DitDit42 and I were going to work on my meditation," Rayleigh replies.

"Would you mind if she joins me?" Tailia asks DitDit42.

106

With a polite gesture, DitDit42 raises their hand implying that the decision is up to Rayleigh. Tailia's gaze shifts to Rayleigh.

"Sure. What's up?" Rayleigh says.

"Would you like to meet royalty?" Tailia asks with a sideways smile giving her a quirky smirk.

"Oh, that would be cool."

"Awesome. If you would like to follow me."

With a nod to DitDit42, Tailia escorts Rayleigh in the direction of Tailia's cabin. "We'll be meeting with the Queen of Yultina, and I thought it might be nice for you to attend," she explains.

"Interesting. So what are we doing right now?"

"We need to dress accordingly. We can't see a queen in what we're wearing."

Rayleigh looks down at her combat gear and then nods. "What does someone wear to see royalty, then?"

"I have some things that will work."

Tailia thinks back to the times she used to visit the royal courts, and the parties they used to have. She allows thoughts to drift as they walk towards her room.

***

As they enter Tailia's room, Rayleigh realises that she has never been inside it before, or even seen inside it, for that matter.

She's surprised to find the room beautifully decorated, almost hiding the fact they are in a spaceship. Artefacts, artwork and ornaments decorate the room, giving it a character and elegance that she had not expected. The room is big, with cushions sprawled over the floor in the back right corner, looking like somewhere you could easily loose yourself. Some of the artwork looks like something that would fit in a palace, while others depict beautfil scenery for worlds Rayleigh could never imagine. There is also a small table, with gadgets that have been pulled apart, making Rayleigh wonder what Tailia might be working on.

Rayleigh wonders, *Is this how the room was already, or did Tailia decorate it this way?* She can see hints of Tailia's personality in the way of colours and style in the room, giving the impression that this is Tailia's work.

"Has your room always looked like this?" she asks Tailia, who has disappeared into a connecting room.

"The boys let me store some things here."

Some things... how much does she have? Rayleigh wonders.

Tailia reappears holding a dress. Rayleigh is unsure how someone would wear such a thing. Her gaze moves from the outfit to Tailia, who is smiling.

"Don't worry, I'll show you how to put it on," Tailia says, handing it to her. "You can get changed back there."

Taking the piece of clothing, Rayleigh heads for the room Tailia had come from. Inside is an abundance of clothing, jewellery and assorted items. *How much stuff does she have?* Rayleigh runs her hand over the garments in the walk in wardrobe. At the back of the room is a wall of jewellery and trinkets on display.

"Do you need help?" Tailia calls from the other room.

"No, no," Rayleigh calls back, realising she has become distracted.

She takes off her clothes and throws them to the floor, then picks up what Tailia had given her, trying to work out what goes where.

"Step through the hole in the middle, and pull the loop over your head," Tailia calls out.

"Ah." Turning the item over in her hands again, Rayleigh begins to understand. Finding a hole in the clothing, she steps through, seeing a secondary smaller hole, she pulls it over her head. She looks at herself in the mirror, checking to see if it looks somewhat right.

Satisfied that she has achieved what she was supposed to, she heads back into the other room. Tailia is standing in the centre of the room, and has changed too. She is wearing a stunning full length gown that leaves her arms and shoulders exposed. There is a collar that stretches up to curve around the left side of her head, running over her shoulder and down over her body and around the waist.

Rayleigh cannot understand with what appears to be no support, how the dress is able to sit the way it does. She realises this is the first time she has seen Tailia dressed like this. She is gorgeous.

Catching herself staring, she quickly moves around the bed and over to Tailia, who is gesturing for her to come closer.

"You look great," Tailia says.

"Thank you. You're gorgeous," Rayleigh responds.

"Why, thank you. It's been a while since I've been dressed up. Here, place this over your head. Pulling some fabric that is drapped down her back up, to drape over her shoulders, allowing Rayleighs back and shoulders to be exposed. Just wait here a moment." Tailia skips into the walk in wardrobe with all the clothes. When she returns a moment later, she has put on a silver twisted necklace and matching earrings and holds out an exquisite diamond studded necklace for Rayleigh.

"Turn around," Tailia says, coming closer. When Rayleigh does so, Tailia places the necklace over Rayleigh's head and connects it at the back.

Rayleigh asks, "Where does all this come from?"

"Oh, this is stuff that I have collected over the years. The ship is my home away from home. There you go." Tailia finishes up and guides Rayleigh to turn around, gesturing to the mirror.

Rayleigh can't remember the last time that she got dressed up. She is a little excited about the prospect of a night out and letting her hair down. She reminds herself that she is going to see a queen, so the event will likely be formal.

As she stands in front of the mirror, Tailia comes behind Rayleigh and takes a look at both of them. "I think we're ready," she says.

Rayleigh nods, then looks down at her feet, realising she is still shoeless.

"Ah yes. Back in a second," Tailia says. She turns and heads back into the wardrobe again, returning moments later with some shoes to go along with the outfit.

Slipping them on, Rayleigh takes a final look in the mirror. She's surprised that everything fits so well, especially the shoes.

"If you're ready, her highness awaits," Tailia says from the doorway.

"Coming," Rayleigh responds, approaching the door as quickly as she can in her new outfit.

In the hallway Tailia is greeted by Allgery, who is coming to inform them that they had landed.

"Wow," Allgery stammers when he sees her.

"Come on. You've seen me like this before," Tailia responds teasingly.

"Of course. It's just been a while. You look amazing."

When Rayleigh emerges from Tailia's room, Allgery nods to her. "My lady."

Rayleigh bows slightly, a little embarrassed at the attention.

"Come, we should go," Tailia says, heading along the walkway to the cargo bay.

Allgery bows to them.

"Just follow my lead and you'll be fine," Tailia says to Rayleigh as they walk. "Oh, and most importantly, enjoy yourself," she adds with a wink.

At the bottom of the exit ramp they are greeted by a beautiful blue sky. The sun is shining and clouds are rolling overhead. The grounds are lush, with an assortment of plants and trees. People move around, taking care of the garden around them.

Tailia moves towards the guards and the awaiting carriage as if she is floating on air, Rayleigh barely sees the dress move and isn't able to hear any sound from the stone gravel underfoot. Rayleigh has not seen her move with such elegance before. The carriage is gold trimmed, looking like a horse drawn ornamental carriage and looks as though it would cost a world to purchase. Rayleigh is confused about how it moves, as there is no horse to pull it, then she notices that there are no wheels and it is hovering above the ground. She's puzzled about seeing something hover above the ground, while yet also maintaining an aged medieval décor to it.

Noticing that Tailia is almost halfway to the carriage, she takes off after her with a trot, before realising she should probably act more elegantly, like Tailia herself. Slowing down, Rayleigh does her best to mimic Tailia's walk in the hope of fitting in.

There is someone perched on top of the carriage, dressed in a sharp formal black attire, who she assumes is the driver. Someone else is standing next to the door, in a matching uniform, helping Tailia into the carriage. They reach out their hand and bow as Rayleigh approaches. Rayleigh takes their hand and allows them to help her into the carriage.

Inside, the chairs remind Rayleigh of beautiful couches back home, so soft and cosy you could lose yourself in them. As the carriage kicks into movement, she looks out of the window at the beautiful gardens, and rolling mountains in the distances, taking in the scenery and the people.

As the carriage moves through the streets, the locals pause from what they are doing, turn and bow as they pass.

Rayleigh finds herself taken aback and uncomfortable at the attention. She looks over at Tailia. *She seems in her element. She makes it look so easy.*

Rayleigh finds herself wondering about Tailia, and what she has been through to get to this moment. Before she is able to ask any questions, the carriage door clicks open and a hand reappears to help them out of the carriage again.

"My ladies," he says, offering his hand to help them out. Tailia gestures for Rayleigh to go first, so she takes the offered hand and steps out of the carriage.

The building before her is extraordinary. She has never seen a building so big, stretching away into the distance. She wonders why someone would need a place so big.

Tailia raises her arm, gesturing to Rayleigh that she should take it. "Shall we?" she asks.

Rayleigh slips her hand around Tailia's, and the two of them begin walking towards the building.

The servants working in the garden leading up to the building stop and bow as they pass, to pay their respects to the guests.

Climbing the stairs in front of the building, Rayleigh looks up at the palace and finding herself questioning what she is walking into. At the crest of the stairs, doors swing open and people hurry out to stand in lines on either side.

As they pass through the doors, Rayleigh sees the servants that pulled them open. Once again, they are bowing as they pass.

"Good day, madam," says a voice. "It is splendid to see you again. Her majesty is excited to see you." The servant is bowing politely and has a gentle demeanour about him. His clothing is crisply pressed and nothing looks out of place on his uniform.

He raises his head and gestures to their right. "Her highness is waiting," he says in a polished voice.

"Thank you Alister," Tailia says, gently touching the man's forearm as they pass. He walks with them.

"It is good to see you again," Tailia whispers.

Alister bows again, allowing Tailia and Rayleigh to pass through the doors, before closing them.

Entering the room, Rayleigh sees a lady sitting at the far side. There are a handful of other people in the room, all keeping their distance from the Queen, moving in briefly to complete tasks before retreating again.

Rayleigh and Tailia walk arm in arm down the middle of the room, stopping several metres in front of the Queen. When Tailia drops to a knee, Rayleigh follows suit.

"Really?" says a voice.

"Just paying my respects, your highness," Tailia says, bowing her head further.

The Queen claps her hands, and the people in the room scurry away through secret doors and passageways.

Once everyone has left, the Queen rises from her seat. She approaches Tailia and pauses in front of her. Dropping to her knees so that she is level with Tailia, she raises Tailia's face with a gentle touch on the chin.

"I thought I had lost you. When I heard what had happened, my heart broke," the Queen whispers. Rayleigh sees tears streaming down her cheeks. It catches her off guard, both the vulnerability and the fact that she is so close.

The Queen caresses Tailia's face. "I've missed you."

"And I've missed you."

Tailia reaches out to place her hand on the Queen's face, mirroring the Queen's own gesture.

The two of them ignore Rayleigh's presence as they look at each other.

Unsure what to do, Rayleigh continues to kneel on the floor, head bowed, not wanting to disturb their reunion.

"My apologies. I am Queen Yutintie. But please call me Yuti," the Queen says, turning to acknowledge Rayleigh.

"Well, unless others are around," Tailia says, winking at Rayleigh.

"Pleasure to meet you, Yuti. I'm Rayleigh," Rayleigh responds, bowing again slightly to pay reverence.

"Please stand. Join me," Yuti says.

The three of them stand and move to the couches. Rayleigh notes the grace with which the Queen moves. It is as though she glides through the air, lowering herself gently to the couch, every action smooth.

"What brings you here?" Yuti asks, offering food and drinks from the table in front of them.

As she watches Yuti and Tailia speak, Rayleigh begins to feel uncomfortable. *I don't belong here. They both look so comfortable with each other, and the world around them.*

Rayleigh is brought back to their conversation when she catches them both looking at her.

"We are looking for information," Tailia says to Yuti. She lowers her voice. "We need information on the jump locations within your dimension."

"You don't ask much, do you?" The Queen chuckles and sits up in her chair. "I'm sure you know that information is forbidden by the I.D.T."

"Yes, I know. But your highness can request this information from the I.D.T." Rayleigh watches the two of them interact, unsure what is happening.

"Oh Tailia. Of course I will help," Yuti responds with a smile, placing a hand on Tailia's. "I will organise a meeting, and inform them you are my envoy. Please take my maid. She is Yurillian." She claps her hands.

"When did you meet a Yurillian?" Tailia asks, sounding a little surprised.

Rayleigh notices a servant appear from the far side of the room. They are covered from head to toe, with no skin or distinguishing features showing.

"No one can know she is Yurillian. She has been with me since she was young. I found her being traded on the slave market, and couldn't leave her to live that life." Yutintie gestures for the servant to come closer. "Tatinet. Would you be able to assist Tailia, please?" she asks.

Tatinet bows to Yuti .

"Thank you." Yuti bows in turn, clasping her hands together. Then she addresses Tailia again. moving closer to her. "I will organise a meeting with the I.D.T. when you leave. Tailia, please be careful. You are important."

"I will do my best," Tailia responds, placing a hand on Yuti's cheek.

"Come – we should leave," Tailia says to Rayleigh and Tatinet. "Your highness," she says, nodding her head slightly before moving towards the door. Rayleigh and Tatinet fall in behind Tailia.

"What is it like working for a queen?" Rayleigh asks Tatinet.

Tatinet looks back at her. Without a word, she nods and turns to face forward again. Rayleigh is a little confused by the gesture, and is unsure how to take it, she decides to ignore it. Upon exiting the room they are greeted by Alister, who is standing on the other side of the door.

"We have prepared the carriage for you, my lady," he says, bowing and gesturing to the entrance of the building.

Tailia nods in approval. Once again, the front doors swing open as they approach, and Rayleigh sees the servants pulling on the heavy levers to open the doors.

Tailia pauses on the top step, looking up to the sky. "There's mischief in the air," she says to Rayleigh.

Rayleigh pauses, looking into the sky, too, and trying to see what Tailia is looking at, but she can see nothing. Noticing that Tailia and Tatinet have continued towards the carriage, Rayleigh gives up and takes off after them. Taking the servant's hand, Rayleigh climbs into the carriage to join her companions.

The door closes and the carriage lurches into movement, turning down the driveway towards the front gate.

"Please let me know if you notice anything," Tailia says to Tatinet, who is sitting quietly, out of the window.

Tatinet nods quietly and returns to watching the world pass.

A voice comes from above. "Excuse me, my lady – we will arrive in a few minutes. Might I advise making the necessary changes?"

"You're right," Tailia responds. She looks at Rayleigh, then pulls a golden rod from beside her, placing it in her lap. She begins rotating several of its sections, and Rayleigh hears a click as it cycles through. Appearing satisfied that she has found the right combination on the rod, Tailia stops and taps the rod on her clothing.

To Rayleigh's surprise, Tailia's clothes change in a shimmer to a beautiful emerald green.

Tailia hands the rod to Rayleigh. "Place it on your clothes and tap it twice," she says.

Rayleigh takes it and taps it on her own clothing. Once again, she is surprised to see her clothing changing colour before her eyes, as if crawling all over her, becoming the same green as Tailia's clothing.

When the colours have settled, Rayleigh hands the rod back to Tailia, who has been talking to Tatinet. Taking the rod, she places it back into her clothing.

"Now, it's important to remember that we're pretending to be envoys of her royal highness – so we should act accordingly," Tailia explains as the carriage swings through a number of turns. "It might be best if I do the talking," she adds as the carriage slows to a stop.

Rayleigh nods. The driver opens the door, and they each take his hand to step out of the carriage.

They are standing before a skyscraper. It looks out of place amidst all the trees and plants. Rayleigh has a feeling that she has seen it before, but the idea is snapped from her thoughts as Tailia and Tatinet start walking towards the front door.

As they approach the building, a flurry of activity bursts from the entrance as soldiers come rushing out, falling into lines on either side of the door with precision. With a clap of feet and weapons, as they come to attention.

Rayleigh jumps slightly at the sound, but tries her best to hide her response.

With military precision, two soldiers extend their hands, grab the door handles and pull the doors open, revealing a man standing and dressed in uniform.

As he approaches them, it becomes clear that the man doesn't have the precise actions as the soldiers, though he has an air of authority about him and doesn't acknowledge or even seem to notice the soldiers around him, as if the world is below him.

When he reaches Tailia, he bows half-heartedly. "My lady, to what do I owe the pleasure?" he asks, then maintains his bow as he waits for a response.

Tailia extends her hand quite naturally, and the man takes it, kisses it, then holds it briefly before releasing it.

"We are here on behalf of her royal highness Queen Yutintie. We seek an audience," Tailia responds, with a royal accent and demeanour that Rayleigh has not seen or heard before.

Rayleigh finds herself believing Tailia's authority, and straightens up her own stance.

"Of course. We have received word of your arrival," the man responds, stepping slightly to one side and gesturing to the door from which he came. "This way," he says, then waits for Tailia to take the first move.

Without missing a beat, Tailia begins moving to the front door. Tatinet doesn't miss the cue, but Rayleigh is a beat behind. Flinching, she catches herself and moves with the group.

Walking past the soldiers, Rayleigh feels uneasiness creep up within her. The soldiers have enough weaponry to constitute being their own army, and Rayleigh finds herself thinking about what Tailia had told her of the war between the Hu Thu's and the I.D.T.

Breathe. Open your mind, she reminds herself, thinking back to her training with DitDit42.

There is a darkness that Rayleigh cannot shake. Something doesn't seem right.

The door clicks closed behind them, and Rayleigh is snapped from her thoughts. The foyer of the building is cold and uninspiring. There are flags of the I.D.T. everywhere, making Rayleigh feel she has entered the lion's den.

The man continues pauses outside a lift, holding the door open for them and ushering them inside.

No words are spoken and the clipping of their shoes echo through the foyer. Rayleigh finds the cheesy *ding* as the lift doors close slightly odd. A thought jumps into her mind: *Even in other dimensions, it's still the same.*

Another cheesy *ding* snaps her back to the present. The room before them extends all the way to the windows on the far side. Unlike the entrance hall, it is beautifully decorated, warm and inviting, with couches and tables spread around the room. The are officers scurrying around the room, busy with their tasks.

Tailia moves with purpose towards a couch in the centre of the room, taking her place centre stage. Rayleigh and Tatinet follow close behind, sitting on either side of her.

The officers shuffle around the room, taking in Tailia's placement and trying to take their seats in front of her.

"How can we be of assistance to her highness?" the officer standing in front of her asks.

Tailia pauses and looks around the room.

"You can speak freely," the officer says.

"Her highness is concerned about reports of jumpers entering our dimension," Tailia states, then pauses to study the officer.

The room tightens as people stop or slow from what they are doing, making it feel like the air has been sucked from the room. Rayleigh holds her breath.

The officer fidgets slightly, then sits upright, looking at Tailia, then the corner of the room and finally back at Tailia.

"We have no reports," the officer responds.

"Then you make her highness question whether you can keep us safe. We have enemies, and we cannot leave ourselves exposed to such weakness," Tailia continues, staring down at the officer.

The officer fidgets, looking around at the people next to him before turning back to Tailia. "We assure you, her highness is safe."

"Her faith in the I.D.T. is being questioned if you are not even informed of travellers within this dimension," Tailia retorts.

"From where has her highness received this information?"

"Where her highness receives her information is none of your business."

The officer looks around the room, as if searching for a lifeline. "But how reliable is her information?"

"Are you questioning her highness?"

"No, no… Just trying to…" the officer trails off. It occurs to Rayleigh that Tailia has total control of the situation. "How can the I.D.T. be of assistance to her highness?" the officer says in an apparent attempt to regain composure.

"She would like the locations and destinations of the jump points within this dimension."

"But we couldn't. That is confidential."

"I'm sorry," Tailia responds quietly, almost delicate. Rayleigh almost feels sorry for the officer. "When her highness meets with Commander Lee several days from now," Tailia says, leaning forward, "should she tell him that you have ignored the request of her highness?"

"No, no. Of course not," the officer responds, trying to defuse the situation.

"Good," Tailia says, sitting back in her seat.

The officer seems to be waiting for something. When nothing comes, he turns to the aides next to him and starts whispering to them. The aides quickly jumps into action, moving towards the back corner, where everyone erupts into a bee hive of activity.

"The I.D.T. would be happy to assist her highness," the officer replies finally with a bow.

Standing from his seat, the officer moves to the back corner of the room to join the hive of activity and to speak with several clerks.

Rayleigh looks around the room, watching all the aides, clerks and other officers. Something doesn't feel right to Rayleigh. Her mind is unable to settle. She looks at Tailia, who is still steadfastly sitting in her seat. Even though she is seated and outnumbered, she still has command over the room. The officers seem not to want to come too close, skirting around her at a distance.

The officer returns and sits down in front of Tailia again, sliding a data slate across the table to her. "Here is the information her highness has requested," he says with a bow.

"Her highness thanks you greatly for your assistance. This will not be forgotten," Tailia responds politely, taking the slate from the table and tucking it into her clothes.

"Is there anything further?"

"No, that is all," Tailia replies. She stands from her seat and extends her hand to the officer.

The officer stands quickly, takes Tailia's hand and kisses it gently, still maintaining the bow.

Tailia turns towards the lift and Rayleigh and Tatinet once again fall in behind her. As they move through the room, everyone steps away, clearing the path for them to exit, as if not wanting to displease Tailia.

The three of them enter the lift, turning to face the room from inside it. Everyone bows as the doors close. The soldiers within the lift stand at each corner, not moving a muscle.

With a chime, the doors open on the ground floor. Without missing a beat, Tailia steps out of the lift, moving purposefully to the front door. Rayleigh and Tatinet scurry to keep up.

The soldiers greet them at the door, bowing slightly as the soldiers pull open the doors for them to exit.

Tailia picks up her pace slightly as she heads for the waiting carriage. Approaching the carriage, the driver opens the door, offering their hand to help the three of them inside.

As she settles into her seat, the tension within Rayleigh's body dissipates.

"Something isn't right," Tailia says, looking around the group. "Tatinet. What do you have?"

"You are right," Tatinet responds softly. "Most of the people in the room were scared, and you did well to keep them on the back foot. When you mentioned jumpers, one officer in the opposite corner stopped what they were doing to listen. They were not scared like the others; they were focused, and unwavering. While the officer you spoke with collected the information for you, this group was investigating, questioning, doubting what you were saying."

"Impressions?"

"Dishonest, betrayal, death."

"That was my worry," Tailia responds, sitting back. "Driver, did you get that?"

"I did," they respond as the carriage jolts into motion.

"I knew mischief was in the air." Tailia says

Rayleigh senses the carriage climbing into the air. She was unaware that it could fly. It begins to climb, picking up speed.

Looking out of the window, Rayliegh sees soldiers from the I.D.T. following them.

"Crap. That was quicker than I expected." Tailia exhales, pushing back into her seat.

Rayleigh hears Tailia call out to Bellery, and then there is an explosion from outside. She looks out to see the I.D.T. vehicles exploding.

"There is no cover in the air," Tailia whispers to Rayleigh, who realises that Tailia must have organised for Bellery to back them up from the start.

Rayleigh notices that Tatinet has taken off her robes, no longer needing to conceal her identity. Tatinet is humanoid, with bright yellow skin and what appear to be tribal tattoos covering her face and disappearing under her clothes, only to reappear and cover all of her exposed skin.

"Her highness says you always keep things interesting," Tatinet says, throwing her robes out the carriage window.

Tailia chuckles. "Does she now?"

The carriage begins to descend. Looking out of the window, Rayleigh sees a flurry of activity below. As the carriage comes to a halt outside the main entrance of the palace, servants are busy rushing around and packing items away.

Yuti is standing on top of the steps, giving directions to everyone as they move around.

When the door for the carriage swings open, Rayleigh can see that the driver is no longer wearing their crisp uniform, but light body armour.

When did... Rayleigh thinks, taking the driver's hand as she steps out of the carriage.

"Tailia," Yuti calls, rushing down the stairs to greet them. "I'm glad you're alright."

"I'm sorry, Yutintie," Tailia responds, placing her hand on Yutintie's arm.

"No worries. I was sick of this place anyway," Yuti says with a smirk, gesturing at the building behind her. "I was tired of the charade and it was time for a change." She turns as Tatinet approaches. "Are you alright?"

"Yes, I am safe, milady."

"Great. Please help Alister with the preparations."

Rayleigh turns towards the roar of engines from behind her, with a crashing sound as their ship lands on top of the fountain in front of the palace. The cargo door swings open and Allgery comes down the ramp wearing full combat gear.

"Sorry about the fountain," he says as he approaches.

"All good." Yuti chuckles. "It was a little ostentatious, so I didn't like it anyway." She turns to head towards Alister at the top of the stairs.

Rayleigh, Tailia, and Allgery take in the people scurrying about.

"Did you manage to find trouble again?" Allgery quips, looking at Tailia.

Tailia laughs and offers a cheeky smile. "Maybe."

"Rayleigh, you should probably get changed and kit up," Tailia says to Rayleigh. "Allgery, you're with me."

With a nod, Rayleigh heads to the ship to change and prepare for the oncoming fight.

***

"What will you do?" Tailia asks as she helps Yuti get into her armour.

122

"We have an outpost from which we have been operating. We will move there."

"I'm sorry."

"That is alright, no need to apologise." Yuti pauses what she is doing to turn towards Tailia. "We've always known that this would happen one day. This place has been a way for us to collect information and build our strength. This place and my position has given us access to things that we never could have reached." She holds Tailia's gaze before resuming donning her armour. "I've always been uncomfortable in this position, but I've held it for the benefit of my people. Now they need me to fight, and I will lay down my life for them."

"I want to stay and help."

"I know you do. We have different paths, and different roles to play. Mine is with my people, and yours is your own path. I will always care for you."

Allgery comes into the room, drawing their attention. "Oh, sorry."

"Not to worry, we are finishing up," Tailia says, stepping back.

"We have incoming," Allgery says, before nodding and exiting.

"We should go," Tailia says, taking Yuti's hand. "I will always care about you, but as you say, we have different paths."

Tailia takes a final look at Yuti, then lets her hand drop and makes for the front door. As she moves through the room, Tailia feels her body pulling against her, trying to will her to stay. As much as she would love to stay, she knows that this place and Yuti is the past and she must focus on the future. She wipes a tear from her eye.

She can hear that combat has begun outside. She picks up her pace to join her companions outside.

The area outside the palace has been turned into a warzone. I.D.T. soldiers are advancing on the palace from their drop ships. The servants have swapped tidy uniforms for combat gear and weapons, and are holding their own against the advancing soldiers.

Tailia sees Bellery and Allgery returning fire. Allgery's heavy weapons are laying waste to incoming transports and ships, while Bellery, perched above him, casually picks off advancing soldiers.

DitDit42 has used their powers to create walls and barricades to protect everyone from the oncoming onslaught. The sprouting trees consume soldiers and ships alike.

Rayleigh moves from barricade to barricade, using DitDti42's trees as cover to allow her to attack the oncoming soldiers.

Tailia tries to determine where she can have the biggest impact. She turns to find Yuti standing next to her.

"We will defeat them," she says.

"We must," Tailia responds.

"Your path is elsewhere. You should leave while you can. Please – take Tatinet with you?"

Tailia hesitates.

"She is safer with you, and she will be able to help you," Yuti continues, still observing the battle.

"I am happy to be of assistance," Tatinet voice chimes in from next to them.

"Are you sure?" Tailia asks, hesitant about taking on another member.

"I am."

Tailia nods and turns back to Yuti. "Please look after yourself."

"You too."

Tailia moves down the stairs towards their ship, giving Yuti and Tatinet some space.

"Thank you for saving me," Tatinet says to Yutintie, giving her a hug.

"You saved *me*." Yutintie responds with a hand on her arm. She gestures at Tailia on the stairs. "She will look after you now. You should go."

As Tailia turns, watching them embrace, she feels her burden of responsibility increase. Feeling the love between them, she knows that she will need to protect Tatinet the way she would protect Yuti. She exhales, pulling herself back into the moment.

"Come on, let's go," she calls out to Tatinet.

The pair break their embrace and step away from one another, though they each hold onto each other's hands until it is no longer possible, before letting them fall. Tatinet takes a couple of backward steps, then turns and jogs to Tailia.

"Thank you."

"No trouble at all. Come on. The others are waiting," Tailia says, looking at the team, who are engaged in all-out war with the I.D.T. Tailia and Tatinet join them, raising their weapons and beginning to fire.

"We're leaving," Tailia calls over the comms.

Allgery, Bellery, DitDit42 and Rayleigh all acknowledge her statement, and begin moving towards the ship.

"Bellery. Get us airborne," Tailia yells over the gunfire and explosions. She fires as she walks towards the ship, while the others scurry inside.

Tailia turns to confirm that the team is onboard. Then she looks up at the palace, where she can see Yuti moving between barricades, firing and issuing orders. She pauses and looks in Tailia's direction. As they make eye contact, Tailia feels the pull on her heart, at the thought of leaving. The realisation that they may never meet again hits her, and a tear runs down her cheek.

"Thank you for everything. I have always and will always love you," she whispers to herself, which brings on more tears. Pulling herself away from Yuti's gaze, Tailia heads into the ship, pressing the button to close the door.

"Let's go," she says over the comms.

The ship's engines roar, and the ship begins to lift from the ground.

***

Yuti looks towards the ship. Tailia is at its exit, looking up at her.

The world stops as she looks down at Tailia. Sadness comes over her as she realises they may never meet again. Her chest aches at the thought. Every fibre of her body wishes she could leave with Tailia, but her responsibility is to her people.

Yuti hears Alister calling out nearby, but she ignores him, wanting to hold Tailia's gaze as long as she can. Seeing Tailia turn only increases the weight on her heart.

"Thank you. I will always love you," Yuti says under her breath, exhaling to let the emotions flow out of her.

"Your highness?" says Alister again, pulling her back to the moment.

"Yes, Alister?"

"We need to go, or we will be overrun."

"Protect the ship."

"Your highness, we need to leave."

Yuti turns to Alister, knowing full well that he is right and that they need to leave. While also knowing, Tailia won't make it off the planet with out their assistance. Fighting back tears, trying to stay strong for everyone around her. She makes eye contact with Alister. His face cracks from the steely combat expression of a soldier to a trusted confidante.

He steps closer to her. "Are you okay?" he asks, and Yuti looks at him.

Alister turns back to the battlefield, yelling out, "Protect the ship."

With trained discipline, all firing shifts to cover the ship.

Alister turns back to Yuti. "We will do what we can."

"Thank you, Alister."

"No problem."

They turn to watch the ship rise into the sky. As it climbs, Yuti feels the worry for its occupants' safety subside, but the sense of loss grows.

"Goodbye."

"I'm sorry. your highness – did you say something?"

"All good, Alister," she replies. "Come on, let's go. We have people to protect."

Alister nods, and they call for the retreat.

***

"Let's get out of here, Bellery," Tailia says.

Breaking through the outer atmosphere, the ship accelerates into the darkness of space. As it picks up speed, the planet begins to shrink behind them.

There is a silence on the deck, which no one is willing or wanting to break. Tailia pulls the slate from her pocket, twisting it in her hands, wondering if it has the information that they need.

Placing it on the table, she taps on the desk to begin downloading the data.

"It looks like we have what we need," Tailia says, drawing everyone's attention. "Bellery, can you see the coordinates?"

Bellery takes a look. "Yes, I see it. If we are going to uncharted territory, we should stop for supplies first."

"You're right. Make the necessary preparations," Tailia says, before leaving the command deck.

***

"Will she be okay?" Rayleigh asks, looking at the door through which Tailia has gone.

"She will," Allgery whispers, lowering his head to look at the bracelet on his wrist. Turning it slightly, he sighs, then stands. "They have history, but she will be fine." He walks past Rayleigh to exit the command deck.

Feeling the tension within the room, Rayleigh doesn't want to disturb it.

"Heck yes," Bellery calls out from the desk, making Rayleigh jump. Allgery pauses at the door at the sound of Bellery's excitement.

Bellery looks around at everyone else on the command deck. "We can get supplies at 8–12-C-14. They have the best noodles."

"Oh, Bellery, you beautiful person." Allgery chuckles, then turns and leaves.

Bellery continues to look around at everyone, as if waiting for some sort of response.

"What do you mean?" Rayleigh asks.

"There is a noodle place there that I have been wanting to try forever," Bellery says.

Rayleigh and DitDit42 look at each other, then back at Bellery.

"I'm open to trying them," Rayleigh responds, and DitDit42 nods.

Not needing any more encouragement, Bellery turns to start punching away at the controls. DitDit42 takes a seat next to him, looking over the information they collected from Yuti.

Realising she isn't going to get any further responses from those two, Rayleigh walks over to Tatinet, who has been sitting at the back of the command deck by herself.

"What are your thoughts?" Rayleigh asks, taking a spot next to Tatinet.

Tatinet looks over at Bellery and DitDit42. "There is a heaviness. They remember loss, heartache, pain," she responds.

"I worry about Tailia," Rayleigh says, looking through the command deck window into space.

"Unfortunately, I am unable to sense her intent," Tatinet responds.

"What do you mean?" Rayleigh asks, confused.

"I come from a race that does not communicate with sounds, as we are doing now. We read bodies, behaviours, patterns. People's intentions. This means we are commonly used for negotiating or diplomacy, as we can see through the words. I have only learned to speak so that I can communicate with others. But vocal communication feels like a primitive form of communication and leads to miscommunication. I'm not sure why, but I can't read Tailia."

She gazes deep into space, then looks at Rayleigh. "I can see that you are scared, confused about where you belong, unsure of yourself and your value to others. You are moving from a past that was created for you by others, towards a future that you are creating for yourself. Look within yourself to try and find a way to trust yourself. You know more than you realise." She stands, placing a hand on Rayleigh's shoulder.

As Rayleigh looks up at Tatinet she feels a pang in her chest. There is truth in what Tatinet has said.

She drifts into deep thought as Tatinet heads for the command deck door, disappearing into the hallway. She wonders what Tom has been up to over the past months. *Has he moved on?*

She watches Bellery and DitDit42, who have such purpose. They act as though they have all the answers, as if they know their place within the world.

Why do I question myself? How can I be more like them?

Rayleigh wishes she felt the same way. She rises and heads for the door, still lost in her own thoughts. Dimly, she hears DitDit42 and Bellery striking up a conversation behind her.

Rayleigh wonders what the future has in store for her.

***

People are milling everywhere, and street markets and stalls fill every available space. The space station feels as though it is going to burst at the seams due to all the people.

The team move through the crowd together, keeping an eye on each other.

"Does everyone know what they need to do?" Tailia asks as they stop at a crossroads.

"Noodles," Bellery calls out. He has talked about noodles every moment he could since the decision to come here.

"I might go with Bellery," Rayleigh says, eager to try these noodles that she has heard so much about.

"Sure," Tailia responds.

"I too am curious," Tatinet says.

"Sure thing." Tailia laughs, Bellery's constant talking has got them all excited. "DitDit42 and Allgery, you know what we need?" she asks.

"Yes," they reply in unison.

"Okay, let's meet back at the ship in a few hours. Bellery, that should give you time to have some noodles." Tailia looks between the device in her hand and the group.

"Yep, yep," Bellery calls as he turns and runs off into the crowd.

"Don't lose him," Allgery says to Rayleigh and Tatinet.

Surprised at the speed with which Bellery has disappeared into the crowd, Rayleigh turns and runs after him. "Bellery, wait up!" she calls out as they run after him. The three of them get absorbed into the crowd.

Rayleigh catches up with Bellery as he pauses at an intersection. Bellery takes in his surroundings, looking down at the device in his hands. He turns around in circles, as if unsure where he is going.

"This way," he calls out, and runs off again.

Not wanting to fall behind, they take off after him only to bump into him again coming back in the other direction.

"Nope. Wrong way," he calls out, heading the other way.

"Do you know where you're going?" Rayleigh calls, but Bellery has already disappeared into the crowd.

How does he survive in combat? Rayleigh wonders.

She and Tatinet head after him. They wander through the streets, following Bellery up and down, going this way and that.

Rayleigh sees Bellery suddenly stop in front of a building, looking down at his device and back up again. Her and Tatinet come bursting through the crowd to catch up with him. He is grinning ear to ear. *This must be the place.*

"See. Found it," he says, with the excitement of a young child.

Without waiting for a response, he disappears into the building, leaving them both standing on the street amid the sea of people rushing about. Rayleigh and Tatinet look at each and chuckle at his excitement. Rayleigh gestures for Tatinet to enter the building, and she bows politely and moves through the entrance.

The interior is small, and there is only a handful of people in the store, all huddled over bowls, slurping down their food. It reminds Rayleigh of the ramen bars in Japan, though with a slightly alien twist due to the people sitting around the bar. Hints of advanced technology poke through, reminding her that she is on a space station.

The smell that greets them as they enter makes her stomach rumble in hunger and draws them further into the store. They pile into an empty stall at the back, where Bellery has already taken up refuge, and pick up menus from the table. The menus look as though they've not been updated or changed in decades; they're full of holes and barely readable.

The waiter calls out from behind the bar, Rayleigh looks at the other two and they both shrug. The waiter pops their head over the counter, they call out again. Bellery, Tatinet and Rayleigh all look at each other, knowing that the waiter is talking to them, but unsure what to say.

Rayleigh raises her menu, pointing to an item at random. The creature nods and looks at the other two, who both nod their heads as well. Satisfied, the waiter disappears behind the counter and Rayleigh hears them yelling at someone in kitchen.

"What did we order?" she asks.

"No idea," Tatinet responds, looking over at Bellery.

"You didn't research what to order?" Rayleigh asks Bellery.

"Nope. I love noodles, and have heard rumours about this place… so I had to try it," Bellery responds with a big smile on his face, looking satisfied with himself.

The girls chuckle, folding up the menus and placing them at the end of the table. They begin a conversation as they wait for their food to arrive.

It doesn't take long for the waiter to appear, sliding bowls of noodles across the table. They look at each other, then down at the food.

Rayleigh picks up what appears to be an item of cutlery with a single spike on the end and a hook just above it, making it look like a small pike.

"It looks edible," she says, poking at the food.

The smell creeps into her nose and her stomach grumbles again, eager and excited about the food. Bellery can wait no longer and dives into his food. Rayleigh notices that he is using the hooks to pick up the noodles and twist them around before scooping them into his mouth.

"This is incredible!" he cries out after a few mouthfuls.

This prompts both the girls to brave the food. Rayleigh soon realises that Bellery is right; the food is incredible, full of different textures, flavours and smells. Things that Rayleigh has never experienced before, and she savours every moment of it.

After finishing their food, they sit back with satisfied sighs, letting the food settle in their bellies. Rayleigh notices movement and sees a group walking passed them. On closer inspection, Rayleigh recognises one of them.

"Rutherian," she calls out, reaching out to touch them on the shoulder.

Before Rayleigh can react, the trio have drawn their weapons and pounced on them, snarling. They all throw their hands in the air.

The store goes silent. Nobody dares move.

"Wait – I know you," Rutherian says looking at Rayleigh.

"I'm with Tailia," Rayleigh replies hesitantly, not wanting to provoke any further aggression.

"Oh, right," Rutherian replies. They all holster their weapons.

Rutherian climbs into the spare seat at their table, and their companions turning to survey the store.

The people in the store come back to life, resuming eating.

"How is Tailia?" Rutherian asks Rayleigh.

"She is good. We are just here getting supplies," Rayleigh replies, glancing at Bellery and Tatinet.

Rutherian looks them up and down as if assessing them. "What have you been doing? I've heard rumours that the I.D.T. have been attacked and that they are hunting someone matching Tailia's description."

"Yeah, we had some scraps, but things are good now. We were attacked after getting information about jump locations in this dimension," Rayleigh explains. The people around them go quiet at the mention of jump locations.

"You might want to keep that down," Rutherian says, leaning in closer to Rayleigh. "Where are you heading?"

"Dimension 16," Bellery says beside them.

"Dimension 16. Really?" Rutherian says.

"Yep," Bellery responds immediately, though Rayleigh questions whether they should be sharing this information.

Tatinet places her hand on Rayleigh's arm to get her attention. "Far side. Deceit, danger." The words slip out of her mouth as a faint whisper.

Before Rayleigh has a chance to react, Rutherian's bodyguards are sent flying, thrown against the back wall by an invisible impact. Rayleigh looks down to where Rutherian had been, but Rutherian has already drawn their weapons and is halfway across the shop, firing upon two figures before crashing into a third.

Chaos breaks out as people climb over each other, trying to get away. Turning around, Rayleigh sees two cloaked figures in the back corner. Rutherian has a sword pointed at one and their gun at the other.

The waiter pops their head over the counter, yelling at the four of them. Rutherian swings the gun around to point at them, and they disappear back into the kitchen.

"We should go. That is going to draw attention," Rutherian says, holstering their weapons. They look down at the bodyguards, climbing over them, collecting some belongings from the bodies.

Appearing satisfied with their findings, Rutherian makes for the front door.

The others don't need further encouragement, and follow Rutherian.

"What hangar are you in?" Rutherian calls out.

Bellery looks down at the device in his hand. "Hangar 6."

"Follow me," Rutherian calls out, moving to the far side of the street without waiting for a response.

The group take off after Rutherian, dashing into the closest laneway, running to keep up. Rayleigh hears the scuffle as officers descend on the store behind them. The waiter yells as they storm the building, but the sounds are drowned out as the group scurry through the back streets, moving through the crowds of people, who yell at them in annoyance as they pass.

"Hangar 6," Rutherian says as they emerge from the crowd.

They look up at the hangar in front of them, where their ship stands. DitDit42, Allgery and Tailia are loading items into it.

"We didn't expect you back this soon," Allgery says as they approach, a questioning expression on his face.

"We should go!" Rayleigh yells, looking back towards the hangar entrance.

Bellery and Tatinet slow their pace slightly, but continue past Allgery and into the ship.

"You! Stop!" someone yells from the hangar entrance.

Allgery looks up to see an I.D.T. officer standing in the doorway. He looks at Rayleigh, then back at the I.D.T. officer.

"It's time to go. Let's wrap it up," Allgery calls out.

More I.D.T. officers come through the entrance, huddling behind crates and pulling out their weapons.

"Hurry it along… Wrap it up, wrap it up," Allgery calls out more urgently, pulling out his weapons and firing off a few shots.

The others join Bellery in packing the last of the crates into the ship. Allgery increases his rate of fire, trying to hold back the I.D.T. officers, who duck down, poking their heads up only to fire. Tailia comes out of the ship, armoured and firing as she walk, joining Allgery in holding back the I.D.T officers, more of whom come streaming into the hangar, pushing their way further into it due to sheer numbers.

The ship roars to life, the engines stirring up dust and debris within the hangar. The deafening sound drowns out the sounds of gunfire being exchanged between the group and the I.D.T. officers.

Walking backwards and firing as he goes, Allgery moves towards the ship, preventing the officers from making further progress into the hangar.

With the last of the crates having been dragged into the ship, Allgery and Tailia slowly make their way towards the ship, firing off a last few rounds before the door closes.

Immediately, Bellery pulls the ship up from the platform, and turns it towards the exit. Rushing out into space, the ship moans under the pressure of the engines, putting distance between the ship and the space station.

As the crew crowd into the command deck, there is a collected sigh of relief.

"Rutherian. Where did you come from?" Tailia says, noticing Rutherian's presence.

"I bumped into your companions in a noodle shop; we were attacked by the I.D.T.," Rutherian responds, looking at Bellery, Rayleigh and Tatinet.

"Oh. Thank you for your help," Tailia responds, moving over to greet her old friend. Then she takes a seat. "Is there somewhere we can drop you off?"

"Well, if you are going to Dimension 16, I would like to tag along," Rutherian replies, taking a seat opposite Tailia.

"Oh. What makes you think we are going to Dimension 16?" Tailia asks, one eyebrow raised.

"Your man there said so," Rutherian responds, pointing at Bellery at his desk.

"Did he now?" Tailia says, glancing at Bellery.

"It isn't every day you get a chance to explore an uncharted dimension. I'm not about to pass up the opportunity."

"Welcome to the team. Happy to have you," Tailia says, nodding to Rutherian before moving to the computer desk. "I guess we have all we need. Bellery, do you have the course?"

"Yes, ma'am. We are coming up on the jump location."

"Then if everyone is ready, let's make the jump," Tailia calls out.

Taking her cue, the crew members each move to the closest seat and strap themselves in.

With a crack of light, the ship makes the jump.

Chapter Eleven

"I'm not sure I'll ever get used to that," Rayleigh says as they come out the other side of the jump.

Her stomach churns as she unclips the harness and gets up from her seat. She looks around at everyone else, all of whom appear completely unphased by the jump.

"I've never seen a dimension so small," DitDit42 whispers, shocked as they take in the new information streaming into the computers. "It looks like it is only one system. No wonder it isn't charted. It must be hard to find."

"Does this look familiar?" Tailia asks Rayleigh.

"I've never been into space, so I can't say for certain," Rayleigh responds, through the command deck window seeing a red planet off to one side.

"There is only one planet with life. This one," DitDit42 says, pulling up the planet on the view screen.

"That looks like it," Rayleigh whispers stepping closer to the view screen, seeing the outline of the continents and their familiar layout. "Home."

She reaches out to touch the map, only to have her hand pass through the hologram.

"They appear to be level 23 development," DitDit42 reads out.

"Let's keep our distance. We don't want to spook anyone," Tailia says. She gets up from her chair and walks to Rayleigh. "Are you ready to go home?"

"Yep." A mixture of emotions swelling inside her; the thought of being home feels strange after her travels with the group. Tom, her family and her old life flash into her mind.

"Home," she whispers, not wanting to shatter the thought of it.

"Allgery, do we still have the small transport ship?" Tailia calls out.

Allgery responds with a thumbs up.

"Great. Rayleigh and I will take that and head to the surface. You all feel free to explore the dimension, but stay out of sight and out of trouble," Tailia says, loud enough for everyone to hear. "I'm looking at you, Allgery and Bellery."

"Hey!" they respond in unison.

"Come on, let's go," Tailia says to Rayleigh.

"Okay."

The pair leave the command deck and walk towards the cargo bay.

"Hang on. Let me grab somethings," Rayleigh says, pausing and turning to run in the other direction, past the command deck doorway. When she stops in front of the door to her cabin, it slides open. Stepping inside, Rayleigh takes in the room: the place that she has called home since coming on board this vessel.

Rummaging around, Rayleigh grabs the small plant given to her by DitDit42 and a book that Bellery gave her. She races out of the room, back towards the hangar and Tailia.

As she passes the command deck doorway, she pauses. Slipping inside, she sees the crew talking eagerly about where they want to go and what they want to see.

DitDit42 turns, noticing Rayleigh standing in the doorway, holding the plant and the book. They walk over to Rayleigh.

"Goodbye, friend," DitDit42 says, leaning down to give her a hug. As they release, DitDit42 bends down further, whispering to the plant in their native language. The plant glows slightly, and then settles back to its normal state.

Having seen DitDit42 break away, Allgery and Bellery stop their conversation and walk over.

"Thank you for everything," Rayleigh says, tears in her eyes, torn between the life she has at home and the life she has on the ship.

"Thank you," Allgery says, stepping forward and embracing Rayleigh.

Allgery pulls a set of cards from his pocket. "I've never had someone beat me so completely. Please, take them," he says, handing the cards to Rayleigh. Rayleigh recalls the nights they spent playing games and drinking, listening to Allgery's stories, and his past adventures.

"Thank you," Bellery says, raising his hand slightly in a wave.

Rayleigh steps forward to give him a hug, then pauses. *He doesn't like to be touched.* She reminds herself.

So instead, she mirrors his gesture. Noticing a tear escape his eye, Rayleigh feels touched at his expression of feelings. Bellery turns quickly and returns to the command desk.

Tatinet and Rutherian are standing next to the desk, looking over at her and the others.

"Goodbye," she calls out to them, waving. "I wish I had the chance to get to know you better."

Rutherian and Tatinet both bow their heads slightly.

"Until we meet again," Rutherian calls out.

After taking a last look at the group, Rayleigh begins running down the hallway, eager to not keep Tailia waiting any longer. As she passes the armoury she pauses, then steps inside, taking in the place one last time, smelling the after effects of the firing range. The memories of going through the drills with Allgery and Bellery swim into her mind.

A tear runs down her face, and a heaviness comes over her as she realises she is no longer the same person that she was.

After a moment more, Rayleigh continues her journey down the hallway.

As she enters the ship's hangar, she sees Tailia sitting in the cockpit of the smaller ship, going through the preparations. Rayleigh runs over, climbs into the ship and takes her seat in the cockpit with Tailia.

Tailia looks down at her bag. "Are you all packed?"

"Yep," Rayleigh says with a nod.

The pitch of the engines increase, taking on the weight of the ship. Lifting off, they exit the ship and begin their journey towards Rayleigh's home.

Rayleigh turns, hoping to see the ship she had called home these past months disappear, but all she sees is the doorway to their current ship.

Turning to the front again, she settles herself for the journey home, back to Tom. Back to her life.

***

"You'll need to let me know where to go," Tailia says.

"Oh, of course." Rayleigh pulls up the map of Earth on the hologram and zooms in on where she lives. "I live here, but we should be able to park the ship down here." Rayleigh says, pointing to a location on the map.

"Sounds good."

Turning off the map, they fall silent again, having not spoken since they started the journey several hours ago.

"Are you ready to go back?" Tailia asks, just loud enough for Rayleigh to hear.

"Yes. Well… I think so. Actually, I don't know." Rayleigh looks down at her lap. "How am I supposed to go back to my life after everything that's happened?"

"You know that you can stay," Talia says.

"I know… But I can't. My life is here… Tom. My family. My work. My life." Rayleigh is unsure whether she is trying to convince Tailia, or herself.

"I'm going to miss you," Tailia says.

Rayleigh hesitates. "I'm going to miss you."

They sit in silence, the sound of the engines taking over.

"We are a few minutes out," Tailia says, breaking the silence.

Rayleigh nods, uneasiness creeping up again inside her. *Is this the right decision?*

The planet grows before her, soon filling the entirety of the window. Rayleigh is able to identify countries, then cities, then her local area and its familiar sights.

Tailia brings the ship down where Rayleigh had indicated, and Rayleigh hears the engines powering down. When the whirr finally dissipates, they are thrown into complete silence. They both sit there, looking out of the window.

"It is beautiful," Tailia says, looking out at the beach and the waves crashing against the shoreline. Rain begins to fall, creating a faint *pitter-patter* on the ship's hull.

I'm home, Rayleigh thinks. It's as if her emotions are trying to climb out of her stomach through her eyes. She fights back the tears, not wanting to let go.

Open yourself. DitDit42's teachings come into her mind.

Looking over at Tailia, Rayleigh sees a tear running down her face, which only makes it harder to keep it all in.

"I have something for you," Tailia says, handing her a duffel bag.

Raleigh puts it onto her lap; she can feel the weight of something hard inside.

"Don't look yet," Tailia says as Rayleigh goes to open it. "I should probably go. Before someone sees the ship."

With a nod, Rayleigh collects her items and heads for the door. She steps out into the rain, the cold wind biting through her clothes and the rain soaking her through.

Turning, Rayleigh sees Tailia stepping out through the ship doorway, and she catches sight of the tears streaming down her face before she steps out into the rain. Feeling Tailia's pain, before the rain washes away the evidence.

Not knowing what to say, Rayleigh steps forward to give Tailia a hug. She holds her longer than she expected to, fighting the urge to let go. They continue to hold onto each other tightly, their hearts beating as one.

Breaking away, they stand looking at each other. Tailia takes Rayleigh's hands, lifting them up and giving them a gentle kiss.

"Goodbye," she says.

After lingering for a moment, Tailia turns. Rayleigh feels her heart being pulled from her as Tailia walks back to the ship. She realises this is the closing of a chapter of her life.

She feels something in her hands. Looking down, she sees that Tailia has slipped into her hands the necklace from their trip to Yutintie. The memories flood back, giving more weight to her emotions. She can't hold on any more. She lets the tears flow out of her as she looks up at the ship and hears the engines reaching their maximum power.

Please don't go. Take me with you. The thought jumps into Rayleigh's mind without warning. She pushes it back. *No, my life is here.*

"Goodbye," she says, pulling the necklace to her chest as if to hug Tailia again.

She looks up at the cockpit, hoping to see Tailia. The ship rocks as it lifts off the ground, rising into the sky.

With that, Tailia is gone, leaving Rayleigh standing in the rain, the waves crashing on the sand, adding to her sorrow. Feeling as though a piece of herself has been taken away, Rayleigh continues looking up into the sky, but there is nothing left to see.

Returning to herself, she picks up the bag at her feet, feeling its weight. She places it back down and opens it to see what Tailia has given her.

At the sight of the guns and weapons she had trained with and used, the memories of her training come crashing into her mind, bringing with them another wave of tears. She doesn't know how she could have been so lucky to meet someone like Tailia. How she wished things could have ended differently.

She closes the bag and picks it up throwing it over her shoulder, then turns to begin walking back to her apartment. To Tom and her life here.

Chapter Twelve

"Tom," Rayleigh calls out as she enters the apartment.

"Rayleigh?! Rayleigh!" Tom yells, running from the bedroom. "Oh my god! Rayleigh!"

Tears stream down his face as he embraces Rayleigh as if it has been decades since they last meet. He hugs and kisses her, then breaks away and starts all over again.

"Come in, come in," he says finally, closing the door behind her.

The apartment feels familiar but different to Rayleigh. It's like walking into a different world. She places the bag on the dining table, the plant next to it.

"Where have you been?" Tom asks, his voice cracking a little with emotion.

"I've… ah… It doesn't matter," Rayleigh responds. *He wouldn't understand – he couldn't.*

"What do you mean?" Tom asks. Then he pauses. "Actually, you're back. That's all that matters." He reaches out to take Rayleigh's hand, kissing it and holding it in his. Then he jumps up and rushes to the phone. "Oh. I have to tell your family! They've been beside themselves."

"Tom! Tom!" Rayleigh calls out. "Can we hold off for now? I just want to sleep and shower"

Tom looks over at her. She can see he is struggling to make sense of her request.

"Of course. We can update them tomorrow," he replies finally, sitting down next to her again. "What sort of plant is that?"

"Oh. I actually don't know the name of it." Rayleigh realises she never thought to ask DitDit42.

Tom looks over at her, as if scanning her to ensure she is still there, then down at the bag. "Okay. Okay. Well you go and shower. I'll put the plant in the window."

"Thank you," Rayleigh says. She picks up the bag, then places the bag at the front door. She disappears into the bathroom, closing the door behind her, giving her a sense of safety.

When she turns on the shower, the room begins to fill with steam. The familiarity brings her some comfort. She strips off and climbs into the shower, letting the water take her in, washing over her.

The bathroom door cracks open, and Rayleigh tenses at the sudden movement.

"Here's a cup of tea for you," Tom says, placing a cup on the bathroom counter before heading out of the room again.

As her focus returns to her shower, Rayleigh feels her tension slipping away. There is something familiar but alien about this place, though she's unable to put her finger on it. She finishes her shower, dries off, and steps out of the bathroom.

Tom is standing over at the window, looking out. As she approaches, she can see he is crying. Startled, Tom turns quickly, wiping the tears from his eyes.

"I'm sorry," he says, fighting to hold back the tears.

Rayleigh finally takes some time to study him. She notices bags under his eyes. *He hasn't been sleeping.* With a pang in her chest, she begins to realise how much he has been struggling. She walks over to him and embraces him.

"I'm sorry," she whispers.

As they hug, Rayleigh feels Tom's guard drop as his weight relaxes onto her and he begins to cry again. As he holds her close, the pain pours out of him. With the weight of the experience leaving his body, Rayleigh holds him close.

"It's okay," Rayleigh says.

Finally, they break away from one another.

"I'm back now. That's all that matters," Rayleigh says, placing a hand on Tom's cheek, looking him in the eye. Tom body begins to relax as he breaths out, slumping slightly.

"I'm going to get ready for bed," Rayleigh says, turning.

"Sure thing. I'll be in shortly," Tom says, wiping away the tears.

144

Rayleigh heads for the bedroom. The wardrobe contains all her items, just as she left them. Tom has looked after everything while she was away.

She pulls out her pyjamas, slips them on and climbs into bed. She relishes the sense of sinking into the bed. She is home.

Rolling onto her back, Rayleigh focuses on the idea of being home. She allows the thoughts to slip from her mind.

In her last moments of consciousness, Rayleigh senses Tom getting into the bed. He slides over to her and pulls her close, hugging her. His familiarity comforts her, but there's also something foreign. She slips into sleep.

***

Rayleigh wakes in response to a beam of sunlight shining through the window. Rolling over, she finds that Tom is already out of bed. Clanking sounds come from the kitchen.

She props herself up against the bedhead and looks out of the window, at the daylight, the clouds, the birds and everything this world has to offer.

She turns her attention to the room, the life that she and Tom had. Her running gear, the books, the pictures and everything that they have collected over the years.

Hearing voices from the other room, Rayleigh pulls herself out of bed to see who is there.

As she opens the bedroom door, she's surprised to see her family rushing around, busily preparing a full spread of breakfast.

When Rayleigh's mother notices her in the doorway, she screams and drops the plate she was holding, which crashes to the floor, grabbing everyone's attention. They all stop what they are doing and look over at Rayleigh.

"Rayleigh," she gasps, raising her quivering hands to her mouth. She crosses the room to Rayleigh slowly at first, then picking up speed. "I thought I'd lost you," she says, tears streaming down her face. She throws her arms around Rayleigh, and Rayleigh hugs her back.

"It's okay, Mum. I'm back now," Rayleigh whispers, trying to calm her down.

Rayleigh's father and brother have come over as well. Her father, normally stoic, has tears rolling down his face. Rayleigh tries to recall if she has ever seen him crying properly. He wipes his tears away, but there was no hiding them. Her brother, on the other hand, is not so controlled, and is sobbing.

Rayleigh moves over to hug each of them in turn. It puts a crack in her father's armour, and tears escape and more roll down his face. As she hugs her brother, he seems to find new strength, hugging her back and wiping away the tears.

Rayleigh looks over quickly at Tom who is preparing food.

"I guess I should get dressed," Rayleigh says, looking down at her clothing. "I'll be out shortly." She turns back to the bedroom to get changed.

Once inside, she feels a little annoyed that Tom would tell her family without checking with her, but she realises he was probably just trying to help, so she pushes the thought aside and continues getting dressed.

After throwing on some clothes, Rayleigh comes back out of the bedroom. Her family have resumed setting up the table. As they all take their seats, Rayleigh can sense the relief, happiness, and pain around the table. There is a collective exhalation before they begin eating breakfast.

As she eats, Rayleigh thinks again of her life with Tom. The times with her family, the meals, the laughs and the heartache come back to her in waves, and with each recollection she slips back into her life.

She catches up on what she has missed. Hearing her family's stories, Rayleigh finds herself looking at Tom, remembering the love they shared. Letting the feeling take her, she slips her hand over to take his.

Rayleigh smiles at Tom and returns to her food, listening to her family converse.

When they have all finished, Rayleigh's dad coughs to halt the conversation around the table.

"So where did you go?" he asks Rayleigh.

Rayleigh hesitates. "Honestly. I'm not sure where to begin." *They would never understand*, she thinks.

"Try."

Rayleigh can see that he is looking for answers, something to fill the hole.

"It's okay, Dad. I'm back now."

"Where have you been the last few months?"

"It's okay, dear," Rayleigh's mother says, placing a hand on his arm. "She's back now."

Rayleigh's heart breaks at seeing her father's pain. She fights with herself to know what she can do to make things right. Getting up from her seat, she walks over to her father and crouches next to him.

"It's okay, Dad," she whispers, rising to give him a hug.

The hug makes him loose a little bit of his armour and some tears slip out. As Rayleigh breaks away, she can see he's struggling.

"I just want to understand," he whispers.

"I know, Dad. I know," Rayleigh responds, placing a hand on his arm. "I don't even know where to begin myself. I still don't believe it, and I was there."

Everybody around the table is silent, looking at each other and Rayleigh.

"She's back now, and that's all that matters," Tom chimes in.

They all look at him. After a moment, each of them nods in agreement. With that, Rayleigh returns to her seat, and return to swapping stories and laughing about the life they've shared.

Chapter Thirteen

After coming up over the dunes, Rayleigh pauses, reflecting on the night she said goodbye to Tailia. The moment still weighs heavy on her heart, despite it being five months ago.

Where did the time go? She turns to head back towards the apartment. As she runs along the beach, the waves continue to crash, reminding her of the cracking sound made by jump points between dimensions. Her body twitches at the thought of taking another dimensional jump.

She turns to head through the park, waiting for other joggers to pass through the gate. She moves through it, making her way down to the pond, then runs around it and up the other side, back towards the apartment.

As she pulls open the front door she sees her neighbour walking towards her, smiling. She holds the door open to let them through, then passes through the foyer and turns to take the stairs up to her floor. It's been months since she used the lift, taking the stairs ever since she came back.

When she reaches her floor, she goes into the hallway leading to her apartment, and opens the door. She hears a clank as the door hits something. Looking behind it out of curiosity, she sees the duffel bag behind the door still.

"Morning," Tom calls from the kitchen.

"Morning," Rayleigh replies, closing the door behind her.

"How did you do?"

"Good. Another personal best." Rayleigh slips off her shoes and moves towards the bathroom.

"You've been killing it," Tom calls back.

She steps into the bathroom and closes the door behind her. She slowly takes off her clothing, dropping the items on the floor.

I have been killing it, Rayleigh thinks. Ever since her return, she has been stronger and faster than she has ever been.

"Probably the training they put me through," she says to herself as she welcomes the warm water of the shower.

"What was that?" Tom says, poking his head around the door.

"Nothing," Rayleigh responds quickly.

"Just letting you know that breakfast will be ready soon, and we also have the theatre tonight." Tom disappears again.

Theatre. That's been a while. Rayleigh realises she hasn't been to the theatre this year.

She turns off the shower, jumps out and dries herself off with the first towel she finds. Throwing it around herself, she dances and skips through the apartment, heading to the bedroom.

The smell of Tom's cooking comes from the kitchen. Rayleigh's hunger begins to set in, her stomach growling. Bouncing into the bedroom, she settles on an outfit, throws it on and joins Tom for breakfast.

Tom is placing the last of the items on the table. He looks up at her with a smile. "You look nice," he says, giving her a kiss on the cheek. "I have a meeting today with the boss, but I'll be off early so we can get to the theatre on time."

Rayleigh nods and serves herself some food.

"I'm aiming to be there around six. Does that work for you?" Tom says.

"Yep. I'll take off a little early so I can get there in time," Rayleigh says. Thinking about the last few months, she's still surprised she was able to return to her job and her old life, with few issues.

Her mind wanders as Tom talks about his day. *He's putting on a brave face, but he's still struggling. I guess I don't blame him, either. I did disappear for months, only to return with no explanation.*

"Rayleigh?" Toms voice cuts through her thoughts.

"Huh?"

"You drifted off again… Are you alright?"

"Huh? Oh. Yes, everything's fine."

Tom studies her for a few seconds. "Well, I guess we better get going. We don't want to be late for work," he says with a wink and a smile as he picks up the plates from the table.

Rayleigh stands, intending to help him, but she slips back into her thoughts as she goes about her tasks.

He has been a little strange these last few months, she thinks, and notes her hesitance about going to work. Since returning to work, she has felt a need to prove herself, as if to make up for the time that she disappeared. *I haven't had the same enthusiasm for this life that I used to have. What happened?*

Catching herself in her thoughts, she returns to the cleaning up. Then the two of them collect their bags and meet at the front door. Heading out together, they say their goodbyes and go their separate ways.

***

The day passes like any other, and before she knows it Rayleigh looks at her watch and sees it's already time to leave.

"I need to take off everyone," Rayleigh says, packing up her items.

"Enjoy the theatre!" one of her colleagues calls out.

"Thank you."

Rayleigh heads out of the office and makes her way towards the theatre, excitement building within her at the prospect of returning to one of her passions.

***

It's a show about lost love, adventures and betrayal. Rayleigh can remember how it made her feel the first time she saw it with her mum, as a teenager. Even after all these years, it still brings a tear to her eye, stirring up all the same emotions.

Rayleigh and Tom exit the theatre hand in hand.

"What did you think?" Tom asks.

"It was good. It still gets me every time. For two people to be so in love," Rayleigh says as they head down the street.

"Just like us," Tom jokes. He winks and bumps into Rayleigh in jest.

There is a hustle and bustle in the street as people stream out of the theatre and into the night air. People are laughing and joking as they dissipate. Tom and Rayleigh head for their apartment, taking the long way down by the park alongside the pond.

As they stop to cross the street opposite the park, Rayleigh's body screams, *Danger!*

Without a thought, she pushes Tom sideways, diving in the other direction and dodging the bullets screaming through the air.

She crashes into a nearby car, leaving a dent in its door. Looking up, she sees two I.D.T. officers in the street, guns raised and preparing to fire again.

What are they doing here?

Tom is getting to his feet, stumbling slightly.

More bullets graze the car as Rayleigh darts behind it. Moving down along the row of cars, Rayleigh flanks the officer. Peering around the boot of the car, the officer catches sight of her and fires again. Three shots ring out, flying by her head close enough that she hears them whistle as they pass.

"Tom, stay down," Rayleigh calls out, seeing Tom rise to his feet.

The officer turns when he sees Tom get up. Taking the opportunity, Rayleigh charges from behind the car, covering the ground between her and the officer in an instant. Catching sight of her, the officer turns to engage.

"Too slow," Rayleigh whispers to herself, catching the officer's wrist as they try to swing the weapon in her direction.

Swivelling, Rayleigh brings her shoulder up, still holding onto the officer's wrist. There is a crack as their arm breaks. The officer winces in pain and drops the weapon.

Catching it before it hits the ground, Rayleigh turns, bringing the weapon up to the officer's head.

Click.

Nothing. The weapon doesn't fire.

"Crap!" Rayleigh yells.

The officer is already on the counter attack, bringing their leg up to meet Rayleigh's ribs. Pain shoots through her body as she's lifted off the ground.

"Rayleigh!" Tom calls out, finally getting to his feet.

Without missing a beat, Rayleigh thrusts her head upwards, connecting with the officer's head as she does. Stumbling backwards, Rayleigh takes the opportunity to throw her leg into the officer's stomach, causing them to buckle over.

Moving around behind the officer, she takes their head and twists. There's a pop, and the officer goes limp, collapsing to the ground in a heap.

Rayleigh looks up, scanning for the second target and catches them moving behind the nearest car. She doesn't hesitate, launching herself in their direction. The officer looks up when she is only a few steps away, but has no time to react as Rayleigh crashes into them, bringing them to the ground. They scuffle, rolling around on the ground. Manoeuvring behind them, Rayleigh manages to get her arm up around their neck. Choking, they begin to thrash and kick, trying to reach up to grab her. Rayleigh gets a fist to the face, but she ignores it, tightening her grip. Slowly, the officer begins to go limp. Rayleigh waits a few moments, then releases her grip hesitantly, wondering if they will jump back up again. But no.

Standing over the body, Rayleigh looks up to see Tom before her. There's confusion, shock and fear in his expression. Stepping over the body, Rayleigh moves towards him. He flinches and takes a step back, but allows her to approach. Rayleigh takes him in her arms, holding him tightly.

"It's okay," Rayleigh says.

Tom calms a little, looking between the bodies and Rayleigh, mumbling to himself.

"Come on. We need to get them off the street," Rayleigh says, moving towards one of the bodies. Pulling by the collar, she drags the body into the laneway.

She looks at Tom. "You grab that one," she calls out, gesturing at the other body.

Tom does nothing, so Rayleigh resumes pulling the first body off the street. Having got the body behind a dumpster, she goes back for the second. Tom is still standing motionless, watching her.

"Tom. Come on," Rayleigh calls out, trying to snap him into action.

Tom stumbles along behind her, still dazed. He watches her drag the second body, to the same dumpster as the first. Rayleigh searches the bodies, pulling out devices and items from the officers' pockets.

"Tom, give me your bag," she says, pointing at Tom's laptop bag.

Tom fumbles a little as he hands over the bag. Pulling out his laptop, she hands it too him. Before placing everything from the officer's bodies into the bag.

"Come on," Rayleigh says, taking him by the hand and escorting him out of the road.

Coming to the street, Rayleigh picks up the soldier's gun, and begins to move faster across the street with Tom in tow. She scans their surroundings for any indication that they are being followed.

She pauses at the corner of their street, checking in all directions. Satisfied that they are not being followed, she continues along the street. Tom, having recovered slightly, is now moving more quickly. Rayleigh can sense his eagerness to get home to safety.

"What just happened?" he asks.

"Those were I.D.T. officers. They must have tracked me here," Rayleigh responds. She takes him by the hand and guides him further into the apartment.

"What's an I.D.T. officer? And more importantly, are they dead?" Tom asks, pulling away from her. There's panic in his voice, and he's shaking.

"The I.D.T. is the Institute of Dimensional Travel – and yes, they're dead." Rayleigh crouches in front of Tom, as he sits on the couch. Holding his gaze, Rayleigh runs her hand down his cheek. "Honey. It's okay. They aren't here for you. They're here for me."

"Why are they after you?" Tom asks.

Rayleigh lets out a sigh and begins to explain who the I.D.T. are and why they are after her. Tom looks at her blankly.

"Tom. It's okay. Breathe," Rayleigh continues. "I'm sorry, Tom, but I'm going to need to leave again."

"What do you mean?" Tom asks, tears welling in his eyes.

Rayleigh hesitates, trying to find the right words. "Now that they've found me, they'll be back."

"But we can go to the police."

"And tell them about dimensional travel?"

Tom sits back, trying to think of another solution.

"Tom." Rayleigh attracts his attention again. "I'm sorry. I need to go. Not only because of the I.D.T. officers, but... If I'm honest with myself, it hasn't felt the same since I came back. I've been trying to convince myself that this is where I need to be. But tonight, when the soldiers appeared, I knew this was no longer my life," she whispers, holding Tom's hands in hers. "I'm sorry. This isn't fair, I know. If there was another way, I'd take it. But I don't feel like my life is here any more."

Tom appears frozen, as if caught between worlds and ideas.

Put words to her concerns and internal world, Rayleigh finally takes stock of her situation and that this is what she believes. Seeing Tom crumble before her as the life they had planned together comes apart at the seams. Tears stream down his face. Rayleigh leans in to give him a hug, then wipes away his tears with her thumb.

"I'm sorry," she says. "This is for the best." She holds his gaze a little longer before pushing herself off the couch. "I should go, before they track me and associate me to you."

"Right now?" Tom asks.

"Unfortunately, I don't know when more will be coming."

As she moves to the bedroom, Tom sits in silence, his head lowered.

In the bedroom, Rayleigh makes her way to the closet to recover the clothing in which she returned, months earlier. She pulls out the box from a shelf, then begins putting on each item of clothing. With each piece added, she recalls her travels with Tailia and the team. The pieces of her decision comes together as she pulls on her jacket. When she looks at herself in the mirror, she sees the person she had been.

She pauses for a moment, looking around the room, at their life. The laughter, the tears, the good and the bad. They have been through so much together.

Is this the only way? She attempts to reassure herself. *I couldn't live with myself if something happened to him… This is for the best.*

When she emerges from the bedroom, Tom is still sitting on the chair. Rayleigh walks to the front door and grabs the bag from behind it. Opening it, she takes out the holster and armour and begins strapping it to herself. Finally, she pulls out the guns and holsters them.

Tom looks up at her. "Do you have to go?" he asks again.

"I do," Rayleigh replies.

She picks up the bag, walks to Tom and places it on the table. She discards all the items from the laptop bag onto the table and places them into her bag. She straps the jump device taken from the I.D.T. officer to her forearm. Pushing the keys, she wonders if she can get it to work. To her surprise, it comes to life as the lights flicker into life and the display lights up. Satisfied, she turns her attention to the officers' guns, placing them into her bag and zipping it up.

She takes Tom's hand and leads him out of the apartment. They remain silent as they descend to the foyer in the lift, neither of them able to say a word. The lift chimes and the doors open, and Rayleigh steps into the foyer, Tom following behind.

Outside, the moon shines down on them. Rayleigh moves down the steps of the building and into the middle of the street. Tom follows her.

"Tom. This is goodbye," Rayleigh says, taking Tom's hand in hers. "I'm sorry it has to end this way. You didn't deserve this." She strokes his cheek one last time.

Tom stares at her, his eyes puffy from crying.

Stepping backwards, Rayleigh begins playing with officer's jump device on her forearm. Finding the last jump coordinates the officer used, she hits the activation button for the artificial jump point. She looks up at Tom one last time and raises her hand.

"Goodbye," she whispers, stepping backward into a flash of light and, with a crack, the world she once knew vanishes.

***

Tom drops to his knees, looking to where Rayleigh was moments ago.

"Rayleigh. Please don't go," he whispers to himself, his head dropping. He remains hunched on the ground, he can no longer hold back the tears as they pour out of him.

She is gone.

Rain begins to fall. He hears footsteps coming up behind, but he doesn't care – he has lost her again.

Seeing feet come into view around him, he still reals with what he has seen.

"Where is she?" one of them yells.

"I don't know." Tom mumbles, not even looking up to acknowledge the figures around him.

"Don't lie to us!" says another. Tom feels a solid whack as something hard hits him across the side of his head, throwing him to the ground.

Lying on the ground, Tom sees the road ahead of him, the place where Rayleigh vanished. His eyes sting as blood creeps into them.

"Where is she?" one of them says, grabbing Tom and pulling him up by his shirt.

"I don't know," Tom replies, turning his head finally to look up at the officer. Looking around at the other three as they watch on, before returning to look at the one holding him. Groggy from the blow, he struggles to keep his head up.

The officer hits him again, throwing him to the street. Tom looks to where Rayleigh disappeared, trying to make sense of what is happening. On his wrists he feels the coldness of what he assumes are steel handcuffs.

"Take him with us. We will want to talk to him some more," one of the officers says.

Tom is struggling to stay conscious, and he wonders how much blood he has lost. Two of the officers lift him up and drag him along with them. Tom tries to lift his head to see where they are going. His body is beginning to tingle.

There's a flash of light, and the road changes from tarmac to polished concrete. Tom tries to move his head again, but can't bring himself to. Letting go, he slips into darkness.

Chapter Fourteen

After stepping through the portal, Rayleigh finds herself standing in an open field. Two suns light up the sky. She can see some animals grazing off in the distance, paying her no attention.

She looks down at her wrist as the navigation display beeps. She pushes keys at random, hoping to switch it off. The device falls silent. With a few more button presses, the screen changes to a set of boxes.

Staring at it, Rayleigh realises it is looking for coordinates.

What where they? Rayleigh tries to remember the coordinates that she had seen with Tailia.

"Oh," she says in excitement, and enters the coordinates. With a few more presses, a map appears with a small dot bleeping. Next to the dot is a timer, counting down.

Looking up from the device, Rayleigh tries to determine where she is in relation to the dot, turning to see if the map gives any kind of direction. Seeing the map rotate as she does, she takes off in the direction shown on the map. She runs through the field, crossing it quickly, and vaults the fence on the far side. She slips into a forest and pushes through the vegetation.

In response to a crack in the distance, Rayleigh stops to look back over her shoulder to where she had come from. *What was that?* She scans all around, but quickly resumes running due to the timer continuing to count down, jumping over logs and ducking under tree branches. When she trips on a branch she's sent crashing to the ground, but she pushes herself up quickly, not even pausing to check herself over.

***

As the I.D.T. officers blip into existence in the field, they take up positions around the jump site, surveying their surroundings for any sign of movement or anything out of place.

"Nothing, sir!" an officer calls out.

"How many jump points?" the commanding officer asks.

"Six in range one, and ten within range two," the officer responds after studying their device.

"Get agents to each jump zone within range one, and get the drones out to range two," the commanding officer orders curtly, then moves into the field.

"Yes sir," the officer replies.

Satisfied, the commanding officer disappears in a flash of light.

"Let's move," the officer calls out to the remaining I.D.T. standing around them, pointing to send each one in a different direction.

As they disperse, the officer pulls off his backpack and throws it to the ground. Pulling a cable out of the arm device, they connect it to the backpack, they punch away at the keys on their arm device. With a click and a hiss, the bag flips open and four drones fly out, heading for jump portals in zone two.

As they head into the distance, the officer picks up his bag. He checks the device to find the last location and head towards it, not wanting to let his commander down.

**

Pausing for breath leaning against a tree, Rayleigh's heart beats in her chest, and her muscles protest at the strain she is putting them under. The countdown timer on the device is still going.

"I can do this," she tells herself. She pushes herself off the tree. As she's about to move away, she hears a hum over her head. Looking up, she sees nothing. *Was that a bird?* She pushes the thought aside and tells her body to keep moving.

She's covered in mud, with scratches over her body from the forest, by the time she bursts out into a field. She sees animals grazing in the distance. She looks down at the map to find her bearings. She points herself in the right direction and starts sprinting across the field, jumping another fence to reach the grazing pastures. She slows to a walk as she approaches the animals, not wanting to scare them.

The animals tower over her and pay her no attention. As they graze casually, the odd animal looks up, chewing on a mouthful of food, before going back to their meal.

When she reaches the edge of the pack, Rayleigh pauses again, looking down at the device.

"I'm close," she says to herself.

Looking up, she sees something hovering over her. She squints. *What is that?*

The device on Rayleigh's arm beeps quietly, making the nearest animal turn its head in her direction before going back to its food.

"Two minutes. I don't have time for this," Rayleigh mumbles.

She launches into a sprint again, bursting out from the pasture towards the spot identified by the device, covering ground quickly.

She notices the hovering object has turned in her direction. It drops to her height, then picks up speed, heading directly towards her.

What now? Rayleigh wonders.

Danger! her body screams as the device launches itself at her. Dropping, she ducks underneath the device as it flies over her. It whirrs as its engines kick up, and it tries to turn around to come at her again.

Rayleigh pushes herself off the ground, turning in direction she needs to be. She picks up her pace again, heading straight for the jump point.

Reaching the location, Rayleigh turns slightly to see where the device is now – but it's too late. It crashes into her chest, wrapping itself around her body. Rayleigh's body burns as electricity courses through her. She screams and fights to stay conscious, pushing her arms to move, fighting against the electricity that is preventing her muscles from functioning.

Gritting her teeth, Rayleigh creeps her hand up to the device on her chest. Adrenaline gives her an extra kick, and her body slowly begins to move. She latches onto the device and pulls it free, ripping clothing and flesh from her body. She cries out in pain as she throws the device away.

It tumbles through the air, bouncing once on the ground, before taking flight again. Hovering above the ground, it turns back towards Rayleigh.

Before she has a chance to think, she's drawn her guns and is pointing them in the direction of the drone. With a crack, she places a round through the centre of the device, and watches as it crashes to the ground. It flutters like a wounded bird trying to take to the air.

Rayleigh walks over to the drone and puts two more bullets into it, watching as it finally falls silent.

"What the hell is that?" Rayleigh mutters to herself. She pokes the drone a couple of times with the tip of her gun, and satisfied that it is dead, she holsters her guns and stands.

It's only now that she realises that both she and the drone have already passed through the jump point together. But instead of the lush rainforest of the Hu Thus's world there is only a black, smouldering forest. It has been decimated, and the green forest no longer exists. Everywhere she looks is charcoal and ash.

"No." Rayleigh exhales, anger, sadness and confusion bubbling up within her.

She begins running in the direction of the village. She pushes her way through the burning forest, avoiding the large fires that are still burning.

When she enters the clearing before the village, she halts in shock.

There are bodies everywhere. Hu Thu's lie where they fell; there is not a sound over the crackle of the fires.

"No!" Rayleigh cries out. The strength leaves her knees, and she falls to the ground. Tears pouring out of her, streaking the ash on her face.

Her heart aches as she looks at the devastation before her. The energy leaves her body, so she sits.

"The elders," Rayleigh says, remembering the Hu Thu's she met at the tree.

Picking herself up, she moves towards the path to the village centre and the tree. With every step, she wishes she were able to escape the destruction all around her.

She reaches the bottom of the cliff to stand before the tree, which is now lifeless. Black, smouldering embers hover around it. She finds still more bodies within the courtyard as she heads to the opening in the tree.

Her heart strains under the pressure as she takes in the elders' bodies on the ground; they are slumped next to the pools within the tree, where they had been struck down. Rayleigh eases closer to them. At a sign of movement, she rushes to one elder's side and turns them over so that they are resting in her lap.

The elder looks up at her with an expression of peace and calm that Rayleigh did not expect. They smile gently, as if to reassure her, then reach up with their hand to wipe a tear from Rayleigh's eye. They rub the tear between their fingers as if studying it, then place their hand on Rayleigh's cheek.

Rayleigh recalls when the tree was full of life, all the elder's huddled around, talking amongst themselves and sharing thoughts and ideas. The sudden flash of an image startles her. She straightens up quickly, breaking the connection with the elder's hand and bringing her back to the present.

"You want to show me something?" Rayleigh says to the elder. Their eyes blink in response. Rayleigh leans forward again, allowing the elder to place their hand on her face again.

An image snaps into her mind of the village when it was full of life, all the elders standing around the pools talking amongst themselves. While she doesn't understand their language, she notices the feelings coursing through her as if she understands what is happening.

They look around at one another as a sound attracts their attention. Turning, Rayleigh sees I.D.T. officers standing with guns in their hands. They open fire on the elders. As the elders try to run, panic

162

flows through her; her heart races as everyone runs in different directions. Standing to flee, she feels a bullet tear through her body.

Her body goes weak, then gives out and she collapses to the ground. When she looks down at her body for the wound, Rayleigh sees the body of an elder rather than her own, reminding her that this is not her memory. She touches the wound, leaving blood on her hand when she pulls it away. She places a hand over the wound to try and stop the bleeding.

She hears the footsteps of the I.D.T. officers as they approach. They pause in front of her, then head off in another direction.

The life begins to flow from her body. She finds herself looking down at her robes, watching as she places a hand on them to feel something solid underneath.

Rayleigh snaps out of the memory, her head swimming and her body fighting against the memory of being shot and dying. The elder in her lap is looking up at her. With a smile and a nod, they slowly slip away. Feeling the energy leave their body, tears well up in Rayleigh's eyes.

She understands what the elder is trying to convey. She reaches into the robes and pulls out an orb.

As the memory fades from her mind, Rayleigh is left with a sea of feelings. Protect, preserve and love. Unsure if these are the lingering feelings of the elder, or her own, Rayleigh tucks the orb into her bag. She edges out from underneath the elder, placing their head gently on the ground, shedding a tear at the remnants of the moments they have shared.

Rayleigh can see other elders nearby, motionless. She turns, catching a familiar form out of the corner of her eye; Dit3 is lying on the ground. Rushing over, Rayleigh slumps beside them, taking their head in her hands, her heart aching.

"Please let DitDit42 be okay," Rayleigh mumbles to herself as she stands.

She returns to the opening in the tree, then out into the courtyard. Overwhelmed by what she's seen, she realises she's slowly becoming numb to it. She no longer knows what to do.

She takes the pathway to the top of the cliff, then begins the climb to the top of the cliff. She pauses outside the apartment where she and Tailia stayed and peers through the front door. She slips inside, running her hand along the items of furniture. She notices a book on the table and picks it up, fondly remembering the time that she and Tailia spent here together.

Placing the book back on the table, she moves to the front door, then halts after a few steps. She turns back to the table and collects the book before scurrying outside.

She heads along the pathway again, towards the top of the village, stifling the impulse to look around or try to determine her next steps. The weight of the orb within her bag reminds her that she will need to find some Hu Thus to give it to.

An idea springs into her mind. She tries to remember the coordinates. As they slip back into her mind, she pushes the keys on the device and it beeps into life, showing the location of the next jump point.

She looks in the direction of the jump point, but then she freezes.

Something isn't right, she thinks as she looks around the village. Hearing sounds of voices in the distance, she ducks behind a wall to hide.

From her vantage point, she sees I.D.T. officers walk into view. Rage bubbles within her as she reaches for her weapons, preparing for an assault.

This is not the way. It's DitDit42's voice, popping into her mind. She remembers them training and meditating together. When DitDit42 talking about their culture and the importance of the knowledge they retain.

Placing a hand on the orb in her bag, Rayleigh looks back at the I.D.T. officers.

"This is not the way," she whispers to herself, holstering her weapons again. She watches the I.D.T. officers make their way through the courtyard, kicking over items and looking into buildings.

Rayleigh turns in the direction of the next jump point. She moves silently, skulking through the rubble. She slips out of the back of the village and disappears into the burning forest.

Chapter Fifteen

As she waits for the jump gate, Rayleigh stands watch. It is eerily quiet in the forest, the only sound the flicker of smouldering embers. She looks down at the timer, which is counting down: 10, 9, 8, 7...

She takes a final look at the forest, and back towards the Hu Thus village. With an ache in her heart, she jumps.

Instantly, she is within a sea of tall crops. She looks up at the clear blue sky. The crops shield her from view but they also prevent her from seeing anything.

She looks at her map, trying to figure out which way she needs to go.

"Please vacate property immediately," says an authoritative voice from above Rayleigh. "You are on private property."

Looking up, Rayleigh sees the automated harvesting machine she and Tailia came across previously on this planet, with their long tentacles dangling below them.

"Ah, crap. What was it?" Rayleigh mumbles to herself. "Ah yes. Agent Rita Ronald, badge 920517," she says in her most authoritative voice.

There is no response at first. The robot hovers above her, putting Rayleigh on edge, and she wonders if she got something wrong. *Can I make a break for it?* She looks along the rows of crops, then back at the robot.

"Authentication failed. Prepare to be detained," the robot booms.

"Oh crap."

Rayleigh starts running through the field. After a few metres, the robot's tentacles reach out and grab her, stopping her from going any further. As it pulls her off the ground, Rayleigh kicks and screams, struggling to break free.

More arms wrap around her, each wrapping around a different limb, restricting Rayleigh from moving. The robot lifts her from the ground, and they continue rising higher and higher into the sky.

Looking down at the ground, she realises that to break free now would result in a long fall to the ground. She settles down, letting the machine carry her.

Looking up, Rayleigh can see a city in the distance. The robot is heading straight for it, picking up speed to cover the distance between the field and the city faster than Rayleigh expected.

It slows on its approach to a landing pad at the top of a building, where four more robots are waiting for them. These looking more human, holding guns, giving them an authoritative presence. The robot holding Rayleigh hovers above the pad, as if waiting for something.

"Unauthorised access, and false verification of ID," the robot announces as it drops Rayleigh onto the landing deck.

Rayleigh climbs to her feet. She doesn't have a chance to say anything before one of the robots shocks her, knocking her unconscious.

***

When she comes to, Rayleigh finds herself in a room surrounded by glass, but she is unable to see out. She notices that there is also no reflection. As the dull pain of the shock creeps into her awareness, she realises she has been stripped and then dressed in a green robe. She feels embarrassed and violated at the thought.

The wall behind her clicks, breaking her train of thought. Pivoting, she sees a tall purple robed figure. She retreats further into the corner, unsure what will happen next.

"Yep. This is her. I want her released to my custody immediately," says a commanding voice from the depths of the robe. The figure looks down at Rayleigh, then rises to full height to turn and exits the room. The wall snaps shut behind the robed figure.

Rayleigh props herself up in the corner, her heart racing at a million miles an hour as she thinks about all the possible things that are about to happen.

Who was that?

She watches the wall, waiting nervously to see what will happen next. Her head begins to dip, and she fights against the urge to sleep, only to have it dip again. She slaps her face, trying to stay awake.

When she raises her hand to support her head, it appears blurry. There are no details on the walls of the room, so she hasn't been able to notice the change in her vision. Now, looking at her hand again, she sees it is getting worse. She's no longer able to fight against her body, and everything goes dark.

***

She jolts awake and rubs her eyes, trying to restore her vision. *Where did the room go?* she thinks, looking around.

The sick feeling in her stomach returns as she realises that her outfit has been changed once again.

The sound of a door opening grabs her attention. She tries to push herself up, but finds that her body won't respond. It still wants to sleep.

"Easy. How are you feeling?" says a voice from the other side of the room.

Craning her neck, Rayleigh sees Leonard entering the room, hovering on his flying device. Rayleigh still feels strange about the idea of a talking monkey, which Leonard resembles. But the familiar face eases her nerves slightly, and she remembers how he helped her and Tailia find the Hu Thu's. She slumps down again.

"Easy. Those drugs are pretty rough. I'm sorry you went through that," Leonard continues as he comes closer. "You should eat. It will help your body." He hands Rayleigh a plate of fruit.

After gently helping Rayleigh to sit up, Leonard moves to the couch opposite the one on which she's lying. Rayleigh looks down at the plate and coaxes her limbs to move so that she can eat.

Leonard gives her a few moments and have a few mouthfuls of food before he asks, "Are you okay?"

Rayleigh ponders her response. "I'm not sure how to respond to that question."

"You're right. I apologise – that was a silly question. Why were you impersonating Rita?"

"I was coming to get your help and didn't know how else to get here."

"Why were you coming to me?" Leonard says, and Rayleigh hears surprise in his rough voice.

"I was looking for Tailia and the Hu Thus," she says, taking another mouthful of food.

"I haven't seen Tailia since you were both here last, or the Hu Thus. Did the last address not work?"

"The address worked. But…" Rayleigh trails off as images of the village flash into her mind. "I.D.T. officers found them." Rayleigh feels a tear creep from her eye.

"Oh, I see… I guess… Let's take a look at the map and see if there is another," Leonard responds calmly.

Rayleigh pulls herself off the couch, and they head into the next room. Leonard approaches the part of the wall with the hidden Hu Thu twig, and pulls out the drawer to retrieve it. Unwrapping it from its cloth, he places it on the table, and begins to go through the coordinates.

"That was the last coordinate on the list," he says quietly.

"Crap…" Rayleigh says. Then a thought occurs to her. "Wait! Where's my bag?" she blurts out, looking around frantically, then coming to the realisation she hasn't seen it since she was in the field.

"Your bag?" Leonard says, watching Rayleigh as she stumbles around the room in her search. "I think we have your belongings from your arrest."

He calls out in what Rayleigh assumes must be the local language. After a few moments, a yellow robed figure appears carrying a crate, which they place on the table before Leonard and Rayleigh. Rayleigh flips it open and rummages through it eagerly. When she finds her bag, she pulls it out, then reaches into it to pull out the orb.

"What the hell! Where did you get that?" Leonard throws a cloth over the orb. "You're lucky they didn't realise what you had when they arrested you."

He floats around the room, checking his own quarters are safe, closing the door to the other rooms as he passes them.

"It's only a matter of time until they figure what you have," he says. "You'll need to leave quickly, before the I.D.T. get here."

Leonard exchanges a few words with the yellow robed figure in his native language. They bow to each other and then the figure leaves the room.

Turning back to Rayleigh, Leonard pulls back the cloth again. As he moves the twig closer to the orb, the list of coordinates explodes, going from a dozen to perhaps hundreds. The information scrolls over the desk too quickly for Rayleigh to read.

Leonard places his hand on the desk next to the twig. Then he turns his hand slowly, like a dial. To her surprise, Rayleigh notices that the flow of information slows and she is now able to see the coordinates flipping through on the desk, finally coming to a stop.

"Here," Leonard says, pointing to a number on the desk. Rayleigh nods.

"You can never let the orb fall into the I.D.T's hands," Leonard says, looking at the orb as he pulls away the twig. "Guard it with your life, or destroy it if you cannot." He wraps the twig in the cloth and then places it back in the hole in the wall. "Don't worry, the twig is only a display; it can only store limited information, which is why it will only hold a dozen coordinates."

There is a click behind them, and they both jump.

Thankfully, it is only the yellow robed figure returning. Holding a small crate in their hands, they cross the room and place it on the table. Bowing slightly, they back away and leave again.

As the door clicks closed, Leonard pushes the drawer into the hole, hiding the twig in the wall again. He returns to the desk where the figure left the crate, and opens it by flicking the latch on its front.

"Here are your fake identification papers," Leonard says, handing a collection of items to Rayleigh. "Your name is Sarrati Suthti, and you are now an agent. I would advise against getting caught by a *real* agent. This box will have your information and badge number, to allow you to move more freely in this dimension. Be cautious how you use it, and don't go rogue. The identity won't hold up if anyone starts digging into it. I had to cash in a lot of favours to get you freed this time. We might not be so lucky next time."

They both freeze again at a knock at the door. A voice comes from behind it.

Leonard pauses momentarily. "You need to leave," he says, pulling open a drawer at the bottom-right of the wall. Reaching inside, he retrieves a purple robe and hands it to Rayleigh, then directs her to the next room. "You will need this. You should leave through that door. Put the robe on and exit through the door in that room."

There is another knock at the door again, and the voice calls out. Leonard responds with a few words in the native language, and closes the door behind her.

Rayleigh finds herself standing alone in some kind of library. Moving quickly, she slings the bag over her shoulder and slips on the robe. She wonders what she ought to do next. Noticing that Leonard hasn't closed the door completely, she looks through the crack.

A group of I.D.T. officers are standing in front of Leonard, and they appear to be questioning him. Leonard sits patiently behind his table, answering their questions calmly.

Rayleigh hears a click from somewhere nearby, and her heart stops. She turns to see the yellow robed figure standing in the doorway, gesturing for her to follow.

Rayleigh doesn't need to be told again. She follows them from the room as they move towards the front door of the shop. When they reach it, the figure bows and opens the door to let Rayleigh pass.

She returns the gesture and slips through the door into the bustle of the walkway outside. As she moves through the crowd to the landing bay, people make way for her; Rayleigh enjoys this newfound ease of travelling.

She glances over her shoulder at Leonard's place just as an I.D.T. officer appears in the doorway, scanning the crowd before turning back to the building.

Rayleigh quickens her pace, not wanting to stay around any longer than she needs to. As she rounds the corner, she sees two I.D.T. officers standing in front of the landing bay door. Rayleigh's heart stops and her stomach performs a somersault.

"You've got this," she mumbles to herself, straightening her posture as she takes a step forward to continue along the walkway towards the doorway.

"Identify yourself," the officer states as she approaches the door.

"How dare you interrupt an agent on business?" Rayleigh says in an attempt to be authoritative, while her stomach does another somersault.

"Apologies. We're looking for outlaws, so we need to see authentication," the officer says, bowing stiffly.

Rayleigh's heart stops again, and her mind races as she tries to think how she will get out of this.

"Madam, remember your identification is in your bag," says the voice from nearby. Rayleigh turns to see a figure in a yellow robe standing by her side.

"You are speaking with Sarrati Suthti, badge number 3268941," the yellow robed figure says, addressing the officers directly.

Rayleigh's stomach continues to turn, but she experiences a sense of relief at seeing the familiar robed figure. She reaches into her robes to find the ID, pulls it out and shows it to the officer, who nods and raises their device to scan the badge. Rayleigh relaxes as the officer looks down at the device and nods.

As Rayleigh puts the badge away, she notices the officer has brought the device close to her face. Rayleigh's heart explodes in fear.

They have me, Rayleigh's brain screams at her, anxiety dancing around in her head.

"What are you doing?" she manages to squeak.

"We are confirming your identity," the officer continues, looking down at the device again.

Rayleigh begins to speak, but the yellow robed figure places their hand on her arm. The moment drags out, lasting centuries as they wait for the response.

In response to a bleep and a chime, the officer looks up and smiles. "My apologies again, ma'am," they say, bowing again.

Rayleigh sees that on the screen of the device flashes the word *Authenticated*. The section that should have had a photo displays the words *Confidential level 3*, with a blank photo behind it.

As Rayleigh's heart begins to beat again, the yellow robed figure moves forward, gently nudging Rayleigh with the hand still on her arm, to guide her forward. In response, Rayleigh moves through the doorway and into the landing bay.

When the doors close, Rayleigh turns to her expressionless robed companion. "Thank you," she whispers.

"I live to serve, madam… Leonard sends his well wishes, and his thoughts. Protect it," the figure responds curtly, bowing again.

Though Rayleigh is still unable to see anything beneath the robes, she interprets the gesture as a positive one.

"You should de-robe now. Safe travels," the figure continues, bowing again and gesturing to the bins in the wall.

Rayleigh pulls off the robe and throws it into one of the bins to disappear down a chute. Turning back to the robed figure, she bows politely.

"Thank you," she says. *I wonder who they are?* she wonders as she studies the robed figure a final time.

The door to the landing bay behind her opens. Hearing the roar of engines, she turns and heads to the landing bay. As she comes closer to the craft that has arrived for her, the roar of its engines drowns out all other sounds. She pauses at the door of the transport, looking back at the doorway from where she has just come.

Leonard's voice comes into her mind: "You can never let the orb fall into the I.D.T's hands. Guard it with your life, or destroy it if you cannot."

Wondering what she is getting herself into, Rayleigh steps into the waiting transport.

"What is your destination?" says an automated voice over the speaker.

Pulling the jump device from her bag, Rayleigh opens the map and responds with the coordinates to a remote location. As the door closes, the automated voice gives a confirmation. Rayleigh watches as they begin to rise into the sky, watching the buildings disappear below them.

"I'm agent Sarrati Suthti, badge number 326894. Please activate codes 56, 42 and 36." Rayleigh commands, settling into her seat.

"Confirmation. Codes 56, 42 and 36 activated," the automated voice responds, before falling silent.

Letting her head drop back to rest on the seat, Rayleigh places her hand on the bag, feeling the orb within and the weight of everything that she has. She reminds herself about what she has to protect.

Letting her eyes rest, she drifts off to sleep.

Chapter Sixteen
(Months earlier)

As the engines lift her into the night sky, Tailia looks down, through the rain streaming across the view screen, to where she left Rayleigh. There is a heaviness in her chest at the thought that they will never see each other again, but she lets herself go. Tears running down her face, matching the rain across the ship window. Letting them continue uninterrupted, she holds on to the flight controls as she breaches the outer atmosphere and into outer space.

"How did you do?" asks a voice over the comms. It's Bellery, checking in from the main ship.

Tailia struggles to find her voice, and it breaks as she begins to speak. "Good. She's home now."

"She'll be missed," he responds.

"She is where she belongs," Tailia mumbles, not waiting to go into detail.

"Maybe. Well, we're waiting for you. Rutherian and DitDit42 are still out exploring this dimension, but I'll call them back," Bellery concludes, before cutting the link.

As she dives back towards the ship, Tailia can hear the engines purring, the familiar sound bringing her some comfort.

Shifting her attention back to the controls, she pushes the craft's engines further, picking up speed as she makes her way back to the others. Tailia sees it come into view, then watches it grow, before she's eventually swallowed up by it.

As the docking guidance system takes over, she lets go of the controls and the computer takes her in. Now that she no longer needs to focus on flying, the tears start up again, coming thick and fast. She lets her head drop backwards against the seat rest as tears run down her face. With each deep breath, she feels as though she is taking a bite of the sadness that is choking her up.

"Goodbye," she whispers, closing her eyes and letting the last tear escape from her eyes.

When she hears the clank of the ship's docking claws securing her vessel, Tailia opens her eyes and slides out of the seat. As she heads to the opened door, she hears Allgery and Bellery talking outside.

She steps out into the hangar, and they both pause to look at her as she approaches.

"Well, what now?" Tailia asks them.

"Trouble?" Allgery says, with a smirk.

"Mischief?" Tailia responds, matching his smirk.

"I think I can manage something," Allgery says. "Bellery, are you in?"

"I'm always up for anything," Bellery says with a smile.

"Maybe Helga has something?" Allgery says, almost to himself, looking upwards.

Bellery stands to attention and gives a salute, then runs off the deck.

"So you and Helga are still in contact?" Tailia asks Allgery with a raised eyebrow.

"She always has things that will get us into trouble and mischief," Allgery replies with a chuckle. Allgery and Tailia walk side by side, as they follow Bellery to the command deck.

"How are you doing?" Allgery asks as they reach the docking bay door.

"I didn't think it would be this hard," Tailia says quietly.

Allgery stops Tailia before she goes through the door. "I worry it might get worse. If you need anything, you know where I am," he whispers.

"Thank you," Tailia replies, placing a hand on Allgery's arm.

The two of them stay this way for a moment, and Tailia can feel the connection between them. Then they step through the door and move along the hallway to the command deck. Bellery comes over the comms to tell them he has located a nearby jump point. They redouble their speed, wanting to reach the command deck before Bellery makes the jump. Allgery pauses to let Tailia enter first, and they step into the command deck to find everyone waiting for them.

Tailia can see that Rutherian and DitDit42 are already in their seats.

"Are you both up for an adventure?" she asks.

They look at each other, and each respond with a shrug and a nod.

Tatinet enters the command deck, having heard Bellery's announcement. "I'm in as well," she says as she finds a seat.

"Alright, I guess we're good to go, then," Tailia says.

As she and Allgery take their seats, Tailia takes a final look around at everyone, ensuring they are buckled in. Then she says, "Ready when you are."

With that, there is a flash of light and they jump.

***

Children run around as Tailia, Bellery and Allgery walk through the street. Allgery feels a sense of conflict build within him at being back in this place. He's unsure how he will be received, and equally unsure whether coming here is the right decision. Some of the kids bump into Bellery as they pass, and Allgery reaches out to grab one of them by the arm.

"Nice try, but I'll need that back," he says, crouching to make himself eye level with the child.

The child shies away, trying to avoid Allgery's gaze. After a moment they raise their hand to show a watch dangling from their hand.

"Thank you." Allgery reaches out and the kid places it in his hand. "Bellery, you might want to keep an eye on this," he says as he hands the pocket watch back to Bellery, who looks confused to see the item in Allgery's hand.

Allgery lets the child's arm slip out of his hand so that they can move again.

"Hey!" Tailia calls out as the child starts to run off.

The child stops. Tailia kneels next to them and pulls some food out of her bag. She offers it to the child with an outstretched hand. The child looks at it, then at Tailia, then at the food again. Tailia gives a wink and a smile, still holding out her hand. "Here you go."

The child looks down at the food, up at Tailia, and then over at Allgery, unsure what to make of the situation.

"It's okay," Allgery says.

With a slight hesitation, the child takes the food from Talia, then darts away into the streets, disappearing from view as quickly as they had appeared.

"So, where are we going?" Tailia asks Allgery as she stands.

"This way," Allgery says, pointing down a nearby alleyway.

"I'm not sure if they'll be happy to see us," Bellery chimes in. But Tailia has already begun walking down the alleyway in the direction that Allgery has pointed.

"Nothing has changed, then," Tailia calls over her shoulder with a chuckle and a smirk.

The alley ends at a cul-de-sac with a bar on the far side. Two men are standing outside, smoking and talking in whispers.

The three of them look at each other, then move slowly towards the men, watching their movements to see if they pose any threat.

"Where do you think you're going?" one of the men says in a low voice barely loud enough for them to hear.

Tailia, Bellery and Allgery ignore him.

"I said, where do you think you're going?" the man says, a little louder this time.

"We're here to see Helga," Allgery responds.

"There's no one here by that name," the man says, finally turning to face them. Straightening to his full height, he stands taller than Allgery.

"Ha. Nice try," Allgery chuckles. He goes to push past the man, slightly annoyed that they are playing this game.

In a flash, all guns are drawn, and everyone is eyeing each other.

"There's no one here by that name," the man repeats firmly as he aims his guns at Allgery and Tailia. His companion covers Bellery and Allgery.

"You're outnumbered here, buddy," Bellery responds.

"No, my friend, you are," the man replies casually, looking up at the rooftops. Tailia can see countless silhouettes standing on the roofs around them.

The atmosphere is tense as they all hold their stance, everyone waiting for the first person to flinch.

Talia looks around, trying to work out how to get out of this situation. Before she knows it, Allery comes crashing to the ground, broguth down in a flash.

"My love," say the person who has landed on top of him.

"Hey, Helga," Allgery responds from underneath her.

She showers him in kisses, pausing intermittently to check every part of his body to make sure that he hasn't been hurt.

"Ah… your friend?" Tailia says.

"Helga, meet Tailia. Tailia, this is Helga," Allgery says as he tries to ward off Helga's advances.

At the mention of Tailia's name, Helga finally seems to take in the people around them. She looks up at Tailia.

"She's attractive. Is she your new lover?" she asks Allgery.

Allgery goes bright red at the suggestion.

"You need to loosen up – it's fine," Helga says with a wink, giving Allgery a tap on the cheek. Standing, she turns to Bellery and asks, "Is it okay to give you a hug?"

Bellery considers this. "That is okay."

"Tight or gentle?"

"Tight, please."

Helga steps forward and gives him a hug. Pulling away, she extends her hand to Tailia. "Any friend of Allgery's is a friend of mine."

"Pleasure to meet you as well."

"Come on, let's go inside," Helga says, walking past the two men standing at its front. "All good. They're cool," she says, giving one of them a slap on the arm as she passes.

Both men holster their weapons and return to their smoking and conversation. The figures on the roof vanish back into their hiding holes.

"Come on," Helga says, pulling open the door of the bar.

Tailia and Bellery look at each other, then down at Allgery, who is still lying on the ground. He takes Bellery's offered hand to help him get up.

"*My love*," Tailia says with a smirk and a chuckle.

"That's a story for another day. Come on, let's get a drink." Allgery dusts himself off and moves towards the door.

The two men smoking ignore the three of them as they head in through the door.

There is a hum in the bar, everyone mumbling to each other in hushed voices. A band is playing in the corner, but most people don't appear to be paying them any attention.

Helga has taken a seat on the far side of the room, surrounded by a group of people who are laughing and joking with her. As Allgery makes his way through the crowd he stops to hug people, nodding at others, and high fiving others. Walking past the bar he nods to the bar tender, who rushes to prepare a drink for him. Finally taking his place at the table with Helga at her table. Talia walks past the bar, raising her hand, signalling with her fingers that she would like two. The bartender nods, and starts to prepare hers with Allgery's. Taking her seat at the table with Allgery and Helga, she looks back to see Bellery struggling to get the bartenders attention.

"He always seems to struggle," Allgery says looking over at Bellery.

He gives a loud whistle, which makes the bar fall silent. The bartender looks over, and Allgery points at Bellery at the bar. Making the Bar tender finally turn to acknowledge him, nodding that he has Bellery's order. Bellery turns and makes his way towards them.

With Bellery joining them, Helga looks over at them all.

"Your weapons will be returned to you when you leave," Helga says causally, before turning to Allgery.

Panic comes over Tailia, as she pats herself down, trying to feel her weapons. But they have gone.

"Don't worry, we're safe here," Allgery says, picking up his drink. "Everyone here works for Helga."

Helga is paying Tailia and Bellery no attention and continues to dote over Allgery. Allgery looks over at Bellery and Tailia, looking uncomfortable with the ongoing attention. He coughs to get Helga's attention and to highlight that they have guests. Helga responds with an expression of disappointment as she turns to the others.

"Sorry about that. He's so boring sometimes," she says, gesturing at Allgery. "How can I help?"

"We were wondering if you might have any work or odd jobs that you might need done," Allgery says.

"I guess there is something… but it might be a bit of a suicide run," Helga replies.

"Sounds like fun," Tailia says, glancing at Allgery.

Bellery nods in agreement.

"We have news on a shipment that you might be interested in," Helga says to Allgery.

Allgery's stops mid drink to look over at Helga. "You've found another one?"

"Yep. It's currently being held on Planet 29 at coordinates 42–12. It will likely be there for another week before it's shipped out. So, if you want in, then you'll need to be quick." Helga finishes her drink and before turning to go back to talking to the group next to them.

"What are the details?" Allgery asks in earnest. When Helga doesn't reply, he says, "Helga?"

"It doesn't look good, and it might be best to ignore it," Helga responds.

"You know I can't do that."

"I know… Expect heavy resistance, as it is a base world. Would you like assistance?"

"We have a small crew, so it might be best to try and slip through," Allgery replies. He picks up his drink again, falling silent as if lost in thought.

"Don't forget, I'm here if you need anything," Helga whispers to him.

"I know… Thank you," Allgery responds, also in a whisper.

Tailia watching the exchange, is a little confused what is happening between the two of them. Not able to shake the cryptic way they are wording the conversation.

***

"Alright, I guess we have our trouble," Allgery says with a chuckle, looking at Bellery and Tailia, who have been watching them.

"Do we get more information?" Talia asks Allgery.

"Bellery, would you be able to look into the coordinates with DitDit42?" Allgery asks.

"Sure thing. I will get on it when I'm back."

"Tailia, do you think Rutherian and Tatinet will be up for the adventure?"

"We can ask them when we get back to the ship, I guess. But are you going to tell us what we're doing?"

"Something to help the war against the I.D.T.," Allgery says, looking down at his drink.

"That's a little vague," Tailia says, placing a hand on his arm to get his attention.

Allgery shies away from her. *They won't understand.* Then a contrasting thought runs through his mind: *But they're your friends… Surely they'll understand… But what if they won't help… This is too important.*

"Allgery?" Tailia's voice interrupts his thoughts, and he looks up to see her looking at him.

"It's important," is all Allgery is able to get out.

Tailia studies him a little longer, then nods. "Come on, Bellery let's go," she says. Bellery nods and the two of them stand and make their way across the bar.

Allgery goes to stand, but feels a hand on his arm.

"You can trust people. You're important to us, and we're happy to help," Helga says, reaching over and placing a hand on his cheek.

Allgery shrink even further into himself, unsure what it is he is supposed to do.

"Hey," Helga says, snapping him from his thoughts. "I'm always here for you."

"Thank you... I..." Allgery exhales, trying to shake the weight from his mind. "I should go... They're waiting for me." Tailia and Bellery are on the other side of the bar, looking back at him.

"Please be safe," she whispers, giving him a kiss on the cheek.

"I will. Thank you again," Allgery responds. Their contact lingers a moment longer before they break away. Allgery makes his way across the bar towards Bellery and Tailia.

When he reaches them at the front door, Tailia asks, "What about our weapons?"

"You have them back already," Allgery responds.

Tailia opens her jacket, a look of surprise on her face at finding her weapons holstered where they should be. "That's a little creepy," she says.

"Don't be fooled – everyone here is highly trained and will give their lives for Helga," Allgery responds, looking over at Helga, who has returned to her party. "Come on. Let's go," he says, pulling the door open. He looks at Helga again as he waits for them to pass through the door. She catches him staring and nods. With a smile and a small wave back, he follows the others through the doorway.

Outside, the weather is still bitterly cold, and the two guards are still at the front, talking and smoking. They watch them all leave, so the group move quickly into the darkness. They cross the street and make their way back down the alleyway, towards their ship.

"So we are about a day out from the coordinates we got from Helga," Allgery says, pulling up the map of the planet they are heading for and zooming in on their destination. "It appears to be heavily guarded, but I'm sure that we'll be fine."

"This is the factory we are aiming for, and we are looking to set down in this area," Bellery says, indicating a building and then scrolling to show their landing site.

"Umm, this is a base. Are we sure we want to do this?" Rutherian asks, looking around at the members of the group and then back at Allgery.

"It will be worth our while," Allgery says quickly, but he feels nervousness grow inside him as they all look at him.

"If we land here," DitDit42 says, picking up Allgery's explanation and drawing everyone's attention back to the map, "it should be thirty minutes or so on foot to the factory. This is an active military planet so we should expect to meet resistance, and once we do, things are likely to get intense. We might need to make a quick getaway."

Allgery zooms the map out slightly so that everyone can see the route and the base.

"Who are we up against? And what sort of terrain are we expecting?" Tatinet asks.

"It is an I.D.T. research facility on one of their military planets," Bellery replies. "We will be landing in the forest, which is as close as we can get, and will be moving through an industrial part of the planet." He looks around at the group, then continues, "We will set up the training grounds using the information we have available, so we can play out some possible scenarios. Let's spend the rest of the day practicing some simulations, so we can get in sync with each other and be ready for tomorrow."

"Are there any further questions?" Allgery asks, looking at each person in turn.

"Yep," Tatinet says. "Do you have more information about the mission?"

Allgery's body tenses up as his mind races for an answer. The sick feeling returns to his stomach. "We have information that the I.D.T. are holding something important there. Unfortunately, that's all I have at the moment." He knows he's not being honest with them. "Are there any further questions?" When no more questions come, he nods.

"Okay, let's meet in the training room in thirty minutes," Bellery says as Allgery switches off the display and the group stand.

"Are you sure this is a good idea?" Bellery whispers to Allgery as the others head to their respective rooms.

"It's too important not to try," Allgery replies.

"But we should give them the choice," Bellery whispers, nodding towards the others.

"I can't risk it. I'm sure they'll understand," Allgery says, trying to shut down any further questions.

"I'm with you, no matter what," Bellery says.

He turns back to the command deck, leaving Allgery alone with his thoughts. For a while he watches Bellery work, then he turns to head to the armoury and prepare for their training.

***

"I feel like he's keeping something from us," Tailia says.

"What do you mean?" Bellery asks, continuing to work at the desk.

"This mission – it seems off. Like there's something we're missing. Does he not trust us?"

"He trusts you with his life."

"Then what is it?"

Bellery pauses, unsure where to look or what to do. Finally, he says, "He means well, and I trust him with my life." He looks back at the controls. "Please be patient with him. I hope you know you can trust him."

"We've been through a lot. I just wish he would let me in," Tailia says, looking out into space. "I trust him with my life. I wish he wouldn't put up so many walls."

"Walls?" Bellery looks at her. "He's human."

"That he is, Bellery, that he is," Tailia says with a chuckle. She places a hand on Bellery's shoulder. "Come on – we should go."

"Yep, I'll be right there," Bellery replies as Tailia walks away. He turns back to the command controls, giving them a final check. Finishing up, he climbs out of the seat and follows Tailia to join the others in their practice.

Chapter Seventeen

The ship shudders slightly as they enter the outer atmosphere of the planet. The team members are all strapped into their seats, waiting for the ship to stop jumping around. Allgery looks around at them all. Each of them has their own unique way of handling the rough ride, with Rutherian sleeping through, while Tatniet holding on for dear life. The ship stabilises and levels out.

"We should all go and get ready," Allgery calls over his shoulder to the others, who are behind him. "Have you got this, Bellery?"

"All on it," Bellery replies chirpily, focusing on the controls. As the ship speeds over the surface of the planet, he looks like he's playing one of his space games. The mountains go screaming by, and then the ship drops into a valley. Allgery is captivated by his friend's skill. *He never ceases to amaze,* he thinks as he looks from the screen to the map beside Bellery's control desk.

"Touchdown in thirty seconds," Bellery calls over the intercom as the team move through the ship towards the loading bay.

"Thank you, Bellery. I'll go and join the others," Allgery says, patting Bellery on the shoulder. Bellery only manages a nod, still focusing on the task at hand.

Allgery makes his way to the loading bay, the ship swaying and weaving as he walks. He reaches out to the wall to stabilise himself while moving as quickly as he can. As he enters the loading bay, he sees the others supporting themselves on the ship's beams, waiting for the touchdown. As if on cue, there is a shudder as the ship settles on the ground. The engines power down. The crew don't need any instruction; the door drops and they head out of the ship.

Allgery follows them out. The clean air of the forest washes over him. After several days in the ship, it's nice to breathe fresh air.

The team move with purpose, not needing to say anything to each other, taking up positions outside the ship. Crouching, they survey the surrounding area.

It doesn't take long for Bellery to join them, coming out of the ship with his weapon drawn. Tailia and Allgery have taken point, standing at the front of the group with Rutherian and Bellery standing on the left and right side respectively, DitDit42 and Tatinet in the back middle.

"Is the ship secure?" Allgery whispers over the comms.

Bellery taps at the controls on his arm. "Ship secure."

"Let's go," Allgery whispers, pointing in the direction they need to go.

With that, the team members move in unison and wordlessly into the forest, which embraces them. Each member scans the forest, watching for any movement.

"Not to worry," DitDit42 says over the comms.

His statement is closely followed by a sound of a stick breaking in the forest nearby. Rutherian swings around in the direction of the sound, and the others stop moving.

"Not to worry," DitDit42 says over the comms again.

At this, Rutherian brings his weapon around and begins move again, the group continuing through the forest as before, trying to move without making a sound and doing their best to ensure they do not leave any trace of their presence.

At the edge of the forest they all crouch down to scan the buildings in front of them.

"Bellery," Allgery whispers over the comms.

"On it," Bellery responds before slipping away from the group and disappearing into the closest building. Tatinet moves into Bellery's position, filling the gap without needing direction.

Allgery pulls out the map to confirm their location and ensure they are heading in the right direction. "Bellery, we need a scan," he says over the comms.

"On it," Bellery responds curtly.

The map grows and fills out with information as Bellery's drones scan the surrounding areas.

188

"Great, it looks like this is the best route," Allgery whispers over the comms, tracing the route on the map with his finger. The team each look down at the devices on their arms, following the line on the map.

"Confirm," Bellery responds over the comms.

"Let's move," Allgery says. "Bellery, please watch over us."

"On it," Bellery responds.

Allgery moves first, the others following him, staying in their assigned positions as they move soundlessly.

The massive industrial buildings tower over them as they move into the streets. The buildings are dark, lifeless and unwelcoming. The group hug against them for cover.

It's late at night, so there is no one out on the streets. At the first corner, Allgery raises his hand to stop the team, and they all drop back against the wall, prepping themselves. Allgery continues holding his hand up, watching guards move on the other side of the street.

There are six guards, all talking and joking, seeming to be unaware of their surroundings and more engaged in what is happening amongst themselves.

After a short moment, they move on.

Allgery lowers his hand and the team all lower their weapons slightly into resting position. Allgery's data slate beeps in his ear, and he looks down to see a message reading, *Love you!*

A *crack* rings out in the distance, snapping him from his thoughts. Each member of the team tenses up at the sudden sound.

"What is that?" Allgery whispers over the comms, looking to see if the guards have done anything.

"Checking," Bellery replies in his earpiece.

The ground shudders, then thunderous cracks ring out in quick succession, intensifying each time.

"It's gunfire and explosions on the far side of the city," says Bellery over the comms.

Allgery looks down at his slate. Images are streaming to his device from Bellery's drones. "She's too good to me," he says under his breath.

"What's that?" Bellery responds.

"It's Helga. She's distracting them," Allgery replies. "Come on – we should make the most of this."

Nodding to the team members, he turns and jogs in the direction of the factory, now taking less care to move quietly. Moving through the streets with new speed, they reach the factory quicker than originally planned. The team fans out on either side of the doorway, preparing to breach the building.

"Ready?" Allgery whispers over the comms.

"Yep," they all respond in unison.

Allgery gestures at the door in front of them. "DitDit42, if you would be so kind?"

DitDit42 walks forward, pulling a small plant from under their robe and placing it on the keypad. The plant grows as its roots push into the electrical circuits of the doorway access pad. After a moment, the door clicks.

"It is open," DitDit42 announces, standing up.

"Thank you." Allgery nod at the group, then swings the door open, entering with the group filing in behind him. They are greeted by a long hallway.

"Rutherian, DitDit42 and Tatinet – you take that way," Allgery says, pointing. "Tailia and I will take the other."

The team nod and break off in their allocated directions.

Tailia and Allgery head off down the hallway, moving with military precision, scanning the doorways they pass. Once they are out of earshot of the others, Tailia finally speaks.

"So, do you want to tell me what this is all about?" she whispers to Allgery, who is coming out of a room he has just cleared.

"What do you mean?" Allgery replies casually, uneasiness climb up inside him.

"What are we here for?"

Allgery doesn't respond and continues checking through the rooms, making sure they are clear.

"Hey, you can trust me," Tailia says, stopping Allgery as he comes out of another room.

"We've found something," DitDit42 says over the comms, breaking the tension between Tailia and Allgery.

"What have you found?" Tailia asks.

Allgery continues into the next room. As he passes through the next door, he finds what he is looking for.

"It might be easier if I show you," he calls out to Tailia, before DitDit42 can respond.

As he looks into the room, he fights against the sick feeling swirling through his body. *How can people do this?* he wonders.

The smell floating from the room adds to the sick feeling in his stomach. He looks down at the children huddled in the dark as the light from his and Tailia's torches move around the room. The children shy away from the light, and Allgery wonders how long they have been in the dark.

He looks over at Tailia, with his emotions taking over.

"Who would do something like this?" Tailia asks him.

"Does it really matter? We need to save them," Allgery says, moving into the room to check on the children. Lowering his weapon, and smiling to the children, he tries his best to reassure them as he moves, but the children move away from him.

Tailia slings her weapon behind her, trying to remove any possible worries for the children.

"Free everyone," Allgery says over the comms to DitDit42, finally acknowledging his question.

"Already on it," DitDit42 replies quickly.

"Who are they?" Tailia asks, the words tumbling out of her mouth.

"Some of them are children of jumpers, some orphans of war. Others were just in the wrong place at the wrong time," Allgery replies.

"Can you help me, please?" he asks, as he moves to free them from their chains.

"Of course, but we'll discuss this later," she responds. She snaps into action, moving into the room to start helping with each child.

The kids huddle together at the doorway, unsure what they should be doing even after being released from their chains, they huddle together.

A loud crack sounds nearby, shaking the building. Several of the children cry out and drop to the floor, whimpering.

"It's okay," Tailia whispers to the children. "We have you." She places a hand on several of the closest children.

They all look at her, and huddle more closely to each other.

"You have incoming," Bellery says over the comms.

"Can you distract them?" Allgery responds.

"Of course."

Sounds of gunfire begin, coming from nearby.

"It's okay, children. That's us," Allgery calls to the children as they turn in response to the sounds of gunfire.

"How are we going to do this?" Tailia asks.

"We'll find a way."

Allgery and Tailia both have try to hide their tears from the children, but can see it in each other as they make eye contact.

"Okay," Tailia responds, placing a hand on his shoulder.

As he looks down at the children, Allgery can see himself in the children, remembering his own experiences as the past comes crashing into the present, making him freeze.

Tailia's voice snaps him from his memories. "DitDit42, we will need protection getting out of here. Rutherian, we need you to cover our escape, and Tatinet, can you help us calm the children?" Tailia says over the comms.

"Thank you," Allgery whispers, reaching out to touch her hand lightly.

"I trust you," she responds. "Come on children. You're with me," she says, breaking away from Allgery and moving towards the doorway, where the dozen children are huddling. She crouches down next to them, pulling them in with her presence. "It's going to get loud, but if you stay close to me and Allgery, we will keep you safe," she says.

Allgery continues to move around the room, freeing the last of the children from their cells, and directing them to the front door where everyone else is gathering.

"We have everyone and are back at the entrance," Tatinet says over the comms.

"We are ready," DitDit42 says.

"We're on our way," Allgery responds as he joins Tailia and the children at the door. "Ready?" he whispers to Tailia.

"We're ready," Tailia responds, looking at the children.

She steps out into the hallway. Two cracks ring out, and Tailia fires in response. Several of the children cry out in fear.

"She will protect us," Allgery says, crouching next to them and placing a hand on some of their shoulders and adopting a smile to reassure them. "Stick with Tailia and you'll be fine."

Tailia has now moved out into the hallway and is scanning for any further movement. After a moment, she looks back and nods at Allgery.

"Right, children, stay close to her," Allgery says, gesturing for them to move after Tailia.

He watches the children scurry into the hallway, then scans the room to make sure that no one has been left behind. Then he steps out into the hallway, looking back along it to see two guards lying on the ground.

Turning, he takes off after Tailia and the children, falling in behind them to cover the rear of the group.

There is little resistance as they move through the hallways, with only a few more guards jumping out, disposed of by Allgery and Tailia. Soon, the children get used to the sounds and stop jumping at every crack of gunfire.

As they round the last corner before the exit, they see Rutherian, DitDit42 and Tatinet standing by the doorway with another group of children.

"Bellery, how are we doing?" Allgery calls out over the comms.

"Busy," Bellery responds curtly. The sound of gunfire is audible over the comms.

Allgery moves to the doorway and looks into the courtyard outside. There are I.D.T. officers scurrying around, taking up positions. When they see him, several of them take potshots, and he ducks into the safety of the entrance.

"Well, that's rude," Tailia jokes, pulling a cheeky face at the children to ease their nerves.

"DitDit42, if you would be so kind," Allgery calls out.

DitDit42 is on the opposite side of the doorway. "Of course," they respond, and move forward to stand next to the doorway.

"You'll love this, children," Tailia says, winking as DitDit42 approaches.

"Rutherian, you're up next," Allgery says over the comms.

"Sure thing," Rutherian responds, moving forward next to DitDit42 in preparation.

"He might be a little loud, children," Tailia says cheerfully, gesturing for them to cover their ears.

Tailia and Tatinet both bring the children in closer to them with a gesture. "Stick with me, and we will get you through," they say to their groups.

The children nod sheepishly, but take them at their word. Tailia looks back at DitDit42 and Rutherian and nods.

With that, DitDit42 slips through the door in an almost elegant manner. Immediately, the officers outside begin to fire. DitDit42 moves through their bullets, almost dancing, pausing and moving with direction and purpose. They cover the courtyard quickly to reach its centre, then raise their staff and slam it into the ground.

An explosion of nature erupts from the point of impact. Branching out from where the staff has made contact with the ground, trees, vines and plants shoot in all directions, stretching over the courtyard and covering everything they touch. The I.D.T. officers hesitate as the plants take hold around them, then continue firing.

DitDit42 now stands behind a wall of plants that have grown up in front of them. The officers' bullets hit the opposite side ineffectually.

DitDit42 looks back at the doorway from where they came. Instantly, Rutherian steps out from behind it, covering the ground from the doorway to a wall created by the plants. Scurrying up its side, they flip over it to bring themselves on top of the barrier.

The I.D.T. officers redirect their fire at the new target, but before they have the chance to hit them, Rutherian swings their gun, which dwarfs them and yet which they move effortlessly, towards the officers.

When they pull the trigger, the world becomes into a sea of bullets. They spew towards the officers, who are now questioning their defences as the buildings around them are torn to pieces, Rutherian's gun eating away into everything.

Chunks begin to fly from the walls, and several of the officers fall over, caught in the sea of bullets. Walls continue to shatter and officers jump out of the way as the gun rips into the protection behind which they were standing. Rutherian moves the gun casually as it continues to roar. The I.D.T. officers shy away from the hail of bullets heading in their direction.

DitDit42 takes the opportunity to create another wall and a pathway behind which the others can hide. It is high enough so that the kids will be safe behind it, but Talia and the others will still be able to fire over the top.

Allgery surveys the chaos unfolding outside as Rutherian and DitDit42 combine with Bellery to hold back the officers trying to stream into the courtyard. Seeing the new wall that DitDit42 has created, he looks over at DitDit42, who is smiling and giving a thumbs up. Allgery returns the gesture before turning back to Tailia and the children.

"Right, children, listen up," Allgery calls over the roar of Rutherian's gun. "We have a path that has been made for us. Keep low and stay with us." He looks up at Tatinet and Tailia, who are standing behind the children.

The children are shaking, and some of them jump at the sounds of the firefight outside.

"You're okay," Tailia calls out over the din, speaking loud enough to attract the attention of the children that are struggling to focus. "Stay with us."

"Ready?" Allgery says to Tatinet and Tailia.

They both nod.

Allgery steps out into the courtyard, moving in the opposite direction that the kids will go, in an effort to draw the attention of the I.D.T. officers.

"Tailia," he calls over the comms, signalling for her to move with the children. Turning, he watches as she ducks out with the first of the children, crouching behind the wall that DitDit42 created.

As she steps into the firefight, Tailia lets out a salvo of bullets, taking down several officers silly enough to expose themselves. The children stream out after her, crossing the distance quickly to join her behind the wall.

Rutherian is still unleashing hell, drawing the officers' attention. DitDit42 is continuing to create defences and taking down any officers that get close to Rutherian.

The children continue to stream out of the building, Tatinet following them. Seeing her, Allgery makes his way back towards the group. As he passes the door, he sees there is a boy, roughly 10 years old, still inside. He slips in and crouches next to them.

"Hey, what are you doing in here?" he asks.

"It's scary out there," the boy reply, looking down at the floor, flinching in response to the cracks and bangs from outside.

"Hey, it's normal to be scared. I'm scared all the time," Allgery says, sitting down next to him. "Do you want to know what I do?"

The child nods.

"I tell myself it's okay to be scared. This is normal… Then I realise I don't want my fear to stop me," Allgery says, resting his head against the wall. "I have a lot to live for, and so much living to do. How about you?"

The child is still looking at the floor. Allgery wonders if his statement might have gone over his head.

"I miss my sister," the child says, and a tear creeps out.

Allgery feels a pang in his chest as memories of his sister come crashing back.

"I miss my sister as well." Feeling the child's pain, Allgery reaches over to place his arm on their shoulder, pulling them closer. "Come on – should we go and live?"

The child sits silently for a moment, their fingers fidgeting. Finally, they look up at Allgery.

"Let's go and live," they say.

"Alright then, let's go. Come on, follow me out. I'll look after you."

The child nods again.

As the two of them stand up, Allgery can still feel the emotions swirling inside him. Allgery find himself wondering about his sister, and whether she would be proud of him. He pushes the thoughts aside to bring him back to the task at hand: saving the children.

"Ready?" he asks.

The child nods, with what appears to be a newfound confidence.

Allgery leads him out the door and into the firefight raging outside. With the child in tow, he makes it to where Tailia and Tatinet have set up with the other children.

"That's all of them," Allgery calls out to Tailia.

She nods in response. "Alright children," she calls out, gaining their focus. "You're all with me. We're going to stay low behind this wall, making our way to that building." She points to the far side of the courtyard.

With explosions rocking the world around them, all the children drop down in a huddle as if to escape the chaos.

"Once we're there, we'll turn right and head down the closest street. Stick with me, and Tatinet will be next to us and Allgery will be following up the rear." Tailia points to them in turn.

Allgery remembers why he would give his life for Tailia. He is in awe of her ability to inspire, while making people feel safe, giving them the courage to overcome the impossible.

People would follow her into hell, he thinks as he watches the children begin to move behind her. *Don't worry, sis, I'll protect her with my life.*

Registering movement nearby, he looks up to see an I.D.T. officer coming around the corner, trying to flank them. Allgery fires without thought, dropping the officer before they are able to get any closer. After performing a quick scan of the area to make sure there are no more officers, Allgery moves after the children.

Looking over the wall, he can see DitDit42, Rutherian and Bellery still slogging it out with the scores of officers trying to overrun them. Allgery crosses the courtyard to join the others on the far side, where they are huddling down. He nods to Tailia as he approaches, letting her know that she can keep moving. Needing no further guidance, she turns and continues moving, directing the children along the street.

Allgery turns back to look at the others in the courtyard. "We're clear," he calls to them over the comms.

"Acknowledged," they each respond.

"I'll set up a distraction," Bellery adds.

"Thanks, Bellery. Be careful," Allgery says.

DitDit42 and Rutherian break away, moving towards Allgery, leaving Bellery perched on the far side of the courtyard. As they withdraw, the I.D.T. officers advance into the courtyard to take up positions inside it, firing at DitDit42 and Rutherian as they withdraw. Allgery supports them by firing at the officers. DitDit42 and Rutherian pass him and take up positions firing back into the courtyard, preventing the officers from moving any further.

Allgery can hear Bellery's drones approaching overhead, their whirr cutting through the sounds of gunfire. He looks towards where Tailia and the children were, but they've already disappeared around a corner. He contacts Bellery over the comms. "We're all clear. The floor is yours. Be safe, my friend."

He turns to DitDit42 and Rutherian. "We better start running."

Allgery throws a smoke grenade into the courtyard. Amid the smoke spewing out, they turn and begin running towards the children. As one of the drones passes over their heads, Allgery starts to run a little faster. After a few moments, the world behind them erupts into a giant fireball as the drones reach their destination, detonating with full force, levelling the courtyard and everything inside.

Despite knowing what was coming, it catches Allgery off guard, making him stumble slightly with the shock wave. The others turn back as they run to see the fireball as it expands and stretches up into the sky.

Allgery follows up at the rear, still feeling pain in his chest at the sight of the children. He rounds the corner and sees the children ahead, moving through buildings and making their way back towards the hangar. Tailia and Tatinet are doing their best to keep them together and moving forward.

Allgery's heart is racing, and he tries to calm himself down. He feels for the children that had to go through such things. He hopes that he has made the right decisions.

"How did you do?" Tailia asks as they approach.

"All good. We got clear," Allgery responds.

"What about Bellery?" Tatinet asks, looking around the group.

"He'll meet us at the ship," Allgery replies. He looks down at the children. "Come on, kids, let's get out of here."

Allgery moves through them all, placing a hand on some of their heads as he makes his way to the front. He and Tailia lead the way back to the ship.

"Can I ask you something?" Tailia asks, without looking at him.

"Sure."

"Why didn't you tell me?"

Tailia's words bite into Allgery, adding to the debate he'd had about whether or not to say anything to the group about why they were here.

"I... I..." Allgery lets out a long sigh. "I didn't know if you would want to help or not," he finally manages to get out.

"Of course I'm going to help."

Allgery feels the tension increase between them, as he struggles to find words.

"But what if you said no?" Allgery says, wrestling with his doubts and uncertainty swirling inside him.

Tailia puts an arm around him as they walk. "Allgery, I'm always here for you. If you wanted to risk your life and limb for an ice cream. I would be right there by your side..." She looks over at him and says, "I'm with you."

Her words wrap around Allgery like a blanket on a cold night, settling his inner doubts.

"Your sister would be proud of you," Tailia adds. As the words pierce through him, Allgery feels the tears rolling down his face. Not wanting the others to see, he turns away and continues walking, placing an arm around Tailia so that she moves alongside him.

"I think of her constantly," he says.

"And so do I."

Allgery glances at Tailia to see that she is crying as well, not holding back. Allgery is annoyed with himself that he didn't come to her sooner.

"Thank you," he says, turning back to look at the path ahead.

"We're in this together..." she says looking up at him, before breaking away. "Come on, we should get back to the task at hand. We have people to protect."

"Look at us, in the middle of a warzone, crying and having deep conversations," Allgery says, nudging Tailia playfully.

"Isn't that what we should do when the world turns to chaos?" Tailia jokes back, giving him a soft punch in return.

"Forever the philosopher."

"That we are. Come on, I think this is us."

They turn into the next building, looking back to make sure that everyone is still following. They sneak through the building, continuing to make their way back to the ship, always scanning for possible threats. They both slip back into protecting the children. With the sounds of gunfire and explosions having stopped the children have begun to settle more, talking amongst themselves and walking with a little more confidence.

When they reach the ship, Allgery opens the door to let them all in. "Tailia, can you help them get settled?" he asks.

"Of course."

Allgery watches each of the children walk in, taking in their faces, trying to reassure himself that he can let people in.

"DitDit42," he says, "would you be able to get the ship ready for takeoff?"

"As you wish."

As the last of the children enters the ship, Rutherian stands alongside Allgery to look out into the surrounding forest.

"Do you think Bellery is safe?" Rutherian asks.

"Of course. He will be here," Allgery says, looking down at Rutherian.

The two of them stand watch, guns ready and waiting.

"What are you looking at?" says a voice from nearby.

"We're looking for unicorns," Allgery says, recognising Bellery's voice. "It's great to have you back, old friend. How did you do?"

He turns to see that Bellery is covered in dust, blood and what appears to be black soot.

"I ran into a couple of squads, but they're amateurs, so it was no issue," Bellery says.

"Should we go?" Allgery asks.

"Let's," Rutherian replies.

Bellery nods, and they turn and head into the ship.

Allgery pauses at the bottom of the ramp, letting the others go on without him. On his device he opens the message from Helga and responds, *Thank you.*

As if on cue, the guns in the distance fall silent.

Love you appears on the screen of his device. Allgery stares at it, feeling the connection between Helga and himself in those few words.

"She deserves so much more," he says to himself. He looks at the message for a little longer before closing it and making his way inside.

The engines are nearing full power. Allgery braces himself against a wall as the ship lifts off the ground, taking them up into the skies and to safety.

Chapter Eighteen

"Who is she? Who does she work for? What is she doing?" The guard's questions come thick and fast.

Tom floats into consciousness, his mind racing. He has asked himself these same questions.

He grapples with other questions, too: *How long have I been here? Who are they?*

"Come on, Tom. We need answers."

Slowly, Tom opens his eyes to look at the two people standing before him. They are both wearing full military uniform, black from head to toe, with full face helmets. Tom can't determine anything about them. The light swings over his head, and his head feels heavy. He pulls at his wrists, which are strapped to the chair. Loosing strength he falls forward, the restraints catch him, sending jarring pain down his arms, shocking him back into focus as adrenaline runs through his veins.

"Who is she? Who does she work for? What is she doing?" It's the other guard speaking this time.

Tom looks up at them. "As I said, her name is Rayleigh. She works at Milford Design and she's an interior decorator," Tom spits out, repeating the same things he's been saying all along.

"You're lying." The guard pushes a button, sending pain through Tom's body. His muscles scream in protest. His body feels like it is on fire, burning with electricity, but he knows it can't be possible, as the guards are touching him and are unaffected.

Is this all in my mind? Tom thinks as he fights his way back to awareness.

They come at him again. "She doesn't love you, Tom. She isn't who you think she is."

What do they mean? Can what they say about her be right? Have I been wrong all this time?

One of the guards punches him, sending shockwaves through his body and making him lose his strength. Falling forward, he is stopped by the straps again.

No. She loves me… Tom's heart tries to wrestle back against his doubts. *Well, she did… Maybe I did something wrong… or I wasn't enough.* His thoughts and feelings pull against one another. His heart tries to push back the doubts as they stalk him. *Is what they say true?*

A little piece of his mind falls away at the thought. *No. She loves me… or loved me.*

Bringing himself back to the present, he raises his head to look at the two guards who have continued to ask him questions, but he slumps again, his head unable to support itself.

"Put him back in his cell," one of the guards says.

There is a click, and a door appears in one wall of the room, out of nowhere. Two more officers step in to collect Tom from his chair and drag him out.

"He's not telling us everything. He knows more," the officer says, looking at the other.

"He does." The two of them turn and walk through the doorway.

***

Tom wakes in his cell. His head is groggy and he struggles to recall where he is. Hurling himself forward, he vomits on the floor.

Not again, he thinks.

He pushes himself up, every fibre of his body protesting at the movement. A question continues to swirl around in his head: *Who is she?*

A hole appears in the wall, and a parcel of food slides through it. Tom doesn't flinch. He stares up at the ceiling, questions running through his mind.

Who is she? Who does she work for? What is she doing? Do I even know? Looking over at the food, he thinks, *I should eat… Otherwise, they'll feed me.* The memory of the last experience sends chills down his spine.

Tom slides his feet off the bed to fall to the floor. He has forgotten all about the vomit, and they land square in it, clumps crawling between his toes.

"God dammit." Tom lets out with a sigh, lifting his feet and shaking them to try and get rid of the vomit. He staggers over to collect the food. Out of energy, he collapses on the floor next to the tray and slides it onto his lap, looking at the slop they have served him. He summons all his strength to get the food into his mouth. Slowly, one piece at a time, he begins to scoop the food into his mouth.

How long have I been here? he thinks. *How long will this go on for?*

Returning his attention to his food again, he continues to eat.

***

Bellery and Allgery sit on the command deck, looking out at the planet. It was several weeks ago that they saved the children, and now the ship is full of them, racing all over the ship, putting their hands into everything, exploring and breaking everything they can find.

But everyone has enjoyed the time with the children, who have brought an abundance of life back to the ship, filling the corridors and rooms with laughter and games.

"Will they be safe here?" DitDit42 asks, coming up behind Bellery and Allgery who are looking at their destination on the holographic display.

"Yep, there's a place for them here," Allgery responds.

The planet grows in the view screen. Allgery issues directions as they go, highlighting a landing spot on the map.

"Prepare yourself for landing," Bellery informs everyone over the intercom.

The kids running around outside the command deck and Rutherian is chasing after them, who squeal as they run into the cargo bay to take their seats.

"I think Rutherian is going to miss them," Tailia says as she enters the command deck.

They all chuckle and nod, none of them willing to admit they will miss the children too.

"Don't mind us," Tatinet calls from the hallway, looking in at the four of them standing on the command deck.

"My apologies. I'm coming," DitDit42 responds as Tatinet chases some kids down the hallway to the cargo bay. "I should go help," they say, then nod to Bellery, Allgery and Tailia before making their way off the command deck.

Tailia takes DitDit42's space next to Bellery and Allgery, looking out at the planet as it expands.

"Will they be safe here?" Tailia asks Allgery.

Allgery laughs. "That's what DitDit42 just asked," he says. "Yep, they have a place here. Decades ago, I helped some refugees settle here. They will know what the kids have been through." He turns back to look out at the trees passing underneath the ship. "The town is simple and the level of technology is low, but for most of the children, slow and relaxed is what they need. It's peaceful here."

"That's good," Tailia says. "Guess I better go help," she says, before turning to leave.

***

"Morning, Tom," comes a voice from the doorway.

Rolling over, Tom looks at the person standing in his doorway.

"Morning, Juilter," he replies, swinging up to sit up in his bed. "Will we have another session today?"

"Do we need to?" Juilter asks, sitting opposite Tom, holding his breakfast.

"I was thinking there might be more," Tom replies as he takes the tray.

"Okay, I will organise a time this afternoon…" Juilter gestures at the food. "We've made you your favourite this morning, because you've been good."

"Thank you," Tom replies, looking down at the sloppy food. He has become used to the food over the last seven months, and has come to enjoy its familiarity.

"I better get back to it. The boss is being hard today," Juilter says, standing up. "Do you need anything else?"

"No, I think that's it for now. I'll see you this afternoon."

"Sure thing. See you then," Juilter says, heading out of the cell. He stops at the entrance. "Do you want this open or closed?"

"Open is fine."

"Sure thing," Juilter says, leaving Tom to his breakfast.

Chapter Nineteen
(Decades earlier)

The waves wash gently against the shoreline, creating lapping sounds and rustling the pebbles. The birds overhead call out to each other as the sun comes up.

Tailia stirs from her sleep, rolling over to take in her surroundings. In the distance, the beautiful mountains stretch up into the sky. Her gaze follows their sides to the ocean. Her eyes chase the skyline, reaching to the room in which she lies.

Seeing the silhouette of her partner lying next to her, Tailia rolls over and pushes in behind Sari. Slipping her arms around her, she pulls her close.

"Good morning, my love," Tailia whispers into Sari's ear.

"Good morning, my love," Sari responds, rolling over to look back at her. A smile cracks her face.

Wrapping herself around Tailia, Sari places a hand on her face as she kisses her. They hold each other softly.

A quiet knock from the door breaks their focus. They both look over to the door.

"Duty calls," Sari whispers.

"That it does," Tailia responds, her attention moving from the door and back to Sari.

The knock comes again. Tailia and Sari hold each other's gaze a little longer, not wanting to move.

"Yes?" Tailia calls out, reluctant for anyone to know that they are even in here.

"Sorry to disturb you, your highness," Bailey, the aide, calls from behind the door. "Your brother and sister wish to speak with you."

"Thank you, Bailey. Please let them know I will be there momentarily," Tailia responds, still holding Sari's gaze.

"As you wish, your highness," Bailey replies.

"I'm sorry, my love. I should not keep them waiting," Tailia says to Sari, giving her another kiss before pushing herself up from the bed.

As she tries to pull away, Sari pulls her closer and holds her tighter. Tailia lets herself be pulled in, and they embrace each other again.

Breaking away, Tailia climbs out of bed and makes her way across the room. Pulling on the free-flowing gown that she wears within the palace, she collects herself, and picks up the royal seal from the dresser. She places the seal around her neck. It will show everyone that she is a member of the royal family, but of course within the palace everyone knows who she is.

Tailia pauses at the door to look back at Sari, who is getting dressed for the day. "See you for lunch?" she calls.

"It would be my pleasure," Sari responds with a smile.

Tailia slips through the door and out into the hallway, where Bailey is waiting. The guards standing on each side of the door nod to Tailia as she exits the room.

"Bailey, Tiir and Miir, good morning," Tailia says, bowing formally before hugging each of them in turn.

"Your highness," they each respond.

"How did you sleep?" Bailey asks as the four of them begin moving down the hallway.

"Well, thank you," Tailia replies. "It's great to hear the birds have returned for the year."

"The red bow bird is amazing, your highness," Tiir chimes in from behind them.

"That it is," Tailia responds.

"Your brother and sister will be in this room on the right," Bailey says, his tone and posture becoming more formal as they approach the room.

Tiir and Miir also adopt a more formal guard position as they round the corner and come into sight of others within the palace. Bailey opens the door for Tailia.

Tailia's brother and sister sit on the far side of the room, enjoying their breakfast as the staff wait upon them. Tailia's sister, who is a few years younger than her, is wearing a similar outfit to her own, so that they look almost identical. Her brother is older than both of them but looks younger. He has defined features, making him look a little sly and cunning. They both move with the presence that is a result of being royals, growing up with the finery of their positions.

"Good morning, brother and sister," Tailia says, walking into the room and smiling to them both. They both look up to welcome her.

Tailia uses a secret gesture to Bailey, Miir and Tiir, signalling that they should fall back. Tiir and Miir stand at the entrance with the other guards, and Bailey sits with the other aids. Tailia takes a seat at the table, opposite her brother and sister, who each reach out a hand so that Tailia can take them with a squeeze of affection.

Tailia eats, and the three of them laugh and joke. They have always been close.

Bailey appears at Tailia's shoulder. "Your parents wish to see you," he whispers just loud enough for her to hear, before backing away.

Tailia nods. "Our parents have requested my presence," she says to her siblings, who stop eating.

"Oh, they must be ready to announce your position," Tailia's sister says excitedly.

"You deserve it," Tailia's brother chimes in.

"Thank you," Tailia responds politely. "If you will excuse me."

Standing, she bows to her brother and sister before turning to head for the doorway. Bailey, Tiir and Miir fall into step beside and behind Tailia as she passes them. The four of them move through the house, each in their formal positions based on their station within the household.

As they pass others in the hallways, everyone bows and steps aside to allow them through. Tailia still finds all the attention odd, but she pushes the thought aside.

They round the final corner, at which point Bailey, Tiir and Miir all pause. Tiir and Miir both taking up their positions with the other guards at the entrance. Tailia walks forward, then pauses in front of the doors.

"Are you ready?" Bailey whispers to Tailia.

Tailia doesn't respond, focusing on the door. Without a word, both doors swing open to reveal a grand room. On the far side, her mother and father sit in chairs placed side by side. Tailia stands still, waiting for her introduction. Bailey taking a single step into the room and bows to the King and Queen, who nod their approval.

"It is with my humble pleasure that I welcome and greet you, to introduce Tailiania Yerullian Therian, second in line to the throne," Bailey calls in a formal voice.

The internal guards snap to attention and a silence falls over the room as everyone stops. Tailia hesitates before walking into the room. her head high and moving with grace, as if she is floating. Her presence fills the room and each of the local governors bow as she passes.

Tailia comes to a halt in front of her parents. She bows, going down on one knee.

"Your majesties. I come at your request," she says with her head still bowed.

"Thank you," Tailia's father says in a regal voice.

"Thank you to all that are present. We ask that you leave the room, so that we may speak in private," Tailia's mother says, projecting her voice so that everyone in the room can hear her.

There is muttering of confused voices. Most of people here are used to being included in all discussions.

The guards snap to attention. Their sudden movement and action prompts silence from the others. Stunned, the local governors and dignitaries begin to file out of the room.

When the last of the guests has left the room, Tailia's father says, "Thank you for your service, guards. We ask that you leave as well."

The commander of the guards opens his mouth to speak, but his majesty raises a hand to stop him.

The commander snaps to attention again. "Guards, you are relieved of your duty," he calls across the room.

With a single movement, all of the guards acknowledge the order, slipping back into private alcoves behind them. As the last of them disappears, the commander surveys the room once more.

"The room is yours, your majesties," he says, before disappearing into his own alcove.

Tailia and her parents are the only people remaining. A room that would normally hold hundreds of people is now empty. The silence is uncomfortable.

"Tailia, my darling," her mother says, interrupting her thoughts.

"Thank you for coming to see us," Tailia's father finishes.

"Why have we broken from protocol?" Tailia asks.

"Unfortunately, the circumstances require that we break from protocol," her mother says.

"We have been thinking and discussing the future and the roles that we all play in society," Tailia's father adds.

"What role have you assigned me?" Tailia asks.

Her mother and father look at each other.

"You will be the next ruler of our world," her mother says finally.

"But what about my brother?" Tailia asks, confused.

"We have been concerned with recent events and believe our people will be safer in your hands," Tailia's father replies. Tailia senses that his words have been weighed carefully.

"Recent events?" Tailia asks, even more confused.

"We cannot discuss them at this time, but everything will come to light shortly," Tailia's mother says.

"We will announce our decision in the coming days," his majesty concludes.

"Does anyone know?" Tailia asks.

"We will be meeting with your brother and sister now and will discuss this with them," Tailia's father continues.

"Until it is announced, we ask that we keep this to yourself," Tailia's mother whispers. She pulls a small scroll from under her garment.

"This is our decree for your safe keeping," Tailia's father says.

Tailia takes the scroll from her mother. Unrolling it, she sees that it proclaims that she will be taking over as ruler. At the bottom are her mother's and father's seals, next to the authorisation code for the decree.

Tailia looks up and nods in understanding.

Tailia's father lifts his sceptre and hits it once on the ground, making a loud thud that echoes throughout the empty room. As Tailia steps back, she hears the clicks of doors opening as the guards slip back into the room.

Tailia slips the decree into her garments as she takes her place in front of her parents. As the last of the guards take their places, she bows. "Thank you, your majesties," she says before standing and backing away. After she has reached a set distance, she turns and walks towards the main doors.

The other guests have not been allowed to enter yet, so only the guards have taken up their positions around the room. As she exits through the main doors, Tailia sees her brother and sister waiting on the other side.

"How did it go?" Tailia's sister asks.

"Huh?" Tailia responds, still struggling to accept what she has been told.

"You look flushed," Tailia's brother says.

"Huh… Oh, sorry, something caught me off guard," Tailia responds. "Let's talk later." She moves past them.

"Sure thing," Tailia's sister responds, nodding as she passes.

"Bailey, I would like to retire to my room please," Tailia says as she approaches her aide. Miir and Tiir are standing at the side of the hallway.

213

"As you wish." Bailey bows curtly, maintaining formal posture and wording in the presence of others.

Tailia continues walking and Bailey, Miir, and Tiir fall in step beside and behind her. The four of them move without talking, passing through the palace, and once again everyone steps aside to allow them through. Tailia doesn't pay any attention to what is happening around her, still caught up in her thoughts.

Why did they give this to me, she wonders. *What's going on?*

The next thing she knows, Tailia finds herself standing in front of her bedroom door. Bailey reaches out to open it for her. Sari is sitting at the desk, but she stands as Tailia walks in.

Tailia hesitates, surprised to see Sari in her room, but also glad and a little relieved that she is there.

"You looked troubled, so I thought you would like her here," Bailey says. "I'm sorry. I hope I've not overstepped?" He bows even further so that he can no longer make eye contact with Tailia.

"That's okay... Thank you," Tailia says, placing a hand on Bailey's shoulder. He rises slightly to make eye contact.

"Thank you. I'm worried for you," he says.

"Actually, I would like to talk to you all," Tailia says, looking around at them.

She makes her way to the couch in the centre of the room. Sari takes a seat next to her, placing a hand on Tailia's back. Tailia looks at Bailey sitting opposite her, then at Tiir and Miir. *Always proper,* she thinks, noticing that they have decided to stand.

"What's wrong?" Sari asks.

"They want me to take over... and rule," Tailia mutters, still unsure of the words that she is saying.

"But... what about your brother?" Bailey asks calmly.

"Apparently something has happened which has made Father and Mother choose me as the successor," Tailia responds, regaining some degree of composure.

214

They all sit for a moment, none of them saying a word. Tailia can sense their tension and confusion. She pulls out the decree, and they hand it around.

"So what now?" Sari asks, breaking the silence.

"My brother and sister should have been told by now, and it will be announced in the coming days," Tailia replies in a hushed tone, as if speaking loudly might shatter the delicate news.

The group all sit back, still surprised at what they have heard, but soon confidence and acceptance starts to take hold.

"I was instructed not to tell anyone, but I wanted you all to know," Tailia says.

They all look at each other nodding before finally settling on Tailia again. She nods, then closes her eyes, trying to imagine what will come. Opening her eyes again, she looks over to Sari, placing a hand on her knee.

"Bailey, Tiir and Miir, if it's okay with you, I would like to be alone with Sari now. We will need to start planning," Tailia says, hoping to get some alone time where she can let her guard down.

They all nod in response.

"As you wish," they say in unison.

"Please let me know if you need anything," Bailey adds as he begins to walk away.

Tailia nods and lets him go.

Then she turns so that her back is towards Sari, then drops into her lap, sinking into her partner's arms.

"Why would they do this?" she muses.

"Your parents wouldn't do this without a reason. We will have to wait," Sari responds. She wraps her arms around Tailia and pulls her closer. "Whatever happens, we will figure it out, and do it together," she continues. She slides out from behind Tailia and lies down next to her. She places a hand on Tailia's face and holds her gaze.

"Thank you," Tailia responds, nuzzling her head into her partner. As they hold each other, Tailia feels the bond between them strengthen. The two of them drift off to sleep, listening to the waves lap against the shoreline outside.

***

Tailia stirs from sleep. It is after sunset, so the room is dark, with only silhouettes of the room. She and Sari are still on the couch, holding each other. Tailia can feel Sari's heart beat, and their love is like a warm blanket over them both.

Sari is everything to Tailia.

Sliding out from under her, Tailia gets up off the couch. She takes a nearby blanket and lays it over Sari. She runs her hand along her face, admiring her.

Moving over to the refreshments bar, she pours herself a glass of water. She looks in the mirror and wipes the sleepiness from her mouth and eyes.

She registers movement in the corner of her eye. *What is that?*

Something slips around her neck and begins to squeeze. Fear jumps up as the arm around her neck tightens, cutting off the life from her body. In the mirror she sees a figure emerge from the darkness.

She tries to scream, but they cover her mouth to prevent her from making any sound. Tailia thrashes frantically, trying to break free. Her hand swings wildly, catching the glass of water with her hand and sending it crashing to the floor. It shatters as it hits the hard floor.

There is a click and a thud, and then the figure behind her goes limp and falls to the floor. As the oxygen rushes back into her lungs, Tailia turns to see Miir standing in the doorway with the light from the hallway behind them, gun drawn and pointed in her direction.

With the element of surprise gone, more figures that were hidden within the room switch from stealth to attack. Miir doesn't give them a chance, switching targets and dropping another of them in one swift movement.

Sari rouses from her sleep to see Miir with gun drawn, and Tiir moving towards Tailia. He covers the distance between the door and

Tailia in an instant, catching her as she staggers and guiding her gently to the floor. He swivels to face into the room with Tailia behind him.

"Get down!" Miir yells. A whirring sound spins up, the room erupts into a hail of bullets that tear through the room, making holes in cushions, furniture and walls.

Miir turns towards the hail of bullets, drawing his second weapon and firing. Bullets course across the room towards her, but they're too slow. Miir places two shots into the figure who fired the bullets. The figure slumps forward, putting a stop to the chaos. Miir continues deeper into the room, heading for the balcony, where the shots came from. On the balcony, Miir throws her arm left, turning slightly to bring the other parallel with the first.

Bullets burst from Miir's gun, taking out two more attackers that have climbed over the balcony. Finally, Miir pauses to survey the scene.

"Clear!" she yells, still fanning his guns around the room, searching for the next target.

"Are you okay?" Tiir asks Tailia, who is still curled up on the floor.

Having regained her breath, she looks up at Tiir. "Yes, I think so," she says, rising slowly. She exhales as she looks towards her partner. When she sees Sari move, the sick feeling in her stomach begins to subside.

"What is going on?" Tailia says, looking around the room and ending on Tiir, who has also taken up a defensive position next to her.

"I do not know. But someone wants you dead," Tiir responds flatly.

As if on cue, gunfire begins to ring out from outside the room, drawing everyone's attention towards the door. It rings out in sporadic bursts, breaking the silence of the night and drowning out the sound of the ocean waves.

Bailey comes crashing through the door into Tailia's room, making everyone tense up at the sudden movement. He freezes as Tiir and Miir's weapons are trained on him.

"Is everyone safe?" Bailey calls out.

Realising that it is Bailey, Tiir and Miir resume scanning for movement. When nobody responds to him, Bailey moves further into the room, holstering his weapons as he approaches Tailia.

Tiir moves closer to Miir to support her covering the room. Bending down next to Tailia, Bailey helps her up. When she gets to her feet, everyone stiffens again as two more people come through the door. Tiir fires at them both, dropping them before they can get a shot off, then resumes scanning the room with Miir, working in perfect unison due to years of training together.

"We need to move from here," Miir states without breaking focus.

"I need a moment," Tailia responds.

Miir and Bailey nod, and Tailia heads for her walk in wardrobe. From the back of her wardrobe she pulls out a crate. She places a hand on top of the box, and it takes a moment to verify her identity, then opens with a click. Lifting the lid, Tailia pulls out her combat gear.

She remembers the time she spent training with her old mentor, the tireless nights running drills, over and over. Never could she have imagined that she would need these, but now she is grateful for the time she spent.

She relaxes a little more with each item of combat gear she pulls on. Taking out her guns, she holsters them at her side. Finally, she places her dagger and sword in their places, appreciating their weight.

Standing, she moves from the wardrobe and out into the room.

"Sorry about earlier," she says. "I was caught off guard. It won't happen again."

"No worries, your highness," Tiir responds casually.

"Assessment?" Tailia asks, joining Tiir and Miir in the centre of the room.

"We should clear out and head for the safe house," Miir responds, retaining her vigilance over the room.

"Agreed," Tailia responds.

"I will follow your instruction," Tailia continues, looking at Miir.

"As you wish," Miir responds, shifting focus and taking command of the room. "Tiir – door. Bailey, you're with Tailia, and I will bring up the rear."

"I can fight," Tailia chimes in.

"I know, but we should keep that as a last resort," Miir replies in a softer tone. She looks at each of them in turn. "Channel 35, cipher ALKU – confirm?"

They each respond over the comms links, and Miir ensures they are on the correct channel.

"Tiir – entrance?" Miir asks.

"No. Unsuitable," Tiir responds sharply over the comms. They step out into the hallway and begin firing at the figures moving down the hallway. They're greeted by a hail of bullets, and yelling in the hallway. Tiir ducks back behind the door, continuing to fire down the hallway to keep them at bay.

Miir surveys the room. "Okay. Exit 12," she says over the comms.

"Affirmative," the group respond.

Tailia thinks of their training, and all the drills they have done together.

"All hostile," Miir adds, which makes Tailia's stomach turn.

This isn't training any more. This is life or death, she tells herself.

"Affirmative," they all respond.

Tiir's movement spurs the others into action. He punches a code into the safe near the doorway and pulls out a bag, from which he takes a string of grenades. He looks over at Miir and the others, who have begun moving towards the balcony. He flips the switch, activating the timer. Counting down, Tiir throws the string of grenades down the hallway towards their attackers. As the grenades land, there is a yell of "Grenade!"

Tiir slams the door and bolts it, preparing for the blast. He punches in a code into the door panel, and its locking mechanisms seals shut. Shortly afterwards an eruption comes from outside as the grenades explode.

"Clear!" Tiir calls out.

"Let's move," Miir responds.

They move towards the balcony. When he reaches the ledge, Bailey jumps without hesitation, throwing himself out into the night air. Tailia and her partner are a step behind, following him over the balcony.

Using ledges and poles to slow his descent, Bailey touches down first. He moves into the courtyard, freeing space for Tailia and her partner to drop down behind him, landing in unison. They move behind Bailey, clearing space for Miir to land. Taking up their positions, they all wait for Tiir to join them, after a moment he touches down as well. Miir nods at Tiir. Seeing the unspoken message pass between them, Tailia glances up at her room. A sense of sadness washes over her as all the memories disappear as the explosion engulfs her room.

"Let's move, south route," Miir whispers over the comms.

Without a word, they move, the embers of the fire falling down around them. Tiir slips away into the darkness to scout the path ahead. Bailey takes front and centre and Miir drops behind. Sari is positioned to Tailia's right, keeping her at the centre of the group. As they move through the palace gardens, no one makes a sound, each scanning their surroundings to ensure that they are not flanked.

Adrenaline courses through Tailia's body. Every fibre of her body tries to reach out into the world, looking for any hint, movement or threat. *How can I not be ready?* She thinks back over the years of training she has been put through. She looks back at Miir with a newfound respect for her bodyguards, who have experienced countless wars, combat situations and all manner of training. *There is no training that could prepare me for this.*

A bullet bounces off the wall next to her, and her heart skips a beat. She swings around towards the direction of the shot. Seeing a figure, she lets out a number of shots. The first three miss but the fourth and fifth find their mark and drop the target.

Hearing more shots fired up ahead, she scans for more targets. After a few moments, everything goes silent.

"Clear?" Miir asks over the comms.

"Clear," everyone responds.

They take a moment before moving again. Tailia looks at Miir, her rock; calm and collected, moving with purpose. Every action is calculated and trained, with no wasted efforts.

When they reach the edge of the garden, they pause for a moment. Tailia can hear her heart beating as she surveys the open space ahead.

"Move quickly and stay low… Go," Miir whispers over the comms, and they all begin moving out into the open field to make their way to the far side.

"Down," Tiir calls out in response to sounds of gunfire and flashes that light up the night.

They all do as he commands, trusting in each other. The bullets scream over their heads, punching into the statues nearby and digging up dirt. Rolling over, Miir and Bailey return fire. Tailia is a beat behind them.

"Tiir," Miir calls over the comms.

"Affirmative," Tiir responds, coming out of their hiding spot on the far side of the courtyard. Together, they try to push the figures back. The attackers scatter as Tiir's presence creates a new threat for them. They turn to fire on him as he pushes himself out from cover and fires on the figures as they move.

"Go," Miir calls over the comms.

The others begin making their way to the opposite side of the courtyard. Miir begins walking in a direct line towards their assailants. With Tiir and Miir now creating the loudest noise, the two guards now have all of the bullets heading in their directions, allowing Bailey, Tailia and Sari to move without notice.

When the reach the protection on the far side, Bailey, Tailia and Sari turn back to look at Miir and Tiir. They can see the bright flashes of their guns, responding to flashes on the other side.

Something moves to the right, and Tailia turns, firing off several shots. The first misses, but the second, third and fourth all hit the two figures that have emerged from the darkness.

As they look back to the field, the flashes of light fall silent. They all look frantically for any sign of life.

"Clear," comes Tiir's voice over the comms.

"Clear," Miir echoes. "Regroup at Section 39."

"Affirmative," they all respond.

Following the new instruction, they head for the meeting point. Bailey takes point with Tailia in the middle, and Sari following up closely behind. The three of them move through the palace garden confidently, having spent countless years here.

Bailey and Tailia take down several assailants unfortunate enough to step out of the shadows. With each use of her weapon, Tailia settles into her old training.

They round the final bend to see Tiir standing by one of the garden walls, waiting for them. As Bailey, Tailia and Sari come closer, Tiir nods to let them know they have been seen. The group move into position to give them the best visibility of the courtyard and its possible entry points.

"Where is Miir?" Tailia whispers.

Tiir shakes his head, and a sickly feeling creeps into Tailia's stomach as she wonders where Miir might be.

"I'm here," Miir whispers, stepping out of the shadows.

Tailia turns to see blood streaming down his arm. She approaches him to check his wounds, but Miir doesn't even acknowledge them.

"Are you okay?" Tailia asks quietly.

"We should get to the safe house," Miir responds, continuing to scan their surroundings.

Tailia places a hand on Miir's right arm, stopping her bodyguard.

Miir looks at her and nods. "I'm okay," he says. "We can patch it up when we get to the safe house." Tailia sees him wince, fighting against the pain.

"Come on, let's get to the safe house," Tailia reaffirms to the group.

With that, the group turns and moves down the closest pathway in the direction of the safe house. They can all hear the sounds of fighting in the background. Small fires have broken out all over the palace, and Tailia finds herself stopping to look back at it every now and then. With each glance, she can feel the added sadness and the burden that it carries. She worries about her family, and whether they are safe. She pushes the thoughts aside, and keeps moving, trusting that her family will have guards protecting them.

When they reach the shoreline, they turn and make their way towards the cliff face, covering the distance quickly. They walk in the shallow water in the hope of hiding their tracks. They don't speak a word, each looking to see if there is anyone following along.

When they reach the cliff face, Miir pulls back the vines that have grown over the entrance. Tailia remembers the last time she had been here decades ago, and wonders what it might be like inside.

As the door swings open, they all stream inside, wanting to get out of the water and into safety.

The interior of the safe house stretches into the mountain, and contains countless rooms and enough space for the entire royal family and its entourage. It is lavish and looks like any other room in the palace. To Tailia's surprise, it has been maintained and is spotless. The housekeepers must have been taking care of this place all those years.

Miir closes the door behind the group and activates the code on the inside of the door. There is a hiss as the door seals shut. The safe house has been built to withstand orbital bombardment and comes with all the necessary supplies to survive for a long period of time.

Miir's left arm has been made worse by all the movement, and he is leaving a thick path of blood across the room.

"Excuse me madam," Miir says to Tailia, bowing slightly.

"Do you need help?" Tailia asks.

"No. It is fine. You should stay here with the others," Miir responds. "I will be back shortly." He moves in the direction of the medical bay.

The rest of them settle down on the couches in the centre of the room. Tiir stands next to the couch near Tailia, surveying the room in combat readiness. Given the safety of their surroundings, Tailia wonders again what could possibly be going on.

"It's okay, Tiir. We can relax now," Tailia says.

"Thank you, madam. I would prefer to stand," Tiir responds, looking at Tailia and then the others.

They all jump as someone emerges from the room next door. They breathe sighs of relief when they realise they are Tailia's brother's guards, who have heard Tailia's group enter and have come to see who it is. They enter the room with guns drawn, but lower them when they see Tailia and the others sitting on the couch.

"My lady. Are you okay?" the commander asks.

"We are fine. A little shocked, but we are okay. How are you all?" Tailia asks.

"We are good. Your brother is in the back at the moment. We are just clearing the remaining rooms."

"Why would you do it?" says Miir from the other side of the room.

They all turn to see Miir exiting the med bay, guns drawn and aimed towards the commander.

"What are you doing?" Tailia cries out to Miir. "Lower your weapon."

"Why would you do it?" Miir says again, standing firm.

The commander looks sideways at Miir, and raises his voice in a show of strength. "How dare you raise your weapon to me."

"Why?" Miir says again.

The two of them stare at each other, neither wanting to back down.

Suddenly, the commander begins to laugh. "You always were perceptive," he says, then pauses before looking around at everyone. "How did you know?"

Miir looks at the commander and the other guards. "You're not wearing your seal."

Adrenaline jumps within Tailia, confusion creeping up from her deep within her.

"You've also not taken your finger off the trigger of your weapon… But more importantly, I could sense your malicious intent from the other room," Miir responds, each word adding to the tension.

"Perceptive as always," the commander responds with a smile.

At the first bullet, everyone brings their weapons to bear, and fire at each other. The commander fires with one gun focused on Miir and another on Tailia, trying to take them both down.

Tailia, Bailey and Sari are caught off guard by the sudden violence. As bullets fly around the room, Tailia scrambles to return fire.

Tiir and Miir push the soldiers back, acting on reflex to the new threat, each firing off a volley of rounds and maintaining in their positions.

Sari moves without thought. She steps in front of Tailia and takes two bullets square in the back, from the commander's gun. She goes limp, dragging Tailia down as she falls.

Tailia instinctively throws her arms out to grab Sari, to stop her from hitting the floor. Holding her, she slows the last of her fall.

"What are you doing?" Tailia pleads with Sari, fear rising up within her as the firefight around her vanishes from her focus.

She wraps her arms around Sari, holding her as she lies with blood coursing out of her wounds.

"Loving you," Sari says, placing a hand on Tailia's cheek, smearing some blood on her cheek. "Thank you for loving me," she whispers. Then her hand falls to her chest.

"No, no, no, no, no... Please don't leave me," Tailia pleads.

Her hands move frantically over Sari's face, trying to will movement back into her. She pulls Sari closer, squeezing her and feeling the wetness of the blood on her clothes. Tears are streaming down her face, seeing them fall onto Sari's face.

Words fall out of Tailia's mouth. "How can I live without you?"

"Tailia, I'm sorry, but we need to leave," Bailey interrupts, hunching down next to her.

"No, Bailey, I won't leave her," she snaps, holding Sari's head and trying to gaze into her eyes. But there is no life behind them.

"Madam, I'm sorry. We need to go," Bailey says again in a voice just above a whisper. He places his hand on Tailia's shoulder to get her attention.

The world around Tailia swims back, with the sounds of the firefight continuing. Miir and Tiir are doing their best to hold the guards back.

"I'm sorry. I can't allow any of you to leave," the commander yells from behind the wall.

Something snaps within Tailia. She places Sari on the floor and stands, bringing her guns around to take on the guards. Her anger takes over. The guards try to use her exposed position to their advantage and turn their fire upon her.

"Tailia, no!" Bailey cries out, launching himself from his position. He wraps his arms around her and they both crash back to the floor again.

"Let me go!" Tailia yells at Bailey, fighting against him.

"I'm sorry. Please don't throw your life away," Bailey says, releasing her from his grip.

"You don't get to decide that," Tailia responds sharply.

Bailey is lying on the floor. Her heart sinks at the realisation that Bailey took the bullets that were meant for her.

"No, no, no. Not you as well… What have I done?" Tailia whimpers, the sick feeling creeping into her stomach.

She watches as the life flows from his eyes. He smiles at her. "Thank you for everything," he whispers as his life leaves his body.

Tailia is in shock. They have been with each other for decades. Sitting on the floor, she looks over at Sari lying on the floor next to her.

Bullets whizz overheard, but Tailia pays no attention to them. Looking at her friend and her partner, she feels emptiness opening up within her.

How could this happen? Who would do this?

Miir's voice breaks through the thoughts whirling in her head. "My lady, I'm sorry to disturb you."

Miir is crouching next to her. There is sweat running down his face, along with blood spatter, but his expression is one of peace and sadness.

"Tailia, we need to move," Miir continues, placing a hand on her shoulder. He continues to return fire at the guards even as he holds Tailia's gaze. "Come on – it is time to move," he says in a hushed tone.

"I'm not ready to move." The words slip out of Tailia's mouth without thought. She's still holding Bailey's hand and looking at Sari's body.

"I'm not sure we are ever ready, but we need to move. If we stay, we die."

This echo of death hits home with Tailia. She looks up, taking in her guard's face. There is a kindness there, and she can see all the times they had. The laughing, the adventures, and all the things they have done over the years.

"Okay, Miir. I trust you," she says finally.

She folds Bailey's hands on his chest and whispers, "Thank you for everything." Then she turns to Sari, touching her face and holding her hand as she leans over her. "Thank you for loving me," Tailia whispers. She can feel the oncoming sadness. The loss of her lover, and the fact that the future they were to have together will no longer happen.

We may go our separate ways, but you will always be with me. Forever yours, thank you. She gives Sari a kiss, tucks a hair away from her face, and places her gently on the floor.

"Okay, Miir, let's move." she whispers.

Miir nods slightly. "Tiir," he says over the comms.

"Affirmative," Tiir responds. There is a click followed by a series of thuds as Tiir throws several grenades towards the guards. They bounce and disappear behind the wall.

Using the explosion as cover, the three of them escape from the room, firing as they head to the front door. None of them say a word as they slip out the door under the cover of the smoke and fire from the grenades.

The night air is cold. The water seeps into Tailia's shoes, like cold steel against her feet it sends chills down her spine.

Tailia stares up into the night sky. *What now?* she thinks. Looking up at the palace, her eyes pass over the bunker before finally settling on Miir and Tiir standing next to her.

"Come on, let's go," Tailia sighs. "I no longer have a home here." Her heart is heavy heart and tears are running down her face.

Miir and Tiir nod, and the three of them turn to head towards the hangar.

Chapter Twenty
Present day

Rayleigh wakes in the flying taxi, having left Leonard and the city. The vehicle is giving off a gentle chime, trying to notify Rayleigh that they have arrived.

Rayleigh has no idea how long they have been sitting there, as the car waited for her to wake up. She reaches around to collect her bag and jacket off the seat, and steps out into the field.

"That was good timing," she whispers, looking down at the jump device. The timer is counting down the last few minutes.

As the vehicle rises into the sky, Rayleigh stuffs the last few items into her backpack. Pulling it over her shoulders, she begins moving towards the jump point.

Looking down at the device, Rayleigh sees the timer getting closer and closer. She pauses to look back towards the city as the device beeps down to the jump. *I hope I made the right choice,* she thinks.

Reaching the last few seconds, Rayleigh tucks it back into her garments. Her hair stands on end as a bright light flashes, and she jumps.

She stumbles slightly, still not used to the sensation. When the world comes into view, she takes in her new surroundings.

She is surrounded by Hu Thus, all pointing their staves and weapons at her and talking loudly in their native language. Tension rises instantly within Rayleigh's body. She raises her hands, and the Hu Thus all jump at the sudden movement.

"Woah woah, easy," Rayleigh calls out, trying to calm the crowd.

A group begins to form around her, and their talking becomes louder and faster.

"I'm sorry. I don't understand," Rayleigh calls out to them, turning around and trying to find someone that might understand her.

The group suddenly falls silent, which Rayleigh finds even more disconcerting. Some of the Hu Thus step back to reveal a figure moving forward.

"Our apologies," the tall Hu Thu says. "We are a little on edge after the last attack. You are the one that was travelling with the person known as Tailia, correct?"

The Hu Thu moves with their hands slightly out to their sides. Rayleigh senses they are trying to show that they are holding nothing.

"Not to worry, that is understandable," she says. "Yes, I was travelling with Tailia. Is she here?"

"No, the one called Tailia is not here, but I believe there is someone here that has travelled with her also," the Hu Thu responds, looking around at the group and saying something in their native language. The group begins to lower their weapons and some back away.

"Would you be able to take me to them, please?" Rayleigh asks, slowly lowering her hands as the tension dissipates.

"Yes. I can do that. Please follow me," the Hu Thu responds, bowing slightly.

The Hu Thu turns to the group around them and makes a series of clicks. The group disperses with the last of them lower their weapons, and going back to their day-to-day lives. A small group of Hu Thus remains around with them, giving Rayleigh the feeling that she is still being watched and guarded.

"Please follow me," the Hu Thu says to Rayleigh.

Rayleigh nods, and they move in the direction of the village centre.

The Hu Thus' village is different to the last. The buildings appear new and like they have been well looked after. In the previous village the buildings had been run down. Rayleigh wonders whether they found an abandoned city and then used their staves to grow the plants or if they built the city themselves.

Rayleigh notices that groups of Hu Thus stop talking when she approaches and watch as she passes, and only then return to their tasks.

"What happened?" Rayleigh asks the tall Hu Thu as they walk.

They stop walking and look at Rayleigh curiously, before setting off again. "We were ambushed," the Hu Thu states plainly. "We lost a lot of our kin there, and knowledge," they add in .

Rayleigh is about to speak but she hesitates, not waiting to push the Hu Thu to relive the experience. She finds herself wondering about what the team is up to. *Are they safe? Do they miss me?*

"This is it," the Hu Thu says, interrupting Rayleigh's thoughts.

Rayleigh looks up to see a doorway, which prompts a sense of déjà vu. She steps forward and through the door. As she enters the room, the sounds of talking from those in the room dies down, everyone stopping to look over in her direction.

"Rayleigh," calls a voice from the other side of the room.

Rayleigh looks over at the figure, trying to see who it is.

"DitDit42, is that you?" Rayleigh calls out, unsure if she is recognising them.

"Yes, that is the name you know me by," DitDit42 responds, walking over to Rayleigh and stopping just in front of her. They perform the traditional Hu Thu bow and greeting. Rayleigh returns the gesture, feeling comfort at seeing them again. "How are you?" DitDit42 asks.

"I'm good – and you?"

"I am good as well. We are trying to rebuild after the last attack," DitDit42 responds, gesturing for her to take a seat nearby.

"While I remember, I have this for you," Rayleigh says, reaching into her bag and pulling out the orb given to her by the elder.

DitDit42 steps back, whispering something in their native language. "Where did you get this?" they ask, reaching out a hand but hesitating to touch the orb.

"I went looking for you in the last village, and there was an elder there still alive. They gave me this," Rayleigh replies, turning the orb in her hands.

DitDit42 lets out a few clicks in their native language, and a hush comes over the room. The sudden silence catches Rayleigh off guard, and she looks around the room to see everyone looking at her.

"What is it?" Rayleigh asks.

"We thought we had lost that information," DitDit42 replies, looking down at the orb and then up at Rayleigh.

The Hu Thus around Rayleigh drop down into low bows of reverence at the information that the orb holds. DitDit42 follows suit, muttering to themselves, echoed by the other Hu Thus.

After a few moments, DitDit42 rises from their position and places a cloth over the orb. They place their hands in front of their face, as though praying. Muttering a few more words, DitDit42 clasps their hands underneath the orb.

They nod to Rayleigh, and she takes that as a sign that she can remove her hands, so she backs away.

DitDit42 holds the orb before themselves. They turn to the Hu Thu next to them, passing the wrapped orb to them. They exchange some words and bow to each other. Rayleigh is unsure what is happening.

As the Hu Thu moves away with the orb, DitDit42 turns back to Rayleigh. "You have our respect and faith. Thank you," they say, bowing once again.

Rayleigh is confused and starting to feel a little uncomfortable at all the attention.

As they walk towards a table in the corner, DitDit42 gestures for Rayleigh to sit. Rayleigh slides into the seat, throwing her bag into the corner with a clank.

"How can I be of assistance?" DitDit42 asks.

"I'm looking for Tailia and the others. Do you know where they are?" Rayleigh asks in a hesitant voice, unsure if DitDit42 will have the answer.

"We saved some children several months ago, and dropped them off at a village where they will be safe. I've not seen the team since then, but I know they also frequent 38–31-U-03, so maybe they are there," DitDit42 says, thinking aloud.

Rayleigh pulls out her device to look for jump points. "It doesn't look like they have jump points, so I'm not sure how to get there," she says, looking at DitDit42.

DitDit42 considers this. "Let me speak with the elders. I might be able to help." They look towards the roof. "In the meantime, we have a place where you can stay. Rest up, and I will come back to you once the elders have reached a decision." DitDit42 stands up from the table, gesturing for Rayleigh to follow.

The two of them exit the building, heading into the street. Rayleigh notices several guards standing by the front door. *How long have they been there?*

They head along the street towards the centre of town. As they walk, DitDit42 tells Rayleigh about the adventures the crew had after they dropped her at home. As Rayleigh listens, she feels a small amount of sadness that she missed out. She can feel herself getting excited and anxious to see them all again. DitDit42 finishes up the stories as they approach a little building next to a tree at the centre of town. Holding the door open, DitDit42 gestures for her to enter.

Rayleigh takes a moment to look at the tree, feeling slight comfort at the familiar sight of a tree that stretches up into the heavens. Then she steps through the doorway into the small house, which is similar to the one that she and Tailia stayed in. The sight of it brings back memories, again stirring the feelings of wanting to see everyone again.

DitDit42 turns and bows slightly. "I will be back once the elders have made their decision," they say, rising to their full height again.

Rayleigh nods and watches as DitDit42 nods to the guards that have appeared at the front door. DitiDit42 talks with them briefly and the guards nod before taking up position next to the door. Rayleigh finds herself a little uncomfortable at the sight. *Why would they be guarding me?*

She pushes the thought aside, and turns back to the room. She throws her bag on a couch, then moves over to a bed, and spins and crashes down onto it. She closes her eyes, relishing its warmth and familiarity.

She finds a weight being lifted by the safety of the vines and trees around her.

A thought pops into Rayleigh's mind: *I should shower.* She realises it has been several days since she last showered.

Willing herself into movement, she heaves herself out of bed and stumbles across the room, leaving a line of clothing in her wake.

As she steps underneath the shower, she smiles to herself. She pulls the lever and water begins to flow like a waterfall from the ceiling. The pressure and warmth gives her comfort.

She loses track of time due to her enjoyment. When she has finished up she feels like a new person, fresh and ready for whatever is to come. She returns to the bed, crashes down again and drifts off to sleep.

***

Birds singing outside stir Rayleigh from her nap. She hears a faint clicking sound, too. She realises that the guards are speaking with someone outside.

Rolling over, she finds that the bed has grown over her, offering her a blanket. While it is made of branches and leaves, it is soft and gentle, warm and cosy, with nothing sticking into her.

She rolls onto her back again, looking up at the ceiling, reviewing her memories of the past months. *Did I make the right decision leaving?*

Sounds from outside bring her back to the present. *I should get up,* Rayleigh thinks, nervousness stirring within her.

Pulling herself out of bed, she crosses the room to her bag, then pulls on some fresh clothing before heading to the front door. She pulls back the vines in the doorway to peer outside. The guards stop their conversation, looking over at Rayleigh as she pokes her head through. Now Rayleigh sees that DitDit42 is standing with them.

"Good morning. How did you sleep?" DitDit42 asks.

"Morning?" Rayleigh responds in confusion. Realisation sets in that she has slept through the night. "Good, thank you. How did things go with the elders?"

"Things went well. Should we go inside?" DitDit42 gestures back into the house.

"Oh yes, please come in," Rayleigh replies, casting a sideways glance at the guards.

DitDit42 says something to the guards before entering, and they turn away. Inside, DitDit42 follows Rayleigh across the room to the couch.

Realising that she has strewn items all over the room, Rayleigh runs around to pick up her belongings before moving to the couch to join DitDit42.

"So, good news," DitDit42 says. "The elders have said that I can assist you with finding your friends. They were incredibly grateful that you have returned the orb to us."

"Oh, that *is* great news. Thank you."

"Before we leave, the elders would like to see you."

"Ah… Okay."

"I'm ready when you are," DitDit42 says, standing from their position.

"Oh. Give me a moment," Rayleigh says.

Jumping up from her seat, she scrambles to collect her clothing and her book from the bedside table. She stuffs everything into her bag, then surveys the room to see if she has collected everything. Satisfied, she zips the bag shut and heads over to DitDit42.

"Ready," she says eagerly.

"Okay, follow me," DitDit42 says.

The two guards snap back as the two of them appear in the doorway. DitDit42 says something to them and the guards appear to gesture acknowledgement.

Rayleigh and DitDit42 cross the courtyard, heading for the giant tree. Rayleigh's pace slows as she looks up in awe at it. Even though this is not the first time she has seen one of these trees, it takes her breath away. Moving through the entrance, Rayleigh sees elders sitting around the knowledge wells, chanting in unison.

As she and DitDit42 approach one of the pools, one of the elders breaks away from a group and comes over to meet them. DitDit42 talks to them and gestures to Rayleigh.

The elder bows to Rayleigh. *That seems lower than normal,* Rayleigh thinks. An uncomfortable feeling rises up within her at the reverence the elder is showing her.

"We cannot thank you enough," the elder says, still in their bowed position, not looking up.

Rayleigh responds sheepishly. "No problem."

The elder looks to DitDit42, who says something to the elder in their native language. Appearing satisfied, the elder returns to an upright position.

"We would like to give you something as thanks," the elder says to Rayleigh.

"Oh. Okay," Rayleigh says, unsure what to expect.

The elder steps forward, reaching out their hands. When Rayleigh takes them, they lean their head forward. Rayleigh mimics the gesture until the two of them are touching foreheads.

Feeling a little silly, Rayleigh looks up to see that the elder has closed their eyes. Rayleigh follows suit. A sense of relief and relaxation comes over her, and she breathes into the feeling. As the touch of their foreheads ends, Rayleigh opens her eyes again to see the elder pull away. Rayleigh straightens up and steps away, dropping the elder's hands.

"Thank you, and welcome," the elder says. They turn to DitDit42. "Please take care of her, Zetzutata. She is in your care."

DitDit42 gestures acknowledgement.

"Shall we go?" DitDit42 asks Rayleigh.

"Yes, let's," Rayleigh responds, bowing to the elder as they walk away.

There is a lingering feeling that Rayleigh isn't able to shake concerning the encounter with the elder. A sense of peace sits with her.

As they walk, Rayleigh turns to DitDit42. "So, what now?" she asks.

DitDit42 chuckles. Rayleigh wonders if she has ever seen them chuckle before. "Well, we head to where I saw them last, to see if there are any clues," they respond. They look sideways at Rayleigh. "Sorry for laughing. It is strange hearing you speak our language. You still have a strong accent, but that will improve."

"Your language?" Rayleigh says, unsure what DitDit42 is talking about.

DitDit42 chuckle again. "The elder has transferred the knowledge of our language and culture to you. You haven't realised it, but you are speaking Hu Thu. Oh, and please call me Zet."

Confused, Rayleigh stops walking. *Their language and culture.* She tries to grapple with the idea that the elder has been able to transfer their complete language to her.

The thought sinks in. *That's why I understand their little gestures now.* She thinks about noticing DitDit42's chuckle earlier. Rayleigh realises that she can feel a tightness in her mouth and throat as she talks, having to use muscle to speak that she has never used before. *That would explain the strange sensation I'm feeling when I talk.*

She can feel more and more knowledge becoming available to her about the Hu Thus and their life, as she starts to know the words for things as she looks around the village.

"Is that why the elder referred to you as Zetzutata?" Rayleigh says finally, returning to their conversation.

"Yes. That is my name in native Hu Thu – but please, call me Zet for short. Names starting with DitDit are for people outside our culture."

"Oh. Okay. Well, it's a pleasure to meet you, Zet," Rayleigh says.

Zet chuckles again. "It is a pleasure to meet you as well. Welcome to the family."

They reach the edge of the village. Rayleigh takes out the jump device from her coat, seeing the countdown timer ticking down for their first destination.

She looks over at Zet, and they both nod at each other, then take each other's hand as they move forward into the jump zone. There is a crack and a flash of light.

Chapter Twenty-one

Coming into open grassland with rolling hills, Rayleigh looks at the new world around them.

It is quiet and peaceful. There is very little movement, but Rayleigh can hear the trickle of a small river in the distance. It reminds her of hiking trips.

"DitDit," comes a loud voice from nearby, snapping Rayleigh from her memories. She looks around to see where the voice is coming from, and sees a small head pop up from behind a riverbank. She wonders who this child is.

"DitDit42," comes a chorus of other voices, followed by several more heads popping up from behind the same bank.

Before Rayleigh knows what's happening, six kids have jumped the bank and are running towards them, all calling out to DitDit42.

"Children," Zet calls out, reaching out to embrace the army of children coming towards them. Zet drops down to the children's level, allowing them to huddle around. They make *ooh*s and *aah*s of excitement and wonderment as Zet shows them an orb of light that throws out images of different planets and places. The kids jostle each other for better positions.

"Tell me, children. Do you know where my friends are?" Zet asks them.

They all go silent, shuffling and looking at the ground. Some of them are courageous enough to look at others in the group.

One of the children finally finds the courage to speak. "No. I'm sorry."

"But maybe one of the adults knows," another adds.

Zet takes a moment, over playing that they are thinking, which plays to the children's amusement Rayleigh is captivated, seeing this side of Zet that she has never seen.

"Well, then. Guess we'd better go ask them," Zet says excitedly, stirring up the children again. When Zet directs them towards the village they all run off, two of them taking Zet's hands and dragging them, another two grabbing Rayleigh's hands and pulling her in the same direction.

Zet begins running after the children, moving quickly due to their long legs. Then Zet pulls away from the children, making a game of it, which makes the children laugh and squeal in excitement. The children race to catch Zet, but Zet evades the kids easily.

Rayleigh catches herself laughing as she watches Zet play with the children. She looks down at the two children pulling her along, sensing their desire to go and play too.

"Go on, kids," she says. "Join the others. I'll catch up."

They look up at her and then at each other, before dropping her hands to run off after the others, with no more encouragement needed. They squeal with excitement and chase after their friends, leaving Rayleigh in the field by herself.

Rayleigh is reminded of her friends' children back home. *Kids just want to play*, she thinks as she watches them run off. The familiarity of children playing is comforting. Realising that she's falling behind, Rayleigh trots off after them all.

She manages to catch up with them all at the entrance to the village. Slowing down, she sees the children scatter to their respective homes, dragging parents out and into the town square.

The commotion brings a number of curious adults into the streets, all of them welcoming Zet back to the village, which is rustic and almost medieval. There is little to no technology that she can see, and the houses are made of stone and straw.

Zet greets each of the adults with their customary bow and greeting. Rayleigh follows along behind. At the centre of town, a tall gentleman comes out of the biggest building in the village. It is modest, but there is a hive of activity coming from it as people go about their business.

The man comes down the steps with arms outstretched, and embraces Zet in a massive hug, lifting them off the ground, which surprise Rayleigh as Zet towers above him. When he places Zet back on the ground, the man is smiling from ear to ear.

"DitDit42, welcome back," he says, looking at Zet and then over at Rayleigh. "What brings you back?"

"We are looking for our companions. Are they here?" Zet responds.

"No. They left shortly after you."

Zet falls silent, considering this.

"Do you know where they went?" Rayleigh asks before Zet can speak again.

The man ponders for a moment. "I'm not sure, but the blacksmith might know." He points to a building on the far side of the village.

Zet bows. "Thank you."

"Will you be staying long?" the man asks, stopping Zet from turning away.

"Unfortunately not. We need to find our friends," Zet replies. Rayleigh notes a little sadness in their voice. She realises that she is noticing the emotion within Zet's words more and more since her experience with the elder.

"Well, you are more than welcome to stay as long as you wish," the man says, slapping Zet's arm heartily.

"Thank you. I will be back again," Zet responds, returning the gesture.

As Rayleigh watches this exchange she notes their jovialness, which is uncommon for Zet, who has been more black and white in the past.

"Any friend of DitDit42 is also welcome," the man says, looking over at Rayleigh and breaking her train of thought.

"Thank you," she responds awkwardly, caught off guard at being brought into the conversation.

"Come, Rayleigh, let's go and see if the blacksmith can help," Zet says to her.

Rayleigh nods, and they both bow to the man.

"Thank you for your help," Rayleigh says.

"Happy to help," the man responds, bowing too before turning and going back in to the building they had exited from.

"Let's go," Zet says, and Rayleigh nods. The two of them head off in the direction of the blacksmith's house.

"Everyone in the village seem to love you," Rayleigh says to Zet.

"These are the children we saved," Zet responds, looking around at the children playing in town. "Allgery has been saving children for a while, apparently. He brings them here, where they will be safe."

Rayleigh is amazed. There is still a lot that she does not know about the group.

When they reach the blacksmith's house, Zet knocks on the front door and they wait. There is no response, so they knock again, and once again, nothing.

"Maybe they aren't home," Rayleigh says.

"Ah, man!" comes a loud voice from behind the building.

"What was that?" Rayleigh asks Zet.

"Let's go and see," Zet replies.

They leave the front porch of the house and go around to the back, where Rayleigh sees several kids standing around two people who appear to be teaching something to them.

One kid is trying to work with a piece of metal with a hammer and anvil, appearing to take out their frustration on it. A man is bending next to the child, giving them instructions. A lady is addressing the rest of the group, giving them a demonstration on striking metal with a hammer. The children watch on in amazement, in awe of the sparks and tools.

When the adults see Zet and Rayleigh approaching, they stop what they are doing.

"Let's take a break children," the lady says.

With no further encouragement needed, the children scatter to play.

"Hey DitDit42, welcome back," the man says, approaching them.

"Hi George. Hi Tilly," Zet responds, bowing slightly.

"Wow. You know everyone," Rayleigh jokes.

Zet smiles and shrugs slightly.

"How have you been going?" Zet asks them.

"Things are good. We have been busy with all the children and keeping the town running," Tilly says, looking around at the outdoor blacksmithing area.

"How are you?" George asks.

"I'm good. We had some trouble on our planet, but we are rebuilding," Zet responds, pausing slightly, presumably thinking of the destruction of the village.

"I'm sorry to hear that. I hope you work it out," Tilly responds in a hushed tone.

"Thank you," Zet says, before moving on quickly. "We were hoping you might be able to help us find Tailia, Allgery and Bellery. Do you know where they went after they left?"

Tilly and George pause, looking at each other.

"What's the name of that place?" George asks Tilly.

"That's a good question," Tilly responds.

"Was it Yopo Bar or something?" George says uncertainly.

"Something like that… Maybe Yoto Bar?" Tilly says.

"Do you mean Yuptu Bar?" Zet asks with a little more confidence.

"Yes, that's it!" George and Tilly say in unison.

"That is the smugglers bar we visited," Zet says to Rayleigh.

"Not sure I know that one," Rayleigh says, trying to remember if she had ever been there. "Thank you," she says to George and Tilly, excited at the thought that they now have a destination.

"Happy to help," George replies.

"Will you be staying long?" Tilly asks.

"Unfortunately, not this time," Zet replies. "We have somewhere we need to be."

"Maybe next time, then," Tilly says.

Zet responds with a bow. "Of course."

"Take care of yourself," George says. He and Tilly stepping forward in turn to give Zet and Rayleigh a hug.

"And you," Zet responds. "Come, let's go," they say to Rayleigh.

Rayleigh nods eagerly, and follows Zet back to the village. "Do you know where we're going?" she asks.

"Yes, it's where we met Bellery and Allgery before we set off on the mission to save the children."

Excitement grows within Rayleigh at the thought of seeing everyone again. As they enter the town centre, the children huddle around them again, begging Zet to come and play with them.

"Sorry, children. I need to leave," Zet says, bending down next to them. "But next time, for sure."

The kids all sigh in disappointment.

"I will show you something special next time," Zet adds in a hushed tone, looking around at the children in a mysterious way.

The children all straighten up in excitement.

"For now, I need to help my friend – but I will be back." Zet looks around at the children, then at Rayleigh.

Rayleigh smiles and waves sheepishly, feeling a little guilty for dragging Zet away from the children and their games.

"Okay," the children respond in unison.

Zet pats several of them on the head, then stands up. "Should we go?" they ask Rayleigh.

Rayleigh looks around at the children, then at Zet. "We will be back soon," she says looking to the children, before turning to Zet and nodding to agree that it's time to leave.

"Take care, children," Zet says.

With that, the two of them head for the next jump point.

Chapter Twenty-two

As they move through the spaceport. Like a child in a theme park, her head swivels as she tries to look at everything. She could never have imagined being in such a place, surrounded by so many different lifeforms.

There is a hustle and bustle to the spaceport, as everyone goes about their business. Zet wears their massive cloak pulled up over their head, and it droops down to drag along the ground. People part in front of Zet to let them through.

Rayleigh shuffles along after Zet, trying not to step on the cloak as it drags behind. Zet stops every now and then to scan the street, and they look back at Rayleigh every now and then, making her feel like she is falling behind.

Rayleigh takes in all the sights, sounds and smells as they go. Hearing her stomach growl, the smell of food enticing her stomach as they walk past. Looking at all the different foods, she wonders what they taste like.

Zet stops suddenly in front of an alley, they turn and head down it. Rayleigh stumbles before following her companion.

The crowd thins as they move further down the alley. Soon they are alone.

Some scraping noises catch Rayleigh off guard, and she jumps. Zet barely acknowledges the sound and keeps moving. After several hundred metres, Zet stops outside a small doorway and gestures towards it.

Unsure what she is walking into, Rayleigh looks up at Zet. She pushes the thoughts aside and pushes open the door and steps inside.

She finds herself standing in a small shop. The staff behind the counter are working away on their food, and Rayleigh's stomach grumbles with hunger.

"I would like the Lukluk, please," Zet says to the waiter, who looks up at them briefly.

"I'm sorry. We are out." They turn back to cleaning glasses.

"Sure thing. In that case, I would like the Lukluk," Zet says again.

The waiter pauses, looking Rayleigh and Zet up and down before returning to their cooking.

"That will be 6.34."

"I'm sorry, I only have 8.23," Zet responds.

Rayleigh is confused by what is going on – why Zet is ordering something that isn't available, and the response of 8.23 if it only costs 6.34.

As if to answer her questions, she hears a click from behind them, and she turns to see a fridge sliding to the right, exposing a doorway. Within it is someone that appears to be welcoming guests, waiting for them.

"This way please," they say, gesturing for them to follow.

"Thank you," Zet says to the waiter, before turning to head through the doorway that has just appeared.

Rayleigh is at a loss about what just happened, but she follows Zet further into the building.

At the bottom of the stairs, Rayleigh sees a room stretching out in front of her. There are different groups spread around, each huddled in their own private little booth.

Zet pauses, looking around the room.

"Would you like me to take your coat?" the server asks with their hand outstretched.

"I am fine, thank you," Zet responds.

The server bows slightly and back away.

"This way," Zet whispers to Rayleigh, before heading into the bar. Rayleigh follows them, continuing to study the room as they move through it.

"Bellery," Zet says suddenly as they come to a stop outside a booth.

"Hey, look who it is!" comes a voice from behind the booth. "Oh, hey. What are you doing here?" Bellery says, sticking his head out to see Rayleigh.

"Bellery!" Rayleigh lets out a squeal of excitement at the sight of a familiar face. She launches herself forwards to give him a big hug. When he squirms and shifts, she lets him go so that he can move away again. "Where are the others?" Rayleigh asks.

"Oh. They're on the ship," Bellery replies. The other 4 people at the table continue to look up at Bellery earnestly.

"Are you coming?" one of them calls out to him.

Rayleigh looks at the group, taking in the strange game where all of them have a cup with dices in front of them.

"What hangar?" Zet asks, grabbing Bellery's attention.

"Hangar 15," Bellery responds quickly, trying to switch his focus between the game and the conversation, only to fail at both. "Do you want to join?"

Zet holds up a hand. "No, I'm fine, thank you."

"I'm fine as well," Rayleigh replies too, when Bellery looks in her direction.

"We will head back to the ship," Zet says, looking at Rayleigh, who nods in agreement.

"Sure thing," Bellery says, finally returning his attention to the table.

"Should we go?" Zet asks Rayleigh.

Rayleigh hesitates. As she watches them shake the cup with the dice, before slamming them down on the table with the dice inside the cup. Looking around at the room, a part of her would like to stay, but she also can't wait to see Tailia. She turns and begins making her way to the doorway with Zet.

Stepping out into the street, Zet looks up, then in each direction along the alley. "This way."

They join the hustle and bustle of the spaceport again. The noise of people, traffic and the city crashes into them, making Rayleigh hesitate, but Zet pushes on. Rayleigh continues into the sea of people.

Rayleigh hears one of the local merchants calling out, trying to get her attention. She looks over in their direction, seeing them stirring the food in front of them. Rayleigh finds herself wondering if it is edible, and what sort of meat it could possibly be. Her stomach does a somersault. At first she thinks it's due to the food, but then she pauses; something is off.

She looks around, trying to figure out what's wrong. She can see Zet still moving ahead through the crowd. She is about to call out, but then a hand slips over her mouth, and another around her neck. The fear shoots through her, as her heart frantically races and the panic sets in.

Pulling her close, the attacker whispers into her ear. "Keep your hands where I can see them."

Rayleigh can see Zet continue to move through the crowd. Her heart jumps. How can she contact them?

To her surprise, Zet stops and turns to face them both. Rayleigh her heart begins to slow at the relief that she is no longer alone.

Zet strolls back casually, stopping a few metres away as the figure brings up a gun.

"Please don't do this," Zet says calmly, holding up their hands.

"The I.D.T. will pay good money for Hu Thus," a voice says.

"I'm sorry," Zet says.

On cue, something comes crashing into both Rayleigh and the attacker, throwing them off balance. Rayleigh tries to figure out how Zet has done this. Throwing them into the ground, she rolls over to face her attacker. She can see Bellery wrestling with the unknown assailant. The two of them scramble frantically and Rayleigh simply looks on, unsure if she should do anything.

Before she can decide, Bellery's fist connects with the assailant's face and they go limp.

"Are you okay?" Bellery asks them both.

"I think so," Rayleigh says. She looks down at Bellery, who has begun searching the unconscious body.

"Bounty hunters. They never change," Bellery says as he finishes up his search of the body. "I noticed him following you out of the bar," he says, standing and flicking through the items from their clothing.

"Come on, we should go," Zet says. "They will likely have backup coming."

Bellery nods in agreement, placing an item he had taken from the bounty hunter into his pocket and throwing another onto the bounty hunter's body.

"This way," Bellery says, moving quickly down one of the streets. Zet and Rayleigh follow his lead, moving through the back streets of the spaceport, hugging the shadows.

At a crossroads, Bellery throws up his hand and the group stops. He scans the road as if looking for something. Zet and Rayleigh don't move, not wanting to break the silence and his concentration.

"We've got company," Bellery whispers, looking towards the other side of the road, where Rayleigh can see shadows moving. Bellery keeps his hand raised, and Rayleigh notices she is holding her breath due to the tension. *Who are they? What is going on?*

"This way," Bellery says.

He heads back down the alleyway, and Rayleigh and Zet follow him. Bellery stops outside a small store before ducking inside; again, Zet and Rayleigh follow.

No one inside the store stops what they are doing, or even looks over at them. Rayleigh feels almost invisible. Bellery walks casually through the store. At its rear, he nods to a staff member in the corner before pushing back a cabinet and disappearing into the doorway that appears behind.

Zet and Rayleigh look at each other, and Zet gestures for Rayleigh to steps through the doorway behind Bellery. She doesn't need any further encouragement.

As Rayleigh heads down the stairs, she can hear Zet's footsteps behind her. They dip into darkness for a moment as the doorway behind them closes. Sensing that she shouldn't stop, Rayleigh continues to move forward, and sees a flashlight turn on ahead of her. She hears another click behind her and then a warm blue light illuminates the tunnel. Rayleigh recognises the light as one of Zet's orbs. She continues on with more confidence.

"What now?" Rayleigh asks Bellery.

"I've informed the others that we have company. So they are preparing to leave. We can follow this tunnel to come out in the hangar," Bellery explains.

Both Zet and Rayleigh nod. Bellery looks at both of them in turn, as if looking for confirmation. Not getting any response, he turns and moves down the old passageway at a slow jog, scanning the junctions he passes. Rayleigh finds herself wondering where each of them leads. She notices an animal scurry away as they pass one passageway, making her jump a little. She pushes the feeling down, noticing that Zet and Bellery both continue moving without flinching.

Bellery pauses at a stairway that leads up. Rayleigh assumes it must be the one leading to the hangar. Rayleigh can hear clicking sounds, and she wonders what is making it, as it seems out of place.

"Right, we can go," Bellery whispers. When he gets a nod from each of them, he begins to climb the stairs. He pauses at the top, leaning against the door for a moment, his ear pressed against it before he pushes it open and steps through.

Rayleigh continues moving towards the door, only to see it begin to close. She throws out her hand, pushing on it, but something on the other side is pushing back.

"Hey!" she calls out.

The pressure stops, and she continues to push the door open, only to be confronted with Allgery standing beyond the doorway.

"Oh, where did you come from?" he asks.

Rayleigh sees Bellery making his way toward the ship, picking up his pace as he goes.

"Maybe we should catch up later?" Rayleigh quips, moving past Allgery so that Zet can pass through the doorway.

"Right you are," Allgery says from behind her as she jogs towards the ship.

"You have a surprise," he calls out over the hum of the engines as they start up. Rayleigh is about to respond, but then realises he isn't talking to her but to someone over the comms.

She continues to jog towards the ship, not wanting to hang around any longer than necessary.

As the three of them reach the doorway, the ship's engines reach full power, overwhelming all other sounds. As the last of them comes through the doorway, Allgery closes it behind them, and they all make their way to the bridge.

As Rayleigh steps through the doorway to the bridge she can see a someone sitting at one of the desks. Her heart jumps a little. *Is that Tailia?*

"Are we good to go?" says a voice behind her.

Rayleigh turns their head toward the voice.

"Oh… Hello… Where did you come from?" Tailia asks in a surprised tone. "Actually, let's talk later. Bellery, get us out of here," she calls out.

The three of them continue moving onto the bridge, findings seats and strapping themselves in as the ship begins to lift off and move through the hangar at a crawl. It covers the distance between the landing pad and the hangar exit, gaining speed. It shoots out from the exit like a bullet from a gun, picking up speed as it heads deeper into space.

When the ship has levelled out, Tailia turns to look at Rayleigh, unclipping herself from her seat and moving towards her. Rayleigh unclips herself too, but isn't able to get anything out before Tailia gives her a hug.

"It's good to see you again," Tailia whispers into Rayleigh's ear, barely loud enough for her to hear.

"It's good to see you as well."

They both hug each other, Rayleigh feeling like it's been a lifetime since they saw each other. She doesn't want to let go.

"I knew this is where I needed to be," she whispers, holding Tailia's gaze as they break away from one another.

Tailia moves over to Zet and greets them in the customary Hu Thu manner.

"What, no love for us?" Allgery jokes as Tailia breaks away from Zet.

"There's always love for you," she jokes, giving him a gentle punch on the shoulder.

They all begin to swap stories of the adventures they have been on, and what they have been up to. Tailia and Rayleigh break away from the group to talk.

"How did you get here?" Tailia asks.

"The I.D.T. came for me, and I escaped. From there, I went out looking for you," Rayleigh says, placing a hand on Tailia's arm.

Tailia is about to respond, but a sound from the command deck interrupts her. She looks over at Bellery, who has also frozen. He begins moving with confidence over the control panel in front of him.

"They found us," Bellery says, looking down at the desk, noticing the incoming ships.

"Where should we go?" Allgery asks, looking around at the group.

"I know of a knowledge well that we could recover, if we are up for it?" Zet says when no one else speaks up.

The members of the group look at each other, no one seeming to want to make the decision.

"Let's do it." Rayleigh chimes in, taking the lead.

When there are nods of consensus, Zet moves to the desk to assist Bellery with the flight coordinates to this new location. Everyone moves to their respective seats and the ship begins to pick up speed. Rayleigh hears the pings of rounds hitting the ship's shields, and excitement rises within her. She's missed it.

"Here we go," Bellery calls out as the flash of light engulfs them, and they jump.

Chapter Twenty-three

After the ship emerges from the jump point, Zet leads them to the location of the planet with the knowledge well. The planet is a great desert, with no life or plants, and they struggle to find anywhere solid enough for them to land. The rocky alcove they find is several hours walk through the sand from where they need to be. As they move through the desert, the wind blows up the sand into their faces. Pulling their clothing tighter around their faces, they try to fight back the sea of sand that is assaulting them.

"Do you know where we're going?" Allgery calls out over the wind to Zet, who is walking ahead of the group.

Zet turns, looking up from the orb in their hands, then nods in response and points in the direction they are heading.

They continue to trudge through the sand, slipping and sliding as they make their way to their destination.

"This is it," Zet calls out, cutting through the wind and the sand that has been constant for the last several hours.

The group huddle around them, looking down at the orb and then out over the sea of sand.

"But there's nothing here," Rayleigh says, looking from the surroundings and back to Zet, who has placed the orb back into their robes.

Zet responds with a smile as they pull their staff from their robes and move from the middle of the group.

"Wait here," Zet says, before heading further into the sandstorm.

Kneeling down, Zet begins to pray, holding the staff in front of them. Standing, they raise the staff to the sky, then ever so gently touch the end of the staff to the ground at their feet.

They all watch on, expecting something to happen when the staff touches the surface, but nothing does.

"Did something go wrong?" Bellery asks.

Zet holds their pose, unflinching.

Rayleigh notices that the wind has calmed. Now she hears a faint hum. Looking around for the source of the sound, she feels the sand shifting underneath her feet.

Zet is still holding their pose. Now, however, the sand several hundred metres beyond Zet appears to be moving. Like water falling down a drain, it begins to disappear into an unseen hole. The size of the hole begins to expand larger and larger, the falling sand creating a hypnotic rumbling sound.

As the group approaches Zet, Rayleigh hears the chant that Zet has been muttering, just above a whisper.

The group stops, not wanting to disturb Zet, and continue to watch as the sand falls away to reveal a deep hole. Rayleigh is now able to see into it, and she's astonished to find a flourishing forest underneath the sand. Somehow, it has survived underneath the sand, despite there being no light. At the centre of the hole there is a giant glowing orb, on the top of a tree, that appears to effortlessly hold the orbs weight. On closer inspection Rayleigh sees that the orb is hovering *above* the tree, casting a blue-green tinge over the edges of the hole, feeding the life within its reach.

As the sand begins to settle, Zet finishes their prayer, stands and turns to face the group.

"We are here," Zet says politely, bowing.

They all stare, stunned at the sight.

"This way," Zet says, grabbing their attention, and begins moving to one side of the circle formed around the forest. Reaching the edge, Zet walks to a pathway, as if they knew it was there all along. They disappear into the hole.

The others look at each other before taking off after Zet, not wanting to fall behind. As they descend into the hole, they look out over the forest below.

Over the following hours, they make their way through the forest towards the orb at the centre. As they approach the orb, Rayleigh is in awe as it continues to grow. Standing at the base of the tree, they all need to crane their necks to look up at the orb, far above them.

"I will need a few hours to transfer the knowledge," Zet says.

They all nod, and Zet turns, walking to the base of the tree disappearing along a hidden path. The others fan out to find places to rest while they wait, telling their tales of the last few months.

***

Rayleigh lies on the grass, watching the clouds pass overhead. It has been hours since Zet left, and she wonders how much longer it will be. She's been listening to Tailia and Allgery, and she can also hear Bellery playing his flute, which produces a soothing tone. Rayleigh wonders if she may have dozed off while they have been waiting.

She feels something crawling over her body – perhaps a bug looking for a home. Looking down, she can't see anything, so she lies down again. The sensation continues, becoming slightly more intense. She throws her hand down, trying to swat away whatever it is, but there is nothing there.

Pushing the feeling aside, she resumes looking at the sky.

"Ah… is something happening?" she calls out.

Everyone looks over at her. Rayleigh looks at the sky again, trying to work out what is going on.

"I don't think so," Allgery responds.

Now they are all looking up at the sky.

"Wait. Look over there," Tailia says, pointing to the edge of the circle.

The group all follow the direction of her pointing finger. With each passing moment, something moves before Rayleigh's eyes.

They all watch in wonder as the trees and plants around the edge of the circle begin to grow – slowly at first, then faster – towards the centre of the circle. Other trees grow from the ground up to the new 'ceiling' forming above them to support the new covering.

"What's happening?" Bellery asks.

They all look at each other, no one knowing what to say. Rayleigh can feel their unease, and she notices that Tailia and Allgery have both placed their hands on their weapons. Rayleigh's stomach turns at the thought of what this might mean. Looking deeper into herself, Rayleigh begins to feel something coming.

The group begin to draw closer to each other, turning to face outwards from the centre, their training kicking in naturally.

Rayleigh hears Bellery calling out over the comms to Zet. The uncertainty of the situation raises her anticipation.

Rayleigh watches as the last of the sky disappears behind the new ceiling that has grown up from the trees, throwing a dark shadow over the forest and adding to the tension of the group. The orb at the top of the tree is throwing a green tinge over the forest, giving an eerie feeling to the shadows that the light creates.

"What now?" Rayleigh says, a sea of unease swirling away inside her.

No one responds and each of them looking around at the others, as if searching for answers. A crack of thunder draws all their attention to the ceiling. A ray of light shoots through the ceiling, and quickly disappears again as the trees grow to cover the hole. Another crack is strong enough to shake the ground, the ray of light shooting through the ceiling before disappearing again. It's followed shortly by three more; none of them are able to break the ceiling, like the first two. They begin to increase in frequency, no longer able to break through the ceiling. The ground rumbles in response to the bombardment.

"What was that?" Bellery asks.

"If I had to guess, I would say it is the I.D.T coming here for the orb," Tailia says.

"How did they find us?" Rayleigh asks in confusion.

"The I.D.T. have a strong presence in this sector," Tailia replies. "It wouldn't surprise me if they picked up the massive hole opening up on this planet when we found the orb. A desert planet with a giant forest is surely something that would stand out, even from space."

"Trust us to find the I.D.T. on a deserted planet," Allgery remarks with a smirk.

"DitDit42 still needs more time," Bellery says, looking up at the orb overhead.

"Agreed. We should prepare for company." Allgery checks his weapon. "Bellery, we need eyes."

Bellery nods before turning to run in the direction of the big tree.

"Where do you need me?" Rayleigh asks Allgery.

Allgery turns to survey their surroundings. "We don't know where they're coming from, so we'll need to cover all sides. If we each take a side, we can then move about as we start to engage."

The group are all looking at Allgery, nodding agreement. They begin to prepare themselves for whatever is coming, pulling out weapons and devices from their bags.

Rayleigh can feel the anticipation and nerves building in her body as she thinks about what is to come. She looks around at the group uneasily as they all look over their weapons and combat gear, as though it is a day like any other day. The certainty of the group gives her some confidence, and she finds her training coming back to her. She pulls out her armour and begins to strap it on, focusing on her breathing and hearing Zet's words in her mind: *Don't overthink it. Trust yourself and feel the world around you.*

With these words running through her mind, Rayleigh begins to feel more at ease. She puts her foot up on a log to strap on her leg armour. Looking at the weapons and items they have placed on the log, she sees a number of small metallic balls in the middle of the pile.

"I have two," Tailia says, pulling out two more of the metal balls from her bag, and holding them in her hand.

"You never cease to amaze me," Allgery says.

"I guess it will be one of those days," Tailia responds. There's a lightness to their conversation, despite what they are preparing for. Tailia picks up the five metal balls and places them in her bag. "I'll be back soon," she says.

Allgery nods and Tailia jogs towards the tree, leaving Allgery, Rutherian and Rayleigh alone. Rutherian is busy working away on their armour and weapons, poring over every detail of the massive gun they are carrying. Rayleigh can see the extendable sword poking through underneath their cloak. Rutherian pauses and looks over at Rayleigh, then pulls the cloak over themselves further, to hide what is beneath.

Allgery asks Rayleigh, "Are you feeling ready?"

When she turns to face him, she sees concern in his face. "I think so," she replies. "Just not sure what to do."

"That's understandable. This is only your second engagement," Allgery says.

"Third, actually."

"Oh, well, you're a pro, then," Allgery jokes. Putting a hand on her shoulder, he adopts a more serious tone. "Sorry. I guess this isn't really a joking matter. It's natural to be scared and nervous. Even after all this time, it still scares me, which is why I make inappropriate jokes." He sits beside her. "We're all scared. All we can do is try. We stand a better chance if we do this together... and never forget, we are all here for each other," he adds in a hushed tone.

He looks out over at the forest, then back at Rayleigh, and gives her another little nudge on the shoulder. "Trust in yourself, your training, and the people around you," he says with more certainty, standing and looking down at Rayleigh.

"I didn't realise you felt that way," Rayleigh says. She has a new impression of Allgery now. *He's just doing his best*. The thought gives her some comfort, making her realise they're more similar than she knew.

"Don't tell the others," Allgery jokes again, breaking the tension.

"There you go, joking again," Rayleigh responds with a cheeky smile.

Allgery picks up his weapon and adopts an exaggerated combat pose.

"Thank you, Allgery," Rayleigh says, ignoring his attempts to break the tension.

"Happy to help," Allgery says. He drops the pose. "Come on. Let's get ready," he says, returning to his preparations.

They both turn as they hear Tailia approaching from the direction of the tree.

"How are things here?" she asks when she reaches them.

"A little nervous, but we're ready to do what we can," Rayleigh replies quickly, with a new confidence.

"Great to hear," Tailia says with a smile.

"More shelter would be nice, but I guess we need to work with what we have," Allgery says, looking around.

"Agreed," Tailia says. "We each need to take a point and hold our positions."

They both nod.

Tailia turns to look over Rayleigh's body armour, checking the straps and pulling on pieces of the armour. She nods to Rayleigh, a look of satisfaction on her face.

"Let me know if you need anything," Tailia whispers to Rayleigh.

"Thank you," Rayleigh says. She feels a moment pass between them, the closeness between them, the memories running through her mind. With a small nod to each other, they both turn back to the group.

The group all split as they head to take their place around the tree. As Rayleigh separates from the group, she feels anxiety creep up in her yet again. As she moves to her position, the rhythm of running and her regular breathing comforts her.

"You've got this," she says to herself as she approaches a fallen tree, then ducks behind it.

"So Allgery, where are we going after?" Tailia asks over the comms. The sudden sound makes Rayleigh jump a little, but despite her momentary shock, she finds comfort in the voice.

"I was thinking about that," Allgery replies, then pauses. "I heard about this bar which is supposed to make these incredible drinks."

Tailia laughs. "Why am I not surprised? It's a date."

"What about you?" Allgery asks.

"I've heard of this waterfall in a valley that's said to be gorgeous," Tailia replies.

Allgery laughs in turn. "Of course. Sounds great."

"Oh, I want to go see this volcano," Bellery bursts in over the comms.

Tailia and Allgery both laugh at his eagerness. "Of course," they both respond in unison.

"What about you, Rayleigh?" Tailia asks over the comms. "What would you like to do after this?"

"Umm…" Rayleigh begins, unsure what to say. "I guess… dinner with you all."

"Of course," Tailia responds after a slight pause.

"Stay safe, and thank you," Allgery says.

"Stay safe, and thank you," Tailia responds.

"Stay safe, and thank you," Bellery chips in.

Rayleigh relishes the bond between them.

"We have company," Bellery says after a few minutes.

Rayleigh's stomach turns. *Am I ready for this?* She focuses on her breathing, trying to calm her nerves. She finds herself thinking about what Zet said to her during training: *Trust your instincts, don't overthink it.* The mantra settles her. She concentrates on the push of the fallen tree behind her back, and the softness of the ground. She takes in the world around her, everything that the universe has to offer her, and all of its possibilities.

You've got this.

She senses movement behind her. Turning, she rises and places two shots into the I.D.T. officer emerging from the trees.

As the officer falls, Rayleigh hears shots ring out. They've caught the I.D.T. off guard, and they begin to fallback for cover, firing as they move. Rayleigh turns back to look up at the tree. She can see the orb above, and the flashes from Bellery's gun.

There! her body calls out to her, and she turns. She fires off several more shots, dropping two I.D.T. officers and sending several more back into the trees for cover.

The officers return fire now that Rayleigh has made her presence known. Pushing herself up against the back of the log, she can feel it beginning to rock as shots hit its other side.

"Trust yourself and the people around you," Rayleigh repeats to herself, stifling her uncertainty and anxiety. Gripping the gun a little tighter, she takes a deep breath and feels the tension leave her body as she exhales.

***

For an hour or so, they have been holding back the I.D.T. officers. There have been running skirmishes with the officers each side continually on the move, trying to avoid being pinned down.

However, as time goes on, Rayleigh and the others have been drawn closer and closer to the base of the tree, losing ground as the officers continue to push with numbers.

"Rayleigh, how are you holding up?" Tailia asks over the comms, breaking Rayleigh's focus.

"I'm… holding… in there," Rayleigh stutters as a steady stream of bullets surround her position. She flinches as the tree next to her crumples. She's pinned down and unsure what to do next.

"Bellery," Tailia says over the comms.

"On it," Bellery says quickly, before disappearing.

Rayleigh hunkers down further as the firing continues, the shots coming more and more frequently as the I.D.T. officers encroach on her position. As they push closer to her hiding place, Rayleigh waits for a space between the firing, so that she can return fire.

After a few quick bursts of bullets, everything falls silent. Rayleigh takes the opportunity and jumps up from her position, pulling her guns around to face the I.D.T. officers, only to see that they're already on the ground.

"Thank you," Rayleigh says over the comms, realising Bellery must have helped out.

"No problem," Bellery responds casually. "You should move. There are more incoming," he adds, before going silent again.

"Come to me," Tailia says quickly over the comms, the sound of gunfire behind her voice.

"Will do," Rayleigh responds, pulling herself up from the tree and beginning to make her way in Tailia's direction. Ducking through the trees, she tries to remember her training. She stops occasionally to take out I.D.T. officers, thankfully catching them off guard. As she pauses behind a tree, she notices the ground beginning to move underfoot. *What is that?*

"Bellery?" Rayleigh calls over the comms.

After a pause, Bellery says, "Crap."

The central tree lights up with a massive explosion, close to where Bellery had been.

"Shit," Tailia says.

"Regroup at the tree," Allgery says quickly over the comms.

The tree erupts in another explosion, shaking the ground underneath their feet.

Not needing any further encouragement, Rayleigh turns and begins making her way towards the tree, picking up speed as she goes. There is continual rumbling and tremors underfoot as she moves as quickly as she can.

Coming out of the forest and into the clearing around the tree, Rayleigh sees Tailia and Allgery running to cover the distance from the tree line to the base of the tree as quickly as they can.

Rayleigh picks up her speed, not wanting to fall behind. She slows as she reaches the tree and crouches next to Tailia and Allgery.

"What's happening?" she asks breathlessly.

"They have armoured guns," Tailia responds.

"Glad you could join us," Allgery says as Bellery suddenly appears next to them, having worked his way down the tree to get out of way of the cannons now firing against the tree.

Explosions rattle away above them, creating flashes of light that drown out the blue light of the orb.

"What now?" Bellery asks Tailia and Allgery.

"We need a little luck," Allgery responds as another explosion rocks the tree. There is a loud crack as something shatters, and they all look up to watch the tree sway under the onslaught.

"That's not good," Tailia says.

As if on cue, the orb's light dies out, throwing them all into darkness. No light from the sun able to break through the ceiling created by the trees.

"Well that's not good either," Allgery says with a groan.

The explosions against the tree stop, throwing the everything into silence. Rayleigh can hear the tree sway and crack, the sounds becoming louder each time. Then they fall silent again. The members of the group look at each other.

Light flashes in the night sky. Swivelling in the direction of the light, Rayleigh sees a flare falling slowly from the sky, others popping up to join the first one. They cast an eerie red glow, a stark contrast to the soft blue of the orb.

"So what now?" Bellery asks.

"I guess we wait for DitDit42," Allgery responds.

They all nod in agreement. Several bullets hit the tree next to them, and they turn to see several squads of I.D.T. officers coming across the open grass land towards them. They all jump up from their position to return fire, taking out the officers that have been silly enough to expose themselves.

"Fan out," Allgery calls out, jumping up and moving away. He fires as he moves, in an attempt to keep the officers in their hiding places.

The others follow suit and move to the closest bits of cover that they can find, firing on the I.D.T. officers as they come out of the tree line. The ground begins to rumble again, and armoured guns push through the tree line and out into the open space. The monstrous machines knock through the trees, not caring for anything. They stop and position themselves to face the group.

Rayleigh's stomach turns at the sight of them. *How can we fight them?* Momentarily, she forgets all about the officers moving in front of her.

The first armoured gun erupts in a flash of light. Rayleigh is confused as to what would make it explode into a fireball. The rest of the group are continuing to fire on the officers running through the clearing towards them. The I.D.T officers that had been standing next to the tank now run in all directions, trying to get away from the fireball that is expanding outwards. As the other tanks continue onwards, unfazed, a second explodes in another flash of light, once again sending the people around scrambling for cover.

The remaining armoured tank stops, as if questioning what has happened to the two tanks next to it. It begins moving forward again, only to be consumed by another flash of light as it erupts into fire.

"So glad we had those," Allgery says over the comms.

"Yeah, not sure how we would have handled those tanks," Tailia replies. Rayleigh remembers the metal balls they shared out earlier.

More flares go up into the sky, lighting up the world. The group begins to fire on the officers that are starting to move forward again, having regained their confidence. The officers come closer and closer to the tree, moving from cover to cover, trying to overrun the group, who are huddled behind fallen trees at the base of the tree.

With each new wave of I.D.T. officers, the cover begins to vanish. Rayleigh wonders how long they can possibly hold out.

"I can taste the cocktail already," Allgery say over the comms.

Rayleigh hears Tailia laughter in response. "I can feel the spray of the waterfall," she retorts.

"I want to see lava," Bellery adds.

At the casualness in their voices, Rayleigh recalls the conversation they had before they left.

"I hope you wouldn't do anything without me," says another voice over the comms. Rayleigh pauses, trying to identify the voice.

"Welcome back," Tailia says.

"We wouldn't dream of doing anything without you," Allgery adds, his laughter coming over the comms before he cuts it off.

Rayleigh looks up to see a figure flying over her head, coming to land several metres in front of her. They raise a staff above their head, then slam it into the ground, creating an explosion of trees and plants that shoot outwards from the point of impact.

"Zet," she whispers to herself.

The vines and trees break free of the ground and climb towards the oncoming I.D.T. officers, swallowing them and building barriers. Zet stands, turning to face Rayleigh with a smile on their face.

"Should we go?" Zet asks, stepping towards Rayleigh.

"I was starting to get worried," Allgery says to Zet.

"It's good to see you," Tailia adds, appearing next to Rayleigh.

Zet nods to each of them in turn, then heads in the opposite direction to the I.D.T. officers.

No one needs any further encouragement. Moving from the safety of the tree, they head towards the edge of the field that has been created by the battle. Rayleigh stops occasionally to look back towards the tree, distraught at the sight of the skeleton of the tree that once stood at the centre of the forest, now lifeless.

She can hear I.D.T. officers calling out to each other as they take the opportunity to swarm into the space the group has left behind. Another flare goes up into the sky, allowing Rayleigh to see the shadowy figures beginning to scale the tree.

What will they find? she wonders.

At the edge of the field of battle, the group pauses. Each of them looks back a final time before stepping into the forest and out of sight of the flares that cast their light over the battle area. Rayleigh lets the forest envelope her as she steps into the safety of the shadows.

Chapter Twenty-four

As the groups sits around the kitchen table on the ship, only a handful of words pass between them. Each of them is processing what they have been through.

"That was a little unexpected," Allgery says, looking around at the others.

Bellery and Rayleigh nod, but Tailia is staring up at the ceiling.

"I'm sorry I wasn't there to help," Tatinet says, twirling her thumbs.

"That's alright; it was good that we had someone back here, looking after the ship," Tailia says, continuing to look at the ceiling.

The group lapses into silence again, adding to the heaviness of the room.

"So what happened to the orb?" Rayleigh chimes in.

"I managed to send all the information to one of our settlements for safekeeping," Zet replies.

"Okay – that's a relief," Rayleigh says.

"Yes. There was a millennia of information stored in that well. It is great to return that information to the collective," Zet says, then takes a sip of their tea. They bow to the others in turn. "We cannot thank you enough."

"Happy to help," Allgery says.

"Hopefully, we weren't too late," Zet responds, dropping their head in reflection.

"What do you mean?" Tailia asks.

"The information was old, but during the transfer, I noticed something. The I.D.T. had a research facility that was researching Hu Thus and our technology. In recent years, the I.D.T. has been attacking our colonies. We've been unsure how they have been finding our settlements, and have heard stories about Hu Thus being taken during raids," Zet continues, turning the mug in circles on the table. "When I saw reference to this research facility, I wondered if maybe they have been able to decipher one of the knowledge wells. And maybe that is where they have been keeping the Hu Thus that have been captured."

When Zet finishes, the group is silent for a while.

"But you said the information from the well had been there for a millennia," Bellery says. "Could any research facility listed really still be in operation?"

"It is possible. It would not be the first time," Zet responds. "If they have managed to keep it hidden this long, it is unlikely they would have any need to move it."

They all ponder this.

"I'll see if Helga has any information on that location," Allgery chimes in.

Zet turns to him, a look of hope on their face.

"Bellery, can you make the preparations for Helga's?" Allgery asks Bellery, who is sitting next to him.

"Of course," Bellery responds causally, jumping up from his seat and heading for the command deck.

"It will take a few weeks for us to get there," Allgery says to the others.

"Let me see what I can find out as well," Tailia says.

"Can I borrow the secondary shuttle?" Rutherian asks Bellery.

"Sure."

"Great. I will see what I can find as well."

"I'll drop Helga a message so she knows we're on our way, and why we're coming," Allgery says.

They all look at each other. There is still a flat feeling within the group, no one moving with much energy. Tailia breaks the stillness by standing and turning to leave the room. Her action triggers the others to move, each standing and offering a gentle nod to each other before they break away from the others.

***

Allgery and Tailia come together as they walk out of the kitchen.

"I've heard stories about that region, and if the I.D.T. are there, that would explain a few things," Allgery whispers.

"Yeah, I've heard stories as well," Tailia responds, matching his tone. "Let's see what we can find out."

They both look at each other and nod before breaking away.

***

There is a tense atmosphere throughout the ship during the following weeks as they head towards Helga's hideout. All of them spend time distracting themselves, some with training, some in meditation and others with reading. No matter what they do, a cloud hangs over them. Even when joking around and laughing, the thought of the facility and the Hu Thus is never far from their thoughts.

As they touch down in Helga's hanger, there each experience unease and trepidation about what is to come.

Exiting the ship, the group walk into the hangar, looking around for any indication of life. Helga appears from nowhere, crashing into Allgery and bringing him to the ground.

"Hey you," she cries out, throwing her arms around him and giving him a kiss on the cheek.

"Hey," Allgery responds blankly.

Pulling away, Helga looks around at the group. "Welcome, welcome," she calls out. Standing up, she gives each of them a hug, allowing Allgery a chance to get up.

"Hey," Helga says quietly to Allgery, tapping him on the shoulder with her fist to get his attention.

Allgery turns to see her smiling face. He nods. "Hey," he responds.

"We'll figure this out," Helga whispers, placing a hand on his arm.

"Thank you. I didn't know who else to turn to," Allgery replies.

"Thank you for coming to me," Helga says in a hushed voice, before embracing him again.

This time, Allgery hugs her back. They hold each other for a moment before breaking away.

"Come on, everyone. Let's go unwind," Helga says loudly again, turning back to the group.

"Food and drinks for everyone," Helga cries out to her crew, who have been filing in behind her.

At her command, they cheer and jump into action, jostling with each other to make sure they don't miss out on the best food and drinks.

"Come, come." Helga ushers the group towards the food hall, where the roar of laughter and partying can be heard already.

As they cross the yard and make their way into the hall, they are greeted with some familiar faces and acknowledgements from some of Helga's crew.

"We should be preparing," Allgery says to Helga.

"We are. You look exhausted, so you should eat and rest. We have a long road ahead of us," Helga says, placing a hand on his arm once again.

Allgery hesitates but goes with it, letting Helga lead him to a table.

"Sit, eat, relax," Helga says to the group. "I had the chefs prepare a special meal for us."

Plates of food are brought in from doorways around the hall. Rayleigh watches as, to her surprise, the plates manage to make their way around the room, passed from one person to the next, despite all the rowdiness and chaos. There is a structure and practiced movement to the distribution of the food. Finally, plates are placed on the table in front of them. The smells make Rayleigh's mouth water and her stomach cry out.

"Please, begin," Helga says.

No further encouragement is needed, and everybody in the room springs into their food, talking and getting their fill, the stories and drinks beginning to flow.

As the night goes on, each of the group begins to relax. They begin to exchange old stories, remembering their adventures together, the close calls, the near death experiences and past lives. It all comes flooding out of them, filling the room with laughter and bringing them together.

The night passes by, then each of them retires for the night, having had their fill. As they head to their rooms, they find the last few weeks catching up with them.

As the last of the group leaves the table, Helga and Allgery find themselves sitting alone in the great hall, amid the roar of the party.

"How are you doing?" Helga asks Allgery.

"Alright. Just worried about everyone," Allgery responds.

"I know." Helga places an arm around Allgery. "I know you want to save everyone, and I wouldn't want to stop you. If you can remember, you don't need to do it by yourself," she whispers, pulling him closer. "You have people here that care about you and that can help." She rests her head on the nape of his neck, and they both look out into the great hall.

Allgery is about to respond, but the words stumble in his mouth and he pauses.

"Can I fall asleep in your arms tonight?" The words slip out of Allgery's mouth.

"Of course. Come on, let's get some rest," Helga whispers, and takes his hand.

The two of them slip out of the hall and head off to bed.

***

The camp slowly begins to stir as Rayleigh stumbles out of her room, rubbing her eyes and heading towards the kitchen. As she moves along the hallways she notices a familiar stillness of the early morning silence and peace.

There is already life in the kitchen: Zet is cooking, humming to themselves as they work, unaware of everything else around them.

Rayleigh stands and watches them, wondering if she should disturb them or let them be, only to be caught by Zet when they turn with a plate of food already in hand for her. She smiles, takes the offered food and heads for the dining table. Once settled, she dives into the food, savouring every morsel.

Tailia swans gracefully through the room, arriving at the kitchen to be greeted by Zet with another plate of food. She takes her place at the table next to Rayleigh.

Allgery and Helga are the last to enter. They arrive together, then break away from one another at the sight of the others already in the room. Zet is already prepared for them, standing with plates for them. They cross the room to take them, then join the others at the dining table.

"How are we all doing this morning?" Helga asks as she sits down.

Each of them nod and respond with a greeting.

"So… we have a big day ahead of us," Helga begins, filling the room with her energy. "This is a bit of a doozy. I've had my crew do some reconnaissance at the location you provided, and… wow. This is going to be a tough one." Casually, she flips up a display showing what they have been able to find out. The hologram springs to life in the middle of the table, hovering over them all.

There is a knock at the door, and they all freeze.

"Yes?" Helga calls out.

"There's someone here for you," says a voice from the other side of the door.

Helga switches off the display and calls out for them to enter. When the door swings open, they see Rutherian standing behind one of Helga's guards.

"Perfect timing, as always," Tailia calls out from her seat.

"I guess they're with you then," Helga says to Tailia. "Please, join us. We're just getting started." Helga points Rutherian towards a space at the table and switches the display on again.

"As I was saying, this is going to be tricky," Helga says as she zooms in on the facility. "The place is heavily fortified and dug in. We almost missed it. There will be heavy resistance in the air and on the ground. This is the information we were able to get."

They all lean in, trying to get a better look at the display.

"It isn't possible. Can you zoom in on that area?" Zet asks, pointing to a section of the map.

"What is it?" Tailia asks.

"It is ancient, but it looks like a Hu Thu building," Zet says.

"Are you sure?" Tailia says in surprise.

"I will need to check with the elders, but it looks like it."

"That might explain it… Trying to get onto the planet comes with its own challenges," Helga continues, zooming in further. "We don't know how this is possible, but we sent in a number of teams onto the planet and they vanished. One team made it back, and they said they were sent to another dimension."

She pauses to let everyone take this in. No one seems to know what to say. They all sit in silence, looking at the map.

"How is that possible?" Bellery asks.

"We're not sure, but we're trying to find a path through to the surface," Helga replies.

"This sounds familiar. It makes me even more sure this is a Hu Thu planet," Zet says.

"What makes you say that?" Tailia asks.

"We used to protect our research facilities by creating a maze of portals. Follow the wrong way, and you will be sent to different dimensions. They were created to prevent people from getting in."

"But those facilities were lost, when we fled the I.D.T.…." Zet trails off.

"Is there a way that we can find out?" Allgery asks.

"Possibly. I will consult with the elders and come back." Zet pulls up some coordinates on the screen. "There is a Hu Thu settlement here, where we should be able to speak with some elders."

"Then I guess that's our next point of call," Tailia says.

"Bellery, can you make the arrangements?" Allgery asks.

"Yes sir," Bellery responds curtly, jumping up from his seat and heading for the ship.

"Guess we'll find out our next steps when we get there," Tailia says, looking around at each of them in turn.

"Thank you, Helga," Allgery says to Helga.

She nods. "Happy to help. Let me know if there is anything further." She places a hand on his knee.

"Thank you for the help with the children," Allgery says quietly, placing his hand on hers. "I'm not sure what we would have done without your help."

The rest of the group have begun moving off already. Allgery stands and takes off after them. At the door, he looks back at Helga, who is looking at him smiling.

"Please be careful – and come back," Helga says before Allgery turns and leaves.

***

As they feel the weight of ship settle as it touches down, the group unclip themselves from their seats.

"Where now, DitDit42?" Tailia asks.

"It isn't far from here," Zet responds, bowing slightly to Tailia.

"Lead the way," Allgery says to Zet.

Zet nods, making their way toward the exit with the others following. As the ship loading bay door opens to reveal the surface, the sounds and smells of the planet crawl into the ship. The bird calls and the swaying of the trees provide a level of comfort after having spent so long cooped up on the ship.

They can hear the animals chirping and making noises in the distance. They have landed in a small clearing within a dense rainforest that creates a wall around them.

As Zet reaches the bottom of the ramp, they pause, looking down at the orb in their hands. Then they look up in the direction they need to head in, and start walking in the direction indicated by the orb.

The group fall in step, and the ship ramp closes behind them. They have brought with them a small assortment of weapons, though they are not expecting anything, this being a Hu Thu settlement. They walk across the clearing casually, taking in their surroundings as they walk.

Zet steps through the tree line and into the undergrowth of the forest, the others following behind, trying to keep up with Zet, who is moving effortlessly through the vegetation.

The sound of a branch breaking grabs their attention. Rayleigh and Rutherian swing around with their weapons to see what is there. Zet doesn't flinch.

When did they get here? Rayleigh thinks as she notices a small group of Hu Thus moving through the forest.

Zet continues towards the village, and the others follow along. Soon, they come upon a clearing, and they see the buildings of the village. Several Hu Thus move about the town, unaware of their arrival.

Rayleigh looks back into the forest for the Hu Thus that were following them, but they have vanished.

When did they leave?

As Zet approaches the buildings, a group of Hu Thus come out to meet them. In the centre is an elder, with two Hu Thus on either side, acting almost like guards. Once they are closer, the elder bows, and Zet returns the gesture.

The others stop behind Zet and copy the gesture, greeting the elder.

"Welcome, Zetuta," the elder says to Zet, rising from their bow. "I hope your journey was safe and that the knowledge holds with you."

"Thank you, elder. My journey has been fruitful, and I come with knowledge," Zet responds.

The elder gestures to guide Zet towards the tree at the centre of the village.

"I wonder what they're saying?" Bellery says to Rayleigh, as the group falls in behind.

It's only now that Rayleigh realises that Zet and the elder are speaking their native language. She had forgotten that she's been given insight into their culture and language by an elder.

"Oh, they were saying hello," she replies.

Bellery stops and turns to Rayleigh with a look of surprise on his face. "You understand them?"

Rayleigh keeps walking. "Yes, they gave me the knowledge of their language when I was looking for you all."

The conversation between the elder and Zet takes her attention again.

"I believe we have found an ancient building," Zet says as they walk towards the tree. "We would like your wisdom and knowledge to confirm if this is the case. If so, we hope there is information about how we can access this building."

"This is great news," the elder responds, making subtle hand gestures and bows as they respond. "We will do what we can to provide you with the knowledge you seek."

Coming into the central tree, Rayleigh sees elders standing around knowledge pools, deep in prayer, mumbling softly to themselves. The pools glow with faint blue light. There is a sense of peace within the tree, everyone moving in graceful and flowing motion.

They follow Zet and the elder to the pool at the centre of the tree. The elders around the pool stop their prayers and look up, then bow their heads slightly as Zet approaches.

Zet steps over the side of the pool and into the 'water', wading into the centre. They lie down, with the elders taking their places around the outside of the pool. Rayleigh is intrigued, so she steps closer as the elders begin to pray.

Zet is floating on top of the pool, somehow. Then Rayleigh notices Zet begins to sink, and her heart stops. Panic rising within her, she steps forward, wanting to save Zet from drowning, but Tailia places a hand on her arm, preventing her from moving any further. She shakes her head before lowering her hand again and looking towards the pool.

"They are safe," Tailia whispers. "Come on – this will take some time. We can rest up," she continues, turning away and walking towards the tree entrance.

The others slowly pull their gazes from the sight of Zet hovering below the surface of the pool, the elders standing around the pool with their hands in front of their faces, chanting slowly.

The group slowly exits the tree to find a Hu Thu waiting for them. They bow slightly and gesture to a hut on the far side of the square.

Tailia bows politely in return and walks towards the building. Everyone else trickles along behind her.

Inside the hut, they place their belongings down and settle into their own areas: Tailia and Rayleigh on the couch, Allgery and Bellery at the table. Bellery pulls out some playing cards and dice and the pair begin to play a game. Tailia and Rayleigh begin to talk to pass the time.

Chapter Twenty-five

When she wakes up, Rayleigh isn't sure what time it is. She lies in bed, restless and looking at the ceiling, recent events running through her mind, struggling to switch off.

After a while, she gives up on the idea and climbs out of bed. Allgery and Bellery are still fast asleep. Bellery is murmuring to himself, but she isn't able to understand what he's saying. Rayleigh watches him for a moment, finding the sight adorable. She pulls herself away and makes her way to the front door.

Outside are two guards. Rayleigh bows politely to them, and they each return the gesture. She continues to the courtyard, looking up at the stars and the night sky.

She can see the faint glow of the pools inside the tree. The low hum of voices chanting continues. *Are they still going?* she thinks.

Entering, she sees Tailia standing nearby, watching the elders work. She heads in her direction and stops next to her.

"You couldn't sleep either?" Rayleigh says.

Tailia doesn't respond for a moment, then looks over to acknowledge Rayleigh's presence. "Sleep is difficult these days," she says, turning back to watch the elders.

"How are they doing?" Rayleigh asks.

"They're still looking for any information," Tailia whispers, barely audible above the chanting.

Rayleigh feels the tension in the air, the uncertainty about what they will find and what the future will bring. She falls silent, not wanting to disturb the elders. She tries to follow the rhythmic chanting of the elders, but the words blend together. As time passes, an uncomfortable sensations begins to push around her body, moving through her.

Something is wrong.

"Did you feel that?" she whispers to Tailia.

"Yes. We're in danger," Tailia responds, scanning the room.

Rayleigh notices Tailia has reached for her weapons, which only adds to her uneasiness. Sensing an oncoming conflict, Rayleigh reaches for her own weapons.

"Allgery, Bellery," Tailia whispers over the comms.

Rayleigh hears their response. "Yep. Let me guess, something's wrong?" Allgery whispers.

The universe responds to Allgery's question with the sound of a scream from nearby, followed by gunfire and more screaming.

Rayleigh and Tailia look in the direction of the screams, already starting to move towards the pool were Zet is still submerged.

There's more gunfire outside the tree. At this latest flurry, the chanting stops and the elders break their circle around the pool to look towards the exit.

When Rayleigh and Tailia reach the pool, one of the elders raises their hand to stop them before they can move any further. "We are not ready; we don't have all the information."

"We're out of time, so we have to take what we have," Tailia says quickly, placing a hand on the elder's shoulder.

The elder looks between Tailia and Rayliegh, then back to the pool, as if struggling to determine what to do. After a moment, they join the other elders, who had started to chant again. The chanting has changed, seeming more urgent now.

Rayleigh and Tailia turn towards the entrance, listening for sounds of combat. Each of them faces a different exit, waiting to see what the world might throw at them. The sounds of gunfire increase continually, the chaos outside intensifying.

Rayleigh sees the elders pulling an orb from the pool, and she wonders what it might contain. It glows with the familiar energy of the Hu Thus. One of the elders pulls out a bag and places the orb inside. Bowing to the bag, they close it up.

The elders continue to chant as this all unfolds. As the glow from the pool begins to subside, Rayleigh sees Zet floating back to the surface again. As they reach the surface of the pool, they begin to twitch, glimmers of life returning after almost a day submerged within the pool.

Rayleigh, still unable to comprehend it all, watches on curiously, forgetting about the chaos happening outside. Zet slowly emerges from the pool, rising to full height. They look over at Rayleigh and Tailia with a smile, and bow a greeting to them both. Tailia and Rayleigh return the gesture, reaching out to help Zet out of the pool. Zet stumbles slightly as they step out, using Tailia and Rayleigh to support their first few steps.

"Easy, how are you doing?" Rayleigh asks.

"Thank you. Just a little drained," Zet responds quietly, with a warm smile.

The three of them turn to leave. Allgery and Bellery both stand at the exit armed to the teeth. They continue firing at I.D.T streaming out of the shadows.

"We need to leave," Tailia says over the sounds of combat.

They all nod in agreement, without breaking their focus.

"You will need this," a voice says from behind Rayleigh. One of the elders is standing with a bag in their hands, holding it out. "Guard this with your life," they say as Tailia takes the bag. "Zet's capabilities have been increased to level 10. From the glimpses of what we saw contained here, you will need all the help you can get. We will be in your debt if you are able to help us," the elder concludes, then gestures goodbye to them all.

Rayleigh wonders what the elders have seen within the well, and what it might mean for the Hu Thu's future.

"We should go," Allgery says, breaking her concentration.

They all look over at him, preparing themselves for the fight ahead.

"What about you?" Rayleigh asks.

"Thank you for your concern. We need to protect the information," the elder responds. "I have a gift for you," they say, placing a hand on Rayleigh's arm, which produces a faint tingle on her skin. "Now go, and may the information protect you." They turn back towards the pools and the other elders.

Rayleigh turns to see that the group are beginning to move towards the exit of the tree.

As they move through the village, they see I.D.T. officers storming into the village, trying to overrun the place due to sheer numbers. Wherever they turn, there are more of them. At the edge of the village, Rayleigh turns back to see fires burning. Sporadic gunfire and screams come from all over the village. Her heart breaks at the thought of another village being taken. *This isn't right.* Tears begin to swell in her eyes.

"Are you okay?" Tailia asks.

"I wish I could do something," Rayleigh says, looking at Tailia for only a moment before looking back at the village.

"I feel the same," Tailia responds after a moment, and Rayleigh can hear the heaviness in her voice. "Come. We should go." Tailia places a hand on Rayleigh's shoulder as she turns away to follow the others, leaving Rayleigh alone to look out over the village.

"Tom, I hope you are safe," she whispers into the night air. As the words come from her mouth, her discomfort rises. It has been so long since she has last thought of him. With a final look at the village, Rayleigh turns and heads off after everyone else.

As they head back to the ship, no one says anything. They all focus on the task at hand, not wanting to think about what had just happened, or the hopelessness that there was nothing that they could do. Rayleigh doesn't remember the ship being so close, but then she realises she has been stuck in her head for the entire journey back.

The ship comes to life at their arrival, and the familiar sounds bring her back to the present. Bellery has moved to the command deck with Zet, working to get the ship in the air. The roar of the engines break through Rayleigh's thoughts, and she looks around to see the members of the group strapping themselves in.

As the ship climbs above the tree line, Rayleigh sees the glow of the flames in the distance. Climbing higher, the view of the forest alight sorrow grips her. *Did we bring them here?* she wonders, realising the I.D.T. never seem to be far behind.

The ship turns and begins heading into space, taking them away from the horrors below.

***

There is a heavy feeling across the ship. No one has really been themselves since they had left the planet, each of them going about their tasks in a daze, finding comfort in the daily routines as they make for Trita spaceport where they will be able to recoup, resupply and look over the information recovered by the elders.

As each day passes, Zet's energy recovers. With each piece of energy they become more themselves, helping the others on the ship find some normality. Once Zet is able, they begin looking over the masses of information uploaded to the orb, spending days and evenings searching for anything that might be useful.

As the ship comes into the spaceport, the jolt of it touching on to the landing pad jogs the group from their work.

"What are your plans?" Tailia asks Allgery and Bellery.

"We might head to HiTop; we could use a break," Allgery replies.

"What about you?" Bellery asks in response.

"I was thinking that I need a break as well. I might try and get some rest," Tailia responds, glancing over at Rayleigh.

"Yeah, I'm with you," Rayleigh says.

They all nod, then turn to look at Zet.

"If it is okay with you, I would like to make some upgrades to the ship," Zet says, looking over at Bellery and Allgery.

"No problem with me," Allgery says with a shrug. "Bellery?"

"As you wish," Bellery says.

"I have some people I need to see," Rutherian chimes in.

"I would like to explore this spaceport," Tatinet adds.

They all nod.

"Reach out if you need anything," Tailia says to the group as a whole.

"And stay safe," Rayleigh adds quickly before they all break away to attend to their own tasks.

"I have a place where we can stay," Tailia whispers to Rayleigh as the two of move off the command deck.

"Sounds good," Rayleigh says with a smile.

Happy with the plan, they both exit the command deck to collect their belongings. They meet up in the ship loading bay and head out into the spaceport. Rayleigh takes in the sights, sounds and smells of the place, looking at all the different things as they go. Still amazed by everything, she moves like a child between the stores, pausing to look at food, clothing, ornaments and strange artifacts as they go. Tailia stops to watch as Rayleigh moves about. The fascination and wonder in Rayleigh's eyes brings a smile to Tailia's face.

As they two of them go, Tailia begins to explain the different items to Rayleigh, helping her understand what she is picking up. They buy a couple of items and some food as they go.

Without them realising it, an hour passes before they make it to the place Tailia mentioned. When they arrive at the tall rundown apartment building.

"What is this place?" Rayleigh asks, looking up at it.

"I bought it years ago, and I keep it as a safe house," Tailia responds.

Heading into the building, they walk up to Tailia's apartment. Inside, Rayleigh throws her bags onto the table and moves to a couch. Tailia heads for the bedroom and crashes down on the bed.

The bed moves as Rayleigh crashes next to her, letting out a long sigh as she does.

"Thank you," Rayleigh says, attracting Tailia's attention.

Tailia rolls over, opening her eyes. "I think I should be thanking you. I needed that," she responds.

"What do you mean?" Rayleigh asks.

"I needed some normal, and what's more normal than friends spending time together, eating food and exploring?"

Rayleigh considers this. "Yeah. You're right, we needed that. Speaking of normal... I was thinking I'd like to cook something for dinner. Are you up for that?"

"That sounds great," Tailia replies.

"Great, I'm going to head out and buy some things for dinner," Rayleigh says, looking towards the door and back again at Tailia.

"Do you want me to come?" Tailia asks.

"No, that's okay – I can manage. Can I take some credits?"

"Help yourself," Tailia says, pointing towards the table in the other room.

"Thank you. I'll be back soon." Rayleigh turns from the bedroom doorway, collects her things and leaves the apartment.

***

Rayleigh heads down the hallway, greeted by the hustle and bustle as she steps out of the building. Turning right, she heads back towards the shops that she saw on the corner.

She's happy to be out by herself. There's something nice about doing things for herself again. With each step she takes, her confidence and normality return to her.

What to make... she thinks as she walks down the street. *How does this feel so normal?* She chuckles to herself and picks up her pace, a bounce in her step as she heads for the local market.

Rayleigh looks through the food in the local stall, trying to work out what they are and what they might taste like. She looks for anything that she recognises, or which might be used in place of something she knows.

After heading in and out of several stores, and speaking with several shop owners, she manages to find vegetables and meats that she feels is close enough to what she knows. She's hoping to make her favourite meal for Tailia.

After coming out of the last store, Rayleigh scans the street. An uneasy sensation in her stomach makes her pause and take another look.

"Look at me… scanning the street," Rayleigh says to herself, realising that she has picked up the habits of the team.

She ignores the thought and steps out into the street, turning to head back to the apartment. She stops at a small little store when she sees a bottle of the drink she and Tailia shared when they first met.

You only live once, Rayleigh thinks as memories of that night come back to her.

Heading inside, she buys a bottle from the store and heads back out onto the street again. At an intersection near the apartment, the uneasy feeling returns. She stops, turning to look down the street, scanning for anything out of the ordinary.

After several seconds of watching, she continues walking. She enters the apartment building and makes her way up to Tailia's room.

Slipping into the room, she looks towards the door to the bedroom to see that Tailia has fallen asleep. Rayleigh tiptoes to the kitchen, not wanting to disturb her. She tries not to make a sound as she places the items down and begins to prepare the meal.

***

Stirring from her sleep, Tailia rolls over to look at the ceiling, trying to take in everything that has happened over the last few weeks. The smell of food from the kitchen wafts through the doorway, grabbing her attention.

What is that? Tailia thinks. Hearing movement in the other room, she remembers that Rayleigh had said she wanted to cook.

Curious, Tailia climbs out of bed. She pauses at the bedroom door, looking out into the apartment, not wanting to disturb Rayleigh.

Rayleigh is in the kitchen, cooking away, singing and dancing as she works. Tailia is captivated by her energy. It brings a small smile to her face.

Finally, she moves into the lounge. Rayleigh turns as she approaches.

"Hello, sleepy head," Rayleigh says, smiling and raising the drink in her hand to greet her.

"Hello," Tailia responds, still a little sleepy. "What is this?" She looks over Rayleigh's shoulder at what she is preparing.

"That is a good question," Rayleigh laughs to herself, looking around at the food. "I don't really know the ingredients, but I tried to get as close as I could to my favourite dish." Rayleigh continues stirring the food as she talks.

"It smells great," Tailia says. "Would you like any help?"

"You can set the table if you like?"

"On it." Tailia collects plates, cutlery and glasses from the cupboard and moves to the table.

The two of them go about their tasks. Tailia turns up the music and they can both sing and dance as they prepare the meal. After Tailia finishes with the table settings, Rayleigh starts to bring the food to the table.

Rayleigh chuckles. "That is an interesting way to set the table."

Tailia looks down at the table, confused. The cutlery has been placed under the plate, like always. *How does she do it?*

"It looks great," Rayleigh says before Tailia can speak. "Thank you."

Tailia takes her place at the table, watching Rayleigh return with the last of the food.

"I hope you like it," Rayleigh says, looking up at Tailia.

"I'm sure it's great," Tailia responds with a smile, and begins to serve out the food.

Placing her plate back on the table, Rayleigh sits up suddenly. "Oh, hang on," she says, jumping up from the table and heading back to the kitchen. A moment later, she returns with a bottle in hand.

When Tailia sees the bottle, she laughs. "Oh, I see."

"I figured we needed to let our hair down," Rayleigh says, pouring them each a drink. "To the future," she says, raising her glass.

"To friends," Tailia says, raising her glass.

They both nod to each other, and drink.

"Now let's eat," Tailia says, looking down at the food before digging in. "Oh wow."

"What?" Rayleigh asks.

"No, no. This is good."

"Oh, that's good. I'm glad you like it."

With that, the two of them dive in, eating and drinking the night away. With each bite, the world outside slips away and they slip into laughter and stories from their past.

As the night passes, they let themselves go, enjoying the downtime before they both head to bed to get some much-needed rest.

***

Rayleigh wakes from sleep and looks at the wall beside the bed, letting the memories of the night before slip back into her mind. *That was nice.* The thought brings with it a peace and a gentle feeling into her chest. She flips onto her back to look up at the ceiling, letting the feeling to sit with her for a moment.

Silly alcohol, Rayleigh thinks, realising that she needs to go to the bathroom. She pulls herself out of bed and moves to door. When she goes to step into the lounge, something catches her eye.

"Tailia?" she calls out, but there is no response.

Looking around the room in the dark, the uneasy feeling she experienced in the market creeps back into her stomach.

"Tailia?" she calls out again. Nothing.

As she turns towards the bathroom, something moves.

Danger, Rayleigh's body screams at her, and she dives backwards.

As she crashes onto the bed, a bullet tears through the air above her head and hits the headboard, punching a hole through it and into the wall. Rayleigh rolls onto the floor as the second, third, and fourth rounds punch through the walls. Grabbing her weapons from the bag near her bed, she props herself up, looking back towards the doorway, and sees a shiloette move through it. Rayleigh doesn't think, firing twice into the centre of the shadow.

It buckles and falls. Rayleigh holds for a moment longer and hears a number of shots ring out from the other room.

"Tailia?" Rayleigh calls out.

"I'm fine!" Tailia calls back.

Rayleigh climbs up with the gun trained on the door. She steps out into the lounge to see a shadow coming out of Tailia's room.

"Tailia?"

"Yep," Tailia says.

They meet up in the middle of the lounge, bumping into each other in the dark. Rayleigh jumps a little.

"Are you ready?" Tailia asks.

"Yep."

"Lights," Tailia's says, and the apartment lights come on at her voice command.

Another assailant at the door moves at the sudden exposure the light brings. Both Tailia and Rayleigh fire at the same time, landing shots to the chest. They drop to the ground.

There are loud footsteps in the hallway outside the house. Tailia fires a couple of rounds into the wall, but the footsteps continue and then fade away. The two of them look at each other and lower their weapons.

"Did they get you?" Tailia asks.

"No. You?"

"Yep. That was close," Tailia looks down at the body outside her door, then at the others in the room.

"Who are they?" Rayleigh says, following Tailia's gaze around the room.

Tailia shrugs and bends down next to the body to go through their pockets. Tailia pauses as she pulls back the face covering.

"I know you," Tailia mutters to herself.

"Where do you know them from?" Rayleigh asks.

"My brother – this is one of his guards."

"What?"

"They work for my brother. I used to train with this soldier," Tailia continues, standing and looking around the room. "We need to go." Her gaze settles on Rayleigh. "Grab your things." She turns towards her room.

Needing no further encouragement, Rayleigh darts back to her room and gets dressed. Collecting her bag, she heads out into the lounge, where Tailia is waiting for her.

"There might be more. So we should be ready," Tailia says as she moves to the front door. She pauses to look at Rayleigh once more, before opening the door and stepping out into the hallway.

Tailia goes left and Rayleigh goes right, each raising their guns to cover all angles, relying on their training together.

"Follow me," Tailia whispers, edging along the hallway.

Rayleigh follows her, knowing no response is needed. As she moves, she covers the other end of the hallway, making sure that no one can creep up behind them. The pair move in unison through the building and out the back exit. As they emerge into the alleyway behind the building, they pause, scanning in both directions.

There is a commotion at the end of the alley. People are moving towards the front of the building. Rayleigh hears the sounds of sirens and sees officers moving down the street.

"This way," Tailia says, gesturing in the other direction.

Rayleigh nods, and they stand, tucking away their weapons as they move to the end of the alley, not wanting to draw attention to themselves.

"We have company," Tailia whispers over their comms link.

"Affirmative," the other members of the group reply quickly over the comms.

As Tailia and Rayleigh reach the end of the alley, they turn into the street and blend into the crowd as they head back towards the ship.

"Why would your brother send people to kill you?" Rayleigh asks as they move.

Tailia stops, looking at Rayleigh. "That's a long story. I'll tell you when we're safe," she says, a tear running down her cheek. Then she turns away and continues to move towards safety.

www.ingramcontent.com/pod-product-compliance
Lightning Source LLC
Chambersburg PA
CBHW020909130726
47904CB00006BA/1792